SP

WASHOE COUNTY LIBRARY

3 1235 03350 4957

SEP 3 0 2007

DATE DUE

OCT 2 8 2007		
DEC 2 2 2007		
JAN 2 4 2008		
FEB 0 6 2008		
MAR 0 8 2008		
APR 3 0 2008		
MAY 0 6 2008		
NOV 2 4 2008		
GAYLORD		PRINTED IN U.S.A.

D0960995

THE
KINGDOM
OF
BONES

ALSO BY STEPHEN GALLAGHER

Chimera
Follower
Valley of Lights
Oktober
Down River
Rain
The Boat House
Nightmare, with Angel
Red, Red Robin

THE KINGDOM

OF

BONES

A NOVEL

Stephen Gallagher

Shaye Areheart Books

NEW YORK

This is a work of fiction. Names, characters, places, and incidents either are the product of the author's imagination or are used fictitiously. Any resemblance to actual persons, living or dead, events, or locales is entirely coincidental.

Copyright © 2007 by Stephen Gallagher

All rights reserved.

Published in the United States by Shaye Areheart Books, an imprint of the Crown Publishing Group, a division of Random House, Inc., New York.
www.crownpublishing.com

Shaye Areheart Books with colophon is a registered trademark of Random House, Inc.

Library of Congress Cataloging-in-Publication Data

Gallagher, Stephen.
The kingdom of bones : a novel/Stephen Gallagher.—1st ed.
p. cm.
1. Theater—History—19th century—Fiction. I. Title.
PR6057.A3893K66 2007
823'.914—dc22   2007013288

ISBN 978-0-307-38280-1

Printed in the United States of America

Design by Lynne Amft

10 9 8 7 6 5 4 3 2 1

First Edition

She is coming, my own, my sweet;
Were it ever so airy a tread,
My heart would hear and beat,
Were it earth in an earthy bed,
My dust would hear her and beat,
Had I lain for a century dead,
Would start and tremble under her feet,
And blossom in purple and red.

ALFRED, LORD TENNYSON
MAUD, PART I, SECTION XXII

THE
KINGDOM
OF
BONES

PHILADELPHIA

1903

O N E

hey were driving sheep through the middle of town again. The office window was open and Sebastian Becker could hear them from his desk. All through the afternoon Oakes, the bookkeeper, had been finding reasons to look down into the street. Now he had another.

Sebastian laid down his pen and tilted back his chair. His eyes hurt. He yawned and stretched and pressed the heels of his palms into them and wondered, not for the first time, whether he needed to be checked out for eyeglasses.

Then he realized what he was doing, and cut the yawn short as best he could.

He said, "Are you expecting someone, Mister Oakes?"

Oakes looked back into the office. "Only the boy with the bag from New York," he said.

"The boy's been and gone," Sebastian said. "There was nothing that can't wait until Monday."

Oakes hesitated for a moment and then moved out of the slanting sunlight and away from the window. There were at least half a dozen other desks in the room, none occupied, but all of them piled high with paperwork. One chair had a waistcoat slung over the back of it. Another, a gun belt.

As Sebastian lifted his pen again, Oakes gathered together some ledgers and moved them from one place to another. The sheep were almost out of earshot now, their eerie half-human cries pursued by the impatient clanging of an obstructed streetcar. Oakes began to straighten chairs. Despite Sebastian's permission, he seemed reluctant to leave.

"Mister Oakes . . ." Sebastian prompted him.

Oakes said, "Mister Bearce has said he's unhappy with my work."

"We'll find some way to change his mind," Sebastian said. "On Monday. Go home, Mister Oakes."

"If you're certain . . ." Oakes said, fishing for further reassurance. But Sebastian just looked at him, so he went.

Alone now and with one less distraction, Sebastian tried to return his attention to the words on the page. Despite having left the room, Oakes was still somewhere in the suite of offices. Sebastian could hear him moving around, bothering someone else, finding a few last things to do . . . almost as if the building might absorb his dedication, and then whisper of it to the absent Mr. Bearce.

The General Business letter was a report on the ongoing work of the agency. Compiled every two weeks and sent to George Bangs in New York City, it covered all the investigations that were under way and any new business that might have come in. Bangs would draw together information from all the agency offices and then deliver his summary to the Pinkerton brothers.

Sebastian had been an assistant superintendent for just over a month. The paperwork called for skills he could muster but didn't enjoy using. It was a warm Saturday afternoon, and he and most of Philadelphia were in a weekend mood. There was also the distraction of the telegraph message that he'd tucked under the corner of his blotter. Personal to him, it caught his eye every now and again.

When the letter was finished, he dropped the handwritten pages into the out-tray for the stenographers and reached for his coat from the back of his chair. He was stiff from sitting, and his eyes ached from the sustained concentration.

Sebastian Becker was a man in his early forties. He had not yet gone to seed, and some thought him handsome—his wife, for one. When he looked in a mirror, what he mostly saw was the face of his father coming through. That, and some of the traces of old pain. Intending no offense to his late father, he didn't see handsome at all.

He folded the telegraph message and slipped it into his pocket. Then he opened his desk drawer, took out a double-action Bulldog police revolver, and checked and spun its chambers before stowing it inside his jacket.

"Is there a problem, Mister Becker?"

He turned around. Oakes was watching him from the doorway, pulling on his own coat as he stood there.

"No problem, Mister Oakes," Sebastian said. He closed the window and then followed Oakes out of the office.

As they descended the building's stairway together, Oakes said, "Any plans for the Sunday, sir?"

"I promised to take the Mrs. and her sister out to Willow Grove," Sebastian said. "She's heard that Sousa's conducting in the park."

"Hardly the music for ladies, I wouldn't have thought."

"Mrs. Becker can be an unusual woman."

The night janitor was waiting by the metal gates. He'd closed up the building and was letting the last few people out in ones and twos. He was a veteran, and never spoke. It was said that cannon fire had made him simple.

Out on Chestnut Street and raising his voice as the metal slid, Oakes said, "Will you take the boy?"

And Becker said, "I rather think we will."

A streetcar ride and a ten-minute walk took Sebastian home. Home was in a narrow, tree-lined alley just off a pleasant square, a neatly pointed brick row house with shutters on its windows and a small garden to the rear. Before he let himself in, he checked around to see if anyone was observing. A nag was pulling a brewery wagon across the end of the alley, and that was about all.

It was a quiet neighborhood, and strangers would stand out. Come eight o'clock, you'd hear the banging of the shutters, and by nine, all would be dark. But that was the life he'd been looking for.

They'd lived here a month. The rent was a stretch even on a super-intendent's pay, but it was worth it for him to know that his family was secure. When they'd made the move after the rise in his fortunes, he'd had no idea how good the timing of it was. Their old Lehigh Avenue apartment had been right in the heart of the Irish quarter, and in the light of that morning's news it would have been no safe place to remain.

As he closed the door behind him, his wife's sister was crossing the hallway with an armful of cut flowers from the garden.

"Good evening, Sebastian," she said.

"Hello, Frances," he said. Before he'd finished speaking, the ceiling above their heads began to shiver with the lowest bass notes of a scale from a tenor tuba.

Becker had called his wife an unusual woman. In most respects she was not. She was slight, dark-eyed, pale and freckled and elegantly pretty—all attractive features, but none of them in any way startling or radical. What *was* uncommon was to find such a woman spending at least twenty minutes of each day in practice on a four-valve euphonium, entirely for her own enjoyment.

He followed the sound up the stairs to the sitting room at the back of the house. When he pushed open the door, there she was. She'd set up her chair and music stand by the window. Against the late sun, not just the brass of the instrument but the entirety of her shone like gold. The floor vibrated like a deck and the very air shook when the low notes sounded. Their son was at her feet, propped on his elbows, oblivious to everything but the magazine he was looking at.

Movement caught her eye, and she saw him. Without missing a beat, she raised her eyebrows in a greeting. Sebastian managed a smile, and wondered at the patience of their new neighbors. They'd discussed the possibility of occasional disturbance with them, of course. Both neighbors had thanked them for their thoughtfulness and insisted that they would not mind. But after a certain amount of *Lohengrin,* anyone could start to regret being quite so agreeable.

Robert was scrambling to his feet, his dime novel forgotten. He'd seen his father. He came running toward Sebastian and, avoiding his offered embrace, punched him in the leg as hard as he could before slithering by and away. Sebastian could hear Frances calling after him as he scuttled down the stairs.

Elisabeth lowered her euphonium and laid it down with care, before crossing the room to her husband.

"What's the matter with him?" Sebastian said.

"He'd convinced himself you were going to be early," Elisabeth said. "That's all."

"I never said I would."

"I know."

She rose on tiptoe to give Sebastian a kiss of greeting, steadying herself with a hand against his chest. He sensed her sudden tension as she became aware of the Bulldog revolver under his coat, even though her outward attitude showed no change.

"What's wrong?" she said, dropping back to her usual height.

"Nothing's wrong."

"I thought English policemen didn't like to carry guns."

"I'm no longer a policeman, and this isn't England."

"Is someone looking for you?"

He thought about showing her the telegraph message, and decided against it.

"Stop worrying," he said. "It's only a precaution."

"Against what? Can we still go out?"

From most of the women he'd ever known, such a question would have been thrown down as a challenge or with a pout. But not from his wife.

"We can still go out," he said.

T W O

fter church the next day, and in their summer Sunday best, Sebastian and his family boarded a trolley to the park at Willow Grove. He wore his dark suit and a straw boater. The women wore long, light dresses and Robert a white sailor suit. In deference to Elisabeth's worries, Sebastian had hidden the revolver in the waistband of his pants. He'd tucked it right around in the small of his back so that she wouldn't be aware of it, even if the movement of the trolley should throw them together. He hadn't anticipated its effect in church, where sitting in the hard pew had made the service into an even greater torture than usual.

But he expected no trouble today. Today he was just a man with his family, one face in a very big crowd. The park at Willow Grove had been opened by the Rapid Transit Company to give people a reason to ride on their line, and its model of free concerts and fairground entertainment was being imitated in cities all over the nation. Brooklyn had its Steeplechase Park, Salt Lake City its church-run Saltair. But Willow Grove, Philadelphia's Fairyland, was ahead of them all. Sousa, the March King, had brought his band to play there two years before, and now his visits were becoming an annual fixture.

Elisabeth loved the sound of a marching band. She always said that she'd inherited the love from her maternal grandfather, an old soldier who would forget everything when he heard one in the street. He would follow the musicians until they stopped playing, whereupon he'd discover himself lost in some unfamiliar part of town and unable to find his way home.

At the terminal station, they moved with the crowd through a tunnel under the tracks to emerge into the park. Frances took the boy off toward the midway while Elisabeth took Sebastian's arm, and together they crossed to the pavilion of music. Elisabeth's sister was good with the child, there was no doubting that. She lived with them for that very reason, and earned her keep as his tutor. He did not attend any school.

Sebastian found his son difficult to fathom. He had not begun to speak until he was five, and now cared for little other than his dime novels. Sebastian had forbidden them at first, thinking them inappropriate. But Robert's interests were not engaged by anything else. He was a shy boy, indifferent to friendships or learning unless it was a subject that drew him. In the end, Elisabeth had allowed him one new dime novel every two weeks. He'd go down to the newsstand with Frances and could take anything up to an hour over his choice. He saved them, reread them, could recite entire passages by heart. Frank Reade, Deadwood Dick, Buffalo Bill. He could give you tables of contents with page numbers, list all the back-page ads for any issue. And yet a schoolteacher, whose name they'd agreed would never again be spoken in their house, had once tried to persuade them that their son might be an imbecile.

The band was playing "The Belle of Chicago" as Sebastian and Elisabeth took their seats. Sebastian cared little for music of any kind, but he cared for Elisabeth and as she watched the band, his eyes were on her. At thirty-one, she was his junior by a number of years.

After a while, she became aware of his attention.

"What's the matter?" she said.

"Nothing."

"You're bored, aren't you?"

"How could I be?"

She smiled and looked toward the stage, where the forty members of the Sousa orchestra were turning pages and making ready to strike up again. She tilted her chin up a little to catch a cooling breeze that came and went in a moment, and Sebastian's heart seemed to swell in his chest.

She said, "Daddy once told me he'd buy me an orchestra to play in."

"The euphonium?"

"The price was that I'd have to learn the cello instead. But that was before he lost his fortune."

That was typical of Elisabeth's father. When her family had money they'd lived in one of the big houses north of Market Street. Not quite the "best" district, North of Market was where the new money settled. Elisabeth had spent most of her childhood in a mansion on North Sixteenth Street, just below Columbia. Their neighbors had included families like the Stetsons and the Gimbels.

Despite his own humble background, her father had been a terrific snob, and even financial ruin hadn't managed to knock any of that out of him. He'd disapproved of Sebastian—too old for Elisabeth, an immigrant, a lapsed Catholic with a Jew name, a paid-by-the-hour Pinkerton Man—and disapproved of him still. Only Frances passed between the two households, and brought them whatever news there was.

Until her teenage years, Elisabeth had been a princess of the nouveau riche. She'd owned several horses and had a servant of her own. She'd had Sebastian walk her by their old mansion once. He'd gazed at it in awe, while she gripped his arm and looked the other way. It had been quite something.

Now he said, "What do you miss most?"

"I'm the richest woman in town," she said. "There's nothing to miss."

The band played "Liberty Bell." Men tapped their feet, and women waved their programs in time. When it ended, Sousa turned and bowed to the applause. He was a slight, balding and bearded figure in pince-nez. As this was a Sunday concert, he wore a white uniform and gloves.

Joining in the applause, Elisabeth leaned over to Sebastian and said, "I wish you could tell me more."

"There's nothing to tell," Sebastian said.

"It's not for my sake," she said, "it's for Frances and for Robert. How can I warn them if I know nothing at all?"

Sebastian looked away, took a breath, and sighed it out. What could he do? It went against his instincts, but she was probably right.

He said, "It concerns two brothers of an Irish boy that I helped to track down. Word has come through that the boy is to be executed."

"And these two brothers are looking for you?"

"It's always wise to keep one's guard."

"*Are* they looking for you?"

He did not mean to hesitate. It was only for a moment, but it was enough to give him away.

"No," he said, regretting his attempt at guile even as it came out.

Her hand came up into view. He didn't see where she produced it from, but she held yesterday's telegraph message in it. Which meant that she'd known the truth all along. Over on the platform, Sousa raised his baton. She raised an eyebrow and waited.

"I'm supposed to be the detective here," he said ruefully.

"Don't shelter us quite so much, Sebastian," she said. "Father kept the worst from us, and I hate that more than anything." And then, as the music began, she started to rise, saying, "I think I've had my fill of marching for now. Let's head on over and rescue Frances."

The midway stood beyond the Electric Fountain and the lakes, with two large carousels at either end of the broad walk. Beyond the midway were the perilous-looking Shoot-the-Chute ride and other big park attractions. New rides were being planned and added every year. The crowds were dense, but should they fail to find each other Elisabeth had determined that they'd meet at the Lakeside Café. Robert generally made for the larger of the two carousels, where he was fascinated by the mechanical arrangement that gave the animals a jumping motion.

But neither he nor Frances could be seen there, and so Sebastian and Elisabeth started a slow walk back down the midway toward their rendezvous point. There was no reason to hurry. They had more than half an hour to waste until the meeting time.

Most of the attractions on the midway were housed in permanent structures, in a row that resembled one side of a small-town street facing out across a green. Some of the vacant spaces had been leased to visiting showmen, and here Sebastian could sense a change in atmosphere and tone. Their put-up buildings were brasher and shabbier than the regular ones, and the show people fronting them were similarly turned out. This was Willow Grove, and so they were on their best behavior. But they were like yard dogs given a bath and a big ribbon.

Nevertheless, they were a powerful draw. Their ballyhoo seemed to attract even the most decent citizens where, by logic, one would expect it to deter. Brazen, crude, and primal, their showmanship appealed to the primitive in all. Exhibitions of natural curiosities stood side by side with novelty acts. Largest of all, and brashest among the sideshows, stood a boxing booth.

It was a big tent of dirty canvas, before which a painted proscenium had been raised on a scaffold with a platform that set the pitchman above the heads of the crowd. He had no megaphone, but intoned his message with a nasal cadence that was unlike natural speech but which fell on the ear like a ship's fog warning.

"Three rounds!" he was saying. "*Go* three rounds *with* the Masked Champion *and* win five dollars *and* compel him to reveal his face to all."

The so-called Masked Champion stood behind him in a dirty robe, his face concealed by a device no more elaborate than three holes poked in a knitted cap. He was tall and heavyset and badly out of condition. He was scanning the mostly male crowd, making a show of seeking out challengers.

"*Nev*er unmasked and *nev*er defeated," the barker went on. "Will you be the man to do it? Have we got any men out there? All I see is a bunch of ladies."

Some of the people booed and the barker continued to scan the gathering, working them with an expression of superiority and contempt.

"You!" called out the Masked Champion, pointing at someone in the crowd and shouting in a whiskeyed voice that barely carried over their heads. "I'll fight *you!*" And when his first random target held up his hands and shook his head, he chose another and pointed and shouted again. "I'll fight *you!*"

Elisabeth nudged Sebastian playfully.

"Go on, Sebastian," she said. "He says he'll fight you."

And for a moment it did, indeed, seem that the moth-eaten Masked Champion had picked Sebastian out of the mob to issue him a personal challenge. Sebastian avoided any meeting of eyes and told Elisabeth, "I somehow don't think so," but already the Champion had moved on and was pointing to provoke another.

"I have never seen a boxing match," said Elisabeth.

Sebastian turned to her in surprise. "Would you want to?"

She did not reply. But there was a sparkle in her eyes as she returned his look, as if daring him to respond to some hint that she'd just thrown out and he'd failed to notice. It was a look that he'd seen from her before. It usually marked the start of a path that would lead, in the end, to a private act. But he'd never seen it quite like this, and never before in a public place.

Before Sebastian could say anything more, there was a roar of approval from those all around them.

"We have a challenger!" the barker announced. "What's your name, boy?"

Sebastian immediately assumed a stooge, but the young man pushing his way to the front of the crowd was surrounded by friends of a similar age and seemed to be a legitimate member of the local public. "Henry Keenan," the young man shouted back, handing his hat to somebody and beginning to struggle out of his jacket as he moved.

"Come on up, then, Henry Keenan," the barker called. At the first sign of a contender, the Masked Champion had lowered his head and disappeared back through the flaps of the tent. "Take your seats inside, folks. No spitting, no gambling, no climbing into the ring. No children, sonny."

Elisabeth was still looking at Sebastian, still daring him. All around them people were starting to push their way toward the entrance to the booth, buffeting them like a passing flood.

Sebastian had seen something of life. He was fairly certain that the experience would not be as she imagined it. But how to explain that to her, without seeming to treat her like a child?

So he inclined his head slightly as if to say, Why not? And they gave in and went with the flow.

On the inside, the boxing booth was like a grimy circus tent over a cattle auction ring. There were shaky-looking wooden bleachers on all sides around the fight area. The place had almost filled up as Sebastian and Elisabeth found seats in the middle of a row. Sebastian had worried that his wife might be the only woman to join the audience, but she was far from alone.

The young challenger, now in shirtsleeves, had been given a well-used pair of gloves and was being laced into them by his companions. In the opposite corner of the ring, the Masked Champion was alone and taking off his robe. He had no second; all available hands were out among the crowd, moving along the rows and taking money.

As the robe came off it revealed high boots, long johns, and a woolen undershirt, with baggy trunks over. This closer look confirmed Sebastian's first impression. The man's body was powerful looking, but neglected and past its prime. There was something touchingly domestic about the way that he clumsily straightened the creases out of the robe before hanging it outside the ring, as if he had no other and it needed care. Sebastian wondered if he had just the one knitted mask, as well. It covered his entire head, showing only his eyes and his mouth.

In the middle of the arena the showman paced and swung around, favoring every corner of the tent with a commentary. He was there to keep the sense of a show alive for as long as the necessary business took.

"The man in the mask has fought before presidents and the crowned heads of Europe," he declaimed. "He has traveled the world and he has never been beaten. He has a special contempt for the males of Pennsylvania, who he says are the weakest-looking bunch of old women that he's ever come upon."

The males of Pennsylvania responded exactly as they were meant to, loudly and angrily, and the atmosphere became even more charged. It was a strange sight, the Philadelphia middle classes hooting and hollering like farmhands at a cockfight. Sebastian looked at his wife. She was slightly flushed, and he could sense the tension in her; she was glancing all around and missing nothing.

He reckoned he had a fair idea of how it would go. The professional went through this every day of his life, several times a day. A young blood in gloves was unlikely to trouble him much, however full of vim. He'd keep it going, giving the crowd their money's worth, making it look as if there was a real chance of an outcome, and then probably put the boy down midway through the third. The boy would be carried off with honor, bearing some manly damage and a tale to be told, and the Masked Champion would go back out front to the platform and do it all over again.

That was unless the boy showed some skill, or presented a genuine danger to the professional. Then it would be in the professional's best interest to floor the challenger quickly, and terminate the boy's luck. The crowd wouldn't like it. But there would be other crowds.

All was ready. "Three rounds," the barker cried out over the racket. "London rules." He then said something in a low voice that the two opponents had to lean in to hear. The masked man nodded, and the boy started to skip impatiently on the spot.

Then the barker raised his voice again. "Gentlemen, go to."

He stepped from the ring as the two men squared off.

The noise in the tent was now deafening. The fighters circled. The friends of Henry Keenan were right up against the ringside and making the most noise of all. The boy feinted a few times, and the fighter did nothing in response. Not even a flinch. When the boy suddenly put in a blow, the seasoned fighter blocked it without seeming to alter his stance by more than an inch or two.

Keenan's supporters grew even more vocal. Sebastian glanced again at Elisabeth. She seemed to be holding her breath.

They continued to circle, the masked fighter lumbering like an ox and the challenger becoming ever more bold. The champion's action wasn't impressive, although personally Sebastian wouldn't have cared to attempt to bring such an ox to the ground. That thought didn't seem to occur to Keenan; the fighter's stolidity and lack of speed were tempting the young man into a display of overconfidence.

Keenan was showing off, wasting his energies, playing to his friends. He got in a couple of body blows that didn't trouble the professional at all, and then a lucky one to the head that did. The masked man didn't stagger; but he took a step back and he closed up his guard, putting himself beyond the boy's reach for a moment. He drew his head back into his shoulders as if to protect it better, as if the punch had jarred him.

At the ringside, the Keenan faction roared even louder. Grinning, Keenan acknowledged his supporters and then turned back to press his imagined advantage.

He turned into the masked fighter's right glove, coming out of nowhere like a rock on a rope and snapping his head around. The left hit him a fraction of a second later, and snapped him around the other way.

One of the two blows broke his nose, but it was impossible to say which. Spit flew, blood flowed. Keenan reeled back, only keeping his balance by a fluke. Flailing his arms, rocking on his heels, he seemed ready to fall. The pro moved around with him, not lowering his guard, ready to give out more of the same.

Glancing at Elisabeth, Sebastian saw the color draining from her face. This was not as she'd imagined. He felt concern, but he also felt relief. Relief that she was still the woman he knew.

Over in the ring, the Masked Champion slammed in another cruel blow with calm accuracy. Henry Keenan wove, staggered, and fell to one knee. The barker was in the ring within moments, stepping between the two fighters with his hand upraised.

"Round One!" he declared. The professional ambled back to his corner, and the young man was lifted back to his own by a couple of his friends. All around Sebastian and Elisabeth, the crowd were getting to their feet in a near frenzy. Only that morning, most of them had been Christians in church; now, with the temporary permission of the sporting ritual, all were pagans in a pit.

She looked back at him and managed a weak smile. He guessed that she'd probably seen enough. Sebastian glanced around them, but between them and the exit was a noisy, heaving mass of passionate spectators. All in Sunday best. All baying like dogs at the scent of a kill.

Elisabeth touched her gloved hand to her lips briefly, as if in need of air.

"Gentlemen," the barker said, "go to."

Henry Keenan, partly recovered, came out of his corner with an angry shout. There was blood down his shirt and madness in his eyes. His opponent stood ready to block any punch he might throw. But Keenan now abandoned London rules. He swung no punch, but hurled himself on and headbutted the pro.

The masked fighter staggered. The barker jumped into the ring and tried to intervene, but Keenan shoved him away and pressed his advantage. The fighter's guard was down. Keenan kicked him a couple of times and then started to beat him about the head, while his friends roared encouragement. The barker seized Keenan from behind, pinning his arms and dragging him back. The masked man had dropped to one knee and stayed there, making a few feeble movements but not rising.

Elisabeth covered her eyes with one hand. Sebastian touched her on the shoulder. Impossible though the crush seemed, he had to get her out of there.

"Let's go," he said, and she nodded. They rose, and with Sebastian leading they started to push their way toward the exit.

Back in the ring, the masked fighter had managed to get to his feet. He stood grasping the rope with both gloves, panting and in pain, while the barker blocked Keenan's attempts to reach him again. Keenan's friends were climbing into the ring to back him up. The crowd was howling, and from all corners of the tent the carnies and bottle men who'd taken the money were pushing their way through to get to the trouble.

Nobody paid any attention to Sebastian and Elisabeth. He gave up on politeness because no one was listening, and started forcing a way.

As they reached the aisle, Elisabeth fell against his side and said, "It was not as I'd thought."

"I know," Sebastian said, putting an arm around her to protect her from further shoving. "But compared to some of the things I've seen people do to each other, I can assure you this is nothing."

It was getting worse. Keenan's friends had their hands on the barker and were restraining him as Keenan crossed the ring to where the masked fighter stood. For a moment it was looking as if he'd attack him again; but instead he put one hand on the man's shoulder. With the other, he grabbed the mask and pulled it off the fighter's head in a single motion.

The crowd gave a whoop as it came off. With the mask went any mystery that it had helped to generate. The man who stood revealed was a battered nonentity. Keenan held up the knitted rag and paraded it around the ring as if it was his enemy's head. Masked or unmasked, the fighter seemed not to care.

There had been no rare beauty hidden under there, that much was for sure. Hair cropped and mousy, a face like something pickled in gin. It was beginning to swell around the eye and cheekbone where Keenan's forehead had made contact. The fighter remained passive, his gloves holding the rope, his chest rising and falling, waiting for the noise to end or for his senses to return.

Out in the aisle, where he should have been helping Elisabeth, Sebastian found himself staring. It could not be. And yet . . .

"Sayers!" he breathed.

THREE

he man was like a train wreck on legs. But the more Sebastian stared, the more certain he became. Only when Elisabeth spoke his name did he remember his duty to her, and returned his attention to her safety.

They reached the outside air just as the park's own security force was arriving. Willow Grove employed a staff of twenty to patrol the grounds and keep order. Standards were set high. Where a man might be escorted to the gates for strolling without a jacket or a necktie, such a near riot in the house of the Noble Art was certain to result in stern measures. Sebastian and Elisabeth were not the only audience members to be leaving; and all, as they stepped out into daylight on the midway, blinked as if emerging from a nightmare.

They did not linger, but moved on toward the lakeside. Frances and the boy would be waiting there by now. Elisabeth seemed dazed, and said nothing about the spectacle they'd left behind them—indeed, she said nothing at all for ten minutes or more. And when she did, it was a weak "Ah. There they are."

Sebastian's thoughts tumbled and spun, but outwardly he stayed calm. He expected Robert to protest when told that the day was to be cut short, but the boy said nothing. Frances was puzzled, while Elisabeth seemed relieved.

He walked his party out toward Easton Road and saw them onto the departing trolley, where it became apparent that he did not intend to travel back with them. He stayed out on the platform and spoke through the open window.

"I can't explain it now," he said to Elisabeth. "I'll tell you everything when I get home."

"Sebastian?" she said. "Is this something to do with . . ."

"No," he said quickly, "it's not the Irish brothers. It's a very old and a very long story."

Her sister said, "I don't understand."

"I saw someone I know, Frances," Sebastian told her, looking over Elisabeth's shoulder. "I have to go back and find him."

"Who was it?" said Elisabeth. "Where?"

"It was someone I knew back in England. Please, just . . ." He made a helpless gesture, stepping back as the conductor signaled for the trolley's departure. "I'll see you at home."

When he got back to the boxing booth, it was to find that the tent had been emptied and the attraction closed down. A pole across a couple of chairs made a temporary barrier for the entranceway. Sebastian stepped over it and went inside, leaving the life of the midway behind him.

Nobody was within. The bleachers were empty and the ring was down, its ropes lying on the floor. He'd hoped to find someone who might direct him. But instead he spied an exit on the far side of the tent, and made his way over to it.

Beyond the exit was a canvas passageway, a square tunnel linking the big tent to a smaller. Rush matting had been laid down to walk on. At the end of the tunnel, the entrance flap had been tied back. From outside the canvas, Sebastian could hear the sounds of dogs and people in the little private Carnytown behind the midway.

The smaller tent had been set up as some kind of a dressing area or green room. A table had been made out of a plank and two barrels, and a mirror with a frame of faded gilt had been set up on it. Once, perhaps, the mirror had been magnificent. Now it was rescued junk, rubbish with half of its silver gone and pieces of its frame broken away.

Fitting enough for the man who sat before it.

He was on a bentwood chair that, like the mirror, looked as if it had been rescued from a bonfire after a long life in some better place. He sat there in his dirty robe leaning forward over an enamel bowl, folding a damp cloth that he then placed against the swelling and pressed on hard. He'd thrown off the gloves, but his hands were still bandaged for combat.

The woolen mask hung on a corner of the mirror. It, too, looked as if it had been rescued after being thrown around and trampled underfoot. Sebastian could see that his approach had gone unheard.

He cleared his throat and said, "Mister Sayers."

For a moment he thought that his attempt at self-introduction had passed unheard, as well. But then the figure at the mirror laid down the compress and slowly turned in his chair.

It took a moment for recognition to take hold, and even then there was little change in the man's expression. Certainly nothing as expressive as surprise. Good God. The last time he'd seen Tom Sayers, the man had been straight-backed and as handsome as they came. This man looked like any beaten old drunk.

"Inspector Becker," he said, in the same boozed-out voice that had challenged him from the platform.

"Not an inspector anymore," Sebastian said. "I'm an American now. A Pinkerton man."

Tom Sayers responded with a polite nod of deference and respect. On such a bruiser, it looked strange. He said, "Congratulations on finding success in your new career." His tone was still that of an educated man, which seemed strange coming out of the fairground fighter.

Sebastian moved around him, and picked the mask from its corner of the mirror. He'd retained that policeman's confidence that could give him an air of ownership over any other man's territory. He held the material delicately between thumb and forefinger, as if it might have the power to infect.

He said, "Speaking of careers. Does this defeat mark the end of yet another of yours?"

The man named Sayers did not exactly shrug, but it was clear that he was not to be provoked. I've come too far to be taunted by anything, that face seemed to be saying. I have seen too much.

He said, "Tonight we'll move on. Tomorrow brings another crowd. I'll put on the mask and go back in the ring. Who'll know? No one will care."

Sebastian threw the rag down before him. "You're past it, man," he said. "Have the sense to see it. Keep on like this, and one day you'll go down and they'll pick you up dead."

Sayers reached for the mask. "I expect that, Mister Becker," he said. "I expect it and I pray for it with all my heart." He smoothed out the mask, and folded it with care. Then he looked up.

"Why are you here?" he said. "I've committed no crime in this country. And whatever you may think that I did back in England, I can assure you that you know far less than half of the story."

"I'm here for the rest of it," Sebastian Becker said.

Sayers continued to look at him. Sebastian noted a slight tremor in the fighter's hands, probably something that Sayers wasn't even aware of.

Sebastian said, "I've waited fifteen years, Sayers. I came to believe you may not have been guilty. Unless you are now going to tell me that I am wrong."

Sayers looked away. He looked down. He rubbed his bandaged hand through his short cropped hair. Then he breathed out heavily, as if even the thought of the challenge was enough to defeat him.

Sebastian looked around the tent and saw another chair, over by a steamer trunk. It did not match the other. He went to it, picked it up, and brought it over.

Placing it squarely before Sayers, he sat down.

"Well?" he said.

THE MIDLANDS

August–September

1888

F O U R

t was on an August night in the year of eighteen hundred and eighty-eight that the curtain fell on the week's final presentation of *The Purple Diamond,* a play in two acts performed by the Edmund Whitlock Touring Theatrical Company.

The Lyric was a small provincial house, and a packed one. The play, which could stand alone or serve as the second half of a variety bill, was a sentimental barnstormer with a leading role full of old-style rant, cant, and claptrap. Actor-manager Edmund Whitlock had honed his delivery over more than eight hundred performances, all of them in theaters and music halls just like this.

If anything, he'd honed it a little too well. The others in the company could see that he was becoming bored in the role. When "the boss" got bored, his performance might carry on at full volume but his mind would start to wander. He'd bought the play from its author and put money into the set, so he was bound to keep it in repertoire as long as there was a venue somewhere in the British Isles that remained unvisited. But tonight he'd missed a piece of business in the second scene, and the Low Comedian had been forced to cover with a lengthy ad lib. Had any other member of the company made such a mistake, there would have been hell to pay. But Whitlock was the boss, so no one would ever hear it mentioned.

The five supporting actors came in from the wings and took their calls, then moved to the sides ready for Whitlock to take center stage.

He sprang through the curtain and then froze there, as if astonished at this unexpected level of attention; a man of sixty in a tight corset, hair blacked and cheeks rouged, fresh—if fresh can be the word—from playing a hero half his age. But so forgiving was the limelight, and so powerful the spell of theater, that nobody ever seemed to find this remarkable.

He came forward to the footlights, hands clasped together, beaming out at the audience with humility and delight. Their whistling and cheering seemed set to go on forever.

And not without reason. Backstage, Tom Sayers leaned out to get a view from the wings. One hand was raised and ready to give a signal to an assembled choir that included the company's carpenter, both stagehands, the teenage Call Boy, and the sewing woman. With slapsticks, rattles, and whistles, they were lined up behind the curtain to give the boss' reception the extra lift that he sometimes felt it needed.

Whitlock raised a hand for calm; Sayers dropped his, and the stage crew immediately stopped making noise and started taking down the set.

As the house quieted, the actor-manager gave every corner of it the benefit of his most penetrating and affectionate gaze. This was a mining town and he gazed out upon starched linen, bad teeth, and brilliantine. The women's faces were mostly indistinguishable from the men's. To a visitor's eye all the children appeared simple, or vaguely criminal.

"My friends," Whitlock boomed. "My friends. My dear, dear friends. The warmth and the love that you have shown to us tonight will ensure that the name of . . ."

Here he seemed to choke with emotion. Sayers knew why. Yet again, the boss had failed to take note of where they were playing. Once, long ago, Sayers had given him a prompt at this point. It had brought the house down, and he would never repeat the mistake. He held his breath.

". . . of *your town* will be engraved forever on our hearts."

Whitlock smacked a fist against his chest, where he kept his heart.

"Ours has been a glorious time together. Tonight we must leave you . . . yes!" he cried quickly, forestalling any cries of protest. "But as our parting gift, let us leave you with a song in the Italian style from the newest addition to our company, Miss Louise Porter."

The waiting cast led the applause as Louise, twenty-two years old and the company's soubrette, stepped forward to join Whitlock. He pressed his lips to her gloved hand and then showed her to the crowd as the other company members melted silently into the wings.

Miss Porter might have been significantly easier on the eye than her employer, but he left no doubt as to which of them was the major figure. Having conferred his patronage, he made an exit through the curtain and left her alone on the stage.

The company had a musical director who played piano in the pit, and conducted the resident band at the bigger dates. This playhouse was on the small side, but it had a good piano and the piano was in tune.

Miss Porter began to sing.

As soon as Whitlock came back through the curtain, he was met with a silver tray bearing a clean towel and a glass of port. The tray was brought by a stagehand who doubled as Whitlock's personal valet, and who was known to all as the Silent Man. He'd been with Whitlock for longer than anyone could remember. He wasn't entirely without speech, but came from some distant part of Europe and spoke no more than he needed to. His wife, inevitably known as the Mute Woman, appeared to have no English at all.

Glass in hand, Whitlock passed within a couple of feet of Tom Sayers. Sayers was supervising the removal of their stage properties and ticking off each item from a list in his leather-bound notebook. The stagehands moved in silence. By the time the audience rose to leave, the stage behind the curtain would be all but bare.

Whitlock lowered his voice and said to Sayers, "I've seen more enthusiastic welcomes for the mortuary trolley in a sanatorium. When do we get out of this godforsaken pit?"

"We've a special that pulls out at midnight," Sayers told him.

"Amen to that," said Whitlock. He raised his glass as if in a toast, and walked off to seek out the house manager.

Sayers, left behind, felt able to relax his vigilance over the striking of the set and to move back to the spot in the wings from where he had a view of the forestage. There was Louise. Here was her song.

And this was Tom Sayers' nightly moment of weakness.

Sayers was Edmund Whitlock's acting manager, charged with all the business dealings of a company on the road. He booked the dates, he arranged the travel, he hired the staff, and he fired those who drank or disgraced themselves. He dealt with correspondence and sometimes stepped in to serve as stage manager or baggage master. To all he was a shoulder to lean upon, and for some a shoulder to cry on.

It was Sayers who'd read *The Purple Diamond* and recommended its purchase to Whitlock, and it was Sayers who had found Louise when their last soubrette had jumped ship in Leicester and left them without cover. Louise was a young woman who had written a letter to Bertram's inquiring about the possibility of a stage career, with no other qualification than that she sang and spoke poetry well.

She'd had little idea of what a theatrical life entailed. Sayers' understanding was that her family faced reduced circumstances after her father's death. Going into service was no option for a child who had grown up in a house with a maid, and life as a governess or companion held no appeal. From the tone of her letter to the agency, it was clear that the stage represented some girlish dream. But inexperienced though she was, she was available to play and willing to take Whitlock's wages.

She'd since begun to mature into a considerable beauty. Not every man's ideal, but enough for most. For those who liked their women big and broad and always ready to scrap, she would never do. But to a man like Sayers, largely inexperienced in romance, she represented perfection.

Every performance ended with her song, and every night Sayers would pause in the wings and watch her. It was always the same: the graceful line of her neck and the angle of her shoulder, that profile when she turned her head. Against the darkness of the house, she seemed to glow. Dazzled by the white of her skin, he could have counted every hair.

Most nights he would stay to the end, and join in the applause. But tonight he dared not. There was too much to be done, and when the sound of footsteps backstage brought him out of his reverie, he quickly consulted his notebook and returned to his work.

Sayers made his way down to the scene dock, where the removers' wagon was due to arrive at any moment. Some of the scenery was already folded and stacked there, and most of the properties numbered and wrapped in sacking and placed in wicker baskets. The costume hampers and the company's personal luggage would be joining them shortly. All was darkness until the scenery doors began to roll back, whereupon a widening crack of light began to reveal the bricks and rain of the gaslit alley behind the theater.

The wagon was already waiting there. It was high-sided, horse-drawn, and on time. The rain was coming down in silver darts under the gas lamps and the drays stood there in harness, stoical and unprotesting as it fell upon them. A man in oilskins was clambering down from the driver's seat and another was around the back and opening up the tailgate.

Satisfied that all was progressing as it should, Sayers went back up the iron stairs toward the dressing room corridor.

At the top of the stairway he met James Caspar, about to descend. Caspar had wiped off his makeup but had done no more than throw a coat over his stage costume of black tie, wing collar, and tails. He stepped aside and indicated, with an overstated grace that had an air of mockery, that Sayers should pass.

"Thank you, Caspar," Sayers said. "Cabs at the stage door in twenty minutes."

Caspar made no comment, and his smile didn't change. He was the company's Leading Male Juvenile and, just as Louise had been "found" by Sayers, Caspar was Whitlock's own discovery. He was very dark, very slick, and very handsome. He had few gifts as an actor, but he moved well and held the eye. Sayers had an athlete's physique, but clothes never sat on him the way they suited Caspar. Caspar dressed like a prince in disguise. Sometimes Sayers would catch sight of himself in a mirror and think that his hard-wearing checked suit and brogues made him look like a country farmer scrubbed up for a wedding.

Sayers felt no reason to envy Caspar. But all the same, he could not like him.

He appeared to be set on leaving the building.

"Caspar!"

Sayers called out his name, but too late. James Caspar had ducked out of the open scene dock and into the rain, slipping out like a cat through a kitchen door. He clearly had plans of his own for the scant hour or so between now and midnight.

Well, so be it. Caspar was his own man. And if being his own man led him to miss the midnight special and so their first date in a new town . . . well, again, so be it. No one here was irreplaceable.

And replacing James Caspar was a job that Sayers would have been more than happy to add to his duties.

Sayers could hear the applause for Louise as he returned to the dressing-room corridor and rapped on the first of the doors. They loved her, all those misshapen miners and their hardworking women. All the shopgirls and the sweepers and the factory hands out there. Their applause echoed through the backstage spaces of the house like that of ghosts from some earlier time. He could picture Louise, giving her single bow and backing through the curtain that one of the stagehands had been assigned to hold open for her.

When a shout came in response to his knock, he swung it open to find the Low Comedian and Ricks, the company's First Heavy, already dressed for the street and removing the last traces of pancake from their faces.

"Cabs at the stage door in twenty minutes," Sayers repeated. "Make sure you're ready."

"Cabs!" the Low Comedian said. "Does this mean the boss finally remembered what his pockets are for?"

"It means we've a train that goes at midnight and if we miss it, no matinee tomorrow."

Usually, a run would end on a Saturday night and then the company would have all of Sunday to travel. All over the British Isles, stations like Crewe or the Exchange in Manchester would be abuzz with actors and stage workers, all meeting on the platforms and in the public rooms and catching up with the news as they awaited their connections. The public would turn out, just to see the spectacle of it all.

But with half-week bookings—Monday to Wednesday in one town, Thursday to Saturday in the next—everyone had to scramble. And when the dates were so many miles apart, as sometimes they had to be, then there was little room for error in the acting-manager's organization.

As Sayers pulled the dressing room door shut and turned away, he had to step back for fifteen-year-old Arthur Steffens, the company's call-boy. Arthur had an armload of newspapers and was moving at his usual speed. He was always running five errands at once, being in no position to refuse any of them. Caspar used him more than anyone, and did not treat him well.

"Arthur!" Sayers called after him.

"Mister Sayers?"

"Don't waste your time looking for Mister Caspar when the cabs arrive. I just saw him leave the building."

"No, sir. I mean, yes, sir. Was there anything else, sir?"

"If he comes back with his costume ruined, you can tell him it'll come out of his wages."

The boy looked so stricken at the thought of the task that Sayers had to relent and let him off the hook.

"All right, then, Arthur," he said. "I'll tell him myself. Get on with you."

Arthur scuttled off down the corridor, and Sayers moved along to
the next dressing room. Without contriving it, he somehow reached the
door in the same moment as Louise.

"Miss Porter," he said.

"Mister Sayers," she responded. Their formality was only half-
serious. It was a joke that they'd been sharing for most of the year.
Sayers liked to believe that her ease in these exchanges signaled the even-
tual possibility of some deeper feeling.

"I watched you sing," Sayers said.

"You always do. I'd think my luck had turned bad if I didn't see my
little mascot standing there."

Sayers affected dismay. "Your little mascot?" he said. "Thank you,
ma'am."

"You know I'm teasing. Was I good?"

"I could hear their hearts turning over. How do you do it?"

"I don't know," she said. "It must be all the great suffering I've
endured. I suppose it's third class again tonight."

"I've reserved a private compartment for you."

"Oh, Tom," she said, genuinely surprised. "However did you manage that?"

"Never ask a magician to explain his effects."

"Bless you, Tom. Whatever would I do without you?"

"I've no doubt some other devoted servant would rush forward in
my place."

"I'd never find one as devoted as you are, Tom," she said, and with
that she seemed to float into her dressing room with the sewing woman
following close behind.

The dressing rooms were small and had bare walls of painted brick.
Louise Porter's had a stove and folding screen behind which she could
get out of her stage costume. As she sat to unpin her hair, the sewing
woman showed her the tray that she was carrying. Silver-plated and a

prop from their last production, it had borne Whitlock's port and towel only a few minutes before. Now it carried a number of engraved visiting cards and a single red rose.

"For you, Miss Porter," said the sewing woman. "Sent through by the stage doorkeeper. With the compliments of various gentlemen."

Louise looked over the cards with the mildest of interest. Gentlemen? Here? Mining engineers and merchants at best.

"Only five?" she said after a quick count. "How ancient and ugly I must have become." And then, shaking her head once so that her unpinned hair fell loose, she rose to go behind the screen.

Raising her voice, the sewing woman said, "Shall I deal with them in the usual way, ma'am?"

"Have the doorman give them each a picture." During their last London dates, Whitlock had sent her along to Window and Grove's on Baker Street to sit for a postcard. She'd posed as Desdemona, a role she'd never played. Then he'd docked the cost of the prints from her wages.

As Louise shrugged herself out of her stage dress and the first layer of the underwear that went with it, the sewing woman moved to the iron stove. She picked up some tongs with which to lift the lid.

She said, "Tom Sayers stopped to hear your song."

"Yes," Louise said absently. "Isn't he sweet." She might share jokes with Sayers about service and devotion. But the truth of it was that the acting manager usually went from her thoughts in the same moment that he left her sight.

"Last night, Mister Caspar did the same."

Louise stopped. She put her head out from behind the screen.

"Did he really?" she said.

The sewing woman made a face of assent as, tongs in one hand and tray in the other, she let cards and flower all slide into the flames together before replacing the stove lid with a clank.

"Well," said Louise.

She drew back behind the screen. But she mused on the thought for a moment before she continued to undress.

Well, indeed.

———

Members of the company were now starting to gather around the stage doorkeeper's office, where Sayers had posted the movement order and from where the cabs would pick them up. Whitlock had stepped inside with the doorman and was still keeping a tight hold upon his cashbox. Usually the Silent Man was at his side, shaven of head and bony of skull, a forbidding presence and a deterrent to all.

When Whitlock saw Sayers through the glass, he beckoned him in. Like all doorkeepers' offices it was a cramped and cozy space, and the doorman was unhappy to share it.

Whitlock said, "What do I hear about Caspar?"

"He didn't wait for the carriages," Sayers told him.

"Does he know where to go?"

Sayers made a helpless gesture. "If he read the order. Who can say?"

Whitlock glanced away for a moment, thinking hard and none too pleased.

"I'll speak to him on the train," he decided.

"Assuming he catches it," Sayers said. "I don't know where he's gone."

When Sayers came out of the doorkeeper's office he was collared by the Low Comedian. The man's true name was Gulliford, but in the profession he went as Billy Danson (a Baggy Suit and a Big Smile). He had his traveling bag in his hand, and he'd been reading the movement order over the heads of the others.

He said, "The train list says you're in with me."

"That's right."

"You always get a private compartment."

"Not tonight," Sayers said, and went off to make sure that the scenery and props were on their way.

F I V E

bout a mile from the playhouse stood an arena of a different kind, the town's cattle auction with its adjoining slaughterhouse. Local farmers drove in their herds at one end, and local butchers carried off dressed carcasses from the other. In between stood a yard like a parade ground with a drain across the middle of it, an auction hall with covered pens and a bidding ring, and an abattoir with two killing floors and a cesspool. Few houses were to be found nearby, but a soap works and a tannery took water from the same river and returned their noxious wastes to it after. The river then flowed through the town, foaming at every bend and weir.

James Caspar had walked here alone. The rain had continued to fall, quickly clearing the streets of departing theatergoers and leaving him unobserved. Now it was driving harder, and it glistened on the cobbles as he looked out across the yard. He was under cover. Behind him, several dozen animals moved uneasily in the pens. They read their own mortality in the scent of the air, but did not understand its meaning.

A high brick wall surrounded the yard and buildings. The main gates were open and a single lamp hung from the center of the archway above them. By tilting his pocket watch, Caspar could just about read the time by its light. This was later than he'd intended.

Someone was coming through the gate. Two figures, running. Crouched against the rain, coats flapping; and there, because he'd missed it at first, a smaller figure in between them. The Silent Man was holding out one side of his unbuttoned greatcoat like a bat's wing, sheltering whoever ran by his side. A few strides back from them came the Mute Woman, his wife, hurrying to keep up.

Caspar flipped down the cover on his pocket watch and drew himself up. It would not do to let his impatience show; but nor would it do to conceal his displeasure. A tricky call.

The Silent Man arrived in front of him. His wife came no farther than she needed to get herself out of the rain. The Silent Man lifted his coat aside to reveal his sheltered companion.

"Well," said Caspar, "let's see what we have here." He came around for a better look in the poor light, and the Silent Man turned with him.

"A boy," said Caspar.

The Silent Man watched him, dark eyes staring from his skull of a face. He was both apprehensive and submissive. The boy just stood there.

It was impossible to tell his exact age, but he was young. Malnutrition probably made him seem even younger than he really was. He was thin, he was awkward, and he was ragged. His ginger hair had been recently cut as if by a novice shearer, leaving bare patches and scabs. His mouth hung open. Only his eyes seemed alive, and they were wide with terror.

"Oh, well," Caspar said. "Time's limited, I suppose. What's your name?"

Not a flicker in response.

"No name," said Caspar. "What's this?" He touched his white-gloved hand to the back of the boy's head and then inspected the stain on his fingertips. The light here was too poor to be certain of the shade, but it might have been purple.

"Some kind of paint," Caspar said. "What's it for? Ringworm?"

Still nothing. Caspar took the boy by the shoulder and started to walk him farther into the building, where candles had been lit. "Some-one cares a little for you, then," he said. The Silent Man and his wife hung back, their part in the entertainment done. Caspar's grip on the child was firm, not enough to cause him pain, but enough to hold him fast should he try to run.

Caspar said, "How would you like to feel clean for once in your life, boy? How would you like to be cleaner than you've ever been before? Because that's something I can do for you. It's an art that I've practiced. Here."

Steering with his hand, he made the boy turn. The boy swayed and staggered, going wherever he was directed but without much grace or elegance. A ramp led to the upper floor of the building. It was long and shallow and scattered with dirty straw. Trapdoors linked the two levels of the slaughterhouse and chains hung straight down through them. As they ascended, the candlelight grew brighter.

Caspar's grip on the boy tightened as they reached the top of the ramp and the open part of the upper floor came into view. Pennies jangled in the boy's pocket. Caspar made a mental note to have the Silent Man retrieve them afterward.

"See, boy," he said. "Here's what I can do for you."

The boy looked, and for the first time gave some sign of awareness and understanding. He started to whimper. The whimper turned into a scream.

"Now, now," said Caspar. Down below, the Silent Man and his wife started to beat with sticks on the sides of the cattle pens so that the animals started to shift and low, drowning out any sounds that might come from above.

"Shouting won't help," said Caspar. "But I'm sure I can show you something that will."

SIX

t was a close-run thing but they were on the station concourse by twenty minutes to midnight, leaving just enough time to get their freight loaded into the goods van and their people into the sleeping cars. The railway's theater man had opened up the goods-yard gates so that the carriages could draw in alongside the platform. The stage crew transferred the flats, properties, and costume hampers with maximum efficiency. The actors fussed and argued and took rather longer.

Whitlock traveled with four heavy cases, a steamer trunk, and a lapdog named Gussie. He was prepared to carry the lapdog, but Sayers had to organize the transfer of his employer's luggage in the absence of the Silent Man. The actors hung out of the windows and watched.

As Whitlock exercised Gussie on the platform, the railway's theater man caught up with him. He was a slight man with a mustache, a long brown overcoat, and a bowler hat. "Mister Whitlock?" he said. "Mister Edmund Whitlock?"

"Here," Whitlock said with his usual conscious grandeur.

"Cooper, sir. Theatrical representative for the Midland Railway. I'm sorry about your missing people, sir, but I can't hold the train any longer."

With one hand, Whitlock scooped up Gussie from the platform; the other he held up for silence.

"Don't say another word, Mister Cooper," he said. "There is only so much spare capacity in any man's head, and I reserve all of mine for the classics."

With that, he swept himself and his dog onto the train leaving Cooper for someone else to deal with. If he thought that Sayers would step into his place, he was wrong. Sayers had already tried his best with the theater man, and at that moment was elsewhere in the station.

Sayers had spotted someone across the platforms. Could it be? It surely was. Leaving the train and the company, he dashed to the iron bridge that crossed the tracks. It took him up close to the roof beams where all the steam and the smoke drifted. "Bram!" he started calling out even before he was safely within earshot. "Bram Stoker!"

The big Irishman on Platform Five turned at the sound of his name. He'd been easy to identify, even at night and at a distance. A man in his early forties, well over six feet tall and solidly built, he was brown-haired and auburn-bearded. He waited with a look of polite uncertainty as Sayers descended to the platform and crossed toward him.

"Forgive me, Bram," Sayers said, getting his breath under control as he reached his opposite number. In the same way that Sayers was Whitlock's man, Stoker was Henry Irving's. Sayers might be hooked up with a modest little touring dog-and-pony show and Stoker with the mighty Lyceum company, but they surely were brothers under the skin.

Or perhaps not. Sayers saw the searching look in the Irishman's eyes as Stoker gave him a moment of study.

"You do not know me," Sayers said.

Stoker took one moment longer and then said, "You're Tom Sayers. The prizefighter. You wrote and played in . . ."

"A Fight to the Finish."

"You took out the number one touring company in 'eighty-three."

"I serve as acting manager for Edmund Whitlock now."

"As penance for what?" Stoker said wryly.

"I beg a favor, Bram," Sayers said, without rising to the implied slight on his employer. "My company's three short, and I don't know where they are. Have you any influence with the railway's theater man?"

"To hold back your train?"

"By any amount of time at all."

Stoker checked his watch against the station clock and promised to see what could be done. As they crossed the iron bridge, he told Sayers that he was on his way to Scotland to join the rest of the Lyceum people in researching settings for a new production of *Macbeth*. He had broken his journey here to discuss arrangements for the provincial tour of *Faust* that was to precede it.

Researching settings! Sayers marveled at the very thought. Sets for *The Purple Diamond* had been picked up cheaply from the Theatre Royal at Bilston, whose scene dock was filled with the props and scenery of companies that had gone bust there.

Whitlock might not be the easiest of managers. He might not play the best houses, or be received by royalty, or be honored by any major institution. But he led a working company in an uncertain field of endeavor. He kept his dates and gave a living to others. Stoker might have the good fortune to be working for an actor at the very top of his profession. But it was thanks to Edmund Whitlock, and the hundreds like him, that the profession existed at all; and had he not been in such pressing need, Sayers would probably have stopped to argue the case.

While Stoker sought out Cooper, Sayers boarded the waiting train. He had to stride over bags and a birdcage in the corridor. As he was making his way down toward Whitlock's compartment, Louise stepped out to intercept him.

"Tom," she said. "Where is Mister Caspar?"

"Nobody knows," Sayers said, perhaps a little tersely.

"Could he have come to any harm?"

"Him? I don't imagine so."

"Something like this has happened before, has it not?"

It had, in Sunderland, and in Sayers' opinion Caspar should have been dismissed for his offense there and then.

But he said, "I really don't think it's right for us to be discussing this. Will you please excuse me, Miss Porter?"

She withdrew into her compartment—the one that should have been his own, and that he had given up for her—and he tapped on Whitlock's door.

"Who is it?"

"Tom Sayers, sir."

There was a pause and then, after a moment, he heard the door being unlocked. When Whitlock let him in, he saw that all the blinds had been drawn and the cashbox was open. Sayers was the company's bookkeeper, but Whitlock always liked to count the take for himself.

He closed the compartment door behind Sayers and secured it again, and then said, "Well?"

"Bram Stoker's on the station," Sayers told him. "He'll speak to the railway company for us. I think they'll hold the train awhile longer."

"So you're telling me that Henry Irving's man carries more influence than Edmund Whitlock's?"

Sayers had no ready or diplomatic reply, but then realized that Whitlock was only making sport with him. Vain Whitlock might be. Stupid he was not.

"Sir," Sayers said. "May I speak openly?"

Whitlock sat. Without the hair black that he wore onstage, his own hair was a fine shade of silver. His eyes were dark and his features were strong. His back was always straight . . . but that could have been due to the corset, which he seemed to imagine that no one was aware of.

He said, "Is it about Caspar?"

"I've held my peace for long enough," Sayers said. "James Caspar is a growing problem for all of us. I think it neither wise nor desirable that we continue to put the company's existence at risk for the appetites of one performer. We are men of the world, Edmund. If he wants to go whoring, that's his concern. But now the women are starting to notice."

Whitlock considered. He seemed unusually drained and weary-looking tonight. Looking down on him, Sayers began to wonder for the first time whether there could be substance to some of the backstage whispers. That there might be more to the actor-manager's lapses than an overfamiliarity with the play.

"By the women, do you mean sweet little Louise?" Whitlock said. "An undisclosed affection there, wouldn't you say?"

"What do you mean?"

"For Caspar."

For *Caspar*? Sayers could not envision a less suitable attachment. Yet he could imagine how a man like Caspar might appear to one so young and impressionable. He felt a dismay that he took care not to show.

He said, "All the more reason to bring it to an end."

"We need him."

"Not so. I can send a wire in the morning and have a replacement letter-perfect by Friday night."

"No, Tom."

"Why not?"

"Please do not ask me to explain."

Sayers was about to reply, but at that moment there was some commotion outside in the corridor. Whitlock turned to stow the cashbox, and Sayers let himself out.

The members of the company had emerged from their compartments and were standing at the open windows on the platform side. Ricks and the Low Comedian and most of the stage crew were whistling and cheering. A couple of people moved to make space for Sayers so that he could look out with the rest of them.

Emerging from a cloud of steam at the far end of the platform were three strange shapes in lurching silhouette: a great winged figure like a flying Mephistopheles, buttressed on either side by supporting gargoyles, all three staggering this way and that as if the earth shook beneath them. Then the steam cleared and detail emerged; it was Caspar, arms outstretched for support, coat flapping wide, with the Silent Man and the Mute Woman attempting to steer him toward the train while his legs pursued some erratic agenda of their own. The company cheered them on, and the Low Comedian opened a door to receive them.

"Stop the noise!" Sayers shouted. "Please! Consider our reputation!"

The Silent Man and his wife got Caspar to the train. Ricks and the Low Comedian reached out and hauled him in by his clothing. Sayers' warning had come too late; they'd drawn the attention of strangers from other carriages. Railwaymen had stopped to watch from the bridge and one or two later travelers had emerged from the station's waiting rooms, drawn by the disturbance.

Landing in the train, Caspar bounced off the paneling and almost fell back out again. But the Silent Man and his wife were now blocking the way. A guard's whistle sounded outside on the platform and the door was slammed from without.

As the train began to move. Sayers spied Bram Stoker standing with the railway's theater man. It was ten minutes after the hour. Sayers raised his hand in a wave of thanks as they went by, and saw it returned.

Then he closed the window and turned to deal with James Caspar.

Most of the others had returned to their berths. Caspar was clinging to a handrail while his silent companions were trying to detach him and get him into his own compartment. Sayers moved down the corridor toward them with mounting anger.

But before he could reach the dissipated Juvenile, Louise stepped out ahead of him. Her back was turned and she did not see Sayers at all. Her attention was directed toward the young man who was now somehow managing to find his feet despite the motion of the train.

"Mister Caspar!" she said. "Are you unwell?"

She spoke without irony and with genuine concern. Caspar drew himself up to his full height, and then threw off the hands that would support him. He raised a finger, as if he'd just been struck by a brilliant idea that he was about to express.

But then, instead of coming out with it, he looked and saw the open compartment door. He went toward it like a falling oak. As he disappeared from sight, the door was slid from within and the blinds pulled with a speed that seemed impossible.

Louise moved to the closed door, head bent and listening, hand raised to knock.

"Mister Caspar?" she said. A sound came from the other side of the door; more than coughing, not quite vomiting. The Silent Man and his wife exchanged a glance and started to back away.

Louise turned to Sayers as he reached her.

"I don't know what to do for him," she said helplessly.

Sayers said, "Come away, Louise. Please."

From inside the compartment, Caspar's audible exertions grew more major.

"But what if he needs a doctor?" Louise said.

"I do think that's unlikely."

Something caught her eye as she glanced down. Sayers looked and saw something pooling under the door. It was a widening fan of red. It was thick and moving slowly.

Sayers hardly knew what to say.

But he did not need to say a thing for Louise's eyes turned upward in her head and she fell against him in a dead faint. She turned as she fell, and her feet kicked up into the air; before he knew it, he was holding her in both arms as if to carry her to safety.

He was too shocked to move. Her body was utterly relaxed and pressed against his, almost the full length of it; her weight in his arms, her head against his shoulder, the warm scent of her hair up close to his face. It was like the first time he had danced with a woman, only more so; the same overwhelming sense of forbidden physical contact, the same heady feeling of time slowing down. And the fact that his first dance had been with one of his aunts left him totally unprepared for this.

"Bring her in here!" Whitlock's voice rang down the corridor. Sayers looked over his shoulder and saw the boss in the doorway to his own compartment, beckoning. He turned around with extra care, swaying with the motion of the train. One of Louise's shoes dropped, and he had to leave it where it fell. Moving sideways, holding tight to the weight and warmth of her, he shuffled along.

"Mrs. Wrigglesworth!" Whitlock called again, and as Sayers carried Louise into the compartment the sewing woman appeared behind him.

"Fetch smelling salts," Whitlock said to her, and she quickly vanished again.

Gussie was removed to his basket and Miss Porter was lowered onto the seat. The sewing woman patted Louise's hand while Whitlock waved the bottle of ammonia salts under her nose. Sayers stood back, feeling awkward and embarrassed but not as unhappy as he might. The sense of Louise so entirely in his arms would take a long time to fade.

"Easy, child," Whitlock said as the ammonia brought her to her senses with a start. "All is well."

Louise blinked dazedly. Whitlock moved back as she pushed herself to sit upright. "I don't understand," she said.

"Young Mister Caspar has rather disgraced himself."

"Is he not dying?"

"By morning, I've no doubt he'll think it preferable to the head that he'll have."

"What about the blood?"

"Blood?"

"Under the door."

"Ah. Sayers?" Whitlock looked up at his acting manager.

"Cheap red wine and ruby port," Sayers suggested tersely. He was in no mood to offer excuses for Caspar. Let Louise see the man as he really was.

Whitlock said, "Let us pursue this indelicate line no further. I have to ask for your understanding." He looked around to include Tom Sayers and the sewing woman. "All of you," he said. "This is not something of which I often speak. I knew Caspar's father. I'll go into no details, but they had been separated for some time. Caspar was a wild child and all but a lost soul then. His father had taken on the work of reclaiming him for God, but died with it barely begun. I swore to him that I would continue the work until its end. I pledged my own soul to the task." At this point, he looked pointedly at Sayers. "Do not judge Caspar too harshly," he said. "One day you will see the good in him, as I do. There has been much to overcome. There is yet some distance to go."

"That is a very noble story, Mister Whitlock," Louise said, and Sayers felt his heart sink a little.

Whitlock acknowledged her compliment with a slight and graceful nod. Sayers, tight-faced, was disinclined to believe a single word of it. He knew Whitlock's technique too well, and was least persuaded when the old tragedian seemed at his most sincere. But he said nothing.

A few minutes later, Louise was well enough to return to her own berth. Sayers would have stayed to present his argument to Whitlock, but a warning look told him that Whitlock would not have it. At least not here, and not now.

Sayers stepped out of Whitlock's compartment and closed the door behind him. It was, perhaps, inevitable that Louise would believe only the best of someone. Had Caspar been a worthier man, Sayers' gloom would have been more profound; as it was, he had to have faith that she would see the wastrel's true nature before too long, and reach the appropriate conclusion. By much the same token, Sayers hoped to have his own qualities understood.

A woman would choose the steadfast man in the end. It was always so upon the stage.

The corridor was empty now. The sewing woman had retrieved Louise's fallen shoe. Everyone else in the company had retired.

Except for one figure, down at the far end.

The Mute Woman was there on her hands and knees outside Caspar's compartment. She had several rags and a bucket of water, and she was cleaning up the stain from the floor.

She looked up, and her eyes met Sayers' own. Her expression did not change. She swayed a little with the movement of the train. Her face remained blank.

And as Sayers turned to make his way to the berth that he was to share with the Low Comedian, the Mute Woman lowered her head and carried on with her task.

S E V E N

he next morning, about an hour before noon, a group of men passed through the gates of the cattle yard. Three were in police uniforms, and two were not. They were led by Superintendent Turner-Smith, a formidable figure with a broad white mustache, a war wound, and a walking stick. Despite his impediment, the others had to hasten to keep up with him.

The group crossed the marshaling area to reach the slaughterhouse. There was a bellowing from the nearby pens, and a foul country smell in the air. The business of the cattle market had been under way since first light, but after the last arrivals the stones of the yard had been swept and most of the dung moved outside the walls. Turner-Smith spied an approaching figure and altered his course in order that the two of them should meet.

The approaching figure was a man of less than thirty, brown-haired and black-suited. He'd a broad forehead and serious eyes, as brown as any Spanish girl's.

"Well then, Becker," Turner-Smith said. "What do you have for me?"

Sebastian Becker, the youngest inspector in the city police's Detective Department, fell into step beside his superior and pointed the way.

"It's the head slaughterman we need to speak to, sir," Becker said. "He's waiting for us upstairs."

"They use stairs?" Turner-Smith said. "Who'd have imagined such talented animals?"

"There's a ramp, sir. Or I could have the evidence brought down. They slaughter the animals on one floor and butcher them on another."

"I think I can manage the ascent. We may be in a knacker's yard, Sebastian, but I'm not quite ready to turn myself in for cats' meat yet."

"No, sir." Becker did not blush, but nor did he smile. He directed them into a whitewashed passage that would take the party away from the auction ring and into the heart of the abattoir.

As they entered the passage, one of the other two detectives knocked him with a shoulder and almost bumped him into the wall.

"Forgive me, brother," the man said without looking at him, and in a tone that did not suggest repentance.

Sebastian knew that he was little liked by his fellow officers. In a force where promotion was mainly a matter of putting in the years and awaiting your turn, Sebastian's appetite for the job seemed to be held against him.

"No harm done," said Sebastian.

Nobody paid them any attention as they made their way through. The work here was hard, and conducted at speed because the killing floor set the pace for the rest of the workforce. The animals came unwillingly from the pens, usually having to be dragged with ropes and driven with sticks; one was in the loading enclosure as they went by, thrashing dangerously and surrounded by slaughtermen in caps and leather aprons. One swung a hammer and stunned the beast; another leaned in with a knife as it dropped, and slit its throat.

In the time that it took the police party to reach the ramp, the others had shackled its back legs and its carcass was being lifted on a chain hoist. The blood came out of it as if poured from a bucket, steaming in the thick air and flooding into a collection trough.

Elsewhere on the same floor, men stripped to the waist were pulling the lights out of carcasses while others flayed the hides off, adding them to a growing heap like bedsheets of bloodied rubber. Sebastian glanced back as they ascended the ramp, and noted that one of the uniformed men had taken out a handkerchief and was pressing it over his face. The sights were no doubt bearable to men as experienced as these, but the smell was unlike anything he'd encountered before. He looked at Turner-Smith, and saw that his superior seemed unperturbed.

Sebastian could guess why he'd faced no competition when he'd picked up this case. Something questionable found in a charnel house— it was a dirty job with no promise of glory, and no doubt his fellow detectives had been amused to see him volunteer for it. If he hadn't, they'd probably have steered it his way. It was their usual practice. If an indigent was found facedown in a sewer, Sebastian could expect to score a day in the muck followed by a week of barbed comments about some imagined stink that followed him around.

He'd grown used to this. It was something that he could endure—if not easily, then at least without complaint. As far as Sebastian was concerned, the death of a pauper was still a tragedy, if only to the pauper. Everybody needed someone to establish their name, to record their passing, to draw out the story of their final moments on this earth. Including those who died unloved and without company.

Especially those who died unloved.

On this occasion, Sebastian was looking for something specific. Within a few minutes of his arrival, he'd known that there was more to this than a routine unpleasantness. After a first look at the evidence, he'd sent a message to the main police office, directly to the great Turner-Smith himself. Turner-Smith, more aware of Sebastian's character and work record than even Sebastian knew, had laid aside all his other duties in order to respond. Eyebrows were raised. It was almost without precedent.

The head slaughterman waited for them at the top of the ramp. He was bearded, with a scarf tied around his head like a pirate's. There was a belt over his apron, and a long knife stuck through the belt. The blade of the knife had been worn down by repeated sharpening, almost to rapier width.

Sebastian explained, "When the carcasses have been eviscerated and skinned, they're brought up here to be butchered."

Lines of men and women worked at wooden butcher blocks. The

men mostly hacked, the women mostly carved. The stench up here was worse than the stench below. The very air was misty and red; muslin had been hung to keep flies at bay, but to no great effect. The muslin had once been ivory-colored, but was now spattered and brown.

"The offal is sorted into these vats," Sebastian said, and nodded to the head slaughterman. They were now at the tripe tables, where the lowest of the workers had the job of scraping feces and worms from the animals' intestines.

The slaughterman ordered one of the tables cleared, whereupon he lifted up a bucket and dumped its contents onto the surface for the visitors to inspect. They landed and spread with a thick, slopping sound.

There seemed little to distinguish this material from the guts, organs, and assorted entrails that lay all around them.

"More offal?" said Turner-Smith.

"Not quite," said Sebastian. "The man knows his meat. And he tells me that these items are almost certainly human."

THE NORTH WEST

1888

E I G H T

nother day, another town, another playhouse. On their arrival, Whitlock and the actors had gone straight to their lodgings while Sayers had arranged the transfer of their stage properties to the Prince of Wales. They were to replace a show called *Memories of Old Ireland,* and when Sayers reached the theater, it was to find the sets only half struck and several members of the cast snoring loudly under the stage.

Things went rather better at the lodging house, where Whitlock had taken the master bedroom. The room above the bay window went to Ricks and his wife, a former soprano who now played mother roles and Shakespearean dames. Everyone else set their bags down in the rooms that Mrs. Mack, the landlady, had chosen to assign to them. The stage-hands, by their own choice, were billeted in rooms above a public house closer to the theater.

There were several hours to be passed until the matinee, and the company chose to spend them in various ways. Some went out to look at the town. Some gathered in the sitting room for idle conversation, while others read alone. James Caspar, seemingly indifferent to his disgrace, went upstairs and threw himself on his bed and slept.

A few minutes after noon, he awoke, changed into a large and threadbare Oriental dressing gown, and went down to the kitchen to beg some hot tea from Mrs. Mack. Mrs. Mack was not easily charmed, but

Caspar seemed to manage. Gulliford, the Low Comedian, heard him on the stairs as he was taking the tea back to his room. He went out to accost Caspar, but he was too late; Caspar was back in his room with the door already closed.

Gulliford went to the door and knocked. At Caspar's response of "Come in, if you must," he opened it and went inside.

It was a bare room, with an iron bedstead and a table and not much of anything else. Caspar's stage clothes had been hung up to dry on the front of the wardrobe, before which stood his cabin trunk. Caspar was rummaging inside this, and as Gulliford closed the door behind him came up with a glass preserving jar. He appeared to have wrapped it in a sock, for safety during transit.

"She's awake, then," Gulliford said, as Caspar set his jar down on the table and pulled up a chair. He gave the Low Comedian a baleful glance and continued about his business, moving with painful slowness as if every part of him gave hurt. From the pocket of the dressing gown he took a fork, which he wiped up and down on his lapel.

Gulliford said, "I've only got one question I want to ask you." He placed his hands on the table and positioned himself in front of Caspar, where he couldn't be ignored.

"Why do you do it?" he said.

The jar contained something pickled in murky liquid. Caspar sprang open the clips that sealed on the lid, and poked around inside with his fork.

"Do what?" he said.

"We're a humble company," Gulliford said. "I can understand if you despise your place in it. But you act as if you despise the very profession we're in."

Caspar speared a morsel of something that resembled a small, dark sausage. "My head hurts," he said. "Go away."

"You're going to hear what I have to say."

"Great wisdom from the company's Low Comedian?"

"That's a role, sonny boy, it's not a rank. You don't seem to know the difference. I've forgotten more about the stage than you will ever know. You never match your business and you pick up your cues the same way you catch your trains. Well, I've seen through you and I know what your game is."

Caspar stopped munching. He became very quiet and wary.

Gulliford said, "We both know there's no other occupation where you can rise from the gutter to the very top of society. And from you, my friend, for all your French cologne and your high manners and your one good set of clothes, from you I get the definite whiff of the gutter. You've no love of the stage. You just like playacting."

Caspar sniffed. "If you're unhappy with my work," he said, "talk to Edmund."

"Edmund to you. Mister Whitlock to the rest of us. Don't think it hasn't been noticed."

"There's nothing to notice. No man has hold over me. Nor I on any man."

"No. But there's something in it for both of you." Gulliford reached over and took the new morsel from the end of Caspar's fork, right under his nose.

"I don't know what the bargain is," he said, "and I don't care. What I want you to remember is this. The rest of us aren't your stepping-stones. This is more than our living. This is our life."

So saying, he flipped the morsel into his mouth.

It was horrible. He was thrown. After trying to contend with it for a moment, he had to spit it into his hand and place it on the table.

"Sack the chef," he said and, still wincing at the taste, moved to the door.

"Anything else?" Caspar said.

"I've said my piece," the Low Comedian said. "I'll see you at the matinee."

Caspar was left contemplating the spat-out and abandoned morsel. He speared it with his fork.

To the otherwise empty room he said, "I'm heading for places you can never imagine, my friend."

And then he popped the appalling pickle into his own mouth, crunching it up as if such was the most natural thing in the world.

N I N E

ebastian traveled back with Turner-Smith in the superintendent's own carriage. Once the ride was under way, he was eager to explain his suspicions and to share some of the conclusions that he'd half-thought through.

But Turner-Smith sat with his bad leg outstretched and his cane across his knees, looking out of the side window as the streets of the town unrolled past it, and said, "How is your mother these days, Sebastian? Is she well?"

The question was a surprise. Sebastian was not sure how to respond, so he simply answered, "She is, sir," and then "I was not aware that you knew her."

"We've never actually met," Turner-Smith said. "But she wrote to me upon your promotion."

"She did?"

Turner-Smith looked at him then, half amused as if he already knew the answers to anything he might ask, and all of his pleasure was in seeing the younger man's reaction.

"She disapproves of your choice of profession and holds me personally responsible for your safety."

"I apologize," Sebastian said. "I did not know of any letter."

"Don't apologize," Turner-Smith said. "You and she never spoke of the matter?"

"We rarely speak at all."

The town's main police office stood next to the magistrates' courts, with a secure passageway linking the two buildings so that prisoners could be walked straight from the jail cells and into the dock. There were public rooms at the front, with offices at the back and the cells below. Its rooms were spare, bare, and high-ceilinged. Despite the presence of gas flares and the most modern cast-iron radiators, those who worked there complained that the small-windowed cells were the only warm rooms in the entire building.

There was a stable yard on the side, hidden from the street behind a high stone wall and archway. It was from the yard that Sebastian Becker and Superintendent Turner-Smith entered and made their way down the central corridor toward the Detective Department's rooms.

Word of Turner-Smith's arrival had preceded them. A uniformed man stood ready to open the door, and the office beyond it was tidy and square. Detectives stood to attention by their desks. The police cat and its new kittens had been swept into a cupboard and would stay confined there for the length of the superintendent's visit.

"Be about your business," Turner-Smith told them as he followed Sebastian. "This is not an inspection."

He lowered himself into a chair with a sound of relief as Sebastian opened a drawer and took out a package. The seal on the package was broken, and it bore no address other than the words *To the Police for their Kind Attention.*

"This was left by persons unknown," Sebastian said, opening it up and laying its contents on the table before his superior.

"When?"

"Some time yesterday morning. The desk sergeant found the package in the public waiting room, but he did not see who'd left it. There is no letter or message. In my opinion, the writing resembles that of a child."

"Or an illiterate."

"It's hard to say. The spelling is correct. But the hand is not a practiced one."

The contents were three sheets of a heavy, cheap paper with a distinct smell of the glue pot. Each bore pasted-on cuttings from a number of different newspapers.

"Perhaps the writing has been disguised," Turner-Smith said, leaning forward with both hands on the head of his walking stick. He peered closely at the sheets without attempting to touch them.

"They are theatrical notices," Sayers said.

"So I see."

"All for the *Purple Diamond* company. All from different newspapers in different towns and cities on the tour."

"And not a good notice among them, by the looks of it," Turner-Smith said. It was not necessary to read the reviews in full to get the flavor of their content; certain negative words caught the eye and told the story. He added, with growing interest, "Each notice appears to have been paired with a crime report from the same pages."

Sebastian said, "Look at the dates."

Turner-Smith looked at them. "They're not the same."

"But there is a consistency. The notices are all from first nights. Which means that each mutilation murder probably coincides with the end of a run. Three days, four days, perhaps even a week later. It varies."

"And?"

Sebastian said, "The *Purple Diamond* company closed at the Lyric last night. They've already packed up and left town for their next engagement."

"Leaving human remains for us to find today."

"So the pattern holds."

"If it *is* a pattern. I'm sure I could throw together a list of dead paupers and foundlings for any set of dates and places you could mention."

"Yes, sir. But all dismembered? Flayed? Eviscerated?"

"I am not disagreeing with you. I think you are probably right. This has the look of insider work, Sebastian. Someone in the company is signaling their suspicions."

"I suspected that, sir, but I could not be sure."

"Where are the *good* notices, Inspector Becker? Show me a tour that could survive on notices like these. The good ones are in somebody's press book. These are the leftovers that no performer would care to remember."

"Of course, sir. Now I understand."

"You're turning out to be not a bad little detective, though. I credit you for it, Becker."

"I credit my teacher."

Turner-Smith considered the pages for a moment longer. Then with the aid of his stick, he rose to his feet.

"I shall act upon this," he said. "Where is the company now?"

Sebastian had already made inquiry of the Lyric's management, and had confirmed the information by telegraph.

"In Lancashire," he said. "At the Prince of Wales Theatre in Salford."

"I'll spare you Salford," Turner-Smith said with a smile, "and I shall pursue this myself. But do not worry. I'll ensure you get full credit for your insight here."

"I do not doubt it. Take care up there, sir."

Turner-Smith raised his walking stick and, holding it horizontally between them, gave it a twist and pulled so that the shaft separated into two halves. The action revealed part of the sword blade that lay hidden within it.

"Have no fears for me," Turner-Smith said. "I know Liverpool Street of old."

T E N

he Prince of Wales Theatre ran a variety bill, and *The Purple Diamond* had been brought in to provide the second half of it. The first part of the program included Felix's troupe of Siberian Wolf Hounds, Nelly Farrell, the Glittering Star of Erin, Medley the Mimic, and "musical wonders" The Avolo Boys. They were short of a second-spot comedian, so Gulliford had seized the chance to resurrect his old act and the baggy suit he performed it in. To his dismay, the suit was no longer quite so baggy as it once had been. But he went over well at the first matinee, so the management engaged him to double up his jobs for the rest of the run.

Friday night brought the best house of the week. Doors opened at six and the entertainment began at six-thirty. There was little for Sayers to do once the play was settled into a new venue, but he would always stand ready to give a correcting hand to any problem that might arise. Sometimes, when everything was running smoothly backstage, he would go around to the rear of the auditorium and watch the show for a while.

As Bram Stoker had so astutely remembered, Sayers had been a performer once. When injury had cut short his sporting career, he had taken to the stage in a sketch dramatizing the events surrounding his most famous bout. Although he was hardly a born actor, he was at least up to the challenge of representing his own history. He'd been a popular fighter, and now found enough success on the Halls to square his debts and discover a new living.

Having managed his own troupe, he now managed others. While he sometimes felt a pang of envy for those to whom the limelight seemed a natural home, he knew that his dramatic talent had already been exploited to its limit.

Sayers stood at the back of the house and watched as Nelly Farrell sang of how one black sheep shall never spoil the flock. She was a strong-featured, short-haired, can-belto performer of Irish comic songs, and Louise Porter's opposite in almost every way.

He listened to a couple of her verses, and then turned and wandered through into the bar where a smaller crowd, drinks in hand, watched the stage through the auditorium pillars.

Sayers felt restless this evening. He often did, when everything was in order and there was little left to occupy him. Without the usual mass of practical detail to engage his thoughts, they tended to turn inward and there, they found uncomfortable issues to fasten upon.

Like, this present occupation of his—how long would it last? Old boxers seemed to fall into two classes: those who'd succeeded and sank their prize money into some enterprise like a small hotel or a beerhouse, and those eternal contenders who stayed too long in the ring, looking forward to success that never came.

As far as Sayers could see, he'd fit into neither category. Nor into any other that he could imagine.

"Tom?" he heard, and turned his head. A woman had called his name from behind the bar counter and was looking at him. Her face was instantly familiar, but for a moment he struggled to place it exactly.

"Lily?" he said, moving over to the counter. "Lily Collins?"

"Lily Haynes, now," she said, and held up a hand to show him a well-worn wedding band that looked as if it had passed through a generation or two, if not a pawnshop or three. "How are you, Tom?"

"Lucky old Albert," Tom said. "I'm doing fine."

Lily Collins. It had been five or six years since he'd last seen her.

They both leaned on the bar so that they could converse without too much disturbance of those facing the stage. And then whenever the bar crowd joined in a chorus, they had to pause because it became too difficult to be heard.

Lily had toured with Sayers' first company, playing in *A Fight to the Finish* as Hester Chambers, the jilted country-girl sweetheart of Tom's opponent. She'd entered the theater as a dancer, and back then she'd been slight and slim and could pass for a girl of seventeen despite her dozen or more years in the profession. Albert Haynes was a tumbler in a three-man act, and whenever their engagements coincided, it was obvious to everyone that they were a destined pair. She'd grown more matronly since then. But her eyes still held their sparkle.

"So you're off the road now?" Tom said.

"Albert got the flu," she said. "It left him deaf in one ear. He could never balance proper after that. He's all right in himself. But he used to stand on one hand, and now I have to watch him on the stairs."

After a pause for a roaring chorus, she told him of how they'd married and put their savings into a pub on Langworthy Road. Albert ran it, and Lily brought in some extra money by working here three nights a week.

"Come and see us," she said. "Any time. Don't worry if we're busy. We'll always make time for you, Tom."

"I will."

"Don't just say it."

"I truly will."

She was looking at him strangely. Not so much at him, as into him. Sayers had always found Lily Collins to be one of those women of intuitive honesty, with an uncanny sense of it in others. They make valued friends. But a woman who can always spot when a man's deceiving himself makes for a discomforting companion.

"How are you really, Tom?" she said. "Are you happy? Tell me you are."

He laid aside all pretense.

"I believe," he said, "that in time I will be."

"Well," Lily said, raising her voice to compete with the final chorus from the Glittering Star of Erin, "That's probably all any of us can ask for. Knowing what will make you happy and feeling you're on the way to it. Everything else is memories."

The end of Nelly Farrell's act brought a surge of customers to the bar, and with quick good-byes and equally quick promises Lily had to abandon Sayers and return to her work.

When Medley the Mimic came bouncing on and started with his imitations, Sayers slipped out to the foyer and made his way backstage. By the time he got there, Medley was off again and the Avolo Boys were out trying to repair the damage.

"Bloody Salford 'eathens," cursed Medley as he pushed his way past Sayers, raw egg dripping from his jacket. "If it don't sing or fall on its arse, they don't want to know."

Sayers checked to see that the *Purple Diamond* stage crew would be ready for an early call, and then made his way back to the green room to give the same warning to the cast.

Most were ready anyway. As he might have guessed, the only one not present was James Caspar.

The dressing rooms were at the side of the building, with high windows overlooking the alley that divided the theater from the public house next door. Sayers climbed the stairs, almost hoping not to find Caspar there. If he wasn't, then Whitlock would either have to cancel the performance or send on a substitute, book in hand. It would be a disaster for the company and the most serious professional lapse imaginable; yet there was something in Sayers that weighed one night's pain against Caspar's permanent departure.

His father had taken on the work of reclaiming him for God, but died with it barely begun. I swore to him that I would continue the work until its end. I pledged my own soul to the task.

Sayers did not believe one word of it. There had to be some more credible explanation for the hold that Caspar had on the boss. Whatever it was, Sayers would welcome any reason that might cause the "task" to be abandoned.

Reaching the top of the dressing-room stairs, he hesitated. The door to Caspar's room was open, and the man was not alone. Sayers could see him reflected in the dressing-room mirror. It was a cheap, old glass and Caspar's image was like that in a dirty window. He was in costume, but his stiff collar was sprung open. Sayers heard him snap his fingers and say, in an imperious manner, "Stud."

"Yes, sir." It was the voice of Arthur, the callboy. Sayers' view was momentarily blocked as Arthur moved across with a stud to fasten the collar.

He heard Caspar say, "Where's my press book?"

"Still working on it, sir," Arthur said. The business with the collar seemed to be a struggle.

After a few moments Caspar said, "You're a slow little weasel, aren't you?"

"Yes, sir."

"Slow of hand, slow of wits. I think I'll ask Edmund to dismiss you. Would you like that?"

"No, sir."

" 'No, sir,' " Caspar mimicked. "Get out."

"Yes, sir."

Arthur came out of the dressing room like a boy with a reprieve from the dentist's chair, and almost ran into Sayers at the top of the stairs. Sayers must have seemed to appear out of nowhere because Arthur leaped back, startled like a buck at a gunshot.

"Beginners, please, Arthur," Sayers said.

"Yes, Mister Sayers," the boy said, and looked faintly stricken at the thought of having to turn around and go back into the presence he'd just escaped.

"Be on with you," Sayers said. "I'll give Mister Caspar the call."

"There's no need," said James Caspar from the dressing-room doorway. Arthur shot off down the stairs. Caspar primped his wing collar, tugged down his white waistcoat, and shot his cuffs. He looked as sharp as a barber's razor.

"It seems that your services are hardly required at all, Mister Sayers," he said, and moved forward. Sayers had to step aside to let him by.

A dozen rejoinders occurred to him as he followed Caspar down toward the stage, but the moment to use any of them had already passed.

The Prince of Wales had its own pit orchestra, so the company's musical director foreswore the piano and picked up the baton for their overture and effects. *The Purple Diamond* overture was a bespoke piece for the play and had not a lick of original music in it, being a mishmash of classic themes and familiar tunes. And a very successful mishmash it was; not a note in it that wasn't tried and tested and free of all copyright fees. It tweaked the mood of every audience. If you like this kind of thing, it seemed to say, then here comes the kind of thing you'll like.

For each member of the acting company, it was an unconscious metronome guiding them to their places and preparing their minds for the performance. Hearing it backstage, they drifted to their entrances like theater ghosts. The curtain would rise on the Low Comedian as the butler, who had a belowstairs monologue to set up the story. Then on came Louise, and the lovers' plot would be got under way. Whitlock would enter then, as the detective in disguise. He usually got a vocal greeting from the audience, but on this run Sayers had sensed the boss's irritation that his reception was matched by the one given to the Low Comedian at the play's beginning, the reason being that they recognized him from his first-half turn as baggy-trousered comedian Billy Danson. But the boss could see that it was to the benefit of the play's overall effect, so he'd made no changes.

As Louise stood in the wings and waited for her cue, James Caspar seemed to float out of the darkness to appear behind her. She did not see his approach; rather, she suddenly sensed his presence. It startled her. Caspar's first cue was a good ten minutes away, and he was to enter from the opposite side of the stage.

He leaned close, so that he might speak and not be heard from beyond the wings.

"I'm sorry if I surprised you," he said. His breath brushed her ear. Louise felt the hairs on the back of her neck rise.

"Mister Caspar," she whispered back. "There is nothing to apologize for."

"I wanted to ask you something."

"Oh?"

"Your song tonight. Would you sing it for me?"

She did not know how to respond. He seemed to sense her confusion, and did not press for a reply.

By the time that she had gathered herself, Caspar had turned away and faded back into the shadows.

In the bar at the back of the auditorium, Police Superintendent Clive Turner-Smith stood among a group of strangers and watched the curtain rise on *The Purple Diamond*. He'd arrived at the theater too late to see the Low Comedian's first-half spot, so he was mystified by the cheers that greeted the sight of a butler in an apron, busy polishing the silverware in a country-house kitchen. Having little interest in the play itself, he scanned the audience. Common folk all, out for nothing more than a good evening's entertainment. One or two types he'd be inclined to keep an eye on, had this been his own patch.

As the butler launched off into one of those *Oh mercy me,* talking-to-myself but really talking to the audience monologues, Turner-Smith became aware of a touch at his sleeve. He looked and saw that a shaven-headed, skull-faced man had appeared by his side and was holding out the same note that he'd sent backstage some ten minutes earlier. It had been opened, and a return message had been scribbled on it.

Turner-Smith took it, read the scribble, and then folded the note and tucked it into an inside pocket.

He said, "I'll be waiting in the saloon bar next door. Tell no one else about this. Do you understand?"

The man remained silent, but inclined his head in assent.

Turner-Smith left the auditorium and crossed the foyer, emerging onto the street by the theater box office. He'd arrived in Manchester little more than an hour earlier. He'd told no one of his arrival, but immediately took a cab across the river and into Salford. He'd made the same journey twenty years before when, as a provost marshal, he'd been in pursuit of a deserter who'd killed a sergeant in barracks and run for home. He could remember a four-roomed terraced house full of children and having to face down the deserter's mother, a woman more formidable than many a man in his regiment. She'd denied seeing her son when, in truth, he was hiding in the privy in a neighbor's backyard. The boy had fled as Turner-Smith's men began to search, and drowned himself later that afternoon. The river Irwell divided the borough from the city; a drowning would bring out the two sets of police with boat hooks, one squad of men on each bank, ready to shove the body toward the opposite shore for their neighbor force to deal with.

Liverpool Street was a wide thoroughfare, with broad stone pavements and tram rails set into the cobbles. Ahead of him, a girl of around eleven was pushing along an old pram loaded with firewood. More children could be seen outside the commercial hotel next door. They sat on the steps, they sat on the kerbstones with their feet in the road. Younger ones played in the care of their older siblings, all waiting for parents who were spending the evening in the public bar.

Turner-Smith bypassed the public bar for the more respectable saloon, where the drink came from another side of the same counter, but the extra penny bought a better class of room with upholstered seating, mahogany paneling, and waiter service. He settled alone in a three-sided booth, ordered a glass of Madeira wine, and paid for it when it came.

He said to the waiter, "I shall be joined by a gentleman, name of Sayers. He'll be coming over from the playhouse. Make sure he can find me when he gets here, will you?"

The waiter dipped his head and went away. Turner-Smith laid his stick across the seats beside him, stretched out his bad leg, and settled back to wait. Behind him in the next booth was a party of commercial travelers; he eavesdropped on their conversation for a while, but soon felt his attention start to wander.

Children of the poor. They were everywhere. He'd been met by a crowd of them begging outside the railway station, and seen them scatter at the approach of a special constable. It was as if the growth of cities was like a gaseous reaction; for a certain volume of prosperity, an even greater volume of poverty was produced. The result was great public works and proud civic buildings and range upon range of desperate hovels, all standing as one under the same dirty sky.

After a while, he took out his watch and checked it. Sayers had undertaken to meet him during the play's second act. He'd addressed his note to the owner of the *Purple Diamond* company, but it was this Sayers who'd responded. More than half an hour had passed since then.

Someone was standing over him. He looked up as the waiter spoke. "The gentleman is here now, sir," the waiter said, and moved aside for his visitor.

"I'm Tom Sayers," the man said, and took a seat on the opposite side of the booth. The waiter hovered for a moment, but the newcomer shook his head.

When the waiter had moved away, the man faced Turner-Smith and said, "What can I do for you, Superintendent?"

"I'd been hoping to speak to Mister Whitlock himself."

"I'm Edmund Whitlock's acting manager. I handle all the company's practical affairs. If I can't help you with it, then it probably can't be done."

Turner-Smith considered the man before him for a moment, and then decided that he could speak as one gentleman to another. They were more likely to have interests in common than in conflict.

"Take a look at this, please, Sayers," he said, and placed before him one of the pasted-up sheets that suggested a link between paupers mutilated without apparent motive and the stage company's progress around the country.

The other man read for a while, and then glanced up.

"Some of our less notable receptions."

"The dates, Mister Sayers. Look at the dates."

He read on for a while. Then he sat back in the attitude of a man conceding an argument that had already been won. "This is very revealing," he said.

And Turner-Smith, who for the past minute had been given the opportunity for a closer study of his visitor, said, "Are you by any chance wearing greasepaint, Mister Sayers?"

The man threw the paper onto the table between them.

"Ah," he said. "There you have me."

Under the table, Turner-Smith reached out for his sword stick. He took care not to signal his intention. "Yet you are not listed on the playbills among the actors," he said.

"Very true." The man smiled. "I can see that you are too good a detective for me, Superintendent."

A few moments later, the man rose from the booth and walked out of the saloon. The four commercial travelers in the next booth were laughing so hard at a story that none of them noticed his departure. One took a draft from his mug and leaned back in his seat, only to splutter it out all over the table.

His fellows were slow to catch on. Their humor ebbed, where his had vanished in a flash.

"What the devil?" he said. "Something pronged me!" And he turned in his seat to find out what it was.

All clustered for a closer look at his discovery. An inch of pointed blade protruded from the horsehair back of the bench on which he'd been sitting. "Lor', Jack," said the one with the walrus mustache. "They've sat you in one of them iron maiden thingies."

"Iron maiden be buggered," said the wounded one, and stood up to look over into the next booth.

There sat the white-haired, stern-looking man who'd come limping in on a stick about three-quarters of an hour before. His back was to them, his head bowed.

The stick was in two pieces now. The hollow shaft lay across the table by his emptied glass. The other, the blade and handle part, had been thrust through his chest and had him pinned in place like a bug.

James Caspar was across the alleyway and in through the stage door in no more than a dozen strides. The Silent Man pulled the door shut behind him and then followed along a snaking route through the backstage areas toward the wings. As he walked, Caspar shed his jacket, his cravat, and his collar. He let them fall and the Silent Man collected all of them in his wake. Out came the cuff links, his sleeves shaken loose. Up five steps and through a door, and ahead of them the fly ropes and the lights of the stage. He put his hand in his hair and tousled it, as befitted a man who'd been unjustly condemned at the end of the first act and was now being returned to life and honor, thanks to the remarkable insight and unstinting efforts of a sixty-year-old detective with rouged cheeks and a corset.

Out on stage, Whitlock had already spoken Caspar's cue. It came at the end of an entire page of speech, delivered to a grieving Louise and building to a rip-roaring climax that usually brought the house to its feet as the lover she'd thought hanged was restored to her with a flourish.

Seeing no sign of Caspar, the Low Comedian had drawn breath for an ad lib to cover a stage wait. Before he could deliver it, Caspar sprang into view, not so much entering from the wings as being ejected from them. He flung down the hooded cloak of the mysterious beggar who had been seen outside the window in the middle of the second act—all part of the detective's brilliant plan to fool the true culprit into revealing himself—and threw out his arms to receive Louise. She ran to him and hit him like a train, and as the audience cheered their embrace, Whitlock quietly moved upstage of the pair ready for his next revelation.

At the back of the auditorium, Sayers had returned to the spot where he'd been standing earlier. As those around him whooped and whistled, Sayers nursed a heart like a heavy stone. The reason for this was a short conversation that he'd had with Louise in the brief interval between the play's two acts.

It had gone like this:

Tom!

What is it?

I need to ask you something.

Anything.

Do you think James—Mister Caspar—likes me at all?

A silence.

Tom?

But everybody likes you, Louise.

Later, when the evening's entertainment was over and the players were all leaving the theater, they were confronted by a considerable police presence around the public house next door. Two wagons were drawn up on the street and a large number of uniformed men had surrounded the building and were turning onlookers away. Lanterns had been set for extra light, and sheets and a stretcher were being taken inside. A man from the *Salford Chronicle* was talking to people on the pavement, trying to separate fact from fiction and getting some of the most enthusiastic accounts from those who had been nowhere near the events. It was a fight over a woman; it was the work of a gang over from Regent Road; two people were dead; three people were dead; everyone in the pub had been massacred. A drunk had run amuck with a knife. Sailors had fought with locals. It was the so-called Buffalo Bill's Gang, local scuttlers stirred to a violent frenzy by their unreasoning passion for the penny-dreadful magazines.

Sayers made it his business to get the women away as quickly as possible.

Caspar was nowhere to be seen.

efore he went for his train, Sebastian Becker went to church. It was his first visit for some time. The doors were unlocked but there was barely any light in the dawn sky outside, and it seemed he would have the place to himself for a while. When he stepped inside and closed the door behind him, the fall of the iron latch echoed like a gunshot all the way up to the vaulted roof.

Perhaps this was a mistake. One look at his surroundings and again he felt some of the deep spiritual terror that he'd known as a small child, making its mark that he knew would never be fully erased. The Catholic Church, the same the world over. Whether it was a cathedral in Cologne or a mission in California, in their essence they never varied. Candles and gilt, darkness and mystery.

And suffering. Always suffering. In every image, in every hymn, and in every prayer; and it was always inflicted by a God who spoke in Latin, and borne by a Christ who resembled no Jew that Sebastian had ever met. As if the real Christ had been insufficient for the Church's purposes, so they'd manufactured their own.

He knelt briefly in the aisle, and crossed himself. It took no effort to remember the procedure. He wanted to ignore it, but could not see how. The training ran too deep and he knew that he would freeze, unable to continue until the omission had been corrected.

Once that was over, he took a seat at the front of the church. Where the congregation sat, right in the front row. There were oil lamps around the high altar that had been burning all through the night. Behind the altar, in an ornate frame, towered some magnificent Renaissance painting that he could barely see. Before this shone a cross; in gold or brass, from here it was impossible to tell. He stared at it almost in defiance; refusing to pray, refusing even to admit the possibility of prayer.

So why was he here?

Last night's news had shaken him. Turner-Smith not just dead, but murdered. Sebastian's insides churned like a bag of snakes when he tried to come to terms with it. He should have been the one to pursue the information. Then Turner-Smith would be alive. But then Sebastian might well have suffered his superior's fate in his place. Unless, by conducting himself differently, he reached a different outcome.

But perhaps his mentor had died because he had made some discovery that would prove vital to the investigation. In which case, his achievement and his sacrifice were bound together. For Sebastian to have replaced him and survived would be to negate both. While to make the same discovery and die in his place . . . well, in considering that one, Sebastian found proof that he did not have the makings of a saint.

There would be a funeral. A police funeral, with full honors. The streets of the town would be taken over for the procession, and people would turn out because all those black-plumed horses and men in uniform would be something to see. But Sebastian could never picture a funeral without thinking of the white coffin of his sister, small enough for one undertaker's man to carry in his arms.

He'd been a few days short of his ninth birthday, and death had meant little to him then. Grief, though . . . that had been everywhere he turned, terrifying and oppressive. The house draped in black, the downstairs rooms crowded with somber people. He hardly dared speak. Even the appearance of his living self seemed to be taken as an affront, and so he kept out of his mother's way as much as possible.

He'd dared to wonder if, given time, this turn of events might mean that he'd receive a fuller share of her affections. But as his ninth birthday came and went without notice, and the birthday after that, each overshadowed by the grimmer anniversary that preceded it, he grew to realize that not only was his dead sibling still loved, but loved more than he.

Why had his mother felt the need to write that letter to Turner-Smith? Did it indicate a concern that she'd never otherwise let him see? The experience of a lifetime suggested not. It was merely her way to place her mark on his affairs. She'd always responded to any of his plans or proposals by pointing out their potential for failure. She considered herself entitled to her opinion.

"Praying's a skill like any other, Sebastian," said a voice behind him. Sebastian looked back and saw Father Alexander, parish priest for the past eighteen years, in the aisle and moving toward him. He must have been elsewhere in the church, and had come in through one of the side doors. "I can't say I've seen you practice it much, lately."

Sebastian said, "Turner-Smith was murdered last night."

"Turner-Smith?"

"My superintendent."

"God have mercy on his soul. How did it happen?"

"The circumstances are unclear. I am to go there with what I know, and if there is an arrest to be made, I shall make it. If there is a God, may he guide my hand."

The priest's eyebrows went up in surprise. "*If*, Sebastian?"

Sebastian rose to his feet.

"Another time, Father," he said.

TWELVE

lthough it stood on a street in where there were a number of lodging houses, Mrs. Mack put up no board or sign, nor did she advertise. A theatrical landlady had no use for business from the public, who might expect to keep normal people's hours. Theatricals and other stage people came home late at night, and many would sleep until midmorning. They'd expect supper at some unsocial time and then an hour or two of society after that. Their talk was of a world known only to their profession. And even now, in the minds of many theirs was not a respectable life.

Constantly on the move, they made few friends in the places they visited. Their only unguarded contact was with each other. Stage folk were like one great, fluid family, and in that family it was often the theatrical landlady who took the mother's role: offering shelter and a welcome, keeping a special lookout for the young, and demanding moral standards from all who came under their roof. The most roaring reprobate of the saloon-bar lock-in would be as meek as a good son in his landlady's presence.

Mrs. Mack was one of the legends. There was a Mr. Mack, but there is not much to be said about him.

It was after ten on the Saturday morning when Tom Sayers woke. He was usually one of life's early risers, but the previous night he had been unable to sleep. Borrowing a latchkey from the kitchen, he had taken himself out for a moonlit walk. He was not a man who feared assault at any hour, and by then it was so late that even coshers and mashers would have crawled off to bed. He got as far as the wide river that divided the two boroughs—slow-moving, sparkling, dirty and dark as oil. He had walked with his mind in disorder, and returned with it feeling no more settled.

Lily's words still rang in his mind. She seemed to be saying that there was no such thing as happiness, per se. It was more a matter of working out what will make you happy, and knowing you're on your way to it. Always believing that it's the destination, when in fact it's the journey.

So, where was he going? Most men of his age had begun to establish themselves in one way or another. Wives, children, some steady form of income. But not Tom Sayers. Sayers performed all the functions of a businessman but he lived the life of a gypsy, always on the move, accumulating little. He had some savings and paid rent on a small house in Brixton that was his home for their London dates, but nothing of any more substance than that.

He'd begun to consider the idea that he might get himself off the road, perhaps set himself up as a personal manager to a select list of clients, dealing exclusively with their affairs. He could picture himself with a small office in Covent Garden, framed playbills in the waiting room and a clerk for the correspondence. One or two performers outside the company had expressed a wish that he might take on such a role, on occasions when he'd helped them out with some personal difficulty. However, when he allowed himself to imagine what form such a new life might take, there was only one client who ever featured in the scene with any consistency.

Louise. At times like this, he ached at the very thought of her. In his mind, he would relive the moment when she'd fallen into his arms. He'd take those few seconds of confusion and tease them out into an entire marriage of their souls that was timeless, graceful, and slow. James Caspar made no appearance in this world of his imagination. Sayers had cut him from the script.

The day would surely come when the *Purple Diamond* tour would have to end, if only because there would be no one left in England who had not seen it. When the end arrived, it was hard to say what might happen; whether Whitlock would pay out money for another play and raise a new company out of the old, or return to good old Shakespeare *(but not his Romeo again, please God, not his Romeo),* or buy himself that cottage down in Kent to see out his time in some more sedate manner.

One way or another, there would be upheaval. With any luck, Caspar would go his own way. And that, Sayers felt, would be the time to broach the subject of offering his personal service to Louise. Anything sooner would not be appropriate.

He'd spent another fitful hour or two lying in his bed and staring at the moonlight through the curtains, until finally sleep had taken pity and claimed him.

His was one of the attic rooms, three flights up with a part-sloping ceiling and a hook on the roof beam to hang his shaving mirror. His window was really a skylight. Between the washstand and his cabin trunk there was little room to spare.

He threw back the covers and sat on the side of the bed. He put his face in his hands and tried to massage it into something that might resemble a man awake. As he was doing this, there was a discreet tap at his door.

Very discreet. Almost womanly.

Panic began to stir in Tom Sayers' breast. Whatever this was, he was unprepared. He slept in his underwear, and his underwear was a testament to the longevity of unbleached wool and his skills with a darning needle.

"Yes?" he said.

It was a man's voice that answered. "Mister Sayers?" But it was not a voice that he recognized.

"Who is it?" he said, reaching for the trousers that he'd hung by their braces on the end of his bed.

Instead of a reply, his door burst open. Two policemen were across the room and onto him before he could respond. They seized his arms and held him fast while another, this one with a sergeant's stripes, came in close behind them with handcuffs at the ready. They hauled him to his feet; and when he began to struggle, they turned him and ran him back to pin him against the wall. The impact drove the breath from his body and gave them a few moments of dominance.

Last into the room came a dark-eyed man of around thirty. He glanced around as the handcuffs were being placed over Sayers' wrists and screwed down, the uniformed men containing his struggles and ignoring his protests.

"Watch those hands," the younger man warned. "He was a prize-fighter, once."

Clearly, the situation was of this man's making. Not in a uniform himself, he commanded those who were. Sayers managed a look at him over the sergeant's shoulder. "Sir!" he said. "This is outrageous!"

The plainclothesman did not respond immediately. When the sergeant was done with the cuffs, he said, "Search his possessions." Only then did he stand before Sayers and weigh him up from one end to the other, before looking him in the eye.

"You dare speak to me of outrage?" he said calmly. "Please do not test me so, Mister Sayers. I have a certain pride in my professional restraint. I would not wish to lose that over someone like you."

Sayers doubled his fists and thrust the handcuffs in the air. "Explain yourself," he said, "and then explain this!"

"I am Detective Inspector Sebastian Becker," the plainclothesman said. "And you know why I am here. Pretend ignorance if that is your only defense. It will not save you from the hangman's rope."

"Sir . . ." said the sergeant, and all turned to look. Becker's threat of the hangman had only served to bewilder Sayers even more. He felt like an actor who'd walked through the wrong stage door into the midst of another company's drama. As he craned to see what new disclosure was to be sprung upon him, he became aware that there were more policemen on the landing outside his room.

With some difficulty, the sergeant had opened up his cabin trunk. As always, it stood on its end, so that it could be opened as a traveling wardrobe. One side contained shallow drawers and compartments. The other was a hanging space for suits of clothes and linen. These had been torn from their hangers and lay crammed into the bottom of the trunk, while the space set aside for them was filled with something else.

In a private exhibition of curiosities in London, Sayers had once been shown an anatomical model in wax; it was of a woman, cut from clavicle to pubis, her belly a removable lid that revealed the gestating fetus within. Perfectly formed, but imperfectly understood, the unborn was depicted as a tightly packed homunculus of adult proportions.

It was in similar manner that the slaughtered body of fifteen-year-old Arthur Steffens had been folded and crushed, upside down, into the confines of Tom Sayers' trunk.

Sebastian Becker crouched by the inverted cadaver and looked it all over with care. He touched nothing until he came to the head and then, with great delicacy and some distaste, he knelt and reached in and teased something from the boy's partly open jaws. It was a piece of paper, screwed up into a ball and stuffed into the young man's mouth. The body had been dead for long enough to grow rigid, and Becker took some time to extract the paper without tearing it.

Sayers felt his legs giving way. The policemen holding him on either side sensed him going, and pulled him back to his feet. His mind had turned blank. He was so distressed at this discovery of the young boy's situation that, for a moment, he had ceased to question his own.

Becker opened up the crumpled sheet and smoothed it out. Still down on one knee, he laid the unfolded paper on the floor and contemplated it for some time.

Then he said, "The last time I saw this, it was in the hand of Super-intendent Turner-Smith." He looked up.

Sayers could offer him nothing.

"Don't play the innocent, Sayers," the detective said, rising. "Clive Turner-Smith is the name of the man you murdered last night. That would have been just before you came back here and did for his informant." He looked to the men holding Sayers. "Get him dressed," he said. "And nobody touch the boy. I'll call for the police surgeon."

They let Sayers struggle into his trousers and boots. They refused to take off the handcuffs and so his shirt, coat, and waistcoat had to be slung over his shoulders. In this humiliating state of disarray, he was bundled from his room and out onto the landing. He attempted at least to tuck his shirttails into his trousers, but was only able to make half a job of it.

The building was full of policemen. He couldn't count them. He could see more outside, through the windows. It wasn't difficult to imagine an entire hostile army of them, with Sayers himself at the center of their inward-facing circle. As they marched him down the stairs, men on each landing held the other guests back and obliged them to stay in their rooms. Once Sayers had gone by the guests were allowed out, and on each level they gathered at the balustrades to look down the stairwell and watch him go.

Down in the hallway stood Edmund Whitlock. For once the old tragedian was stricken by genuine emotion; his eyes were watery and red, and his hand trembled as he folded and refolded a handkerchief to dab them with.

As they went by him Becker said, "Thank you for your cooperation, Mister Whitlock."

Whitlock seemed not to hear the detective. He was looking past him, and at Sayers.

"Oh, Tom," he said, helplessly. "What have you done? I feel only a great sadness for you."

"I have done nothing," Sayers began to protest, but a shove in his back propelled him onward.

Out on the street, the police were holding back a crowd. A horse-drawn Black Maria van awaited him. Windowless, its panels riveted and strong, its rear door open and ready.

Sayers looked back toward the lodging house. It was a tall, narrow building, with steps up to the front door and railings to the pavement. There, in the sitting-room window, stood Louise Porter. Her face was a pale mask of disbelief. Behind Louise stood James Caspar.

As Sayers watched, Caspar placed a solicitous hand on Louise's shoulder and leaned in to murmur something in her ear. It seemed to Sayers that, despite the distance and the window glass between them, Caspar was making the gesture as much for Sayers to see as for Louise's comfort.

His escort took his hesitation for rebellion. Seizing him by the arms, they ran him up the steps at the back of the wagon and propelled him inside before slamming and padlocking the door.

THIRTEEN

he wagon measured about eight feet by six. There were two plain benches, one down either side; after the first lurch into motion he sat with his feet braced wide against the bench opposite, as the handcuffs made it difficult for him to steady himself any other way.

He could barely see. The only light came from vents in the roof and a single barred window in the door, through which he could hear boys following in the street and shouting something he couldn't make out. As the wagon bounced along, Sayers desperately tried to make some sense of the past half hour. He could not.

There was no doubting that his situation was dire. He'd begun by thinking that there had been some terrible misunderstanding that would be cleared up by a closer investigation, but that clearly would not do. No misunderstanding could explain the death of Arthur Steffens or the presence of his remains in Sayers' room; no simple human error could have placed him there. This was an act of deliberate and double malice, both in the murder and in the directing of blame for it.

Sayers had last seen Arthur in life at the playhouse. He was not lodging at Mrs. Mack's, but with the stage crew over the pub in Cross Lane. He must have been killed and his body carried up to the attic room sometime between the end of the night's performance and Sayers' return from his small-hours walk. Which suggested to Sayers that only someone inside the lodging house would have been positioned and able to take the opportunity.

All of his instincts pointed him to James Caspar. Unfortunately, no evidence did. Caspar's dissolute habits and their shared antipathy were proof of nothing; Sayers could speak of them and hope that the police might be moved to uncover some damning new information, but such effort on their part was unlikely. They were in no doubt that they had their man.

He heard the driver calling to the horses, and felt the wagon slow. The bone shaking grew more intense as it went into a turn, and Sayers had to brace himself harder or be thrown onto his side. To be shackled in handcuffs was a greater torment than he could ever have imagined. The physical discomfort was bearable, but because of their restriction he fought a constant urge to panic.

The wagon came to a halt. Nothing happened for a while, and nobody came to speak to him. He went to the door and, looking out through the bars, saw that he was in a police yard with a high brick wall around it. An ostler was leading horses across open ground while, over at the yard's far side, the gates by which they'd entered were being closed by an elderly watchman. The watchman had lost a limb, but moved with speed and skill on his remaining leg and a wooden crutch.

Sayers settled again, and after a while they came for him. He heard the padlock being removed, and then one of the uniformed men looked in through the bars, in case the prisoner should decide to come out fighting.

Six of them were waiting for him in the yard. Big, experienced-looking men, and their sergeant the biggest of them all. They had truncheons at the ready, and for a moment Sayers thought that he was to be driven with a beating toward the police station's jail entrance. But they formed a group around him and he was pushed, prodded, and generally herded toward the grim redbrick building overlooking the yard.

During the next hour, he was given a prisoner's examination and photographed. The handcuffs were removed and he was finally able to button his shirt and put on his waistcoat. He moved wherever he was sent, stood where he was told to stand. He resisted any urge to argue or rebel, knowing that neither would go well for him. He needed to maintain his composure until given the opportunity to speak. Any protest before then would be wasted indignation.

At no point was he left alone or unsupervised. Finally, he was walked into a room where Sebastian Becker and two much older, more senior-looking men were waiting. Both were high-collared and bearded and had small, hard-button eyes. The big sergeant from the yard stood just inside the door, and a shorthand clerk sat ready to take down anything that Sayers might say. The room had bare walls of painted brick and a cellar-style window that was too high to reach, and too small to escape through if anyone ever did.

There was a chair, and he was allowed to sit. Sayers was told of the charges against him, and at last had the opportunity to provide an account of himself.

After giving his birth date and such other details of his life that he could be sure of, he started to speak in the knowledge that whatever he said now would be an important record for the days ahead. Forthright or evasive, self-possessed or sniveling, here would be set down his character as the world would know it.

"I was a prizefighter and professional sportsman for seven years," he said. "I was in training at Chesham for a bout with Charles Wainwright, and I was attacked and struck on the arm with an iron bar. It was an attempt to influence the result, I'm certain of that. But they did their work too well and I was unable to fight at all. I'd borrowed one thousand pounds from the Marquis of Reddesley in advance of the match, and it had to be repaid.

"I wrote a boxing sketch and got up a small company to play it around the halls. As a fighter I had a certain popularity, and I repaid the debt. But people's memories fade very quickly, and so I turned my hand to management. I've managed for several companies since. Whitlock's for the past two years."

The two senior men continued to sit without expression throughout, while Sebastian Becker listened closely. He seemed to be searching for some particular meaning or enlightenment that he did not, could not, find.

He said, "I don't understand you, Sayers." The story he seemed to understand well enough; it was the man he could not fathom.

"There is much here that I do not understand, Inspector Becker."

"Is it some form of a blood lust? Something you could no longer satisfy in the ring and so you had to turn it onto the rest of us instead? I've seen murder for gain. For revenge. Out of rage or for passion. But never before have I seen such cruel and unusual murder for sheer love of its horror."

"I've harmed no one."

"You blinded a man in the ring once."

"I fought by the rules. The man knew the risks."

"What am I looking at, Sayers? Are you an aberration? Or are you something terrible and new?"

"You are looking at an innocent man, Inspector Becker."

"Don't you realize that only cooperation can help you now? You'll still hang, of course. Nothing can change that. But there's more than one path to the gallows."

"You speak of hanging. You found a boy in my room that I neither harmed nor placed there, and you speak of crimes against people that I do not know nor have even met. At no time did I ever hear the name of Clive Turner-Smith until I had it from your lips."

"You arranged to meet him in the saloon of the public house by the theater during the second act of last night's performance. Your note was still in his pocket when you speared him with his own blade."

"I put my hand to no note. And at no time did I ever leave the theater."

"The saloon bar was a matter of yards from the stage door. No one saw you backstage in that time."

"I went to look at the play from the back of the auditorium."

"Where everyone's attention was on the players. How very convenient."

"Ask Lily Haynes. She works behind the bar. She saw me. She spoke to me."

"Not in the second half of the evening, she didn't. Admit it, Sayers. Stop lying. Behave like a man and not the base thing you have descended to. You've left a trail of blood that matches your company's dates exactly. Did you think that by targeting paupers and unfortunates in different places you might escape notice for your crimes? A fifteen-year-old boy saw through you. And the evidence he provided will damn you."

Saying this, he picked up the page of pasted newsprint that he'd taken from the body in the lodging house, and thrust it out for Sayers to see. Suddenly, instinct and reason moved a step closer together.

"Caspar," Sayers breathed.

"Mister Caspar was onstage throughout the evening. He has seven hundred and fifty ticket-holding witnesses. How many could have spoken for you? One. Whom you strangled and stuffed into a box with your second-best suit."

"In God's name, Becker, don't close your mind to me or a terrible injustice will be done!"

"Don't quote the name of God at me, Sayers. If God exists, you serve a different master. I take it you will not confess." He rose to his feet. The clerk stopped writing, and began to pack away his notebook and writing kit. One of the two senior men muttered something inaudible to the inspector, and then he and his colleague left the room.

Sebastian Becker came around to stand in front of Sayers. He crouched a little and looked into the prizefighter's eyes, as if in search of something.

"Help me, Sayers," he said. "It cannot change your fate, but help me to understand. Lily Haynes would believe no ill of you. Clearly, she is wrong. But how can a man who inspires such loyalty in his friends be capable of such deeds as yours? How can a fiend be in any way human, Sayers? Or a human being truly a fiend?"

"You'd have me explain what I do not know," Sayers said. "I tell you once more, I am innocent of these deeds. Call back your clerk, and I'll tell you again."

Sebastian Becker straightened up and said, "You have killed an officer of the law. That means he was a brother to every man here. But we are not beasts as you are, Sayers. You *will* face the ultimate penalty, but there will be no rough handling. The true test of justice comes in moments like these."

Sayers had the impression that these words, though directed at him, may have been more for the benefit of the uniformed man by the door.

"Sergeant," the inspector said, "take him down."

F O U R T E E N

he sergeant's grip was tight on Tom Sayers' arm as he was walked down the corridor, away from the interview rooms and in the direction of the lockup cells. As well as being an effective form of restraint, it allowed the sergeant to sense the intentions of the man in his charge. Any impulse to bolt or rebel would signal itself, even as the thought was beginning to form. Sayers could see that any such attempt would be futile. However he considered it, his position seemed bleak.

He needed friends outside this place, and he needed them urgently. He thought of Edmund Whitlock, his employer, and almost in the same moment dismissed all hope of help from that quarter. The thought of him so teary-eyed and regretful in the lodging-house hallway was still fresh in Sayers' mind. For all his playing of kings and heroes, the actor was not a steadfast man. He clearly took Sayers' guilt at face value, as would many. Whitlock was unlikely to be an effective ally—especially if it meant that he'd have to turn against James Caspar.

Sayers still could not fathom the hold exercised by the younger man over the older, but he had seen its effects over the months. In Caspar's presence the normally intolerant actor became indulgent, and forgiving of his protégé's faults to the point of embarrassment. The younger man's influence was like the sergeant's grip; where it bound, it also gave control.

As they drew level with a door in the jail corridor, the sergeant forced him to a halt. It was a heavy door, reinforced and painted gray, but it was not like those to the cells. The sergeant rapped on it twice, and within seconds was answered by the sound of a turning key and the door swinging open into daylight. Sayers was shoved through without ceremony. He tripped on the threshold and only regained his balance once outside.

He found himself in a cage within the police compound. It resembled a large zoo enclosure and appeared to be a corner exercise yard for prisoners. Although open to the sky, it had a roof of bars that cast their shadow across the ground. Over on the far side of it three men waited, spread out in a line. They'd removed their helmets and tunics and rolled up their shirtsleeves.

When Sayers looked to the sergeant for an explanation, it was to see him unbuckling the wide belt that he wore over his own tunic. The constable who'd unlocked the door was now securing it after them.

"I see," said Sayers.

"No rough handling," said the sergeant pleasantly. "But you being a sporting man, we thought you might appreciate a little friendly competition."

His tunic came off to reveal a shirt and braces that clothed the wide chest and thick belly of a natural brute. Ugly as an afterbirth, here was a man who need live neither cleanly nor well to give off an air of physical threat.

"You wish to fight me?" said Sayers.

"You were the famous Tom Sayers, once," the sergeant said. "Call it a private demonstration of the fistic arts."

With the door now secured, the constable took the sergeant's tunic and helmet and carried them across the cage. He passed the other three, less hefty than their sergeant but born brawlers all. Outside the enclosure, police wagons had been drawn forward to screen the area from general view. Dropping the tunic and helmet onto a general pile, the constable now let himself out through a gate and took up a lookout position in the yard.

Sayers' heart had quickened, and without even thinking he shifted his weight to a more ready stance. He said, "And by what rules would such a friendly competition be conducted?"

"Newton Street rules," said the sergeant, turning away. Sayers began to reply, but mistook the man's intentions. The sergeant came back with his elbow raised and smashed the point of it into Sayers' upper arm, as hard as he could.

Sayers staggered back, clutching at his arm just below the shoulder. The pain was sudden and enormous. It was the same limb and almost the same spot at which he'd been struck and disabled by the mob that had ended his career. Back then, they'd cornered him in an alley and over-whelmed him. He managed not to cry out, but tears came to his eyes and for a few moments he was blinded.

Had they gone at him right there and then, all would have been lost. But the men stood back and watched, one or two of them grinning. Say-ers let go of his arm and flexed his hand, trying to set his face so that he would not wince further and show them weakness.

He said, "I think I have grasped the basic principles."

He could see their intentions now. Each man wanted to be able to brag that he had taken on the celebrated prizefighter and beaten him, yet none had any interest in an equal contest. However they might dress it up as sport, in the final reckoning this was to be rough justice over the death of one of their own. Should the magistrate query his condition in the morning, it would be explained that he had become violent, or had attempted an escape. Five witnesses would all agree. More might be found if required.

He said, "Will you allow yourselves the dignity of coming on one at a time, instead of all in a gang?"

"Certainly," said the sergeant, and moved around to the middle of the yard to be first.

Sayers raised his fists, and worked his shoulders a little to relax them. The pain in his upper arm still raged, and he knew that he would have to protect it. He felt no fear, even though there was little chance that this would go well for him. Fight back with any success, and they'd be on him like dogs. But like the onetime professional he was, he concentrated entirely on the task in hand.

The sergeant squared up, mocking Sayers' stance in a womanly way. Sayers felt dwarfed and slight in comparison to the quarter-ton of beef in shirtsleeves before him. The sergeant was clearly a man who had both dealt out and taken a good deal of punishment in his time, and had no need of grace or finesse.

Suddenly, the man came on. No circling, no testing out of his opponent's defenses, just a straight walk toward Sayers for the purpose of landing a blow. Sayers aimed a jab, but it was weak because he was trying to hit his man and back off at the same time. The sergeant didn't stop, but came crowding on in. He got one arm around Sayers and a fist in against the side of his head, a knuckle-skidder that hurt but did no resounding damage.

Sayers got out from under and circled around behind his man, as the sergeant turned around to keep facing him.

"What's the matter, Molly-boy?" the big man said. "Old men and children more to your taste?"

This was like fighting an ape or a bear. Had this been the ring, the sergeant would have been booed out of it or disqualified within a round or two. But he wasn't here to play by the rules. He was out to slap down and maul the little dancing man for the amusement of all.

Sayers stayed out of reach, and tried a couple of feints that the sergeant didn't fall for. When one of the policeman's big fists took a swipe for his head, he ducked it and got in a couple of body blows that the sergeant seemed hardly to feel.

As they continued to circle, the sergeant turned his own trick back on him, moving as if to strike without actually striking. Sayers overreacted, provoking derision from those watching. As one made noise, another cautioned silence. The man outside the bars looked back at them, anxiously.

Sayers saw an opening, and aimed a hook. But the policeman did no less than catch Sayers' fist in his own enormous hand and hold it there in midair, squeezing it hard and laughing as Sayers tried to pull it free. The sergeant had caught it in such a way that the bones of his hand were being mashed together, causing him cruel pain.

Newton Street rules, thought Sayers. And much as it went against every one of his instincts, he raised his leg and aimed the heel of his boot at the inner side of the big man's kneecap.

As his heel made contact, he felt the edge of it hook under the bone. In the same moment, he felt the gristle rip as the entire kneecap dislodged.

Instantly, the grip on his hand was released. The sergeant's jaw had fallen open in a big O and his eyes bulged wide. He made no sound.

Sayers took the opportunity to choose his move with science and care. He put in a right uppercut that slammed the sergeant's jaw shut with an audible snap, and then a left hook that made the big man's face ripple from one end to the other like a reflection in water.

The sergeant seemed to hesitate in the air. Then he went down.

The others were rushing at Sayers before his man had hit the ground. When he did, the air came out of him like a canvas bag.

Sayers struck at the first oncomer. He hurt him, but did not stop him. The other two were grabbing for his arms, but he knew better than to allow himself to be held. He winded one and butted the other.

The winded man was out of it, but the others came back on. Sayers grabbed the nearest and ran him back into the bars of the cage, hard; he could feel the other trying to get a grip on his shirt to haul him away, so he spun with his man and brought the two of them together. They collided shoulder to shoulder like carcasses swung on chains.

One dropped to his knees, spitting blood from a bitten tongue. The other fell to Tom Sayers' right cross. All four men were down, but only one of them was fully unconscious. Now the lookout was on his way to join in.

As he came through the gate, Sayers met him with the only sure takedown blow that he could see an opening for: a straight-on, bare-knuckle poleax strike between the eyes, almost as much agony to land as it was to receive. More agony, probably, because to the recipient it meant instant oblivion and freedom from all care. His man rebounded from the blow, the drawn truncheon falling from his grip and clattering on the stones. Beyond him stood the now-open gateway into the police yard.

Sayers did not hesitate. Jumping over the fallen constable, he ran through the gateway and out between the screening wagons. A law-abiding man for his entire life so far, Sayers saw little future in trusting to the law now. The law would have him buried for a deed he had not done. Ahead of him lay stabling for horses, with the ostler leading a pair across his field of view. To his left were the main building and the stone archway that led to the street.

The gates were being opened. The Black Maria that had brought him here was on its way out again. As he ran toward it, the sound of a Hudson whistle rose from the exercise yard behind him; as two more shrill notes were added, the one-legged watchman pinned back the gate and the Black Maria started to pass through.

Putting the wagon between himself and the gatekeeper, Sayers used its high sides as cover in the hope that he could slip out along with it. But the Black Maria's driver had turned in his seat at the sound of police whistles, and saw him right away. With an alarm-raising cry of "Prisoner on the loose!" he leaned right over and lashed at Sayers with his horse-whip. Sayers crouched and raised an arm to protect himself, but the whip was short and cracked harmlessly in the air above his head.

He was right by the wheels, only inches from them as they rumbled over the cobbles. Ahead of him there was about two feet of space between the wagon and the gatepost. The driver pulled hard on the reins, trying to use his vehicle to close up the gap and cut off Sayers' exit; the horses, surprised and confused by this sudden move, jumped in the traces and clattered sideways onto the pavement instead of out into the road. The wagon swayed dangerously and swung across, so that the side of it ground into the post right in front of Sayers with a sound of splintering coachwork. Sayers had to throw himself back, or be crushed.

The wagon rocked and was jammed at an angle in the gateway, its horses panicking and at least one of its wheels raised up off the ground. Sayers dropped and scrambled underneath it as the watchman came around the back. For a man with but one leg and a crutch, he was moving at a surprising speed.

The watchman was shouting after Sayers, the driver was shouting at his horses, and the horses were rearing in the traces and in danger of destroying the wagon to wrench themselves free. Their hooves came down like riveters' hammers, striking sparks from the stone pavement, while the robust shell of the Black Maria rocked back and forth like a wardrobe stuck in a doorway. Sayers came out onto the street, touching a hand to the ground to keep himself from falling and feeling a double lance of agony in his arm—once from the sergeant's disabling blow, and again from his own knuckle-busting punch to the lookout.

As Sayers came up to his feet, the coachman lashed out again with the whip. This time the tip of it caught Sayers across the back, splitting through shirt and waistcoat and the skin underneath. He was so close to the horses that he almost lost his footing and fell under their hooves; but then he was out and running, and leaving their chaos behind.

He'd little idea of where he was. It was a Saturday afternoon street in an unfamiliar town, with trams and wagons and horses and a Saturday crowd. A running man in shirtsleeves would draw attention, for sure; especially a running man with an injured arm and the shirt on his back split in two. He could not be halfhearted in his flight, but knew that he must put as much distance as he could between himself and the police station. He needed to disappear into the byways before any kind of a hue and cry could begin.

After dodging through people on the pavement, he jumped into the road. On the far side of it, barrow boys were pushing handcarts along. Which meant that somewhere close by, there had to be a market.

Caught for a moment between two passing trams in the middle of the road, he skipped along sideways until his way was clear. Then he pressed on in the direction from whence the barrows came.

FIFTEEN

t that same moment, Sebastian Becker was emerging from the central police station's main entrance. He was in his topcoat for the return journey and carrying the bag that he'd brought in case of an overnight visit. The day's business had been concluded so quickly that there was no point in him staying around any longer, not when a train on the half hour could have him home by midevening.

Sayers would go before the stipendiary magistrate in the morning to be remanded for trial, and then the business of constructing a detailed case against him could begin. As Sebastian had been discussing with the assistant commissioners, this would be a complicated process. Sayers' stroke of genius had been to commit his crimes in a variety of locations, all policed by different forces; no one force had been allowed a chance to see any pattern to them. It had fallen to a fifteen-year-old boy to lead them to it.

Arthur Steffens. His name would be recorded with honor. There was little that Sebastian could do for him now, but he could ensure that much.

That, and bring his murderer to the public gallows.

He saw no further point in trying to understand the man. There could be no mitigation for the things he had done. Perhaps some deeds truly did defy explanation, while their authors defied comprehension.

The police station entrance was a grand affair with double doors and a broad flight of steps leading down to the pavement. Sebastian was watching his feet as he descended, and glanced up to see a running man in the act of crossing the road. Even as the movement caught Sebastian's eye, the man stopped to let a tram go by. In that same moment, another tram passed before him and the man disappeared from his view.

Sebastian stared in disbelief, waiting for the second tram to clear. There he was . . . on the street in shirtsleeves where everyone else, even the meanest artisan, was properly dressed. Sebastian got a better look at his face as the man glanced to check his way before starting forward again. Tom Sayers, or his ghost.

Sebastian Becker did not believe in ghosts.

He dropped his bag and barked, "See to that!" at a hapless stranger who happened to be climbing the steps to enter the building, and then leaped across the pavement and into the road. A good citizen on a bicycle saw him, assumed him to be a man in flight from the police station, and tried to intercede. Sebastian handed him off and dashed through the traffic after Sayers, who by now had disappeared in the direction of a street market. Sebastian could hear police whistles as he crossed the road, and knew that an organized pursuit would not be far behind; but by then Sayers might have rendered himself invisible . . . all that he needed to do was to stop running, pick up a coat, and turn around to blend with the crowd.

But only the most practiced fugitives could think so clearly. Was Sayers one of those? By the time Sebastian reached the far pavement, Sayers was out of his sight. But he'd marked the man's direction and followed after him. People saw him coming, his dark coat flapping out behind him like a rider's cloak, and scrambled out of his way.

A blue-gowned factory girl who must have seen Sayers pass by only moments before shouted, "That way! He ran that way!" and pointed him toward a street of warehouses. Sebastian took her at her word.

The street held a shoe market, its narrow way choked with temporary wooden stalls and canvas rain awnings. The buildings to either side were of sooty brick, and so tall that only a strip of sky was to be seen above them. Much of the fresh air and daylight was shut out, and as a result the market was all gloom with the stink of used leather.

Sebastian was slowed by the people that he had to push and dodge his way through, but as he looked over their heads was rewarded by what he thought was a glimpse of his quarry.

It was. It was him. Sayers was being slowed down, too. Fighting through the stalls was like swimming through a river filled with furniture. Sebastian saw Sayers look back, and thought he saw recognition in the man's eyes; or it could have been the general anxiety of the pursued, with Sayers not spotting him at all.

Either way, he saw Sayers turn and duck down into the mass, leaving him with only an idea of the man's direction. Another street joined this one just ahead, and his guess was that the prizefighter was making for that.

There was a public house on the corner. He stopped to speak to the children on the doorstep.

"Did a man just go inside?" he said, and they stared at him as if he'd spoken in some foreign tongue.

Leaving the warehouses and the market behind, Sebastian found himself in an area of mean-looking dwellings of a much greater age. They stood three stories high, the holes in their windows stopped with all manner of devices—strips of blanket, brown paper, the crown of an old hat. The overall impression was that of buildings stuffed to bursting point, so that clothing and rags pushed out at every seam. The remaining glass was so filthy that it might as well have been painted wood.

By now, he had no idea where he was. But in the comparative quiet of the street, he could hear running footsteps somewhere ahead.

Sebastian put on a spurt. But it cost him, and he had to slow to a walk for a few strides before launching off again. He was no weakling, but he was unused to this kind of exertion for such a sustained period of time. The effort, combined with the excitement of the chase, was taking a steady toll. He was beginning to feel drained and light-headed. If he *did* manage to lay an arresting hand on Sayers, he could only hope to find him equally diminished.

The street ended in a bridge. Sayers was nowhere to be seen. Sebastian slowed to a walk. By now his lungs hurt and his saliva had become a corroding fire at the roots of his tongue. Even his teeth had begun to ache. His walk was unsteady.

Out on the bridge, Sebastian stopped to listen. All that he could hear was his own uneven breath, raging in his ears. He couldn't calm it, so he held it for a moment.

Down below, a dog barking.

He went to the side of the bridge and looked over. Instead of the railway line he was expecting, he found himself looking down onto a canal basin. A hidden canal, cutting right through the middle of town. The canal and its towpath went off in a curve around the backs of the warehouses, brown water in a man-made canyon. Directly below him were the ends of a number of barges, poking out from under the bridge. Releasing his grip on the parapet, Sebastian turned to the other side. A wagon went by, its ironbound wheels vibrating the cobblestones under his feet.

As he crossed the bridge, he was beginning to think that he should perhaps go back and look more closely at the public house. He had not noted its name. Some of them were known for having stakes and ropes in their garrets where illegal fights could be staged. Older pugilists were remembered and revered while the young contenders pounded at each other. A man like Sayers might be a stranger in the town, yet still find himself welcome if he made himself known.

But then Sebastian reached the opposite parapet. The side of the bridge was a series of panels of riveted iron, a parody of classical architecture put together with the crude confidence of this industrial age. The top of the parapet was widened like a handrail and worn shiny by use.

He looked down into the larger part of the canal basin, where a veritable fleet of barges had been herded and tethered into one great floating raft. All ages, all sizes . . . Sebastian had no idea whether they were awaiting cargo (many were empty), or mustered here for repair (most appeared to need it), or simply as living space (no actual signs of life, but washing hung out on decks, and he could see several smoking chimney stacks).

The dog that he'd heard was tethered on a narrowboat's deck. It was smallish and particolored, like a Punch-and-Judy man's Toby dog. It danced at the end of its rope, still barking at the solitary passerby, who was now some yards on up the towpath.

It was Sayers.

The fighter was walking—limping, actually—with one arm held out from his side, as if it somehow pained him. He looked beaten and tired, but far from resigned; it was as if he'd only slowed because he believed he'd outrun the possibility of capture.

There was another road bridge about a hundred yards on, but the only way up to it was from a wharf by a lockkeeper's house on the other side of the canal. As far as Sebastian could see, his quarry had trapped himself on the towpath. He looked around for the way down.

An iron gate led to a narrow stairway in dark gray brick. It was open to the sky but enclosed on all sides, and it brought him out into the shad- ows underneath the bridge.

It was strange. It was as if the town had vanished and he'd entered a different world. Something rumbled over the bridge, but all of the aboveground sounds of the city had faded away. There were birds on the water and wildflowers growing alongside the towpath. There ahead of him was Sayers, still plodding on, still oblivious. He'd seized his injured arm with his other, as if he might squeeze out the pain.

Sebastian's confidence grew. He started forward, moving as quietly as he could. If he could surprise Sayers, so much the better. The man might have been a professional fighter, but he was damaged and had run a hard chase, and Sebastian was determined to come up with him at whatever risk to himself.

How had Sayers managed to escape the cells? Desperation could drive men to extreme deeds. Sebastian had once known a prisoner to leap from the dock and flee the courtroom after a drop of eight feet, flooring two officers of the court and a passing soldier who'd joined in the chase;

then there had been the thief who'd climbed three stories up an air shaft so narrow that one would imagine a cat could barely slide through it, before crossing the courthouse roof to descend by a waterspout.

He would not be surprised to learn that Sayers had killed again to secure his freedom. He would have to take care. But he did not dare flinch.

Sayers continued to limp along, grimy and torn, clutching his arm, a sorry-looking spectacle. Sebastian closed the distance between them and continued to approach unnoticed, until the dog on the boat began to bark all over again.

Sayers looked back and saw him. Then the man's energy seemed to return. As Sebastian started forward, Sayers took a second to check his options and then broke into a run.

Sebastian had been thinking that he had his man trapped on the tow-path, but now he realized his mistake. There was, indeed, no access to the next road bridge from this side of the canal. But before the bridge there was a set of lock gates, and across the top of the gates there was a rampart just a few inches wide.

Sayers reached this walkway and started across. Sebastian was there only moments after, and he was on it before Sayers had made it to the other bank.

The gates were massive. On this side, only the top edges of them were visible above the water. But looking over, he could see that the level on the other side had fallen to reveal the deep trench of the lock. Below him was the sheer fifteen-foot drop of solid timber necessary to hold back the enormous weight of canal water behind them. Where the gates met in a V, jets were spouting through the slightest gaps under tremendous pressure.

The walkway was nothing more than a plank fixed just below the edge of each gate. There was a handrail, painted white. The crossing took some care, but it did not feel unsafe.

In the middle where the gates met, Sebastian missed his footing and fell.

He hit the canal without grace, and went under. The sudden plunge in temperature was the greatest shock. Sebastian had no fear of water, and he knew how to swim. But his topcoat tangled around him and grew heavy, and he took a long time to rise. The water around him was so dark that the play of light above the surface was all that he could see.

Just as he was beginning to wonder if it was the last thing he ever *would* see, his face broke the surface and he was able to draw breath. He was right up against the gate, and he reached out to pull himself up.

But something was wrong here. Something was holding his arms down. He couldn't raise them more than halfway. He was held like a drowning sailor, being dragged back under by creatures from the deep.

He started to struggle. It was his coat, his damned topcoat. It was halfway down his arms and pulling him under. But surely even the coat plus the weight of water could not draw on him so hard. He fought to get free of it, but only seemed to become more entangled, and its pull on him, if anything, seemed to increase.

Then he realized. It was not merely the sodden weight of the material that was drawing him down. His coat was being sucked through one of the gaps between the gates.

He braced his feet against the wood and tried to wrench himself free. He had to grab a breath as his face went back under, and hold it in while his efforts came to nothing. When he stopped trying, he did not bob up to the surface again. He stopped about an inch short of it.

And still the suction drew him down.

He started to fight. Not in an ordered way, but as a child in a panic might, frantically and without any thought-out purpose. The dead breath came out of him in a bubbling stream. It was a simple enough matter to get his arms out of the sleeves, but the harder he tried, the worse he seemed to make it. Without ever meaning to, he gulped in a lungful of water. The reflex of spluttering it out only caused him to draw in more. He realized with dismay that not only was he going to drown, but that his body was an eager participant in the process. His will no longer mattered.

Then something got a handful of his hair and yanked him upward. His body was racked with coughing, and he couldn't see.

"I can't hold you," Sayers said. "Grab hold of something."

Sebastian could not answer, nor could he free his hands. He shook his head. Which, under the circumstances, was a mistake.

"God Almighty," Sayers swore, and released his grasp. Sebastian started to submerge again but it was only for as long as it took for Sayers to switch his grip to the detective's shirt collar.

"Don't just thrash around," Sayers told him. "Think. Use your right hand to pull off the left sleeve."

It was simple enough when someone said it. Not so simple to do. Sebastian felt around with fingers numbed by cold, and plucked at material he couldn't take hold of. Even when he got it, it wouldn't come. But Sayers was pulling him upward, and between that and the suction from below he suddenly felt his arms come out of the sleeves and found himself floating free.

Sayers was grasping his collar with one hand and holding on to the flimsy handrail with the other, leaning right out over the water in a dangerous way. Moving in a crouch along the narrow plank, he guided Sebastian to the canalside as if steering a log.

There was a short iron ladder fixed to the timber on the back of the gate. Sebastian had not even the strength to grasp its rungs. Sayers hung him on it, and he clung there.

Sayers leaned down to him and said, "I know what you think you see. You think I am running from the gallows. Well, you are right. I am. But that is not because I am guilty. I am not a guilty man, Inspector Becker. And somehow I swear I will convince you of it."

Sebastian had not the power even to attempt a reply.

He went, then. Sebastian learned later that he'd knocked on the door of the lockkeeper's house in passing, and told the keeper of a man in distress in his lock basin. The keeper had hauled Sebastian out with a boat hook, and given him an earful of abuse for his foolhardiness.

By then, Tom Sayers was nowhere to be seen.

S I X T E E N

rs. Mack did not provide an early evening meal, but would cook the guests' own food if they brought it to her kitchen. At around five, she would lay on an afternoon tea in the dining room, consisting of bread and butter with the occasional slice of seedcake. Basic fare though it was, it was usually appreciated by a profession for whom there could be few things to recommend a job more than the inclusion of a practical pork pie in the third act.

Today, however, appetites were at a low. It would be hard to say which had shocked the company more—the violent death of their callboy, or Tom Sayers' arrest for the deed. There had been some talk of canceling the matinee performance, but Whitlock would not hear of it. The show went on; all the cast performed efficiently but as if in a daze, and quietly returned to the lodging house afterward. Only Edmund Whitlock and James Caspar were to be found in the dining room at ten minutes after five o'clock. Whitlock was feeding pieces of seedcake to Gussie, and Caspar was pacing the carpet.

It could be an oppressive room, with its heavy lace curtains and dark furniture and Mrs. Mack's collection of hideous ornaments in every available nook and on every imaginable surface. Enlivened by company and conversation, it would be transformed. But for the moment, the only sounds were the tick of the pendulum clock and the spitty working of the little dog's jaws as one tidbit followed another.

Caspar stopped, and watched the spectacle for a while.

Then he said, "They eat dogs in China."

Whitlock broke another piece off the seedcake and held it up between thumb and forefinger. The little dog froze, watching it intently, and then snapped it out of the air as Whitlock pitched it within reach.

The actor-manager's moods had darkened considerably over the past few months. Everyone had noticed it, but no one knew the reason why. Except perhaps for Gulliford the Low Comedian, who reckoned he knew a sick man when he saw one.

"Contain yourself, James," Whitlock said now.

"For how long? They can't hang him if they don't catch him."

"We'll be back in London in less than three weeks. If you don't manage to conserve your appetites until then, you'll as good as exonerate him."

Caspar drew a chair out from under the table and sat. He placed an elbow onto Mrs. Mack's best lace tablecloth and rested his chin on his hand.

After staring at the dog's performance for a moment longer, he said, "I could join in the search."

"No."

"Well, I've got to do *something,* Edmund. I'll go insane."

"I really don't believe so, James," Whitlock said. "Don't be such a child."

Caspar made a face that could only be described as a smirk, and sat back in his chair.

"Miss Porter doesn't think me a child," he said.

"You have a child's want of education," Whitlock said with weary patience, his attention still on the dog as it throttled down the last of the cake. "A talent for darkness has brought you this far. But the deeper meaning of it all escapes you still."

Caspar leaped back onto his feet in irritation. "Why is it," he said, "that when I complain of anything, I always get a lecture?"

"Then stop complaining. And find yourself something useful to do."

"How can I?" Caspar said. "You've just forbidden me the pursuit of any satisfaction."

Dusting the crumbs from his hands, Whitlock looked up at Caspar and laid out his meaning.

"Learn subtlety, James," he said. "It is perfectly possible to destroy something innocent, yet leave no public mark."

The best daylight in the house was to be had in the sitting room, at the front of the building overlooking the street. This was the room where Mrs. Mack kept her piano polished and her damask cushions plumped— her showpiece room, with grand curtains gathered back like a theater of Varieties and enough memorabilia to stock a museum. There were framed prints on the walls and china figurines along the mantelpiece. A doily on every table, and a vase or statuette on every doily.

In a high-backed chair by the window sat Louise Porter, studying a playbook. More affected by the day's events than almost anyone else in the company, she sought distraction in her craft.

She was distressed to think of the time that she'd spent in Tom Sayers' presence, never suspecting any part of the true nature of her "devoted servant." Those constant small services, the innocent-sounding banter . . . all now took on a new and sinister aspect. Little had she known of how closely she'd been consorting with danger. The very thought of it now was enough to turn her skin to gooseflesh.

Sayers was a monster, and she'd been an object of his attentions. She'd allowed this—encouraged him, even, in her innocent way. And to what terrible end might it have led her, had his crimes not been discovered in time? The convincing way in which he'd dissembled showed him to be a better actor than any in the troupe.

And yet it was a strange kind of distress. It quickened her pulse, but it did not make her timid. Far from making her fearful, it seemed to increase her confident sense of her own existence. Yesterday, she'd known little of the world; today, she felt able to take on whatever else it might offer.

And some better acting parts would be a nice beginning.

She often felt at a disadvantage when she heard the conversations of the other players, offhandedly referring to this scene in "the *Dream*" or "the jewel scene in *Faust*." Most of them had toured or played in stock for years. Unless she wanted to be locked into this one play until Whitlock had run it into the ground, her best chance of expanding her professional experience lay through reading.

She held the text up close, and wore a pair of small-lensed, wire-framed spectacles to aid her. They'd belonged to an aunt who had died; helping to go through her rooms after the funeral, Louise had given in to the temptation to try on the spectacles and had been startled at their improving effect. She'd meant only to study the look of herself wearing them in a mirror, having no notion until that point that her power of vision was less than it might be. Now they were a guilty secret. Not just for the fact that she needed them, but because of the embarrassing impulse that had led her to discover it.

At the faint sound of the door hinge creaking, she looked over the top of the book. Seeing Caspar standing in the doorway, she quickly snatched off the glasses and hid them behind the covers.

Caspar seemed not to notice. He was too busy looking downcast.

"Mister Caspar," she said.

Caspar raised a hand. "I did not know there was anyone here," he said. "Forgive me."

"Please do not feel you have to leave."

Caspar shook his sorry head. "I would not inflict my presence upon you," he said, and he moved as if to leave and draw the sitting-room door closed after him.

"Wait!" Louise said, laying her book aside, and he stopped. "Please explain."

He made as if to speak, and then sighed and shook his head. "What can I say to you, Louise?" he said. "I am ashamed to be of the same species as a man like Sayers."

"His crimes are not yours."

"But I despair."

"Why?"

Caspar moved across the room to the chair that faced her own. As he lowered himself to sit on the edge of it, he said, "Because all is tainted by his base and perverted passions. What must you think when you look upon me now?"

Louise considered his words, and then chose her own with the greatest of care.

"That there are passions and appetites which are neither loathsome nor unnatural," she said. "But which celebrate God and the way that he meant us to be."

He gazed at her with a kind of growing wonder, as if she had shone an unexpected light into his personal darkness.

"I wish I could believe it," he said.

She grew bold.

"I wish I could persuade you," she said.

And at that, Caspar somehow managed to give her a fair impression of a man who might be open to persuasion.

Later that evening, high up in the ironwork under one of the town's many railway bridges, Sayers found himself a spot to settle where no one could steal up on him, nor any bobby's lantern seek him out. He could look out through the spans and girders across the rooftops of the city: its gaslit streets, its distant chimneys, the caul of smoke that covered its sky and forever blotted out the stars. He huddled there in a coat that stank of the beerhouse he'd stolen it from, and he tried to set aside all inclination to bewilderment or self-pity and address his thinking to the greater problems that faced him.

He was satisfied that nothing in his hand was broken. As far as he could tell, the pain in his arm did not represent a new injury but a reawakening of the old. As such, it ought to fade.

But what to do with himself? Where to go? He'd no friend in this town other than Lily Haynes, and he had no intention of blighting her new life with his problems. He knew that he ought to leave, make a run for London, perhaps, but for one good reason could not bring himself to go.

He feared for Louise. There was a madman in the troupe, and she was close within his orbit. Sayers had no doubt that it was James Caspar who should now be in shackles, not he. The man killed paupers for sport and gratification. It was obvious that young Arthur had spotted the series of fatal coincidences during the months that he'd spent combing local newspapers for notices, while at the same time enduring Caspar's unremitting and casual abuse. Passing the information to the police had been his revenge. Alas, the act had rebounded upon him.

Becker had spoken of a note, sent backstage by Clive Turner-Smith. It had supposedly been returned to its sender with an inscription from Sayers—the inscription that had led the superintendent to his end. Sayers had seen no such note. Which meant that another had intercepted and responded to it in his name.

Could Caspar's grip on the boss be such that Whitlock had chosen to hand the policeman's note to his Leading Male Juvenile instead of his acting manager? There could only be one reason for making such a choice—Whitlock must have guessed the significance of Turner-Smith's arrival. Which meant that he must already have been aware of James Caspar's crimes. Thinking back to that tearful display in the lodging-house hallway, Sayers was inclined to think that he had underestimated his employer. Perhaps the man was a greater actor than could be imagined by anyone who only saw him perform upon the stage.

It would not have been impossible for Caspar to keep the appointment in Sayers' place. He was offstage for most of the second act of *The Purple Diamond,* apart from one appearance as a mysterious hooded figure outside a window. This was always an occasion for screams from the audience, and cheers when the mystery was explained—but because his face was never seen at that point, almost anyone might have doubled for him. He could easily have left the theater for twenty minutes and returned to pick up his cue. And then later, back at Mrs. Mack's, he'd need only to choose his moment to hide the slaughtered callboy in Sayers' room.

The bridge began to shake. Up above, a mighty engine passed over. First came its thunder, filling the archway, and then an aftermath of clouds and cinder sparks falling outside like fairy rain. To the damp and soot of the archway it added a familiar smell, of coal and steam and long journeys and places to be, of schedules and order and purpose. Only a few yards above him was the life he had now lost.

Somewhere beyond his sight, the town hall clock was chiming. The second-house performance of *The Purple Diamond* would shortly be under way. Sayers leaned his head back against the stonework and closed his eyes.

He'd tried to approach the lodging house, but had managed to get no closer than the corner of the street. From there he'd seen that the police had left a man outside, and so he'd turned up his collar and walked on without stopping. It was the same on Liverpool Street; constables were all around the theater and when the matinee performance was over, cabs arrived to take the women home.

Somehow he had to warn her. She would not want to listen, but he had to make himself understood.

After all, he was, even in his supposed disgrace and enforced exile, the most dedicated of her devoted servants.

Although the matinee had been a strange and muted affair, by the evening word of that morning's events had spread all over town. By seven, the house was packed and the atmosphere was electric. Clearly, the *Purple Diamond* company had become a major and morbid attraction.

During the opening turn, Gulliford hovered backstage in his Billy Danson makeup and seemed agitated and almost too distressed to go on. The resident stage manager all but had to give him a shove to propel him

THE KINGDOM OF BONES

out of the wings when the band launched into his walking-on music, but he steeled himself and conjured the nerve, and then off he went.

He would later say that once he was out there, it was as if he'd been handed complete power over some gigantic thousand-headed entity; that he had never known an audience like it, or exercised such control from the stage. The same act that he'd done for twenty years, that had drawn polite applause in Whitehaven and with which he'd "died on his arse" in Glasgow, went over like bread to the starving. They were hungry, they were ready, and they would grab and shake and devour whatever he cared to throw at them.

"Better have your mop ready, Charlie," he said to the SM as he came off after his comic song to a storm of applause. "They're wetting the seats." And then he skipped back on and took another call, more like a big-name headliner than a second-spot man.

The mood stayed up throughout the entire first half of the bill, and when the curtain rose on the opening scene of *The Purple Diamond,* the noisiest of welcomes was followed by the most tense of silences as all strained to follow every nuance and development in the unfolding story . . . although it would have to be said that this was a drama in which the nuances were very few, and very far between.

But while it may not have been great art, it was damned good carpentry. Primed by the day's news, the night's audience had perhaps come along anticipating a drama of shock and sensation rather than intrigue and mystery. If they did, it was of no matter, because they took to the play's actual narrative with no less enthusiasm.

Whitlock was at his bombastic best. In the climactic scene, although nominally addressing the stepfather as played by the First Heavy, he turned to the audience and cried out, "Let everyone in this house bear witness! Every man, woman, and child down to the smallest babe in arms! This boy is, indeed, your long-lost son, and a finer man to bear your name you could not wish for!"

And the First Heavy replied, "Yes! I knew it not, but know it now."

James Caspar, as the falsely accused, was standing upstage with Louise

Porter's Mary D'Alroy. Now the First Heavy turned to him, saying, "Speak, my boy, and say what would repair the wrong I have done you."

"I ask for nothing, sir," Caspar replied, "save this; the hand of your stepdaughter, to exchange my newfound liberty for a sweeter bondage, and to make my happiness complete."

"I cannot speak for her," said the First Heavy, which allowed Whitlock to take the reins again.

"Then let her speak for herself!" he cried in a voice that sent a thrill through the audience and a rattle through the chandeliers. "What say you, Mary? Do you find him true?"

The house seemed to hold its collective breath as Louise turned to Caspar. It was as if the personal happiness of each and every ticket holder would depend on her next words.

Caspar gripped her arms and held her, gazing imploringly at her. This was a new and unexpected piece of business, but it seemed so natural and truthful that she was neither surprised nor thrown by it.

"With all my heart," she said, and the house exploded.

For a while it was impossible to continue. They roared, they stamped, they cheered, and they whistled. Never had the company known a reception like it. Those onstage had to hold the tableau for a minute or more. Louise gazed steadily into Caspar's eyes, her breathing shallow and excited, her heart pounding. It continued to pound through Whitlock's closing speech and on until the moment when, standing in the wings and awaiting her call to sing, she became aware of a presence and realized that James Caspar was standing close behind her.

When he whispered close to her ear, his breath fanned her neck and stirred the odd wisp of hair.

She shivered, deliciously, as he said in a low voice, "Now I can see that there are passions and appetites that are neither loathsome nor unnatural. But which celebrate God and the way that he meant us to be."

When she turned to look at him, it was to find that he had faded back into the shadows.

When Louise sang her song, it was as if a mist of tears hung in the air above the stalls. Even the uniformed policemen at the back of the house were dabbing at their eyes. Halfway through it she found herself thinking about young Arthur Steffens, taken from the lodging house to the mortuary, and her voice almost gave way. The women had not been allowed to see his body.

When she returned backstage to join the others, most of the company were moving around as if they'd been deafened by a blast. After the morning's sobering events, the last thing they'd expected to experience was this heightened sense of communal passion. It was as if the atmosphere throughout the theater, both before and behind the curtain, was a potent combination of elation and terror; in the midst of death, they were in life's most vibrant grip.

The theater had been constructed less than ten years before, but its backstage facilities resembled those of a much older building. Two shows a night, six nights a week, plus matinees and benefits, were bound to pile on the wear and tear. If the management were to spend any money, they'd be sure to put their cash into places where its effects would be seen.

Someone had taken the screen from Louise's tiny dressing room, so the house carpenter had rigged a corner curtain for her to change behind. Stepping out of her Mary D'Alroy dress, a rugged piece of working costume that would pass for a fine lady's garment to anyone standing farther than ten feet away, she heard the door to the corridor open and close. A shadow crossed the curtain, cast by the oil lamp that stood over by the dressing-table mirror.

She said, "Mrs. Wrigglesworth? I think I felt some stitches go. It was under the left arm, during the swoon." She held the dress out through the curtain, and it was taken from her.

"Is there anything from the stage door tonight?" she said as she released the corset and then dropped the first of two petticoats that gave the dress its shape.

There was no response, and so she said, "Mrs. Wrigglesworth?" and put her head out from behind the curtain.

James Caspar stood there. Still in his stage clothes, he was alone in the tiny room and no more than three or four feet away from her. His hands were out in front of him and her heavy stage dress lay across them, like something drowned and brought to shore.

"Mister Caspar!" she said. And then, "James!"

Caspar's face was somber.

"Send me away," he said.

"I certainly should."

"Then send me away."

"I shall."

Neither of them moved.

She said, "Mrs. Wrigglesworth will be coming in here at any moment."

"I suspect not," Caspar said. "I believe that she is presently stitching Mister Whitlock into his rather tightly fitting lucky silk jacket. He says he wishes to feel at his best when negotiating with the management."

Nothing separated them other than the flimsy curtain she held in her hand, and the chemise that hung from her shoulders. Which in itself was almost nothing; it was cut straight for a décolleté effect and hung from two thin straps. She felt all but naked before him.

"Well?" he said.

"Well," she replied.

She realized that she did not want to send him away; she did not actually *have* to send him away; and nothing, other than custom and convention and the disapproval of the world, actually obliged her to send him away.

Her only thought was of the embarrassment she'd feel if others in the company were to know of this impropriety. And there was God, of course . . . but had they not dealt with him already?

"This has been . . . ," she said, searching for words that might be equal to her feelings, and failing to find them, "a very unusual day."

He turned and, carefully, laid her empty Mary D'Alroy dress over the back of the nearby chair. Originally tailored for the role of Ernestine in *Loan of a Lover*, it had been acquired from the Theatre Royal as part of the Bilston stock and altered to fit.

"And an evening like no other," he said. "What say you, Mary? Do you find me true?"

"Mister Caspar!" she protested. But by now her heart was pounding as it had on the stage.

"Then send me away."

On any other day, and under any other circumstances, Louise would have conducted herself in the manner expected of her sex; where young men were wild, it fell to young women to be their governors and leaders in decorum.

But this had been no ordinary day. It had been a day charged with an awareness of life's brevity, and the immediacy of its potential end. A day with a simple lesson: that all is fleeting, and whatever is not seized with boldness, whether rightly or wrongly, is soon gone.

She drew the curtain aside and stepped out.

"Secure the door," she whispered, "and do not speak again."

SEVENTEEN

ouise was completely lacking in experience, but not entirely without understanding. Three summers spent with cousins on a country farm had given her plenty to muse upon when it came to the ways of nature. Observation had helped her with many of the questions that an education in classical art might raise, but then stop just short of answering. All those nymphs and shepherds surely had something in mind when they were coming away, but it fell to the barnyard to provide some suggestion as to exactly what it was.

The surprise lay not in her own uncertainty, but in Caspar's. Where she expected him to be bold, he was hesitant. Where she'd assumed he'd be experienced, he seemed innocent. He clearly was not quite the man of the world that she'd assumed him to be.

Far from this being a disappointment, she could imagine nothing that might have endeared him to her more.

It was a hasty coupling, but an effective one. She was almost dismayed by her eagerness for it to succeed.

Afterward, on the floor of the dressing room by the dim light of the oil lamp, tangled in the folds of the curtain that they'd pulled down from the rail to serve them for a hasty bed, she stared up at the shadows on the ceiling and thought, So now I am fallen. The thought amused her so much that she convulsed in a moment of silent laughter. Were she genuinely fallen, she would surely know it in her heart; and her heart was telling her no such thing.

"What?" said Caspar from beside her, breaking their silence for the first time.

"I was thinking that I am a fallen woman," she repeated aloud, and fought the urge to giggle again, as it would not do to be heard from outside.

"Forgive me," he said, and started to rise.

"No!" she said, sitting up quickly and reaching for him. "You misunderstand."

"I *do* understand," he said, adjusting his clothing. "I cannot stay. Let us speak of this in earnest, tomorrow."

He listened at the door for a moment before unfastening it and slipping out, opening it no wider than was necessary.

Louise was left, half out of her chemise and alone, entangled in a makeshift coverlet on a dressing-room floor, her stage costume scattered around her and her going-home clothes hung up on the back of the door.

Her euphoria lasted awhile, but in solitude it began to fade. What was the hour? The theater emptied quickly when the night's work was over, and she could no longer hear sounds from the corridor outside. She got to her feet, and began picking up the various items to gather them together.

She lacked organization. Bending to pick up one thing, she felt something else slip from her arms. But she could not leave the room in disarray, however late it was. Tomorrow was Sunday and another traveling day, although at the end of tonight's performance a rumor had gone around of a return engagement.

Perhaps that was the reason for Whitlock's best-suit meeting with the theater's management. He was dressing to play the Man of Business, and probably meant to negotiate an improvement in the terms. This was a task that, under more normal circumstances, would have fallen to Tom Sayers.

Louise was uncertain how she would feel about extending the run. It seemed uncomfortably close to profiting from a tragedy. But the company had a living to make, and so did she; without her income, she would have no form of support at all. Her father had died leaving her mother with neither money nor property, but with significant debts. Mrs. Porter, once used to presiding over a household of her own, had chosen kitchen work in a vicarage over the poorhouse. Louise had elected to pursue a life on the stage rather than to follow her into service.

Her mother's greatest concern for her had been over the moral quality of the world she had chosen. As if no maidservant had ever been seduced below stairs, or no cleric ever strayed!

And, besides, she'd found that actors loved the Church; they seemed to look upon it as a related branch of their art.

The house was silent as she made her way down to the stage door. She'd dressed in haste and bundled her costume items into the theatrical hamper, ready to be transported. Someone had been around and turned out all the gas, so she carried the oil lamp from her dressing room to light her way. She was beginning to fear that she might have been locked in, but the stage doorkeeper was waiting for her.

She said, "Has Mister Caspar left?"

"Ages ago," the doorkeeper said. "Ah've been waitin' to lock up."

"I'm sorry," Louise said. "I lost all track of time."

The doorkeeper said nothing and his expression, mostly hidden behind an enormous mustache that turned a youngish man's face into an ancient's, gave very little away. But she was convinced that he must have guessed her secret, and she tried not to blush while avoiding his eyes. She handed over the oil lamp and stepped out into the alleyway beside the theater, and the doorkeeper stopped to snuff out the various remaining lights before following her with his enormous bunch of keys.

It had been raining. The stone flags of the alleyway were slick and shiny, reflecting the lit windows of the public house next door. There was a big crowd in there, making a lot of noise—most of them had probably moved over from the theater when the play had ended. Someone had told her that the landlord had closed off the saloon bar and was charging a penny for people to enter and look at the murder scene.

She could see a policeman in a rain cape standing at the end of the passageway, and behind him a hansom cab waiting to take her back to her lodgings.

She thanked the policeman for his patience, and made some excuse about having to look for a lost bracelet. He said it was of no matter. He sent off a couple of passersby who'd lingered to stare, and lent her his arm to climb up into the cab.

The construction of the hansom was such that the driver's position was above and behind her. She called up to him, "Forgive me, driver, but I can't recall the exact address. It's Mrs. Mack's. Do you know it?"

He did not speak, but for a reply cracked his whip across the horse and set the carriage into unexpected motion. She was taken by surprise and fell back roughly in her seat; although the seat was padded and buttoned, the breath was driven from her for a moment.

She supposed she must have annoyed him by keeping him waiting for so long. But this really would not do. They were barreling along as if the ground under their ironbound wheels were a compact sandy beach, not the cobblestones and tram rails of an industrial town. She was shaken back and forth and had to hang onto one of the side straps; she genuinely feared that the next rut, jolt, or bang into a kerbstone might throw her out of the cab altogether.

"Driver!" she called over her shoulder. "Driver, what are you doing? Slow down, please!" But if the driver heard her, he did not respond.

As they tore down the length of Liverpool Street, she began to get the impression that they were only speeding because the driver did not have complete control of the reins. She could hear him calling to the animal, to no great effect.

They did not slow for the next crossroads and barely managed the turn as they cut across before a late tram; she could hear the angry ringing of its bell as they left it behind, plunging on into darker and less-populous streets.

Needless to say, this was not the way to Mrs. Mack's. They were heading into an area of tall, dark factory buildings and railway viaducts. A train thundered over as they thundered beneath, and in the shadows of a brick archway where a single streetlamp burned, the driver finally managed to bring his horse under control and rein it to a halt.

Louise wanted to jump from the cab before it could set off again, but could not turn her intentions into action; she stayed frozen in her seat and clinging to the strap, while the carriage shifted and rocked as the driver tied off the reins and climbed down from his post.

He was coming to speak to her. A fine time to show concern for her welfare! She might have been shaken to death already, or flung out on some corner.

The cab rocked again as the driver put his weight onto the step and drew himself up to look in on her.

"Louise," he said, and he reached up and pulled down the coachman's muffler that had been wrapped to cover the lower half of his face. "It's me. Don't be afraid. Everything you've heard is untrue."

She stared in horror. By the light of that single lamp, he stood revealed. Tom Sayers.

She'd supposed him long gone in his escape but here he was, an immediate presence with nothing to protect her from him.

"Stay away from me," she tried to say, but he climbed up into the cab to join her on the seat. She pushed herself back across it, as far as she could go until the armrest stopped her.

Not even seeming to notice how she shrank from him, he kept on moving in closer to her and said, "Caspar is debauched, Louise. He is the author of all those crimes of which I am accused, and the engineer of my entrapment. He's not some errant angel that you can save and subdue. He is a beast among men."

"I want to go back," she said.

"Have you ever known me to break a promise, Louise? Or known me to go back on my word? Or tell a lie when the truth was inconvenient? Think hard now, it's important."

His manner was so intense that she hardly dared offer an answer.

"Never," he said. "Isn't that right?"

She nodded, too eagerly.

"So, listen to me now. I will walk with you into any police station in the land, if you will let me get you away from that man and if you promise me that you will not return to him."

"I beg of you, Tom," she managed then. "Please let me go."

"Have you heard nothing of what I've been saying?"

"Yes," she said.

"And you believe me?"

She tried to answer, and to say whatever he might want to hear. But it was too late. He could already see that she did not.

"Then what, Louise?" he said. "I've shown you the truth. What more do I have to say?"

"Tom," she said. "The whole world knows what you did. Can't you see that I'm afraid of you?"

This was clearly not a possibility that had occurred to the former prizefighter. For the first time, he seemed to see this situation through her eyes. It was as if he had not been able to imagine that she might ever believe him guilty.

Until now.

His face showed his dismay. He drew back, raising his hands to show that he meant her no harm.

"I understand," he said. "I had thought that you might . . ." But he did not pursue this.

Instead, he said, "Louise, whatever you may think of me now, promise me for the friendship we once had. Will you at least stay away from him?"

"How can I promise that?" she said. "I love him."

He was about to say something else, and stopped. It was as if her words had settled before exploding, changing his world instantly and for all time. Whatever else he had been preparing to say, it would count for nothing now.

He turned his head aside. He looked at his hands. He rubbed distractedly at his brow for a moment, then he seemed to remember where he was and started to climb out of the cab. Louise slid down a little—she had been so tense and fear-stricken that she'd pressed herself against the side of the carriage and had risen several inches in her seat.

She felt sick and weak. It was late and she would have to walk alone in darkness to find some kind of safety, but that would be as nothing compared to what she might otherwise have been forced to endure. She tried to summon the strength to climb out of the cab but knew that she dared not move until Sayers had gone; she could hear him out there, pacing up and down and raving aloud to himself in the echo of the viaduct archway, words that she could not make out but which confirmed him to be the madman suggested by his deeds.

All she could be sure of was a cry of "No," anguished at first, repeated with defiance, and then repeated again with determination as the carriage rocked on its wheels once more; she realized then that her chance had come and gone before she'd known it and that Sayers was now climbing back up to the driver's position. She wondered if there might still be time for a rash leap for safety, but even as she began to move the whip cracked over the horse again. Like Pegasus, he took off. It was all Louise could do to grab hold of the strap and hang on.

For a moment she entertained the faint hope that she had somehow touched Sayers' heart, and that he was taking her back to light and life and the safety of the lodging house.

But as they galloped on into deeper and deeper darkness, leaving even the factories and the gasworks behind them, she knew that her hopes were unfounded.

At the public counter in the police station that served the Knott Mill district of Manchester, an aggrieved cabbie was giving his details to the night sergeant and watching as the officer painstakingly wrote them down in the station's incident book. The sergeant had a neat hand, but a slow one. But then again, the nights could be very long. There was rarely anything to hurry for.

"Anything else taken?" the sergeant said.

"What's left to take?" the cabbie said. "'E got me cab and me 'orse and me 'at and me scarf."

"What did he look like?"

"I dunno."

"You saw him, didn't you?"

"But how do you say? Ordinary." With this, the cabbie pointed to his cheekbone. "Wi' a big bruise just 'ere."

For some reason, that seemed to make the sergeant take notice.

"*Did* he?" he said.

"'E did."

"Stay there," the sergeant said, and disappeared into the back.

The cabbie leaned his elbow on the counter and looked around. Behind him was a wooden bench, and on the wooden bench sat an assorted group of low-living characters who seemed to be assembled there for no obvious purpose. None were clean, and most were missing teeth. Two appeared to have been in a fight, perhaps even with each other. All sat in silence. None seemed bright enough to be bored.

The sergeant reappeared with a well-read copy of the late edition of the *Manchester Evening News,* which he slapped onto the counter in front of the cabbie. It was opened and folded to show the account of the arrest for murder and sensational escape of former prizefighter Tom Sayers, lately of Edmund Whitlock's touring theatrical troupe. The three-columned story was accompanied by an engraving of Sayers in his boxing days, stripped to the waist, fists raised, hair slicked down, standing with all his weight resting on his back foot. The cabbie looked at the picture and then looked at the headline across the columns beside it.

"Blimey," he said.

"Follow me," said the sergeant, beckoning him around the counter.

ebastian was woken early by an urgent knocking elsewhere in the house, followed by the sound of voices in the street just under his window. When he climbed out of his unfamiliar bed and looked down through the curtains, he had a partial view of two uniformed men on the doorstep in conversation with his host. Letting the curtain fall, he reached for his trousers and quickly stepped into them.

Within a minute or two, he was on his way downstairs, dressed as well as any man whose tailor is a pawnbroker. He was in the house of Thomas Bertorelli, an officer of the Detective Department upon whom he'd been billeted. The Bertorellis were between lodgers, and happy to have a contribution to their rent. Their second bed was lumpy, its covers heavy, the room oppressive; Mrs. Bertorelli was very young, and a terrible cook. Sebastian had felt very much at home.

Bertorelli looked back as Sebastian descended the stairs. The house was too small to have a hallway. The stairs came down the middle of the building between the front and back rooms, their width creating a short passageway between the two. The Bertorellis' front door opened directly onto the street outside.

Bertorelli waited until Sebastian was close enough for him to speak in a lowered voice.

He said, "One of the actresses didn't return to the lodgings last night. It seems that Sayers picked her up in a stolen cab."

"What about our man at the theater?"

"He failed to recognize him."

Sebastian managed to restrain himself from emitting an oath.

"There is more," Bertorelli said, and indicated the waiting men with a movement of his head. "We're assembling a raiding party. The two of them have been located."

"Where?"

"Just outside of town, in the waiting room of a branchline station. Sayers thinks he can go on fooling us by crossing boundaries. But we'll have them before the county bobbies get their boots on."

"This actress," Sebastian said. "Did she go willingly or not? What I mean to say is, is the woman his victim or his accomplice?"

"According to her employer, Sayers looked upon her with an affection that she did not return. Imagine that, Sebastian. Her situation is not good."

It was the work of a few seconds for Sebastian to be ready to run. Bertorelli shrugged into his coat and had his necktie in his hand, to fiddle with later. Before Sebastian left the hallway, Bertorelli's young wife appeared from the kitchen and pressed something into his hand; he looked down and saw that it was a slice of bread, folded over generous dollops of butter and jam.

"Thank you," he said in genuine appreciation, and then he and her husband set off up the street after the uniformed men.

It was a wide cobbled street with terraced housing down either side. Fifty years before, this had been an area of fields and meadows, but after the building of the local cotton mill and printing works a good seven acres of it had disappeared under brick and stone. At the end of this street, another one ran across. On every corner stood a shop or a pub.

A police transport wagon was drawing into view as they hastened across. Its rear doors were thrown open, and those already inside shouted and beckoned as the four came toward it. The wagon slowed, but didn't come to a complete stop. Sebastian and the others had to board it on the move. Hands grabbed his shoulders and sped him inside. There was no waiting to get everyone seated; the horses were urged to a trot as soon as all were off the street, and Sebastian had to grab a man's shoulder or fall. Everyone shifted around to make room on the benches, and he dropped into a seat with his breakfast still miraculously intact in his hand.

Now that all were on board, the officer in charge of the so-called raiding party began to explain what would be required of them. Besides himself and Bertorelli, Sebastian counted ten men in the wagon. One had a shiner of a black eye, and at least two of them bore other signs of battery. All but the officer in charge had turned out with an untidy, unshaven look that would have been frowned upon were they on normal duty. Their officer had a full, dark beard and a center parting.

He said, "A signalman was cycling from his cottage to his work in the early hours of this morning. He passed an unattended horse and hansom in the lane behind the station. The cab was empty and the horse had been set to grazing among the weeds at the roadside.

"He found this unusual. A private carriage left abandoned would be odd enough, but a city cab, so far out of town . . . When he reached his signal box, he telegraphed up the line to report it.

"When the news reached us, we had him go back to check the number on the carriage license. It was then that the stationmaster told him a man and a woman were in the station's waiting room, and had been there when he'd arrived. The carriage license matches the cab that Sayers stole."

Sebastian said, "Are they in hiding? Or do they intend to travel?"

"No one can say." The officer took out his pocket watch and checked the time. "The first train on the Sunday timetable is due to pass through around now. I've ordered the signalman to hold it back until we get there."

They traveled west, out toward the mill towns and coal-digging communities that marked the spreading edge of the urban sprawl. Here, the future was arriving all of a piece, the canals and the railways, the factories and houses, rising from the green earth like some invader's machinery of war. It was as if two very different lands occupied the same space. A person could live in a slum, and walk to his twelve hours of labor through fields of grazing cows.

During the last part of their journey, Sebastian shared the breakfast with Bertorelli, and took care not to get jam on his new clothes. His own had been ruined in the canal basin. They'd checked the property store for him but found nothing to fit, which was how he came to be wearing some stranger's Sunday suit from Uncle's around the corner. Appropriate, really, as it was now Sunday morning and soon the church bells would start to ring.

The man with the spectacular black eye caught Sebastian's look, and grinned.

"Don't worry," he said. "This time he'll get as good as he gave."

"I don't understand," Sebastian said.

The officer in charge, who was sitting in the opposite corner of the wagon with his arms folded, said drily, "I've heard it suggested that some of these lads may have had it in mind to take Sayers out into the yard and try their luck in a pugilistic contest," he said. "And that they got a little more competition than they bargained for."

One of the others, seeing Sebastian's expression, said, "Our visitor doesn't approve."

"Our visitor should remember that he's a bloody long way from home," muttered another.

The signalman was waiting for them at the end of the lane. He'd left his apprentice in the box to watch the operating levers and to listen out for messages. Now he stood here with his bicycle, guarding the way. As the men climbed down from the police transport, the officer in charge had a brief consultation with the railwayman before turning and calling Bertorelli forward.

"Take four men and follow the signalman," he said. "He'll show you a pathway that crosses the line to the other side of the station. Once you're in place, spread out so we'll have Sayers encircled. Whatever happens, we've got him now. So let's not take any chances with the woman's safety."

Then he turned to Sebastian.

"You stay close to me," he said.

Bertorelli and his men crossed the tracks and disappeared into the woodland on the opposite side. The uniformed policemen produced truncheons and the officer in charge took out a small revolver, which he checked and cocked. Sebastian had no weapon.

Cautioned to silence, they fell into single file and started down the lane—the officer in front, Sebastian behind him, and the uniformed men following. The only sound was that of birdsong.

After two hundred yards, they came to the abandoned cab and the grazing horse. The horse paid them no attention. It had been released from the traces, but had not wandered. The morning sun was shining down through the overhanging branches and the scene was one of complete rural tranquillity.

A white picket fence ran down past the station. The station was a small country halt in painted wood, looking vaguely Alpine with all the gingerbread edging along its roof and platform awnings. A single long building incorporated waiting rooms and a ticket office, and an iron footbridge ran over to a second platform on the far side of the tracks.

While the officer and the remaining men carried on to enter by the gateway at the far end, Sebastian hung back. Nothing was set to happen just yet; they had to allow time for Bertorelli and his men to get into place, in case Sayers should try to cross the tracks and disappear into the fields and woodlands beyond.

He was less than happy with what he'd heard on the journey out here. Summary justice, making sport with a prisoner . . . what next? Public lynchings, and trials by ordeal?

It was positively medieval, and he'd have no part of it. No matter that he was a long way from home. If he could put an arresting hand on Sayers before any of the others got to him, he would.

Left alone now, Sebastian climbed over the picket fence, taking awkward care and making no noise. He stepped through a flower bed to reach a point where he could peer around the building to see what was happening on the platform. When he reached the corner, he positioned himself to lean out and then froze at the sound of nearby voices.

"It's running late," he heard Sayers say.

Sebastian risked a look, leaning out an inch or so and holding himself ready to pull back.

The prizefighter was at the platform's edge, looking up the track. It curved off into deep countryside past the signal box about a quarter of a mile away. The young actress was right beside Sayers; he had his hand on her arm and was holding her close, as if she might otherwise flee. Sebastian thought that he recognized her from the lodging house, but he could not be sure. All he could see for certain was that she was ghastly pale.

Her words were a surprise to him.

"Please, Tom," he heard her say. "Let me speak for you. I can tell your story to the police. Perhaps I can convince them as you convinced me."

Something from Sayers then, that Sebastian could not hear.

"But I see the truth of it now," she said. "James Caspar is to blame and has bound our employer to him in some secret pact. I can explain all this. Will you not let me be your advocate?"

"How can I do that?" Sayers said. "Knowing the danger I'd be placing you in? No, Louise. I'd rather see you safe."

"But now you've warned me of the danger," she said, "I'll know exactly how to protect myself."

At that moment, there came a sound from down the line. It was a train whistle. The locomotive's approach was further signaled by a moving tower of white smoke against the blue of the sky. Almost immediately after, the engine came into view.

They would later learn that the apprentice signalman had taken his master at his word that they were to "hold the train until the police arrived"; looking out of the signal-box window and seeing men in uniform gathering at the gateway on the north side of the station, he'd taken that as his cue to raise the signal and let the train through.

For Sebastian, it was an unwelcome complication but not necessarily a disastrous one. They all but had Sayers now. Even if he succeeded in boarding the train, they could close in and take him from it. But Sebastian had no intention of allowing him to board.

Sayers had his back to him. He was watching the engine as it came into the station. Sebastian grew bold, and started to emerge from his hiding place.

If he could get up behind Sayers without being seen, he might be able to pinion his arms. The officer and the others could rush forward then, and all would quickly be over. It could be carried off without violence or bloodshed.

"Please, Tom," the woman said. Sayers looked at her.

"You truly believe I am sincere?" he said.

"Tom," she said. "I know of no more sincere man in this world."

Sayers seemed to realize that he had been gripping her arm hard enough to cause her pain. Sebastian was out in the open now, but Sayers had not yet seen him.

"Forgive me," Sayers said to Louise, and released his grip on her.

Whereupon, without any warning, she shoved him hard. He stumbled back. He was close to the edge, and missed his step.

Her action sent him tumbling from the platform, right in front of the moving train.

NINETEEN

t seemed to Sayers that he fell with grace, but landed with none. The track bed was around five feet below platform level, a darkened pit of oil and stones and spilled coal. Only the rails were clean, their surface ground to the bare metal by constant use. He hit the sleepers with his face only inches from the ties; he had about a second to roll into the space between rails before all was plunged into darkness and flooded with steam, accompanied by the deafening racket of steel on steel as the engine passed right over him.

Inevitably, he'd landed on his bad arm. He might have cried out. No one could have heard it if he had. He tried to make himself as small as he could without risk of touching the wheels; they were enormous, and would easily take off any body part that got in their way.

The axles and the undercarriage passed above him, spitting grease and steam as the engine slowed to a final halt. First the engine, then the coal tender behind it, and finally a little more headroom as the first of the passenger coaches came to a stop overhead.

Steam continued to billow all around, pressure driving it along the track and out through the understructures of the carriage. He was unharmed beneath the train, but no skill had saved him from decapitation or a maiming; it was sheer luck, and nothing more.

He could hear voices, shouting, an urgent commotion. And in his mind's eye he saw the expression on Louise's face, captured in his memory as if in a photographer's flash.

It had all been an act. This past twelve hours, she'd been performing to save her life; or so, at least, she must have believed. She'd deceived him into thinking he'd convinced her. He'd thought that he was winning her over when, all along, she'd been playing on his trust and looking for her opportunity.

He scrambled out from under the passenger wagon, emerging into the middle of the open trackbed. Now the train stood between him and the platform. For the moment, he couldn't get back. From down here, the carriage looked enormous, an unscalable wall.

They were calling his name. Who knew his name? And were those police whistles that he could hear?

Sayers turned and crossed the empty track to the opposite platform. A jump and a scramble got him up onto it, with his good arm doing most of the work. As he was getting to his feet, he heard answering cries from the woodland close by.

They were here, and he was surrounded. Almost. He glanced back, and saw curious faces looking at him from the windows of the train. Those on the platform were probably assuming that he was underneath it, mangled or dying. But any moment now they'd learn the truth, and would need only to run to the bridge or fling open both sets of carriage doors to get through to him.

There was no time to waste. Louise was lost to him. There was nothing for it, but to run.

So he ran to the end of the platform and hurdled a picket fence, landing in brushwood on the other side before descending an embankment to an open field.

He had to forget her. He had to forget that look. He had to think only of himself now. Otherwise, they would have him.

He took a moment to check out the landscape. Behind him were the station and the woodland. Ahead of him lay open fields. Across the nearest of the fields ran a cart track that met the railway embankment farther down. The track passed under the embankment by means of a brick tunnel.

Sayers made for the tunnel, valuing speed over concealment. The track was churned and muddy. The tunnel was taller than a house but barely more than one cart's width. For the few seconds that it took him to run through it, he could hear his own ragged sobbing echoing all the way up to the vaulted roof.

Sobbing? He was astonished.

Back in the open air, he stopped and fought for control. This would not do. He wiped his eyes on his sleeve and then walked forward slowly until his breathing steadied. He was on a fenced lane now, and ahead of him was a crossroads. He broke into a cautious trot. He had no idea how close his pursuers might be.

When he reached the crossroads, he chose the way to his right. After a while this lane began to climb, and when he saw that it would end in a farmyard, he left the road and struck out across moorland. On high ground, he stopped and looked back into the valley that he'd left. He expected to see it swarming with men, all spread out in a long line and sweeping their way up the slopes toward him. But there were none.

He couldn't make out the railway station for the tree cover, but he could see the track and the fields that he'd crossed. Way down there moved the merest handful of men, a dozen of them or less, tiny figures making slow progress in entirely the wrong place.

At that his spirits lifted, just a little, and he turned and walked on.

After two hours or more, he was growing breathless and light-headed. He drank from a peaty stream, which left him hungry. He'd eaten nothing in more than a day, apart from a pie that he'd bought with pennies that he'd found in his stolen coat's pocket.

As the day wore on the skies darkened again, and some time later it started to rain. When he came upon an abandoned cottage, he sheltered and waited for the clouds to pass over. The doors and windows of the old house had gone, as had part of the roof. But the beams were intact, as was most of the upstairs floor, so there was enough to keep him dry. No one had lived here in years, and only sheep seemed to use it now. Some farmer had dumped a sackful of cut turnips as winter feed in the place that had once been the sitting room.

Most of the turnips had now rotted away. Sayers found one that hadn't and tried to bite into it, but spat it out. Perhaps boiling for an hour or two might have made it edible. But he had nothing to hold water to boil it in, and no way of making fire even if he did.

The outlook seemed bleak all around.

Insofar as Sayers had a plan, it was to make his way south. He certainly had few friends in this part of the country, and the sensational nature of the accusations against him would keep them fresh in people's minds. They'd continue to study every lone stranger with suspicion.

The farther away he moved, the farther he'd be from the common people's thoughts. If he could get as far as his house in Brixton without being noticed, he had a little money and some valuables stashed under the floorboards. The Tom Sayers hoard.

After a while, the rain began to ease. When it finally stopped, he looked at the skies and decided that if he didn't get off the moors now, he'd be stuck out here for the night.

That wasn't an enticing prospect. Nor were stealing food and sleeping out under hedgerows, but either was preferable to staying where he was. He'd realized that sheep used this building for rather more than feeding and shelter—it was going to take him a while to rid himself of the stink.

He turned up his collar and set off across the hill, picking up another lane on the other side of a gate in a wall. This lane was well used. After a while, it brought him within sight of a village: some rows of houses with the winding tower of a coal pit rising up behind them. It looked like the size of place that had grown up around a single family owned mine and could grow no more; colliers with their wives and children living in the cottages while the shops, school, and Wesleyan chapel were sized to their needs.

A bed for the night would be too much to hope for. Even if he was offered one, it would be too big a risk to take. But perhaps he could work for some food, before slipping away into darkness to seek out a suitable barn or outbuilding. He had to take *some* chances, or else he'd starve. It was probably no more dangerous to show his face here than anywhere else.

With this in his mind he walked into the pit village from its outskirts, passing through a row of allotments and pigeon sheds behind one of the streets.

The village had a store and a public house and a main square and a memorial. The chapel was the most imposing building in the square, and the memorial stood before it. Sayers would never know what loss or disaster the memorial had been set up to commemorate. He stopped at the sight of all the men mustering in front of it.

Before him milled a small army of policemen and special constables. Some had their helmets off, and most had mugs of tea. Trestle tables had been set up to serve them. Local women were handing out sandwiches. A number of volunteer miners in flat caps and silk mufflers had turned out to play a part, armed with staves and pickax handles. One man was sitting on the side of the public horse trough, rewinding the homemade puttees around his ankles. Behind them all, the town's drill hall stood with its doors wide open and lamps blazing inside. Some police officers were walking out studying written orders, while civilian workers in brown coats and bowler hats were carrying in movers' boxes and bundles of maps tied with ribbons.

Without realizing it, Sayers had walked into a place that, in the course of the past few hours, had become one of the base camps for his manhunt. Everyone here was so taken up with the business surrounding the chase that not one of them had yet noticed his presence.

A perverse thought crossed his mind. Did he dare to push his way through the crowd and help himself to sandwiches?

Alas, he did not. This was not some tale of adventure. His liberty and his life were at risk. He took a step backward into the shadow of a wall and, careful not to make any hasty movement that might attract the eye, he turned to walk away.

In three or four strides, he was again safe from view. He was learning; he did not run. He walked back through the allotment section behind the houses. As he passed by the pigeon sheds, a number of the birds suddenly fluttered up, startling him. He glanced back, but no one had followed.

He had thought himself safe. He was not. Those men back at the railway station had been only a beginning. His mind reeled with it.

Sayers was no criminal, and could not begin to think like one. The English countryside might be vast, but his pursuers had maps, manpower, and method, and he had none. His one thought was to keep moving. In an hour or less, it would be dark. The search might stop for the night, but he could not.

If he gave up, they would hang him. A few grim weeks of preparation might pass before it happened, but the outcome was assured. Strangers would strap his arms, bind his feet, put a bag over his head and a rope over the bag, and then drop him so hard that he broke. He could tell them his story as often as he liked. They would ignore it, just as Louise had. Even God would turn his face away as they dumped his remains into unhallowed ground.

For Tom Sayers, the hope of justice was no hope at all.

He'd now reached the spot from where he'd first set eyes on the pit village. He took a few moments to stop and look back for any signs of pursuit. As the daylight faded into a deeper and deeper blue, warm lights were beginning to show in the windows. The lights of home. Somebody's home, if not his own. Those distant lights began to blur; he was growing so weary. His senses were no longer sharp. These people must have been all over the local countryside in the course of the afternoon; sheer ignorance had protected him as he'd walked through their lines.

Or perhaps God was not quite so set against him as he'd imagined.

Could that be it? Heartened by that slender dash of hope, he turned to go on.

But he could not. There was a white horse blocking his way.

He blinked to rid himself of this hallucinatory image, but it did not go away. Astride the horse sat James Caspar. They had appeared as if from nowhere. Sayers had heard nothing of their approach.

"You've been standing there for the past ten minutes," Caspar said. "I thought you were never going to move."

Ten minutes? He exaggerated. Sayers was sure that he'd paused for a few seconds, at most. But the light had faded appreciably. Suddenly he was sure of nothing.

He stood, disoriented and probably exhausted, as Caspar walked the white horse toward him. Caspar was immaculate in heavy riding tweeds, as if the costuming for the part had been a significant element in the hunt's attraction for him. He was also a surprisingly good horseman, stepping the horse sideways like a dressage animal with almost no obvious show of control.

He said, "I volunteered to help. What more can a good citizen do? Edmund's offered to pay for a team of dogs to hunt you down." He reached down across the horse's shoulder. "But I don't think they'll be needed, do you?" He straightened up again as, from a saddle holster down by his leg, he drew out an expensive-looking shotgun.

Sayers did not run. He did not even move. It was as if he'd finally burned off all his fear and energy and had none left to spare. Caspar stretched out his arm and leveled the shotgun at him from about four feet away. It was a beautiful weapon, with a polished walnut stock and scroll engraving on the action. The single barrel was steady, and pointed at a spot somewhere in the middle of the prizefighter's forehead.

Caspar said, "I could walk you back into the village and hand you over to the police. But who's to say they won't lose you again? How inefficient they are." Without changing his aim he gave some invisible signal to his mount, which took a couple of sideways paces, bringing Sayers even closer.

Caspar said, "I was trying to think of a word to describe them and, do you know? It just came to me."

He leaned forward slightly. The cold metal ring of the shotgun barrel pressed firmly into Sayers' forehead, pushing his head back a little.

"Scatterbrains!" Caspar said brightly, and pulled the trigger.

Even allowing for the shifting of his mount, it was the first movement of Caspar's trigger finger that gave the signal of his intention. Sayers reacted in the same instant. He knocked the barrel upward and the firearm discharged above his head. He felt its heat and, for a few moments, was completely deafened.

In silence, he saw the white horse rear up. In silence, he saw it spin around as Caspar fought it for control, the firearm now an awkward liability in his hand. Sayers felt the ground shake as the horse slammed its hooves down in an attempt to dislodge its rider and then reared again, this time casting him free. When Caspar was parted from the saddle he did not simply fall, but hurtled toward the ground as if flung. He bounced and rolled and lay still. All without a sound.

Sayers moved to the fallen shotgun and picked it up. The white horse had backed off to a distance and then stopped, shaking its head and stepping about and looking bewildered. Caspar, equally stunned and bewildered, was still on the ground but was attempting to move. Sayers put his free hand to one of his ears, expecting to find blood, but instead found that his hearing was beginning to return.

Caspar, it seemed, had fared rather worse.

Sayers circled all the way around him at a wary distance. Caspar had rolled over and was trying to crawl. But there was something serious and horrible about the way that he had bent in the middle.

"Caspar!" Sayers said, crouching down before him. Despite his injuries, Caspar was succeeding in starting to drag himself along. He was hooking his fingers into the dirt, like claws.

"Caspar," he said, "your back is broken. Don't move, you're making it worse."

But Caspar did not seem to hear. In fact, he no longer seemed to be aware of Sayers' presence at all. It was as if the only thing that mattered to him was somehow to crawl his way back toward the pit village. He moved in sharp, sudden jerks, his nails breaking on the stones, his twisted body dragging behind like a sackful of dead things.

Sayers had to move back as Caspar managed another pull forward.

"Caspar," he said again helplessly. He was torn between relief at his enemy's fall, and dismay at the state of him.

Caspar was voicing something as he struggled. The words were unclear to Sayers' abused ears, but the tone was one of entreaty. He was repeating the same things over and over.

"*Cartaphilus!*" he seemed to be pleading. "*Ahasuerus!*" He cried like one who had been abandoned or betrayed.

"What?" Sayers said. "What are you saying, man?"

"*Salathiel!*"

Another grab at the dirt, another mighty effort to drag himself on. This attempt seemed to run out of steam before it was completed. Caspar did not exactly die. Like machinery running down, he simply stopped. He lay there with his expression unchanged and his eyes wide open.

Sayers laid the shotgun down. Carefully, as if it might discharge again without his intending it. They'd be certain to have heard that first blast, down in the pit village, and they were hardly likely to ignore it.

If he stayed here, it would all be over in a few minutes. No doubt with yet another capital offense to be added to his list of crimes. But what could he do? He'd been running for two days and a night, and that was after fighting his way out of captivity. He could run no more. He could try, but they'd be on him within a mile.

Unless there was some other answer. Something obvious that he was failing to consider.

He raised his gaze from the dead James Caspar to Caspar's white horse, all saddled and ready to run, fretting unhappily just a few dozen yards up the lane.

"Hey, old sport," he said. "Come here, why don't you." He held out a hand in reassurance as he started walking toward it.

LONDON

|||||||||||||||||||||||||||||||||||||||||||||||||

December

1888

TWENTY

aith," Bram Stoker once said, "is to be found more often in a theater than in a church." And in this last decade of the nineteenth century, London offered no greater Temple of the Arts than the Royal Lyceum, just off the Strand. Leased by actor-manager Henry Irving some ten years ago, it had become, if not a national theater, then the closest thing to it that the nation had yet seen.

It was late in December, the last Saturday night of the year and the first night of Irving's *Macbeth*. This was his second crack at the part and was the production for which, some four months before, he had taken his company north of the border to research background and atmosphere.

Stoker stood at the heart of the theater's empty auditorium and called out to each of the ushers by name, receiving echoing responses from their posts at the different levels of the house. The idea was that his voice would be recognizable to all of them, should he need to give out instructions in the event of an emergency. But in that great, dark, waiting space, there was a sense of something more. As with any ritual, it seemed to evoke a mystery beyond its meaning.

When his inspection of the house was done, he moved out to the upper lobby. Stoker was in evening dress, and it was his custom, on every Lyceum first night, to stand at the top of the wide carpeted stairway and greet the evening's more prestigious patrons as they ascended.

Promptly at seven-thirty, the Wellington Street doors were opened and in they came—gowned, bejeweled, buzzing with first-night excitement. Outside, three braziers above the theater's Corinthian portico threw a dancing firelight across the waiting crowds and the arriving carriages. The noisy gallery and the even noisier pit started to fill. In the Dress Circle and the boxes, London's great, good, and merely fortunately born took their seats under the auditorium's high gilded ceiling.

"Mister Archer," said Stoker.

"Mister Stoker," said the critic from the *World*. "I have heard it said that your employer is finally beginning to heed the advice that we all keep giving him."

"You should know that Mister Irving listens to every opinion that is sincerely offered," Stoker responded diplomatically. Archer had been allowed into the theater for a couple of hours during a rehearsal one night. There he'd been heard to say of Irving, *What can I say of his walk? It isn't* walking!

It was true that Stoker's master was an unlikely looking theatrical hero. With his stick-thin legs and his long, thin-lipped face, along with a style of diction that could be mannered to the point of peculiarity, Irving could more resemble an eccentric country parson than a Benedick or a Hamlet.

Yet he brought to the stage a vital energy like no other since Kean, a presence that raised the pulse and drew the eye to him wherever he stood. He chose his roles with care, and put on plays with a canny blend of intelligence and spectacle that stirred the blood while it satisfied the mind. Irving's style was not to everyone's taste, but he drew grudging respect from even his critics . . . including, on occasions, George Bernard Shaw, who griped at Irving's artifice but turned up for everything, besotted as he was by the charm of leading lady Ellen Terry.

Like Shaw, Stoker was a Dublin-born Protestant whose passion for the theater had brought him across the water. A civil servant and amateur critic with a few pieces of newspaper fiction to his name, he'd met and been befriended by Irving during the actor's Irish tours. When offered a position in the new Lyceum venture, he had given up everything and followed with his new wife to London. He'd been Irving's devoted lieutenant ever since.

At seven-forty, the overture began. For this night only, Sullivan was conducting his own incidental music. Some ten minutes later, the house was stilled and the curtain rose. Stoker went down to the box office to check on receipts and then took a look around backstage, where Irving's usual army of supernumeraries was assembling for the first big crowd scene. After that, he moved silently into the back of the Dress Circle and, himself unobserved, observed the audience for a while.

Down on the stage, in a setting that re-created a typical main hall in one of the drafty stone castles that they'd visited, Ellen Terry's Lady Macbeth was reading her husband's letter by the light of a practical fire. Over in her regular first-night box sat Irving's estranged wife, the usual waves of silent hostility flowing from her toward the stage. Stoker scanned the audience for Florence, his own wife; there she was, seated with Sullivan's working partner, her escort for the evening.

It was at this point that the head usher appeared at Stoker's side and signaled for his attention.

They withdrew to the corridor behind the circle, where the usher said in a low voice, "Word of an intruder, sir. Spotted backstage."

Stoker nodded and sent the man back to his duties, before returning to the pass door into the theater's backstage area. The Lyceum was a tight ship, but because of the large numbers of people working behind the scenes it was sometimes possible for a trespasser to get in. Newspaper reporters of a particular type were a particular problem. But if they came looking for evidence of any impropriety between the actor-manager and his leading lady, they were looking in the wrong place.

A quick whispered consultation with a couple of the flymen sent him in the direction of the wardrobe and property store, down in the basement. Most of the Lyceum's drop cloths and scenery were now stored in railway arches across the river, but there was much that remained here in the way of cloaks, chairs, goblets, and paste jewelry. There were weapons, there was armor, there was a ship's wheel from *Vanderdecken.* And rack upon rack of costume, for everyone from Digby Grant to Robespierre.

Stoker descended in silence, feeling his way down the handrail of the open iron staircase. He was wary, but unafraid. He had right on his side, and the physical authority to ensure that any intruder would be left in no doubt of it. To make doubly sure, he was carrying a heavy wooden belaying pin from the theater's rigging, courtesy of the flymen.

Up above, muffled by the thickness of the theater's floor, the thirty-piece pit orchestra could be heard playing Sullivan's second-act prelude. Down below him, somewhere deep in the basement area, he could see a glimmer through the maze of gas pipes that told him someone had set up a lamp.

He couldn't see the lamp itself. Mostly he could see the shadows that it cast up the walls. He reached the bottom of the staircase and started toward the source of the light, moving carefully in the darkness. There must be no commotion that might be heard from above; any moment now, the prelude would end and, since this was not *Hamlet,* ghosts in the cellarage were not called for.

Something caught at his foot. He started back a little, and then crouched down and felt around ahead of him. Something, perhaps one of the costumes from the rack beside him, lay in a heap on the floor. Picking it up with care between finger and thumb, he raised it into the dim light.

It appeared to be an extremely grimy set of combination underwear. Wincing, he let it fall and then wiped his hand on his side. All his senses were telling him that the grime was not stage dirt.

Some tramp, then. Out to steal. No one stole from the Chief. Stoker kicked the foul clothing aside and strode around the rack to the other side, where the lamp was burning.

The lamp had been set up beside an ornate full-length mirror. The mirror was dulled with wax for use onstage, but a patch in the middle of the glass had been scrubbed clean to make it reflect again.

Before it stood a man. He was knotting a tie. As he stood there, he shifted his weight and flexed his shoulders a little, as if enjoying the very fit of the suit of clothes he wore. He was clean-shaven, and his wet hair was freshly combed.

In as bold a voice as he dared with the stalls directly above them, Stoker said, "Those are stage properties that you are wearing, sir. This is neither an old-clothes shop nor a public bathhouse."

The man jumped in surprise, and then turned to face him.

"I'm sorry, Bram," he said. "I was desperate to regain a little dignity. This is not a way I would normally choose to conduct myself."

Stoker peered more closely in the bad light.

"Tom Sayers?" he said.

The man acknowledged himself to be the same. He said, "Half an hour ago, you wouldn't have known me at all."

Stoker hardly knew him now. He was shocked at how gaunt and hungry-looking the former prizefighter had become since last they'd met. He said, "What are you doing?"

"I'm in hiding, Bram. You must have heard the accusations."

"I doubt there's a single theatrical who hasn't. You're the talk of every green room in England."

As he was saying this, Stoker glanced back toward the stairway. Sayers noted the action, and quickly raised his hands as if to show that he meant no harm.

"Don't bring others, Bram, please. You're one of the most loyal men I ever met. I'm begging you to extend a little of that loyalty to me, at least until you've heard my side of it. I know we're not friends. But are we not fellows in our trade, you and I?"

Stoker looked him over. The suit was a few years out of style, but Sayers had been lucky to find it. Most of the Lyceum's stock was for the classical repertoire, or for historical subjects.

Stoker said, "How have you been living?"

"Nights in ditches, a few fights for money in fairgrounds. Since I reached the city, I've been sleeping on a rope in the Minories. If any man in London can help me to unravel this, it's you. And if you won't help me . . . then let them hang an innocent man, for what can he care if his last hope has left him?"

Stoker considered the fugitive for a moment, and then he glanced upward. The second act was under way; no clear words could be heard, but Stoker could hear the swoops and cadences of Irving's unique delivery of the dagger speech. Irving did not play Macbeth as a man wracked with doubt, or as a good man turned bad by an ill-timed prophecy. He played him as an arrow of evil, a man who had always been set to hack his way to the crown. For him, the witches merely opened the door that he'd been seeking.

Stoker said, "Stay down here. There's to be a private supper on the stage after the audience leaves. I expect you'll be hungry—I'll bring you some food when I can. Don't make a sound until I come to you."

LONDON

| | | | | | | | | | | | | | | | | | | | | | | | | | | | | | | | | | | | | | | | | | | | | | | | | |

January

1889

TWENTY-ONE

t around two-thirty on a cold winter's morning, Tom Sayers woke for no reason. It was probably too cold to rise but he threw back the covers and rose anyway, hoping to shake off his melancholy frame of mind and then, after a look at the moon and a few minutes of night and silence, to return to the warmth of his bed and find sleep again.

He was in a temperance hotel, the General Gordon, which stood on a corner of one of the main streets in Spitalfields. When he looked out of his second-floor window it was through the gilded wooden "A" of the hotel's name, the letters of which ran the full width of the building's frontage. He was registered here as John Thurloe, a cabinetmaker seeking employment. He'd inquired about a room to let, and been offered "a part of a room"—which, he soon discovered, meant that he had it to himself but had to vacate it by seven in the morning, whereupon the bed would be taken by a young woman who worked all night in a bakery. At seven in the evening, she would leave for her work and the room would be his to return to.

There was no moon. Just a dense, dark cloud pressing low over the roofs of the houses. Any lower, and it would descend into the streets and become a fog. These were mean houses, row after row of them: the City of Dreadful Monotony, London's East End.

Stoker had been cautious toward Sayers that night in the theater, but had not betrayed him. Three hours of suspense had ended in relief. Sayers would not have been surprised to see the acting manager return with the police instead of a basket containing half a loaf, a decent slice of ham, and six hot potatoes wrapped up in a napkin.

In between gorging on the food and washing it down with beer, Sayers had told his story. He later learned that Bram Stoker did not simply take him at his word, but over the next few days found ways to raise his name in conversation with a number of people they might have in common. Music hall managers, players, booking agents . . . none had any special knowledge that enabled them to declare Sayers innocent, but all, without exception, had expressed astonishment at his apparent guilt.

It was no public trial, but coupled with what Stoker had seen of James Caspar on the railway platform in the Midlands that night, it had supported the fugitive's story and tipped the balance in his character's favor. Staggering, insensible, disgrace-bringing, blood-puking Caspar . . . Sayers could see that Stoker's was a world of little shading, where those who stayed true were all pure, and those who'd been tainted were damned.

Thank the Lord.

As Sayers had expected, the death of Caspar had been added onto his own list of crimes. There were those who would add him to the suspects' list for the recent string of slaughtered East End whores as well, despite the fact that he'd been begging food and shivering in the hedgerows of Oxfordshire at the time of their murders.

He could have found somewhere safer than this to hide, but he'd tried in vain to find anywhere in London that was cheaper. Stoker had let him take clothing from the Lyceum's stock and had given him money to help prevent him from starving, but he could hardly expect the Irishman to keep him like a dependent. He'd gone along to his Brixton house quite early one Sunday morning, but had found new tenants in residence—his lease had been paid to the middle of the year, but it seemed that in the light of his supposed crimes the landlord felt no duty to honor it.

This was but one small injustice heaped on with all the others, and yet it was the one that he seemed to feel most bitterly.

Down in the street outside the temperance hotel, a police patrol was going by. Patrols in the East End had been stepped up since the Whitechapel murders, although there was a rumor—one among many—that the killer was known to the police and had drowned himself. Sayers turned from the window and climbed back into bed. As usual, he tried not to think about the sheets. On the two-relay system, they went unchanged. And this was a comparatively respectable house; at the lowest end of the scale there were lodgings on a three-relay system where not only did the occupants change every eight hours, but the spaces underneath the beds were let in exactly the same manner.

He shuddered, and put his face under the covers, and then slowly started to warm by his own breath as its heat filled the space in which he lay. He was to meet Stoker later that day, in the time between the acting manager's early Lyceum business and the hour or two he spent at home before the evening's performance. Stoker had something of interest for him to hear, the message had read. Sayers faced a long walk from the East End into the middle of town, but it would use up his morning and save him some money. He had no idea how long his funds would last, or what new turn his life would take. Something had to happen. Things had to change somehow.

For this life that he had now . . . what was it? Without home, without love, without friends—without even the name he'd been born with. This was no life at all.

Early in the afternoon, by the iron railings that ran before the British Museum on Great Russell Street, Sayers waited for Stoker to appear. He arrived on foot a little after 2:15, as big as a bear and full of apology. Sayers was nervous, and tried not to show it.

"Come," Stoker said, using their handshake to pass him a square of pasteboard as they started toward the entrance steps. "Take this and show it as your own. It's a copy of mine. I had our property man make it. I wrote in a name for you myself."

It was a reader's ticket, required to enter the library. They went in through the museum to the open courtyard at the heart of the building wherein the circular reading room stood. Stoker was recognized, and did not need to show his own ticket. And because he was with Stoker, Sayers' forgery was passed without a close inspection.

It was a vast, airy dome of a room, almost as wide and high as Rome's great Pantheon, the readers' desks radiating outward from a central counter like the spokes of a cartwheel. As Sayers followed Stoker, he saw that every position at the long desks was numbered.

In some of them sat old men who looked as if they'd been cobwebbed into place. Here was a young, intense student, leafing fervently through a high pile of journals; there a ginger man of great girth, breathing noisily as he read. At some seats the books were piled high, but with no reader present.

Sayers could only wonder what it was that Stoker had brought him here to see. They'd walked half the circumference of the room before he cut inward and led the way to a spot where one scholar worked alone.

Keeping his voice suitably low, Stoker said, "May I present my good friend, Mister Hall Caine."

The man looked up at Stoker, and then at Sayers. He was a man of some thirty-five years, balding like Shakespeare, bearded like Christ. He nodded, and Sayers offered his hand. The grip that returned his was limp, and slightly damp.

Stoker said, "Caine knows only as much of your story as is necessary. For the rest of it, he trusts to my honor as I am trusting to yours." He signaled for Sayers to draw in a chair from an unoccupied carrel, and reached for one himself.

Hall Caine said, "I have some thoughts I can offer you. I know that Bram will not endorse them all."

"Spin your tale, old friend," Stoker said. "Let us judge it for ourselves."

Sayers knew of Caine by name, but had read nothing of his writing. Stoker's novelist friend had been making notes on unlined paper, in a hand so small that Sayers hardly believed that even its author could read it. He'd been working back and forth through a stack of volumes of various ages. Most had places in them marked by call slips.

He closed and moved aside the book he'd been consulting and then, running his finger down the lines that he'd written, read aloud, "Cartaphilus. Ahasuerus. Salathiel." He looked at Sayers. "You say these were the words of a dying man?"

"As I heard them."

Caine reached for another of the volumes and opened it, first at one marked page and then another.

"Over recent months," he said, "Bram and I have spent time and energy and some imagination in an effort to fit Irving with a part. Most of our subjects have dealt with the supernatural. The Wandering Jew, the Flying Dutchman, and the Demon Lover . . . these are themes around which our imagination has constantly revolved. The words you heard from Caspar are all names used by the Wanderer."

Sayers must have been looking blank.

"A man who trades his soul for prolonged life and forbidden knowledge," Stoker said.

By now, Caine had found the passage he was looking for. He said, "In the earliest form of the legend, Cartaphilus insulted Our Lord on the way to Calvary and was doomed to wander until Judgment Day. But in later versions, he is shown as a man who has entered into an unholy contract for extended life and fortune. He bore the name of Ahasuerus in Hamburg in 1547. Salathiel came later. Close to seventy years ago, the Dublin cleric Charles Maturin recorded the story of Melmoth the Wanderer."

Sayers, ever a man of practical mind, said, "Perhaps that's the explanation for your legend, then. There's no one man living through all eternity. The role has a different player in every age."

"That may be closer to the truth than you think, Mister Sayers," Caine said, and turned the book for him to see. The page carried an engraving of an elderly man, leaning on a staff as he made his way past the crucified Christ in a deep canyon under a stormy sky. Christ looked down, the old man looked up at him; no love appeared to be lost between the two of them.

Caine said, "The Spanish call him Juan Espera en Dios, John who waits for God. He was reported seen in Paris in 1644, in Newcastle in 1790. In fact, there are sightings of the Wanderer going back to 1228. But the names often differ, and the descriptions sometimes change. In Melmoth, we find a possible explanation. There is an escape clause in the demonic contract. If the Wanderer can recruit another to take his place before his long life reaches its end, then he can avoid his fate. All men eventually die, while the role of the Wanderer becomes truly eternal."

"Take his place?" Sayers said. "How?"

"By assuming the Wanderer's burden of certain damnation."

Stoker was less than happy with the direction this was taking.

"Melmoth's a fiction," he said.

"All fictions have their originals."

"And are told through devices. Demons through trapdoors, and contracts in blood. Stuff for the pit and the gallery."

"And what are such devices," Caine pressed on, "but outward symbols for a life within? Consider it, Bram. To turn knowingly from the face of God. To hurl oneself into the darkness and certain damnation. Would such an act not create the kind of delinquent soul the tales describe?"

"Embrace damnation?" Stoker echoed. "Willingly? For what conceivable reason?"

"Advantage. Defiance. Self-hatred. Each heart has its own."

"No," said Stoker. "No one man can live forever."

"No one man is required to," said Caine. "That is my point."

As the two friends' disagreement had increased in passion, it had also begun to increase in volume. They were now attracting attention, and none of it was friendly.

Sayers rose to his feet.

"I am grateful to you, sir," he said, inclining his head toward Hall Caine in acknowledgment of his researches.

"Have I brought you some illumination?"

"I very much fear that you may have."

———————

Out in the city garden at the heart of nearby Bedford Square, Sayers strode about with such nervous energy that Stoker was hard-pressed to keep up with him. He took no specific path, walked with no specific purpose. The agitation was all, and it threw him this way and that like a dancing flame.

"Something moves in me, Bram," he said. "It made sense to me. I can imagine it. To dismiss God's will, and be rewarded for it. What a gift it must seem at the beginning. What a curse it must be in the end."

"This wasn't the kind of enlightenment I had in mind," Stoker said. "Caspar's was a natural evil, Tom. The rest is mere fancy."

"Not Caspar, Bram, although I've no doubt that he'd have taken over his master's contract once his education was complete." He stopped and turned to Stoker.

"Edmund Whitlock's powers are fading," he said. "Many have noted it, and Gulliford claimed he was ill. I think it's more than that. I think he is a dying man, and knows it."

"And?"

Sayers took a step closer to Stoker, seizing him by both his arms and shaking him once as if to make his point.

"Can't you see?" he said. "It's Whitlock! *Whitlock* is the demon! And into that devil's hands I've delivered Louise!"

PHILADELPHIA

1903

TWENTY-TWO

t this point in his long tale, the battered prizefighter paused, and Sebastian began to think that he might not continue. Outside the tent, some kind of an argument was going on. By the sound of it, the stakes were to be pulled and the booth taken down as soon as the park closed for the day. The billboards outside might promise an exhibition of the Noble Art, but the reality of it had too quickly degenerated into scrapping and riots. So now the show folk were being moved on, and in future Willow Grove would stick with its more respectable entertainments.

Sayers listened for a few moments and then said, "They'll soon be calling for me. Everyone is expected to pitch in on a teardown."

But he made no move.

Sebastian said, "So, after all the time that had passed, and everything that had happened . . . you still harbored strong feelings for Miss Porter?"

The boxer in the dirty robe turned his head slowly, and looked at the detective. Then he looked away again.

"I knew what a man in my position ought to do," he said. "Walk away, close up his heart, forget the life he'd once had, and try to make a life elsewhere.

"But I also knew what that would mean. It would mean living as one haunted for the rest of my days. A rootless, aimless man with my heart and mind tied up in a secret past that I could never discuss or reveal.

"And that was only a part of it. Because to walk away then would be to abandon Louise to her fate."

"She shoved you in front of a train."

"A measure of how far she'd been misled. Make no mistake, Inspector Becker, my eyes were opened. All of my romantic illusions now hung in tatters. But you can imagine my dismay on finding that the framework on which they hung remained as strong as ever."

Sayers went on, "In those first weeks after I reached London, I saw Louise only once. Bram arranged it for me. He may not have shared my certainties, but he was my rock from the day I confided in him. I could have asked for no better friend.

"No man of his honor would ever knowingly give shelter to a criminal, but he saw no evil in me. He could see, however, that as far as any living man could be, I was in hell. He thought that for me to see her might bring some relief.

"The death of James Caspar had forced Whitlock to cancel the rest of the provincial tour and make an early return to London. Rather than see the company split up, he engaged a replacement juvenile and took whatever dates he could find in town at short notice. One of these was at the Middlesex Music Hall on Drury Lane. I don't know if you've ever been—it used to be the Mogul Saloon and has the decor of a Turkish palace. I had to take care because many of the names on any music hall bill were likely to know me on sight. On this evening there was Nelly Farrell, who'd been with us on the bill in Salford. Daltry, Higgins, and Selina Seaforth had a comic boxing act that I'd helped them to stage. James Fawn had a drunk act. I'd lent him two pounds once, and he'd been avoiding me ever since.

"I couldn't risk being recognized, so I stood at the back of the gallery to watch. *The Purple Diamond* played in the middle of the evening, and it did not go well. Caspar's replacement was an inexperienced boy in a crepe mustache. There was some new business with a clay pipe that didn't come off. Caspar had been no great actor, but at least he could look the part by just standing there.

"The entire company seemed without spark. Only Whitlock stood out, and he played his role with a kind of suppressed fury, as if he was about to turn on the audience at any moment. The first few scenes were received in silence, as if everyone feared he might do exactly that. But then after a while someone called out something disrespectful, and for the rest of the piece it was 'Come on Edmund' and 'Give us a dance.'

"I watched Louise closely whenever she was on the stage. I had eyes for no other. I mean it as no criticism when I say that as an actress, she is artless; what I mean is that her very soul is what you see. Her nature shines through her roles. Except that on this night, I saw a woman whose thoughts were elsewhere. She ran through the lines and the moves, but it was not exactly a performance—it was more like a polite but unenthusiastic reading of the part.

"I began to dread her song at the end. I began to hope that Whitlock might have cut it. They cheered at the final scene, all right, but it was not a healthy response. There was a note of derision in it. I wanted to leave as soon as the curtain fell, but I could not. It would have felt like a betrayal. Whitlock brought her out and gave her the briefest introduction and then left her to it, alone and unsupported. She looked so fragile and I had to grip the rail before me, to prevent myself from leaping up and calling to her.

"Despite my apprehension, the audience behaved. Only when she faltered did they begin to whisper. The whispers grew to a rumble of concern, as she lost her way in a song that she must have sung on a stage more than a hundred times.

"Our company's musical director was down in the pit with the house band. I saw him mouthing the words from his score as he conducted, trying to prompt her. But I don't believe that memory alone was her problem.

"After a while, the one we called the Silent Man opened the curtains and reached for her arm. He led her off and she went with him like a child. The band struck up something jolly and the chairman banged his hammer and started talking up the next turn as if nothing had happened.

"I rushed out into Drury Lane and around to a spot from where I could see the stage door. I cannot tell you how I felt. It was as if something was swelling and about to burst within me. I wanted to go to her, but I dared not. I remembered her terror at my last appearance.

"After a while she came out with Whitlock, and they got into a carriage together. She had his coat around her shoulders. I was able to follow the carriage on foot for a distance—long enough to observe that it was heading into the area around Marylebone High Street. Whitlock had kept a set of apartments there for longer than anyone could remember, and lived in them when the company was not touring. When he was at home, the Silent Man and his wife served as housekeepers.

"I went out there the next day, and contrived ways to observe his building without drawing attention to myself. I did not dare to get too near, but I could not keep myself away. I needed to know if Louise was his guest, and that she was well. I saw the Silent Man go out in the morning, and return in less than half an hour. I saw no sign of Louise until the afternoon, when a cab drew up and waited until she and Whitlock came out to it. He wore a dark suit, and she a veil.

"Their journey was a brief one, down Wimpole Street and into Henrietta Place, and I had no trouble keeping the cab in view. They went into a house with a brass plate alongside the door, one among many—these were the streets where the city's wealthiest doctors lived and kept their consulting rooms. I had a premonition even before I walked past and read the name on the plate.

"This was the home of a physician well known in theatrical circles. I had heard it said of a number of actresses that they had gone to him for their 'irregularities,' always said in such a knowing way that I had been sure it was a code for something more, and eventually, without ever pressing for the knowledge, I came to understand what it was. Although a specialist in chest and voice complaints, this man had a sideline in dealing with the inconvenient unborn.

"Whitlock was compelling her to it, of that I'm sure. She could not have gone on to serve his purpose otherwise. I did not stay to watch them come out. I could not bear to."

He looked at Sebastian then. The detective had not moved, nor made any sound that he was aware of.

Sayers said, "I know what you probably think of me. That I am one of those men who worships a certain kind of woman and thinks himself a knight of old, a hero in his own eyes and therefore, he imagines, in hers.

"There was a time when this might have been true. That time ended as I walked the streets in the hours following my discovery. I did not flee the abortionist's doorstep through anger, nor through jealousy. I began to understand the true nature of my feelings when I realized that I wept for her distress, and not my own.

"I have learned that a man who offers his worship to women fails to realize how wearisome that gift soon becomes. Mere worship is a trinket to them—nice to receive, but one to pop in a drawer and forget.

"It would have been so easy for me to imagine her defiled, and to make her an object of my anger or even drive her from my thoughts. But in the course of those next few hours, I came to realize that there would never be anything I could not forgive her."

Sayers paused for a while. He folded his scarred hands and rested his lips against them. He did not look up, and Sebastian began to wonder if his story had come to a premature end.

But then Sayers said, "I did not see her again for a while. My money was getting low and I had to take casual work in a fruit broker's on the docks, or else be turned out of my lodgings to live as so many had to . . . moved on by the police all night, and sleeping in public parks by day. Once a week, I would meet with Bram Stoker, unless he was away from town on Irving's business.

"It was Bram who showed me the lines in *The Era* announcing Miss Louise Porter's retirement from the stage. There would be no farewell performance, no benefit night. From that time onward, she was rarely out of Whitlock's company. He became her guardian.

"Although hardly of the top drawer of society, Whitlock had an 'in' to many a fashionable gathering. That is the peculiar thing about our profession: You can be born the son of a costermonger, but play a few kings and it sticks to you. I've even seen a clown talking to a duchess, where the duchess was the one making a fool of herself.

"Whitlock was escorted by Louise wherever he went, and the way he dressed her and presented her, you would have taken her for some foreign princess and the highest-born woman in the room. She was pale and beautiful, and she rarely spoke. Old rakes and young men would vie for her attention; Stoker said that there was always a group of them around her, and that she only ever half listened and seemed to be looking beyond them as if through cloudy glass. This made them see her as some kind of goddess of ice, and they competed for her attention all the more.

"Stoker said he saw it differently. He said that to him it was as if the very soul had died in her."

Sayers hesitated. First he seemed about to say something more; but now he seemed to be done. Then he started to rise.

"The rest of it," Sebastian said quickly.

"You know the rest of it. You were there."

"Only for a part of what happened. Good God, Sayers, you can't stop now. This is the very thing I came back here for."

Someone outside was calling a name. The name was not Sayers' own, but it caused him to look up sharply.

"I'm needed," he said.

"I don't care," Sebastian said. "If I let you out of my sight now, then you'll vanish with the circus and I'll never know the truth."

"You have most of it."   •

"I want it all."

Sayers gave a resigned sigh, then started gathering together his few possessions from the makeshift table.

"Then we must move to another place," he said. "Or they'll have the tent down around us." He went over to his steamer trunk and raised the lid. A shabby but serviceable suit of clothes lay folded on top of the contents.

"You say that after persuading her to lose the child he became her guardian," Sebastian said, rising from his chair, "and that she served some purpose for him. Is it your belief that she became his mistress in return?"

Sayers was stowing his few trinkets and taking out his street wear. He paused in what he was doing, as if the suggestion was an unexpected one that he had never considered before.

"No," he said.

"Then . . ."

"There is much more to it than that," Sayers said. "The sorcerer had lost his apprentice. He had been grooming Caspar to take over the Wanderer's role, but now Caspar was gone. He needed new cover, and time was getting short. His deal with darkness was about to expire. From his increasing desperation, I would not have been surprised to learn that his doctors had put a number on his days."

Sayers let the lid of the trunk fall with a bang.

"Louise was not his mistress," he said. "She was bait."

LONDON

|||||||||||||||||||||||||||||||||||||||||||||||||

March

1889

TWENTY-THREE

n sixteen acres of Southeast London's Forest Hill stood Surrey House, the residence of Quaker tea trader Frederick Horniman. Originally the family home, it had come to hold so many objects, books, and pictures gathered in the course of Horniman's travels that a few months ago he'd thrown a part of it open to the public, by appointment, so that anyone with sufficient interest could come in and view his collections.

Sayers and Stoker were met at the gate by a man with a strong-looking frame and a starved-looking face. He wore a brown velveteen coat, and Stoker introduced him by the name of Samuel Liddell Mathers.

"You've the hand of a boxer!" Mathers said as they shook, and Sayers gave Stoker an uneasy glance. "I box every evening myself," Mathers added.

Stoker returned the look with a slight shrug and a raise of the eyebrows, as if to say, I told him no such thing.

They walked up the circular driveway to the square-set, ivy-covered house. It was shabby and rambling and comfortable. Mathers led them around to a side entrance, where he produced a key to let them in. The house was mostly dark, and the furniture sheeted—the Horniman family was not at home. The two men followed their guide through the kitchens to a door that opened onto a stairway, which in turn led down into the cellars. The house had electric lighting but the cellar did not, and he stopped to light a lantern before carrying it ahead of them to show the way.

As they descended, he said, "The place is full to bursting point. This is where they keep the pictures no one cares to see."

Sayers said, "Do we have permission to be here?"

"I'm a friend of the daughter. We both belong to a little order of Christian kabbalists. Bram picks our brains every now and again, but he refuses to join us. Don't you, Bram?"

Stoker, at the rear of the party, said, "You know my interests have been entirely academic."

"Really," Mathers said. "This might end your sense of detachment." Whereupon, he winked at Sayers.

He had Stoker hold the lantern while he looked through a stack of unframed pictures that were being stored side-on. He knew what he was looking for, and it took him a while to find it. Finally, he drew one of them out. It was mounted in cards and protected by a large sheet of paper that he lifted and flipped back.

The picture was a head-and-shoulders sketch in charcoal and oils, possibly a preliminary rough for a full theatrical portrait.

Mathers said, "The portrait is dated seventeen-seventy-five. The actor is not named, but does he look familiar?"

"It could well be him," Sayers said, peering more closely and having to move to keep his own shadow out of the way. "I believe it is him, Bram."

"His very last mistake, I imagine," said Mathers. "A Wanderer would soon learn to permit no record of his image."

To Sayers' eye, the sketch showed a younger but no less magisterial and cynical Edmund Whitlock. The hair was brown, the face tauter and unlined. Given the freedom of the artist's hand, there was scope for saying that there was merely some physical similarity across a century's gap. But Sayers' first instinct had been to recognize the face as that of his former employer.

Stoker, who seemed to have been hoping for something more persuasive, was clearly less convinced.

"A resemblance," Stoker conceded.

Sayers said, "You brought me to this threshold. Can you not cross it with me?"

"At heart, I'm a rational being," Stoker said. "I've always placed my trust in science and nature."

"Yet you'll publish fairy tales. You have friends"—this with a glance toward Mathers—"who'd raise the devil if they could. And do your best to talk Irving into *Faust* and *The Flying Dutchman*."

"No one talks Irving into anything," Stoker said. "A man can disagree with his friends. And one does not have to believe in ghosts to enjoy a good ghost story. I'm prepared to believe that Whitlock charts his life by the symbols in which he places his faith. But this . . . this is the point at which men are seduced into co-opting history to support the impossible."

Mathers, who had been inspecting the tag on the portrait before returning it to the stacks, now joined them and said, "But do you believe in evil, Bram?"

"As an abstraction, yes."

"What exactly do you think it is?"

"A word that describes a condition of the human soul."

"Not a force in itself? With its own life and substance?"

"No."

"My considered understanding is that evil lives," Mathers said. "It moves. It finds places to show itself whenever it can. A being can be emptied and shaped into a vessel to hold it. We have a term for such a person. We call them . . . godless."

Sayers said, "But how can even a godless being defy the very processes of nature?"

"By embracing the idea that one is cursed, lost, beyond the very sight of one's creator," Mathers said. "Cruel deeds are the means of ritual affirmation. Evil enters the vacuum from where man's natural spirit has been driven. And, of course, in a vacuum . . ."

"There can be no decay," said Sayers, with the wonder of discovery.

———————

"He ages slowly," Sayers said excitedly, as they walked along London Road toward Forest Hill station. "But he ages. He's flesh and blood like the rest of us, Bram. Cut off his head and he'll streak down to hell like a comet."

"Speculation," said Stoker.

"Think of it, Bram. He cannot hold off damnation forever. But he can escape it by influencing another lost soul to take his place. Caspar was to be that soul. He'll seek another."

"And you believe you'll stop him?"

"I care nothing for Whitlock or his future! I think only of Louise in his foul company. I'd go straight to hell myself to make her safe."

At this, Stoker took his arm and stopped him so that he could look him in the eyes.

"I can smell the gin on you," the Irishman said. "Edmund Whitlock is no more than an ordinary man, seduced by a legend. Be very careful, Tom."

Sayers pulled his arm free.

In an uncomfortable silence, the two men walked on toward their train.

TWENTY-FOUR

s soon as he received Edmund Whitlock's telegram, Sebastian Becker sought permission from his superiors and then caught the next train down to London. By this time, Whitlock had wound up the *Purple Diamond* company and was playing a fifteen-minute sketch titled *He Knew It, All Right*. It was a four-hander he'd revived from some fifteen years before, inexpensive to stage and for which he could reuse props and costumes from the last production. He'd sold the *Purple Diamond* sets and the rest of the properties, and used the proceeds to pay off the cast.

Some thought it an odd choice. It was a comic piece set in a draper's, with no songs and no girl. Four skilled comedians might have carried it off, but Whitlock held an open call at which every dodgy character from the twilight fringe of the theatrical world turned up. Of the three that he cast, one had the nasty ticket-of-leave look of a man who'd spent time in prison—hardly the type for a draper's boy—while another was regarded with wariness by all the chorus girls. No one could give a specific reason for it, but if this man happened to enter a room where one of them was alone, she would quickly find some excuse to leave.

So the sketch, as they performed it, was no better than passable. Some suggested that Whitlock had taken a big step down in the world and was showing desperation, although others reckoned that he hardly needed the money. He was said to own property, and had been coining it in as an actor-manager for longer than anyone could actually remember.

Sebastian caught up with him during the first house at Gatti's Music Hall in the Westminster Bridge Road. Whitlock's little troupe was playing the sketch on three bills in the same evening; from Gatti's they'd go to the Canterbury, then to the Camberwell Palace, then back to Gatti's for the final show. Gatti's had only two dressing rooms behind its small stage, one shared by the men and the other by the women, so they met in the manager's office.

Whitlock was in full makeup and a draper's apron, his costume for the skit. He said, "We'll be following the Coulson Sisters in about ten minutes' time. I am at your service until then."

"Your telegram said you had letters to show me," Sebastian said.

"I have." The actor-manager reached into his waistcoat behind the apron and brought out a small bundle of assorted and very cheap-looking papers. "I've been keeping them about me. I would not want Miss Porter to see them."

"Weren't they addressed to her?"

"They were, but I recognized the hand. So I intercepted them. She is suffering enough distress without having to bear the ravings of a lunatic."

The clock on the manager's wall ticked the minutes away as Sebastian read the first of the notes, and then the next.

"Hard enough for you to read such a personal tirade," he commented after a while.

"I've been reviewed by Shaw," Whitlock said. "Believe me, those letters are nothing."

Sebastian glanced up. "Do you have the envelopes?"

Whitlock made a sign of regret. "There were no postmarks," he said, "but the content alone proves that Sayers is here in London. If I were you, Inspector, I would investigate the public houses around St. Martin's Lane."

"Why so, sir?"

"They're a home to the boxing fraternity. And one sniff at the paper should tell you those letters were written on a beer-stained table. You're far away from your own territory, Inspector Becker. I suggest you share this bounty with your brothers in the Metropolitan Police. Or else how effective can you really hope to be?"

"As effective as my dedication can make me, Mister Whitlock. I must keep these, and study them further before I decide what best to do."

"As you wish," Whitlock said. "I feel I have done my duty."

Sebastian moved to put the letters safely inside his coat. "Rest assured, Mister Whitlock," he said, "I shall have him."

"Then I am certain we can all sleep safely in our beds." Whitlock rose and put out his hand. "Tell me, Inspector. What exactly do you believe you are pursuing? Some man, or some fiend?"

"I do not believe in fiends," Sebastian Becker said as he took the actor's hand and returned his grip. Whitlock held on and looked into his face for a time that bordered on the uncomfortable.

Then he said, "Quite right," and released him.

A boy looked into the manager's office and said, "They're playing out the Coulson Sisters, Mister Whitlock."

"You must excuse me," Whitlock said. "I wish you all the success you deserve."

"Where is Miss Porter now?"

"She is a guest at my apartments," Whitlock said, as he followed the boy out of the door. "She no longer has the heart to perform."

He paused.

"Nor for anything, much," he added, and then he left the room.

The actor had gone off without leaving him an address, but it was the work of only a few minutes for Sebastian to find what he needed in the manager's files. Whitlock was still onstage when Sebastian left the theater and walked in the direction of Waterloo Station, hoping to pick up a cab to take him back across the river. Perhaps Whitlock had been expecting him to go straight to the boxing dens on St. Martin's Lane rather than seeking out Miss Porter, who had, after all, had no knowledge of the letters that Sayers had intended for her.

But Louise Porter was some essential factor in the prizefighter's mystery. In all that he'd done so far, he seemed to care more for her well-being than for his own survival.

In everything he'd done, that was, apart from killing her beloved.

Whitlock's housekeeper said nothing, pretended not to understand anything that Sebastian said, and seemed determined not to admit him until there was the call of a young woman's voice from within, which she understood well enough. Louise Porter received him in the parlor, that little-used, overornamented, excessively proper space set aside in the Victorian household for the sole purpose of making an impression. She was in a dark dress. It was not formal mourning wear, but she moved and spoke like one recently widowed.

Sebastian asked her to look at one of the letters. It hardly mattered which one she chose; they all said more or less the same things.

She glanced through one, then another. She seemed unsurprised by them.

"These are the milder ones," she said. "There have been others. These omit the strangest claim of all."

"Mister Whitlock thinks you know nothing of them," Sebastian said. "He thinks he intercepted every one."

"Everybody wants to protect me," she said.

"So what is 'the strangest claim of all'?"

"Tom Sayers would have me believe that my former employer and present protector is a devil in human form. One who has turned from the face of God and now seeks to avoid just punishment as his days approach their end. He says that my late fiancé was being made ready to replace him.

"I ask you, Inspector Becker. As we speak, Edmund Whitlock is running from one music hall to another, in costume, to perform a piece of nothing before a pack of drunkards. If they should laugh at his antics, then that is the most he can hope for. And he is not a well man. If such is a reward of long life and good fortune, I call it a poor sort of bargain."

"Tom Sayers is quite mad."

"Will they still hang him if you catch him?"

"I cannot say. How will you feel if they do?"

She looked toward the window. The main curtains were tied back, and a streetlamp outside could be seen through the lace. "They should spare him," she said. "He believes I'm worth saving. What better proof of a man's lack of reason?"

Sebastian said, "Is there anything more you can tell me?"

She looked down.

"Hell is not a warm place," she said. "It is a place where ice becomes ashes."

Sebastian waited, but that was all she had to say. Nonplussed and a little disturbed, he got to his feet.

"Then," he said, "I'll thank you and say good night."

She rang for the silent woman to show him out. Somewhere in another room, a small dog started to bark at the sound of the bell. Louise Porter raised a hand to her head and settled into the attitude of the irrevocably depressed.

She said, "Tom Sayers does not understand. Even if Mister Whitlock *were* a demon, I would not care. I care for very little, these days."

Sebastian could think of nothing else that he could say to her, other than "I am so sorry, Miss Porter."

There was an uncomfortable silence as he waited for the silent woman to appear.

Looking down, he noticed a stack of engraved postcards, freshly cut from the printers', on the side table at her elbow. He saw the word *discretion* in flowing script. Obeying the impulse that it inspired, he slipped the topmost card from the pile. He flipped it up so that it was hidden by his sleeve as the mute woman came in.

It was still in his hand when he reached the street. Under the lamp, he looked up at the parlor window, but saw no one there. He raised the card to the light. It was a formal invitation and it read, *In the presence of Miss Louise Porter. Selected gentlemen of discretion only.* That was all. Below it was a time—midnight, two days hence—and an abbreviated address.

Selected gentlemen of discretion only. The phrase seemed to have something decadent about it. Almost an air of degeneracy.

How strange, he thought.

How very, very strange.

Over at the Lyceum, the so-called Scottish Play was still running. Its critical reception, though generally positive, had been qualified; William
Archer had written to the effect that Irving had managed to "keep a rein
on those peculiarities of gesture and expression which used to run away
with him." Ellen Terry's Lady Macbeth had been greeted with similarly
faint praise, and she was rumored to be considering giving up her part.

But as Bram Stoker knew, those rumors were false. The voices of the
critics were drowned out by the voice of the public, every night. The
company played to capacity houses. Ellen Terry swore that she would not
budge an inch in her reading of the role. Sargent was asking to paint her
in character, all dark red hair and a dress that glittered blue and green
with real beetles' wings. The advance bookings were tremendous, even
by Lyceum standards.

When Stoker left the theater late that night after another full-house
performance, he did not go straight back to Chelsea and his Cheyne
Walk home. He walked instead the half mile or so to St. Martin's Lane,
where he sought out a yard close to Leicester Square. He paid sixpence
to the doorman of a sporting public house there, and received a metal
token to be exchanged at the bar for beer or grog. Intending to take
advantage of neither, Stoker climbed the stairs to the upper room.

Over at the bar sat the broken-nosed owner with his bullnecked
friends, ex-fighters all. In the early part of the evenings when the room
was full, any two of them might strip off their shirts and don gloves to
spar for a while, before taking up a collection from the crowd. Around
the walls hung the portraits of boxers long dead: lumbering Bill Neate;
Bob Gregson, "the Lancashire Champion"; Jack Randall versus Ned

Turner. Alongside them hung an engraved picture of the owner himself in a posture young, fierce, and challenging, while his older and even uglier modern-day self nursed a gin just a few feet away.

In this company, it was plain that Tom Sayers, alone at a table and some distance from the bar, had managed to escape their common disfigurements due to the brevity of his fighting career. His nose was straight and his brow unscarred. His ears resembled ears, and not bloated fungi.

He looked up sharply as Stoker came in. Stoker was in no doubt that he would have an escape route planned, but, by the look of him, he'd have a struggle to make use of it. Sayers had papers spread on the table, and was composing a letter. A bottle and a glass stood close to hand. The glass was unwashed and the bottle was half empty. Sayers was flushed, and the gaze that he turned on his visitor was unsteady.

"Tom," Stoker said sadly, and gestured to the bottle as if to say, And this will help you how?

"I know, Bram, I know," Sayers said. "I've had one or two, just to steady me."

He needed no explanation. Gin dulled pain. It was the remedy for all those whose lives were such that they had no other.

Pulling out a chair to sit down, Stoker said, "Letters are a waste of time, Tom."

"I can't get them to her anyway," Sayers said. "I send the potboy with orders to place them only in her hands. Whitlock stops them."

"He's hired the Egyptian Hall for a night." Stoker slid a printed card in front of Sayers. The prizefighter struggled to focus his eyes on it in the candlelight.

Stoker said, "I know the floor plan of the house. Maskelyne's rigged it for his magic shows. There's no easy way to get backstage."

Sayers would understand what he meant. Most of the major illusionists prepared their venues in the same way; it meant sending in a team of carpenters to panel around the backstage areas, effectively boxing them in. With a boxed stage, no one could get into the secured zone to interfere with apparatus or observe trade secrets.

Still with his eyes on the card, Sayers said, "Who are these 'gentle-men of discretion'?"

"Well-born young men who've already wasted fortunes. They're the reason why he's been parading Louise at social gatherings all over town."

Sayers nodded. "Then I am right. He means to recruit his new Caspar. It's not just a matter of finding a rake or a dissolute; they're ten-a-penny, and not fit for purpose. He seeks a Caligula for our age, one who cannot fail to understand the full import of the choice before him. Louise is the bait on his hook. What can we do, Bram?"

Stoker looked at the gin bottle.

"With your head skewed by that? Nothing. I liked your company better when all you could afford was half a bed in a temperance hotel."

Sayers raised his hands, as if calling an entire crowd to silence.

"Don't judge me, Bram," he said. "Please. You cannot know. I pray you never will."

Stoker was about to say something else, and then changed his mind. He stood up. He left the printed invitation on the table, and.threw his sixpenny token down with it.

"God be with you, Tom," he said, before he turned away and walked back to the stairs.

TWENTY-FIVE

wo nights later, at an hour when most people were thinking of retiring to their beds, Louise descended to the street outside the apartments where a four-wheeler waited. The Silent Man had gone on ahead of them, and his wife accompanied her now. They were to pick up Edmund Whitlock from the stage door at Gatti's and then proceed to the evening's destination.

The Egyptian Hall stood in Piccadilly, and had been England's Home of Mystery for the past sixteen years. It had the frontage of an antique temple, four stories high and with the look of something hewn from the rock of the Nile Valley. Two mighty columns braced the lintel above its entranceway. Two monumental statues stood upon the lintel. All illusion, in plaster and cement. To either side of this slab of the ancient desert continued a row of sober Georgian town houses.

Within the building there were two theaters. One had been taken by Maskelyne and Cooke for a three-month run of magic and deception that still showed no signs of ending, more than a decade and a half after it had begun. The other was used for exhibitions and the occasional show.

A few minutes before midnight, their four-wheeler drew up outside. Edmund Whitlock stepped down to the pavement, where he turned and offered his arm to Louise.

To an observer's eye, the halls were closed and dark, but a watchman waited to let them in. Louise moved with her eyes downcast, looking

neither to left nor right. They went directly backstage, where the Silent
Man waited to lead them to the auditorium.

It was an intimate house, with a small stage and a runway out from
the footlights across the orchestra pit. The houselights were on and the
curtains were up; Maskelyne was between shows, so his sets were half
struck and the theater's back wall was visible. About a dozen figures were
out there in the stalls, all male, no two of them sitting together although
some were conversing across the rows in raised voices. They fell silent as
Whitlock led Louise to the center of the stage, where a chair waited. He
left her there and moved to the footlights.

"Gentlemen," he said, his voice ringing all the way up to the hall's
domed ceiling. "Welcome. I have spoken to each of you in turn before
this evening."

Louise sat on her chair and continued to look down at the stage.
Whitlock had taken her to Bond Street the day before, to be fitted for a
new dress that the milliners had run up overnight. Her hair had been art-
fully pinned by the Mute Woman, who had a talent for such. Her face
was powdered and her natural pallor relieved by the merest hint of rouge.

Over by the wings, she was aware of the Silent Man easing out of the
shadows and into a spot from where he could observe the auditorium.

"I know you are intrigued," Whitlock said. "I know you will be discreet. And I know the fascination that Miss Porter holds for each of you.
Tonight, I offer the chance for one man to pursue that fascination to
the full."

Hearing mention of her name, Louise raised her head to look at
him. Slowly. She saw him outlined against the footlights with the pasty
gloom of the auditorium beyond. The men out there were but shadows
in shadow. The white fronts of their dress shirts outshone their faces.

"Know that I am hiding nothing," Whitlock was saying to
them. "I am damned. I have lived a life beyond the sight of God and it
has been . . . wonderful. To be free of conscience is the greatest freedom of all. Christ hung upon the cross, and I feel nothing for his pain.
Guilt does not chain me down. God is not my master. I have no
master."

A voice from the stalls called out, "What of his final retribution?"

"Avoidable," Whitlock said. "By handing on the gift to another as I offer it to you now."

From a man somewhere close to the footlights she heard, "There's always a reckoning in the end," but Whitlock had a ready reply.

"True, sir," he said, "but I chose your company tonight because every single one of you is skilled at passing a reckoning on to someone else."

This caused some nervous laughter, and Whitlock took the moment as an opportunity to turn his back on them and move to Louise.

She looked up at him. "Are we done here, Edmund?" she said.

"Just a little longer," he said. "Stand up." He offered her a hand that she did not need, and she rose to her feet. He smiled, and she saw a muscle in his cheek quiver uncontrollably for a second or so. Far from being in full command of the situation, he seemed to be in a state of quiet terror. When he turned again to face the auditorium with her, the telltale sign was gone, masked by the actor's show of confidence.

He said, "Here is your way in, gentlemen. You can do anything to her or with her. She does not care. There is nothing in her heart."

Unexpectedly, he raised his hand and slapped her across the face, hard. Her head snapped around. She did not fall.

Out in the stalls, one or two of the young men were on their feet. Any urge to protest was stilled as their attention was drawn to the Silent Man over at the side of the stage. In the emptiness of the theater, the sound of his revolver's hammer being cocked was impossible to miss. Once it was readied, he held it with the barrel pointing upward, all set to level and fire should it be necessary.

Whitlock said, "What do you say, Louise?"

"Thank you, Edmund," Louise said.

He turned back to his audience.

"Well?" he challenged them. "I seek a man without fear. And I offer him the world."

The man just beyond the footlights was on his feet.

"Not for me," he said, and he started to make his way out. After a moment, two or three of the others started to follow him.

"As you wish, gentlemen," Whitlock called after them, trying to make the best of this unwelcome response but failing to disguise a growing anxiety at a plan that was falling apart before his eyes. "This prize is not for all."

"You're afraid, sir," one of them shot back. "You're no advertisement for your own bargain."

"If damnation's such a prize," called another, "how come Irving's in the Lyceum while you scratch for pennies on the circuit? Who did *he* sell his soul to? I'll go there!"

Some of them laughed. Another said, "Your gift is no gift, sir, it's a burden. I'd happily take the lady. But I'll have none of you."

By now, the sounds of people rising and leaving were coming from all parts of the stalls. Dark shapes were moving across the rows like ghosts, heading for the aisles and the exits.

Whitlock lost his composure. He took Louise by the arm and roughly thrust her forward to the footlights where, with a savage jerk, he ripped open the front of her new dress. In that one move, he tore open her bodice, her chemise, everything. The force of it almost threw her off her balance. She grasped at the ripped material and held it together. She was embarrassed, but she did not actively resist.

"One man!" Whitlock roared at the departing group. It was a tragedian's yell, meant to stir and inspire, but it did no more than betray his desperation. "One man with real blood in his veins!"

And from the back of the hall came a voice that said, "May one inspect the merchandise?"

With the sudden focus of a wolf spotting the weakling in the chaos of a panicking flock, Whitlock turned all of his attention to the tall figure that was moving down the center aisle. Or perhaps it was the drowning man's interest in the one line that he might be able to reach.

Dressed like all the others, no more recognizable in the shadows than any of them, the man was raising a hand to shade his eyes against the footlights' glare.

"An inspection?" Whitlock said. "But of course." He pushed Louise, propelling her forward, and she took a couple of stumbling steps toward the runway. It extended out from the footlights and across the orchestra pit to end over the front row of the stalls.

Recovering her balance, holding her ripped bodice together, she walked with some recovered measure of dignity to the end of the runway. There she stood, self-conscious but straight-backed, to present herself for inspection. Alone, with the darkness of the empty orchestra pit to either side of her, she looked ahead and waited. He was interested, or he wasn't. Whichever it was, she did not care.

From down in the stalls, the man said in a low voice, "Is this what you want, Miss Porter?"

"No, sir," she said. "But it is what I deserve."

"Do not believe that," he said. "And do not dishonor yourself for his purposes. You are worth so much more."

She looked then. He was standing down there with his face upturned, still using one hand to shade his eyes.

She saw that this gesture was meant as much to conceal his features from the others as anything else. She saw him glance in the direction of the Silent Man, still armed and ready for trouble. Then he held out his other hand toward her, as if she might crouch and take it and so be helped down from the stage.

"Tom?" she said in a small and broken voice.

"Come," he said, low enough for only her to hear. "You have seen the man's nature and learned his purpose now. Can't you see that I spoke the truth?"

For those out in the auditorium and in the wings, she betrayed no sign of having recognized him. She kept her face blank, and barely spoke.

"Leave here," she said. "Leave while you can, before it is too late. Forget me."

"How can I?"

"You must. He has me. I am lost. Go, Tom. Save yourself."

Sayers began to say something more. But at that moment, the shooting began.

Splinters flew. Bullets were thudding into the seats around him. The Silent Man had stepped forward and taken aim, and he was emptying his revolver in Tom Sayers' direction. Sayers knew that he'd been recognized. He threw himself down.

Up on the stage, Louise did not move. She barely flinched as the theater echoed with a tattoo of pistol shots. Those who'd been halfway out were diving to the floor or scrambling for the exits; those who had not yet left their seats were jumping up out of them now. There was panic, with little sense of how best to achieve safety. Sayers was aware of at least one man clambering onto the stage.

The shooting stopped as suddenly as it had begun, all chambers emptied. None had touched Sayers, but a rising cry from the other side of the stalls suggested that at least one of the bullets had found a living target. Up on the stage, Whitlock had grabbed Louise and was dragging her toward the wings.

There was a rumble from above. Sayers looked up and saw the descending safety curtain; someone backstage had tripped the counterweight release, and the five-ton sheet of asbestos and metal was coming down like a guillotine.

Sayers took a leap at the end of the runway and pulled himself up onto the stage. "Iron flying in!" he roared in warning to anyone within earshot. Once the fire curtain was down, there would be no way to move between the auditorium and the backstage area. And anyone standing in the wrong spot when it fell would be crushed, or worse.

The "iron" hit the stage within a second of his passing under it, the weight of it shaking the boards and sending a booming echo through the cellarage below. Dust rose from the wood as if from a beaten carpet.

If the stage had been boxed in for magic, as Stoker had said, then Whitlock and his cronies would now have only one way out. But where would their exit be located? Sayers had never played the Egyptian Hall or brought a company here, so he could only guess. He guessed stage left, trying to remember the layout of the building as he'd seen it on the way in.

When he reached the back of the wings, it was to find the pass door closed, with the inert body of the Silent Man sprawled before it. Another man was standing over him, looking down at the body while barring any exit from the stage with the Silent Man's revolver in his hand. Sayers did not recognize him until he looked up and spoke.

"My God, Sayers," Sebastian Becker said. "Tell me what I've walked into."

Sebastian had entered with the ticket he'd stolen from Whitlock's rooms, and had taken a seat to one side of the auditorium. He'd had no idea what to expect. When he'd seen Whitlock stepping forward and offering his young ward for immoral purposes like a slave at the block, he'd been dismayed. He'd never known such a thing—at least, not outside the pages of banned fiction. The lower orders might trade their women and slap them around, but these were not brutes. These were men with clean shirts, and fortunes.

He'd hesitated to act until the shooting began. Then his duty became clear. As the others panicked, he moved down the rows and when he saw his chance, he climbed onto the stage. When the safety curtain fell, he was already behind it. His first aim was to surprise and disarm the gunman. The man was looking out for his master and failed to see Sebastian, who took no chances and felled him with a blow.

Now Sayers said to him, "If you were there when Whitlock spoke, then I need tell you nothing more. Did he leave this way?"

"No one has gone by me."

"Then they have trapped themselves, and are looking for another way out."

"I believe that's so."

Sebastian crouched down, and went through the shaven-headed man's coat. He was looking for further ammunition; finding none, he got to his feet and stuck the revolver into his waistband.

Sayers hadn't waited. He was away already, looking for his Louise,

the woman who'd once pushed him in front of a train and had since
grown indifferent to her own fate. How much more dedicated to his
purpose could a man be? Sebastian listened, and could hear him calling
her name; he also heard something else, from under his feet . . . a thump,
like a slamming door in some other part of the building, but coming
from below.

"Sayers!" he called out. "They are under the stage!" But either
Sayers could not hear him or was already on his way down there.

Behind the scenery at the back of the stage there was a lifted section
of the floor. It was about four feet square, and there was a ladder going
down into the darkness below it. Without any hesitation, Sebastian
descended.

There was lighting down here: a few weak electric bulbs casting a
dim yellow glow, enough to move around by but nothing more. The
underside of the stage was a maze of wooden beams and cross bracing, as
if the floor above was built to support far more weight than could ever be
required of it.

"Sayers!" he called up the ladder. "Did you hear me? Whitlock is
trying to reach the orchestra pit!" He heard a scuffle in response to his
voice; the noise might have been made by rats, because the movement
that caught his eye was from another direction altogether.

There was Whitlock, clambering through the timberwork toward
the front of the stage. He was finding no way through. Those who had
sealed the theater to protect the mysteries above the stage had taken similar care to protect the further secrets below it. Now Sebastian understood the reason for such a complicated understructure. The entire stage
floor above them was a grid of squares, any one of which could be lifted
to give secret access or escape from a piece of magical apparatus.

Whitlock had a grip on Louise and was dragging the young woman
along with him: his one prize, his last asset, his bait. But she was slowing
him down. The new dress was so full that it was getting caught up almost
everywhere. Sebastian moved to follow, and immediately banged his
head on a low bulwark.

The blow was a glancing one and not too hard, but it was enough to disorient him for a few moments. He used his few seconds of unbalance and uncertainty to draw the empty pistol from his waistband.

"Whitlock!" he shouted, and raised the pistol. He held it level as if he would fire. A man might take a while to climb through the understage timberwork to reach a fugitive. A well-aimed bullet would make the same journey without interference.

Had he a bullet. His gun was empty. But Whitlock could not know that for sure.

He saw Whitlock turn his head and spy the firearm. With a terrified jerk, the actor-manager thrust Louise around into the line of fire so that her body shielded his. She had to catch hold of one of the wide timbers to prevent herself from falling.

"You coward, sir!" Sebastian called to him. "You cannot hide behind a woman! Surrender yourself. You have no way out!"

But the move was only meant to buy Whitlock a moment or two of time. He had an escape in mind, and now Sebastian could see what his plan was. Fixed under one of the floor squares was a movable apparatus of pulleys and counterweights. Its purpose became clear as Whitlock stepped onto the platform in the middle of the frame.

"Sayers!" Sebastian shouted, hoping that wherever he was, the fighter might be warned in time to prevent Whitlock from making his way back to the pass door. "He's on the star trap!"

Whereupon the actor-manager threw a release. The counterweights dropped, instantly speeding the platform and its occupant up toward stage level.

Sayers had heard every call that the policeman had made, beginning with the very first, but had been unable to reply. He dared not take his attention from the Mute Woman. She was before him now, one of Maskelyne's trick swords in her hand; whichever way he tried to feint or dodge, the blade was there before him. He knew the blade was sharp. She'd cut him once already.

She'd stepped out from a collection of wooden crates and illusionists' properties, confronting Sayers as he was searching the scene dock beyond the wings. Sayers had never really paid her much attention before now; back in the *Purple Diamond* days, she'd been the sewing woman's lowly assistant. He'd paid out her wages every week, but had very little to say to her. If asked for an impression, he'd have described a dark-complexioned woman, one who avoided all company and never met one's eye, a menial worker bundled up in so many layers of old clothes that her shape was indeterminable.

She'd shed her coat, so that she might move with greater ease. Now her eye was fixed on his. Seeing her as if for the first time, Sayers realized that she was far from the bent harridan of his imagination. She was not a young woman, but her frame was trim and strong and she stood and moved with uncommon grace. She held the sword with a confident hand.

Her purpose was plain: She was here to buy time for her master. She would hold Sayers' attention until Whitlock had escaped to safety, and if Sayers would not be held, then she would almost certainly cut him down. Sayers had made one attempt to disarm her, and was now bleeding freely as a result. She'd backed him out onto the stage, and he dared not turn away. One thrust would end it if he did.

He could hear Sebastian Becker shouting somewhere down below, but it was impossible to be sure of what the policeman was saying. He heard him call out Whitlock's name, and then he heard his own—Becker was trying to warn him of something. But Sayers dared not move his gaze from the Mute Woman, and she did not take her gaze from him.

What came next was unexpected—there was a rumble of weights and pulleys almost directly under their feet. Neither meant to look down, but both of them did. Sayers knew the sound well. It was the machinery underlying a star trap.

A star trap offered the most spectacular—and potentially the most dangerous—entrance that a performer could make. Coupled with a flash of magnesium powder, it could make a player seem to appear out of thin air. A heavily counterweighted platform shot the actor up from the basement through a star-shaped trapdoor. The trap's hinged leaves would flip upward, opening like a flower. Once the body was through, they would drop back into place to conceal the point of emergence.

A good star trap took about half a second to do its work.

Half a second was just enough time for Sayers to place his foot upon one of its sections.

The floor jumped. Sayers felt the full force of a body hitting the trap, only to fall back again. Some of the pointed sections flew up. Even the one that he was standing on bounced an inch or two.

Then nothing, until the Mute Woman started to scream.

TWENTY-SIX

*artaphilus!"* she screamed at the floor. *"Salathiel!"* And she would have screamed more had Sayers not taken advantage of her distraction to floor her with a neat right-cross clip. In some secret and shameful corner of his heart he'd always wondered what it would be like to hit a woman, in the way that the mind tends to dally with the taboos it most ought to shrink from. Like defiling the cross, or dissecting a fairy. It was the thought that could not be entertained, the awe that one sensed before a door that one never dared to open.

Yet when the moment came, it gave him no trouble at all. He responded as he would to any armed man who had cut him and now threatened his life. Only as she hit the floor, with the sword clattering away from her outflung hand, did he recognize the wrong in it. But by then she was down, and he was safe.

He tried to prize open the leaves of the trap, but the stage carpenter had done his work well and they were too close a fit. From the stalls, an onlooker would detect no sign of any device. Sayers crossed the stage to where the sword had fallen, and picked it up. The Mute Woman was stirring slightly, but was no threat to him for the moment. Using the tip of the blade, he levered out one of the star sections and then was able to lift the others and so open up the trap completely.

The first thing that he saw when he looked down was the body of

Edmund Whitlock, sprawled across the apparatus. The platform had jammed about halfway up and his limbs were hanging over its edges. There was little blood, but by the look of him his neck was broken. Sayers swung himself down into the hole and, placing his feet with care so as to bestride the body, he lowered his weight onto the platform. With a load of two grown men on board, it slowly descended in its runners. When he could reach the lever that would lock off the counterweights, Sayers secured it.

Whitlock was dead. There was no doubting it now. But where was Louise? When he'd seen the two of them last, they'd been together. He looked around in the gloom of the stage basement, but the only face that he could see was Sebastian Becker's. The policeman was sitting on the ground a few yards away, with his back against one of the hefty wooden pillars. There was soot and dust everywhere, but he seemed not to care. He was staring at Whitlock's outstretched body.

"Where's Louise?" Sayers said. "Becker, where is she?"

Becker didn't respond until Sayers climbed through the woodwork to where he was sitting. Then the policeman finally seemed to become aware of him, without actually taking his attention from the body.

"I do not know what I saw," he said.

"You saw a man meet an end he well deserved," Sayers said. "But what happened to Louise? Was she with him?"

"She went to him," the policeman said. "He'd flung her aside, but she went to him. She took the blood from his face, and she drew it onto her own. Like tears. I called to her. I would have gone closer, but she signaled me a warning."

"Against what?"

"I cannot say. But it stopped me as I stood. She took his face in both her hands and placed her lips against his. I do not know if he was dead, or on the point of death. But she drew out his last breath and made it her own."

Finally tearing his gaze from the dead actor-manager, Sebastian Becker turned his head to look at Tom Sayers.

He said, "It was not physical. Nor material. I don't know what it was I saw. But I can swear to you, Sayers. I will swear it until my dying day. I *did* see something happen. I swear that something went from him to her."

As Tom Sayers had been entering the basement through the star trap, Louise had been leaving it by the ladder. Her heart was calm and her head was clear. For the first time in many weeks, she felt that her life now had a shape and a purpose.

What shape, and what purpose, she did not yet know. She merely sensed the presence of meaning, where before there had been none. It flooded her, it filled her. It was as if she began to have an exact sense of her location in the great scheme of things, all the way from the center of her being out past the sun to the cold, cold stars.

She found the Silent Man and his wife on their way to the pass door. They were a sorry-looking pair. It would have been hard to say which of them was holding the other up.

She stopped them and said, "Listen to me. Whitlock is dead. I have bared my soul to God and offered myself for damnation in his place. I believe that God has considered the condition of my soul, and has accepted my offer. I am in hell already. Let Whitlock find peace. As God is my witness, for the things I have done I will not be redeemed. I have opened my heart to the Wanderer's burden. Will you guide and serve me as you served him?"

They stared. But she did not doubt that they understood. The Silent Man released his wife and took a step closer to Louise. He was studying her, looking into her eyes as if for signs.

She waited, and allowed it. Her dress was torn to the point of indecency and filthy as well, while her cheeks were marked with drying blood. But she stood there, straight and confident and entirely without shame.

After a while, the Silent Man looked back at his wife. She was waiting for his assessment. When her husband nodded, it was as if she filled out and grew an inch or two. The woman's eyes brightened and her cheeks flushed with life.

"Come," the man said to Louise, and led the way out of the theater.

PHILADELPHIA, RICHMOND, AND BEYOND

1903

TWENTY-SEVEN

hen Elisabeth Becker came down early on Monday morning to set breakfast for the family, she was not expecting to find a visitor already at the table. Especially not one who looked like a convict on the run. He sat like one, too, head down with his arm around the plate as if someone might try to reach in and steal his food. He was wearing the pants and waistcoat of a checked suit that looked as if it had once been loud, but had faded to a sludge color as it lost most of its shape.

She stopped in the doorway. He must have heard her breath catch in surprise, because he looked up at her. He'd just shoveled in a good half a pound of pancakes and corn syrup, and he struggled to swallow so he could speak.

"Please," she said, raising a hand. "Please continue. Don't trouble yourself." Then she backed off into their little hallway. She was still moving backward when she bumped into her husband.

She was about to say something, but Sebastian signaled for her to hold it for a moment and then moved her farther down the hallway. She could still see the visitor from here, but they could speak with more privacy.

"Sebastian," she said, "who is that man?"

The man at the table had grown self-conscious. He tried to carry on as before, but clearly knew that he was being discussed. He'd straightened in his seat and taken his elbows off the table, as if conscious of the need to make a good impression.

Sebastian said, "His name's Tom Sayers."

"Has he been here all night?"

"I let him sleep on the divan."

"Why?"

"He has nowhere of his own."

It wasn't exactly the answer she was looking for. She glanced back at the man again. He shifted uncomfortably on his chair.

"He's the man from the boxing tent," she said.

"So he is," Sebastian said, which brought him a stern look.

"Sebastian," she said, in a voice with a definite edge of warning to it.

"He's someone I knew in England," Sebastian said. "We've unfinished business. From the old days."

"He looks like a criminal. Is he?"

"Things aren't always how they look."

They went back into the kitchen, and Sayers got to his feet. Sebastian introduced them. Elisabeth told Sayers that he was welcome in their house and then urged him to sit down again and continue.

When Sayers had finished his pancakes he tried to wash the pan, but Elisabeth took it from him. She sent the ex-fighter and her husband out into the garden, where they could sit and talk while the rest of the family breakfasted.

It was more of a brick-paved yard than a true garden, but it supported a couple of flower beds and a Carolina allspice bush right next to the door. They had a water pump and a bird table, and Elisabeth would have planted a cherry tree as well if she'd been able to squeeze one in.

"You have a nice home," Sayers said.

"Thank you," Sebastian said. "It's a little beyond our means, but I do my best to hang onto it."

Sayers sat on a wrought-iron bench and Sebastian on a chair that he'd brought from the dining room. They continued the conversation that they'd had to suspend the night before.

Sayers had already told Sebastian of how he'd run straight from the theater to the Marylebone apartments that evening, but either he'd reached them too late or Louise and the two servants had never returned there. He'd waited on the street for hours, keeping watch on the building. After a while, he could hear Whitlock's lapdog begin to bark. He did not know what had happened to it after that night.

"So Whitlock cheated on his bargain in the end," Sebastian said. "Where his soul is now, we cannot know."

"Pursuing Louise was like chasing a wraith," Sayers said. "She changed her name. I imagine she changed her appearance. In Yarmouth, I heard that she had fled to the Continent. The trail went cold for a while after I tracked her to these shores, but in every new town or city I search for signs of her presence. Every now and again I learn something more. I joined that dog-and-pony boxing show because I heard she had come to the East. She is here somewhere. I know it."

"Still chasing her after all these years? There's a thin line between devotion and obsession, Sayers. You can easily cross it."

"You're probably right. But on that night at the Egyptian Hall, I saw how she'd changed. Her time spent with Whitlock had driven her illusions away. She now understood that she'd no reason to fear or despise me. But instead, she'd begun to despise herself."

"And in consequence she abandoned all that was proper, and chose a life of moral decay. Haven't your inquiries confirmed as much? She considers herself lost."

"She can believe it, but that does not make it true. What I saw was a woman worth saving. She could forgive me, but she would not forgive herself. Tell me, Inspector. Is that the sign of a bankrupt soul?"

"Call me Sebastian," his host said. "Or Becker, if you must. I am an inspector no longer."

"I believe that she's only held to her choice by the life she now leads and the company she keeps. Whitlock's servants may try to teach her the ways of the damned. But it's my belief that her nature will temper the excesses of the fiend they would guide her to become."

"Nature can be beaten," Sebastian said. "I once had to deal with a man who'd drowned himself. He put stones in his pockets, to make sure that his will to die would prevail over his instinct to survive. If she's determined to see herself damned, there's nothing you can do that will stop her."

"I'll have to find her to know," Sayers said.

Sebastian went on to recount his own experiences in the aftermath of that momentous evening at the Egyptian Hall. He'd made the profound error of telling his story in full to the Metropolitan Police, without even thinking of how it might be received. In retrospect, he should have censored himself. They listened attentively at first, as officers to an equal. Then they began exchanging glances. Then they moved to another room to discuss what they had heard.

His account was deemed unsatisfactory. None of the well-heeled witnesses ever came forward. The watchman who'd admitted the audience confirmed that they'd existed, but said that their printed invitations had carried no names. When Sebastian was finally allowed to return home, he was suspended from duty and required to appear before a tribunal.

In the days before the tribunal, Sebastian went back to church. He did not pray, but spent several hours discussing myths and miracles with Father Alexander.

Father Alexander could teach others that Christ had risen, while declining to argue whether an intelligent person should allow that a rotten corpse might reverse its decay, heal its injuries, and clamber to its feet. For the priest, God was not hiding in the impossible tricks, but was to be found somewhere in the act of accepting them.

That was of little help to Sebastian. A readiness to believe in wonders might make the believer holy, but it didn't make the wonders true.

The tribunal had recommended his dismissal from the force, the reason to be recorded in the remarks column of the police register as "want of sobriety and contradicting himself in his evidence." Becker's new superintendent had persuaded the chief constable to amend this to read, ". . . in consequence of his health." The original wording would have kept him out of a job in this, his second life. The character of a Pinkerton operative had to be above reproach, with only those of strict moral principles and good habits being permitted to enter the service.

The time came for Sebastian to leave for the office. Sayers went to thank his hostess. He was awkward, she was gracious, and her sister and the boy sat in embarrassed silence while this rough-hewn stranger took up space in their familiar little room.

Then he joined Sebastian and they walked from the house to the streetcar, and rode it into town. The day was warm, and its windows were lowered to let a breeze pass through the carriage as they moved. Sayers sat with his elbow over the ledge and mused, "A Pinkerton man."

"It's like being a policeman," Sebastian said. "Except that people respect you and you make a living."

"If I walked into your office and asked you to find Louise for me, could you do it?"

"Could you afford us?"

That seemed unlikely. Sayers was patently not prosperous, and the years had not been kind. Steady drinking and regular poundings in the boxing booths had affected his bearing. Sebastian had not actually seen him take any drink during the few hours that they'd spent in each other's company, but the need would probably catch up with him soon.

Sayers said, "I've tracked her up and down this country. She knows

I'm looking for her. Once I came this close." He held up one hand with his thumb and forefinger held barely apart.

Sebastian said, "Do you know how she lives?"

"Performing, singing . . . in Pittsburgh, she gave dancing lessons. She's a widow when it suits her. She has an eye on society. I think she'd like to settle in one place. But there's always some reason for her to move on."

The streetcar reached Sebastian's regular stop, and they squeezed their way out through all the standing passengers to disembark.

"Sayers," Sebastian said when they were on the sidewalk and heading toward the Pinkerton offices, "I'm grateful for the answers to questions that have been haunting me for more than a decade. But this life you still lead is the life I left behind. I've no wish to return to it."

"With such a wife and such a home," Sayers said, "I'd be astonished to hear otherwise. All you have is all that I envy."

"Then understand. I'll see what I can find in the office files. Be our guest for a day or two, and we'll get a few good meals down you, see if we can put a spring in your step and a shine on your shoes. If you need money . . ."

"I'll take no money from you," Sayers said. "But I'll be grateful for your hospitality. And if anything in the Pinkerton files can bring me closer to Louise, then I'll be on my way and you'll hear nothing more of me. Will I need to pay your employers for the information? That could be a problem."

"I'm an assistant supervisor. I'm expected to pursue new business. Not everything turns into a paying case. That's expected, as long as it's all within reason."

The building's war-veteran janitor had brought a chair out onto the sidewalk, pretending to look out for a delivery while he was really just taking the air. He'd seen the slaughter at Antietam, they said. Now he just watched the living go by.

"If anyone should ask you, you're a client," Sebastian told Sayers, and led the way into the entrance hall.

TWENTY-EIGHT

he paragraph in a corner on page 17 of the *Echo*—
"A Magazine devoted to Society, Literature and Stage
in the South"—read:

> *Miss Mary D'Alroy, the dainty little actress who has won so*
> *many admirers here with her recitation of "Agnes Lane" and*
> *readings from the works of Mrs. Henry Wood, will give an*
> *informal reception to the ladies and children of her audience on*
> *the stage of the Academy of Music next Tuesday afternoon.*
> *The reception will take place immediately after the matinee.*
> *These functions are always attended with great relish by those*
> *who desire to shake hands and exchange a passing word with*
> *the pretty star.*

Louise had used the name of Mary D'Alroy in Richmond some years
before, and had resumed it on her return. As far as this part of the South
was concerned, she was well on her way to becoming a respectable performer with a verifiable past—one that could be supported by local
sources, at least. Elsewhere in this vast nation she'd moved under other,
similarly established names.

It was still a dangerous life. A man from San Antonio had recognized
her in Chicago, and she'd had to spin him a story. Almost any other

profession would have been safer to follow, but she had to make a living and support two servants, and knew of no other way. She could not sew, or cook, or do any other womanly thing of practical use. And the stage offered advantages that no other kind of living could; who but a certain kind of theatrical could arrive in a new city, offer a demure demeanor and a program of high-minded readings, and within a matter of days be on first-name terms with ladies from the best families in town? The *Echo*'s masthead rolled together society, literature, and the stage, and so, in her chosen way of life, did Louise.

After the matinee, the audience moved out into the foyer. Those with tickets for the reception gathered in the ladies' parlor on the balcony floor while the stage was being reset, and then were led backstage and on through the wings.

Louise was waiting on the stage, along with the chairwoman of the Richmond Women's Club, who made a short speech of welcome. Those who had never crossed the footlights before were suitably excited and awed by the experience. Some of the children stared out into the empty auditorium, row after row of seats from the parquet all the way up to the peanut gallery, stricken by a little taste of stage fright as their imaginations peopled the house.

Louise gave thanks for the welcome, told a couple of stories from her travels, gave them an extra bit of Tennyson that she claimed had been commended to her by the poet himself, and then invited their questions. The questions were usually predictable, and her responses polished.

"What drew you to the stage?"

"Seeing Shakespeare performed when I was a little girl."

"Did your father object to your taking up a career in the theater?"

"He was in no position to. It was he who had taken me to the Shake-speare."

Little of this was true; she'd seen no Shakespeare until her seventeenth year, and her father had died before she ever went near a stage. Indeed, it was his death that had sent her to it. Without that, she would probably have limited her performing to playing the piano and singing in various drawing rooms until some young man of suitable prospects caved in and proposed marriage. By now, she'd have been running a household that she'd filled with her own children.

She looked at these children—scrubbed, scared, bored—and, as she often did, wondered about what she was missing. Her own child, had it lived, would have been—

But at this point, she stopped the thought in its tracks, as she always had to.

One of the women said, "Will you be staying in Richmond for long?"

"For as long as Richmond will have me," Louise said. "Much as I love to tour the world and meet new people, it cannot compare with a home of one's own. There was a time in my life when I thought that such things could wait, and would not matter. Now, as time goes by, I find that they matter more and more."

They seemed happy with that. After the questions, there was fresh lemonade for the children, brought onstage by the Mute Woman, and a chance for all to meet and circulate. Louise moved through the crowd, speaking to each woman as if to a sister, and marveling at every child she was offered as if it was the heartbreaking beauty or infant genius that its mother believed it to be.

She found herself confronted by the woman who'd asked the question about her father. With her was a small ginger-haired girl of about five or six years old.

"She has a question for you," the woman said. "But she won't tell me what it is."

"What's her name?"

"Alice."

Louise got down to the child's level and said, "Well, Alice. Oh Alice, where art thou. That's a lovely bonnet. What did you want to ask me?"

The girl, who was snub-nosed and freckled and seemed genuinely sweet, stared past her and spoke so softly that Louise had to tilt her head to one side in order to make out her words.

What she heard was "My daddy says an actress isn't as good as a horse."

"A *horse*?" Louise repeated, momentarily thrown and trying not to look it. And it would have stayed at that, with Louise assuming that what she'd heard was just some piece of childish whimsy, were it not for the mother's reaction. She reddened, caught up the child's hand, and said, "Forgive me," before tugging her daughter away.

She took her off so quickly that the child could hardly keep up, being swung by her arm into the skirts of some of the others.

Louise straightened up and the chatter around her died down for just a moment or two, as the people closest to her sensed that something was wrong; but no one else had heard the child's words, and Louise's calm smile was back in place by the time she was turning to the next person.

The reception continued for another half hour. Louise signed her name—or rather, the Mary D'Alroy name—to a few copies of the program card, and fielded a few more questions like "Did you see *Her Wrong Righted* at the Bijou?" ("One of the disadvantages of performing is the lack of opportunities to see others perform.") She did not see the woman with the ginger-haired child again, and supposed that they'd left early.

Louise ended the event by thanking everyone and leaving the stage, to polite applause.

As the visitors cleared, she went down to the manager's office to sort out the division of the take. The Silent Man joined her in the wings and followed her down. There had been a fifty-cent cover charge for the reception, children free. Take out the house's share and the cost of the refreshments, and it didn't leave much. Louise signed for the money, then handed the purse to the Silent Man for safekeeping.

As they were leaving the manager's office together, she said to him, "I want a good carriage. Same as the ladies are getting, or better."

He nodded and moved off. Before he'd gone a couple of strides, she stopped him.

"Not *too* much better," she cautioned.

She knew that she did not need to explain. It was necessary to make an impression, but not a vulgar one. She needed these people to see her as a natural equal, and had only a few such well-chosen properties with which to dress her character.

Back on the now-empty stage, she collected her personal pieces together. The Mute Woman had cleared and swept up, and would meet her at the carriage. From the lectern, Louise took her copy of Tennyson's works. Tastefully bound in green with stamped gilt covers, it was a book that she had used in many a reading, whether Tennyson featured or not. She had all her pieces by heart, rather than struggle with her poor sight or appear wearing her glasses.

Raising her voice, but without looking up, she said, "Will you come forward, or hide there in the shadows until you know for sure that I've gone?"

Her voice rang throughout the empty theater, but no sound came in response.

"Yes, you," she said. "In box twelve."

Box twelve was almost at stage level, only slightly elevated from it. It was long and deep, and backed with a thick velvet curtain.

After a few moments, something moved in the shadows, and then a man of around twenty-five years stepped forward into view.

Louise said, "I believe you owe me fifty cents."

"I engaged the box for the season," the young man said, unembarrassed. "Does that not cover it?"

"Not if it puts no food on my table."

He dug in his pocket and found a silver dollar. He put his other hand on the brass rail along the box's front edge and swung himself over onto the stage, not quite as elegantly as he'd perhaps had in mind.

Louise waited as he walked toward her with the coin held out before him.

"You have change for a dollar?" he said.

She took the money from him before she said, "I'll owe it to you. Why did you hide yourself?"

"My understanding was that the event was for the ladies and children of your audience," he said. "I could have worn my best dress, but I don't think I'd have fooled anyone."

She looked him over. He was long-limbed and moved easily. He had a heavy mustache and a rather weak chin. He seemed entirely sure of himself.

She said, "Next time you want to spy on me, Mister . . ."

"Patenotre. Jules."

She blanched at his pronunciation, which was a pure American rendering of the words as the eye might see them, and not a sound that any European would recognize.

"Is that supposed to be French?" she said.

"My family's from Louisiana."

"Well, the next time you feel the urge to spy on a woman, Louisiana, make yourself known. Nobody likes to be watched without their knowledge."

"But you knew I was there all along."

"Nevertheless. You intended I would not. To me, that makes it a strange business."

"Some people thrive on strange business. What was that about a horse?"

Louise finished gathering up her books, then held them to her in a stack like a schoolmistress. She said, "I think I can guess it from her mother's reaction. The child probably overheard her father say that actresses are no better than whores."

The young man mused on this, not at all shocked by her forthrightness. "Do you know her father?" he said innocently.

She gave him a sideways look.

"You speak very boldly," she said. "For one whose preference is to hide and observe."

"Yet when I speak boldly, you do not take offense."

She turned square on to him. "What would you have from me?" she said. "A lock of my hair? A button from my coat? My signature on your program?"

"I'd settle for a kiss," he said.

"For fifty cents?" she said. "*Now* I take offense. Good day to you."

He watched her walk across the stage, away from him and into the wings. When she got there, he called out, "When do I get to collect?"

She stopped and looked back. "Collect what?"

Again, he made a show of his innocence. "My change," he said. "If I don't get the kiss, I want my money."

"Where can you usually be found, Jules Patenotre?"

"I have rooms at Murphy's Hotel."

"Then that is where I will find you," she said, and left him standing on the stage.

TWENTY-NINE

ach Pinkerton office had a criminal department. They had card files and a rogues' gallery and the resources to track certain kinds of criminal activity. The information held by the Philadelphia office didn't compare with the criminal departments in New York and Chicago, but it gave a good account of all the local activity. The room was stuffy and high-ceilinged, and there was a fly somewhere loose in it.

"This one may fit," said Sebastian, pulling out one of the cards to read it more closely.

"How so?" Sayers was in one of the office's captain's-style swiveling chairs, hands on his knees, looking ill at ease. He was out of place in here, and he knew it.

Sebastian read for a few moments and then said, "It's one of our closed cases. A woman engaged us to look for her husband. Forty-two years old. He owned a company making optical and scientific instruments. Happily married, five children, and he disappeared without any reason or warning."

"People disappear all the time. That's not enough."

"Wait. We closed the case after a farmer found his body. At first, it was assumed that he'd fallen from a train. He lay by the tracks for a month until the farmer came along. After all the animals and insects had been at him, it was impossible to be sure of the cause of death. But in the

214

space of that month, our agent found out a few things about him that his family would have preferred not to know."

Sayers had been swinging the chair from side to side. He stopped.

"Don't tell me," he said. "He led a double life."

"He liked the vaudeville. The chorus girls best of all."

"Louise Porter is no chorus girl," the prizefighter said.

"I use the term loosely."

"As does everyone."

"I mean young actresses of any kind. He'd take a box at Keith's theater or the old Trocadero and send notes to the stage door. Once in a while, he'd get lucky."

"Louise has a particular method," Sayers said. "I've seen it develop over the years. She arrives in a new city, sometimes with a letter of introduction to someone in society. That gets her an invitation to one salon or another, where she sings and recites and always causes a stir among the men. She might hire a hall to give a reading, but never a theater. She keeps the title of an actress, but she is never part of any cast or company. She dare not be."

Sebastian held the card up, as if it might offer the proof of something.

"This man's wife was on the committee of the Philomusian Club," he said.

"What's that?"

"It's a women's club. Arts, music, poetry. For all we know, some of their events could even have been hosted at his mansion."

Sayers thought about that one. It did, indeed, seem to put a different light on matters.

He said, "Is there anything there to say how he died?"

Sebastian had to go deeper into the file for an answer. He read for a while and then, with his eyes still on the paper, said, "Our police contacts say they found needles in his body. A dozen of them. All in a cluster. Pushed in where no needle ought to go. All else might decay, but the needles did not. The family were never told."

Sayers asked to see the paper. Sebastian checked for anyone passing the room before he handed it over, but no one was there. Bearce wouldn't like it if he saw an outsider reading a confidential file, potential client or not.

Sayers read for a while and then said, "I believe this may be evidence of her work."

"Her work?"

"I have learned so much about my own sex in these past fourteen years, Becker. There are men who hold that they worship innocence while they seek to consume it like dogs. And there are upright, respectable citizens whose secret dream is of pain and humiliation at the hands of another. Of a mistress, or a lover. To undergo such is an almost unbearable ecstasy for them. Most stay well within the safety of the dream. Some would go to its limit. And at that limit, there is always the possibility of something going wrong."

"These are the men she seeks out?"

"She does not need to seek them out. Whatever signal they are looking for, they seem to find. They pursue her. Most of what I know came from the case of a man in San Francisco. He had survived her attentions, but was left damaged. His consent to what had happened meant nothing in law. There was a scandal. After that, she had to stop using her own name."

"Good God," said Sebastian, who until this moment was certain that he'd pretty much seen everything there was to see of human nature.

Sayers said, "Don't you see what she's doing, Sebastian? She's fulfilling the letter of the Wanderer's contract without being entirely true to its spirit. She dispenses suffering, all right, but only to those who actively seek it. If a death occurs, it's more by their misadventure than by her intent."

"A nice distinction," Sebastian said drily. "As I'm sure the widows would agree."

———

Alongside the post office building stood the square-towered headquarters of the *Philadelphia Record*. They waited in the foyer as Sebastian had a message sent upstairs, and within a few minutes one of the regular staff came down, greeted him as an old friend, and led them through to the archive rooms.

Here, recent copies of the newspaper were piled flat on shelves. Older editions could be consulted in huge bound volumes that needed a rolling ladder to get them down and specially built lecterns to hold them open.

They were interested in those issues that covered the weeks before the dead man's disappearance. Sebastian wasn't entirely sure of what they were searching for, but Sayers seemed to have more of an idea.

"Here's one," Sebastian suggested, and read aloud from the classifieds. "Miss M. S. Lyons. Private instruction in all the latest and most fashionable dances. Classes taught out of town. Private lessons any hour."

Sayers glanced up from his own pages. "A dance instructor?" he said. He didn't seem persuaded.

"You said she tried something like it before," Sebastian suggested.

"I don't think so," Sayers said. "I'm in the society pages, here . . ." He ran his finger down an entire column in a second or two. Sebastian realized that he wasn't so much reading it as taking in the text as a block of print and extracting from it such detail as he needed. Was that how actors got their lines so quickly? Not so much learning the words as absorbing the sense of a piece, and then re-creating the words from it?

Sayers' finger stopped on the page.

"Here she is," he said excitedly.

Sebastian moved to his side, and both read together. It was a small announcement in the society column for a literary lunch to be held at the Rathskeller Café and Ladies Dining Room in the Betz Building on Broad Street. The guest speaker was to be the noted actress and *récitateuse* . . .

"Mrs. Louise Caspar," Sebastian read aloud. "That must be a cruel twist of the knife for you. I'm sorry, Sayers."

"Ignore it," Sayers said. "I can."

There were only two photographs accompanying the society columns, and neither was of Louise.

Sebastian reread the piece and said, "I see no actual mention of the Philomusian Club."

"The name places her in town. That's good enough for me. And look at the date. The trail is fresh."

They looked through more issues, but found no further reference. As they were leaving the *Record* building, Sebastian said, "We need better information. There are other newspapers."

"Never mind newspapers," Sayers said. "Find me a dozen rich women with time on their hands. Find me the clubs and the literary societies. The lecture circuit and the private library. Those are the fields where she beats for her game."

They stopped at the Automat for coffee and sandwiches. It was early for lunch, and the office crowds hadn't built up yet. Despite the morning's excitements, or perhaps because of them, Sayers appeared to have a healthy appetite. His color was better than the day before, his eyes brighter. The cuts about his head were beginning to heal . . . although for the moment he continued to have the look of a barroom brawler, taken out of his element and tossed into the daylight.

Sebastian said, "Say you find her. What then?"

Sayers was oddly silent.

Sebastian said, "I don't believe you've never thought about it."

"I have thought about it," Sayers said. "I have written the scene in my head a thousand times. But until I face the moment itself . . . I have no idea what will happen."

Rather than return to the Pinkerton office, where conversations might be overheard and questions raised, they stood outside Wanamaker's and pretended to study the window displays.

Sebastian decided to be bold.

"You drink, Sayers."

The prizefighter took this without embarrassment or any show of defensiveness. "I have been known to," he conceded.

"It will not help you from here."

Sayers gave a wry smile. He said, "It is very hard for a man to deny something whose companionship has sped the passage of the harshest of days."

"Nevertheless. If you're staying in my house, it won't do to be three days without a shave and have gin on your breath."

"I can easily get a shave," Sayers said.

THIRTY

or the rest of the afternoon, Sayers walked around town while Sebastian Becker returned to the office to look up some names and send out a few messages. Some of the theaters on Eighth Street were running a continuous program of variety acts and Sayers considered passing an hour or two in the cheap seats, but he hadn't the heart or the energy to lay down his money at the box office. He already felt that he'd seen enough comic singers, tap dancers, and unsteady acrobats in his life to last him until the end of it.

And besides, his thoughts would not settle. He was looking for Louise in every woman who passed him on the sidewalk. He ended up sitting on a bench in Rittenhouse Square among all the nannies and their baby carriages, until he became aware that a mounted policeman was eyeing him while circling the gardens a little more often than seemed necessary.

He went home with Becker at the end of the day, and that evening he dined with the family. Elisabeth Becker asked him about his life with the carnival, and his time on the stage before it. She spoke to be polite, but he was quickly able to convince her that he was not the brute he might have appeared, and that the brawl at Willow Grove had not been typical of the booths. He did, however, confess that fairground contests were perhaps not as equal as they might be made to seem; often the challenger would be given eight-ounce gloves to fight with, while the house fighter was able to punch harder with gloves of half the weight.

"How fascinating," she said, seeming to be genuinely captivated by this piece of showman's tradecraft.

"Yes, ma'am," said Sayers. "As you see, it's not just a sport, it's a science."

"So if you ever get to meet Thomas Edison, Elisabeth," Sebastian said drily, "he'll whip you in a straight fight, no problem."

Once it was clear that Sebastian had not introduced some belligerent animal into the household, the atmosphere eased. Elisabeth's sister, Frances, said almost nothing to Sayers, but stared wide-eyed at him all evening as if storing up something she was ready to blurt out. Robert also stared, but at the table. He'd been forbidden to read his latest dime novel at mealtimes but remained inseparable from it. If it wasn't in one hand or the other, it was tucked under his arm until he had a hand free again.

Sayers spotted its title and said, "Did you know that Buffalo Bill once took his Wild West show to England?"

It was as if he'd snapped his fingers to bring the boy out of a trance; Robert's attention went from the table to the dinner guest, with no distraction in between.

"Twice," the boy said, the first word that he'd spoken all evening. "Once in Eighteen Ninety Three, and again in Eighteen Ninety Seven when he met the queen. He goes again this year."

"This year? Well, there I was thinking I'd tell you something you didn't know, and now you've told me something *I* didn't know." Sayers held out his hand. "Shake this. Go on, it's not a trick." The boy stared at the outstretched hand, and then awkwardly took it and gave it a single shake, as if tugging on a bellpull.

"Now," Sayers said as the boy let go, "you can tell all your friends that you shook the very same hand that shook the hand of William F. Cody."

Awe followed. It was a private awe, that Robert kept all to himself; nonetheless, it was heartening to see.

Later in the evening, Sayers kept out of the way while some intense family discussion went on between Sebastian and Elisabeth. It continued for an hour or more. When Sebastian returned to the sitting room alone, he gave Sayers a nod.

Sayers said in a low voice, "What have you told them?"

"That there are two Irish brothers out gunning for me, and that your presence in the house for a few days will bring us an extra measure of security."

"That sounds reasonable."

"Because it happens to be true." Sebastian glanced toward the door, as if there was a risk that Elisabeth might come through it before he'd finished speaking. "It's also true that the brothers were arrested on the Boston train on Saturday. I saw the bulletin when I went back to the office. But they'll serve me for an excuse."

Sayers slept on the divan again that night.

The next morning, Elisabeth told him, "Mister Sayers, I apologize for your discomfort. I have made up my sister's room for you to use during the rest of your stay here. Frances will move in with Robert."

"I don't know what to say," he said.

"She gave it up willingly. I daresay there'll be more lace and ribbon around than you're used to, but I think you'll be comfortable."

"Thank you."

"Don't just thank me," she said, suddenly turning so serious that Sayers found himself reacting as if she'd unexpectedly shown him a glimpse of a knife. She glanced in the direction they both knew her husband to be, and said, "If anything happens to him, I'll hold you responsible. You don't really think I believe that this is all about two Irish boys? I don't know what's going on between the two of you. But if anything happens to cause him harm, may the Lord help you."

It was probably the Buffalo Bill dime novel handshake that had ensured Sayers' extended welcome. The Beckers worried about their son, there was no doubting that. Robert's intelligence was undeniable, his emotions profound; but he rarely showed one or expressed the other, and so was misunderstood by almost everyone outside of the family.

There was a new doctor at Friends' Asylum up in Oxford Township, some five miles to the north of Philadelphia. He'd been recommended to them as a reputable specialist in emotional disturbance. Elisabeth had waited over a month for an appointment to see him, and it fell that afternoon.

Sebastian took them to the station. Less than half an hour after the family had departed, a two-horse wagon drew up in the alley outside the Becker house. It was a carnival wagon, but the elaborate decoration on its side panels had so faded that the paint was almost indistinguishable from the dust that covered it. The team was driven by a boy of about fifteen years old. Beside him sat a much older man, wiry and with a walrus mustache that gave him a look of permanent melancholy. He had a telegram in his hand, against which he'd been checking the street names as they passed.

The boy kept hold of the reins and the man climbed down as Sayers went out to meet them. Sebastian had gone to the station to see his family onto the train, while Sayers had stayed behind to sit on the front stoop and wait for his possessions to arrive.

The man was named Axel Hansen, and he and his brother owned the boxing booth. His brother was the barker. The boy at the reins of the wagon was his grandson.

Together, Axel Hansen and Tom Sayers lifted the steamer trunk from the rear of the wagon and carried it to the house, and then returned for the suitcase. With the Willow Grove engagement cut short and no others lined up, the brothers had tried to find another pitch elsewhere in the city. That hadn't worked out, and so the show was moving on.

When they'd managed all the baggage and set it down by the stoop, Axel Hansen said, "Well, Tom, it's been a time, and no mistake."

"It has," agreed Tom.

Axel reached deep into the leg pocket of his voluminous trousers and brought out a bottle of Green River whiskey, unopened and with its seal intact. Holding it up, he said, "I do believe you forgot to pack this before you left us."

"You know I didn't forget it, Axel," Sayers said. "And I appreciate the thought behind the gift. But hard liquor's not the best thing to have in front of me right now. Why don't you and the boys open it tonight and raise a glass to me?"

Axel's watery blue eyes studied him. Some blue eyes are cold, and make their owner seem hard. With Axel's, it was always as if he was on the verge of tears.

He said, "You cleanin' up?"

"I think I might."

Unoffended, Axel returned the bottle to its hiding place and said, "Then God bless you, Tom, and all who travel with you. I hope the day comes when you find who you're lookin' for."

The two men embraced there in the middle of the sidewalk, and then Axel returned to his wagon.

"Always a place for you," he called down from the seat.

"I know it," Sayers replied, and raised his hand in farewell as the wagon set off to rejoin the rest of the show on its way out of town. When they'd turned the corner, Sayers went and sat on his trunk to await the family's return.

The doctor had spent no more than ten minutes with Robert, and had then turned him over to his assistants for tests and observations that would take up the rest of the afternoon. Elisabeth wouldn't leave him, so she and Frances stayed while Sebastian returned.

When he arrived back from the hospital, the sight of Sayers and his luggage by the doorstep made him feel like a mean-spirited host. But Sayers was a stranger to his family and hardly less of a stranger to Sebastian himself, and it had hardly seemed proper to give him the run of the house.

He unlocked the front door, and they carried the trunk inside and up the stairs into Frances' room, which had been emptied of her more personal possessions to make it into guest quarters.

"We've a woman who collects the washing twice a week," Sebastian told him. "If there's anything you need to get clean, here's your chance."

"I may have been living in wagons and sleeping in my underwear," Sayers said, "but one of the many things I've learned along the way is how to wash through a shirt."

Sebastian watched as he opened up the trunk and, in the space of a couple of minutes, set out the few items that would make a corner of any place his own. A hairbrush, a few souvenirs, a picture for the mirror—the picture was a theatrical *carte de visite* from the *Purple Diamond* company.

"I take it that you don't have another suit to wear?" he said.

"This one's my best," Sayers told him, and a look inside the trunk was proof he did not lie.

Sebastian said, "Don't take offense at this, Sayers, but if you're going to chase Louise through high society we need to make you a little more respectable."

Sayers said, "First things first. I need a bathhouse and a barber." He looked at his battered hands. "In my experience, the first step toward looking human is to start feeling like it."

There was a barber within two blocks' walk, and a public bathhouse just a couple of streetcar stops away. Sebastian began to offer Sayers money, but Sayers stopped him. He had a stash of bills in a secret pocket of the trunk. His emergency fund.

So Sebastian sent him on his way, waited ten minutes or so, and then went upstairs and performed a thorough search of the fighter's trunk and suitcase, taking care to note how everything lay and to replace all as he found it.

In the trunk were two stolen Bibles that Sayers had been using to keep newspaper cuttings from all over the country, slipping them between the pages to keep them flat. All of the San Francisco cuttings could be found in Ecclesiastes. The first book of Kings told the story of a cold trail that he'd followed all the way up to Washington State. In the book of Job was a list of all the soup kitchens in Denver.

He would not throw in his lot with Sayers, but he would offer such support as would send him on his way with a goal to pursue. The prizefighter's reappearance in his life had awakened all of the detective's turbulent feelings over scenes he'd once witnessed. A rational man by inclination, he'd seen his world upturned by the seemingly supernatural. He wanted his world to make sense again. And if there was a slim chance that the search for truth might turn up some final proof of the occult . . . well, no man was an atheist except for want of a more convincing alternative.

But an old painting in a museum basement proved nothing. One thing he had learned from the church was that the credulous would co-opt anything to support a belief.

Edmund Whitlock had been mortal. Louise Porter was no more than human. All else, Sebastian concluded, was human psychology, preserved for the ages in tales of wonder.

In the Acts of the Apostles, Sebastian found two yellowing slips of folded newsprint, each with a marginal note that identified their source as the *Norwich Mercury* of 1891.

MYSTERIOUS DISAPPEARANCE OF A CHILD
Taken from the Rows
Man and Woman Sought

The first clipping told of a child's disappearance in the British coastal town of Great Yarmouth, and of the search that had followed. Eight-year-old Eliza Sewell, a resident of one of the narrow medieval alleys known as the Rows, had been sent on an errand by her mother. Her four-year-old sister was in her charge. The bottle shop was no more than ten minutes' walk away, but she'd neither arrived there nor returned home. The abandoned younger child had walked into a neighbor's house, where she said nothing of what had happened. She played with the neighbor's children and no one raised the alarm until midevening, when the oldest boy took her back to her own home.

Each Row was a close-knit community. Neighbors could, quite literally, lean out of their windows and touch each others' houses. There was a large turnout of volunteers to join in the search. All that the four-year-old could say was that Eliza had been spoken to by a woman, and had gone off with her. In another part of town, a signwriter had seen a brown-haired child walking toward the docks with a similar-sounding woman and a man. He described the woman as looking like a witch, with layer upon layer of ragged clothes. The man was thin-faced with a shaven head.

The search concentrated around the docks, and the worst was feared. Several shaven-headed sailors were dragged out of public houses, and a Swede who spoke no English was thrown onto the cobbles and beaten.

LITTLE ELIZA FOUND SAFE AND WELL
Discovered in Marketplace by the Night Watch
Mystery of the "Weeping Lady"

The second news clipping picked up the story a couple of days on. Eliza had been found by the late-night police patrol. She was wandering in the town's deserted marketplace at two o'clock in the morning. By this time, she'd become "Little Eliza" in print and in the public's imagination, and her fate was the subject of speculation in every backyard and taproom. The reporter's language was oblique, but Sebastian's reading of it was that she'd been found barefoot and without clothing.

Under the heading of ELIZA'S OWN STORY, the child's account was reported. Eliza, though eight years old and unschooled, appeared to speak with the kind of rhetorical flourish appropriate to the middle-aged editor of a provincial English newspaper.

A woman had stopped the two children by the gates of St. Joseph's Church. She knew Eliza's name. She said that she was a dressmaker, and Eliza's grandmother wanted her to have a new dress for the next Whitsun walks. Eliza would have to be measured. Her mother knew all about it, she said. Her sister was to return home. Both would get a penny for being good.

When she turned to go with the woman, Eliza saw that a man had moved in to stand behind her. The woman explained that he was a friend of her grandmother's. He showed her the pennies. They walked toward the docks and Eliza remembered passing the signwriter, who was lettering gold leaf onto the painted glass of a moneylender's window.

They took her to a place near the ships and up some stairs into a big dark room at the top of the building, where Eliza described being able to see the big timbers that held up the roof. A beautiful lady was waiting there.

This lady smiled at her and said that the man had two pennies, one for Eliza and the other for her sister. Eliza could have them when she'd tried her new dress on. She couldn't see any new dress. She didn't want to take her clothes off, but the woman who'd brought her changed her manner and spoke sharply, and she was frightened.

She did as she was told. Then the beautiful lady asked her if she would like to be clean. Eliza said that she *was* clean. Bath night was every Friday.

Something in what she said seemed to upset the lady. She stroked Eliza's hair, and would not look at her. She told the woman to give Eliza her clothes back.

Then it all turned ugly. The man grabbed the lady by the arm and drew her away. They started to argue in low voices, all three of them, and the beautiful lady began to cry. Nobody noticed Eliza creeping away. She got down to the next floor and, when she heard someone coming down the stairs, she hid under some sacks. It was the younger woman, the so-called beautiful lady. She hadn't entirely stopped crying, but now her face was all twisted and red. She carried a sharpened stick or a pike of some kind, and she went from room to room with it calling Eliza's name.

Eliza was too frightened to answer. She heard rats in the sacks around her. When the young woman was out of sight, she got out of the pile and hid behind a dresser instead.

The young woman came back. She heard the rats and mistook them for Eliza. She plunged the pike into the sacks, sobbing all the time, and kept on plunging it in until the man and the other woman came. They took the pike out of her hands. The shaven-headed man moved the sacks to look for a body, but found none. They gave up after that. When they led the young woman away, they had to hold her up.

Eliza waited for several hours, and then found her way out of the house and through the empty streets to the market.

An enthusiastic hunt for the three adults was now under way, the report said.

Sebastian returned the clippings to the place in the Bible where he'd found them. Something had clearly gone wrong. The child had never been meant to survive Louise Porter's attentions, much less be able to tell the tale and describe her to others. The Silent Man and his wife—not so mute, if she'd done all the talking—had set up the child's fate in a manner so heartless it was hard to imagine.

Louise had wavered, and had to be bullied into seeing it through. But once she got started, she quickly went out of control.

Sayers could idealize her all he wanted. But in Sebastian's eyes, she was only one act of cruelty away from becoming another James Caspar.

Sebastian took the *carte de visite* from the mirror. It had been much handled, but carefully preserved. It showed Louise Porter as Desdemona, with her name and the role and the address of the Baker Street photographic studio below the picture. The card was worn around the edges and nearly fifteen years out of date, but Sebastian doubted that she'd have allowed any image since.

He couldn't decide whether she looked disturbingly young, or disturbingly old. The world had changed considerably in the space of fifteen years, and a sepia photograph like this one had the feel of another era altogether. Anyone pictured from those times—babies, even—made him think of them only as those who'd passed by long before. How might she seem now? She'd be well into her thirties. Good Lord, she was practically an old woman!

Unless, of course, life mirrored the legend, and she had not changed in any appreciable way.

There was a knocking at the door. Sebastian quickly restored the fighter's possessions to their former order and went downstairs.

There on the doorstep stood Mr. Oakes from the office, a parcel of brown paper and string under his arm.

"Mister Bearce has been called to Chicago," the bookkeeper said. "He told me to deliver the office keys and tell you that he's left you in charge for tomorrow. I took the chance to bring you this." He showed the parcel.

"You got my message, then? Assuming that's what I think it is."

"I did and it is, sir. I've done everything you asked."

Sebastian ushered him in and led the way through to the kitchen, where he took a knife from the drawer.

"I hope it's the right one," Oakes said. "Everything else was either a uniform, or unfit for wear."

Every Pinkerton office kept a stock of disguises for its operatives. In truth, these days it was more a part of the romance of the company than a feature of its day-to-day running, but there were still occasions when an employee might need to pass as a streetcar conductor or a factory hand, and needed quick access to the clothes to play the part. Sebastian slid the knife under the string and cut through it, and then he unwrapped the parcel on the kitchen table.

When the bundle opened up, it revealed a pair of brogues sitting on a more-or-less neatly folded suit. The suit had belonged to a temporary named Epps, who'd been sent into a construction company as an undercover steamfitter to check on employee dishonesty. He'd been discovered and beaten, and had walked off the job and never returned. It must have been quite a beating to discourage him so; by his clothes, he was roughly the same size and build as Tom Sayers.

"These are fine, Mister Oakes," Sebastian said. He felt a little guilty. Oakes was going out of his way to please, and although Sebastian had promised to put in a good word about his work to the dreaded Mr. Bearce, he'd so far done nothing of the kind.

"I canvassed all the hotels as you asked." This was not quite the momentous task for the bookkeeper that it might have appeared. Most of the big hotels in the middle of town had telephones now. "There was a Mrs. Louise Caspar staying at the Walton, but she checked out almost two weeks ago."

Sebastian raised an eyebrow. The Walton on Broad Street was one of the city's highest-class hotels. Its outer appearance was that of a grand Bavarian palace. On the inside, the foyer alone was like the vault of a Renaissance prince. For the rest of it, he could only guess. Given his income, Sebastian was never likely to see any farther than the foyer.

He said, "Could they tell you where she went from there?"

"They'd love to know," Oakes said, and went on to explain that she'd left with her bill unpaid and no clue as to where they might find her. He'd talked to the doorman, the bell-hopper, and the housekeeping staff who'd serviced the room.

"Well done, Mister Oakes," Sebastian said.

"Thank you, sir."

"You're quite the detective."

"Now you're mocking me, sir," Oakes said. "But I'll let it pass."

THIRTY-ONE

ram Stoker sat at a strange desk in an unfamiliar office at London's Theatre Royal in Drury Lane, writing up the latest set of accounts for Irving's *Dante*. Although the Lyceum company was gone and Irving's tenancy at the Wellington Street theater was no more, Stoker had stayed on as one of the few remaining members of the actor's personal staff.

He could hear the sound of someone approaching down the corridor. A few moments later, Belmore, the assistant to Irving's long-serving stage manager, reached in and tapped on the open door to get Stoker's attention. When Stoker acknowledged him, Belmore came into the room and laid a small envelope on the desk.

"Beg pardon, Mister Stoker," he said. "Addressed to you and delivered by hand."

Stoker picked up the envelope. It was, indeed, addressed to him by name. He pinched it between his forefinger and thumb, as if assaying it for density and value.

"Another request for house seats, at a guess," he said. "Strange how people can be so generous with their praise for the guv'nor while balking at the cost of a ticket."

"Yes, sir."

Belmore went off, and Stoker opened the envelope and took out the note inside. It was not a request for free seats. Nor was it an appeal for him to approach Irving to make some public appearance—a common request, whose authors usually presumed that the actor would gratefully bear all expense and inconvenience for the honor of being asked. Instead of either, it was a note from Samuel Liddell Mathers.

Stoker hadn't seen Mathers in years. They'd met seldom after that night in the basement of the Horniman Museum with Tom Sayers, and not at all recently. He knew that the would-be mystic had landed a full-time job as assistant librarian at the museum, but he'd argued with the management and the job hadn't lasted. The last Stoker had heard of him, he was living in Paris. He'd added the name MacGregor to his own and had been seen bicycling through the French capital in full Highland regalia.

The request was for a few minutes of Stoker's time, at his own convenience. A boy would be waiting to take back his reply. Stoker quickly wrote a response across the bottom of the note, placed it into the neatly slit envelope, and had it taken down to the street.

When he was done with the figures, he locked his notebook away and reached for his hat. He needed to speak to the manager of the Criterion about the arrangements for that evening's *Dante* supper. It was an expense that he'd advised against, but Irving had insisted on it. Despite a mixed critical reception, *Dante* had to be made to succeed.

As usual, Stoker chose to walk rather than take the tram. From Drury Lane he cut through the Covent Garden market, so busy at dawn's first light, so dead by midafternoon. The gutters were strewn with spoiled fruit and leaves, and a small number of costers threw empty crates around. As Stoker walked down the curving lane of Long Acre past the furniture makers and coach builders that lined it, he reflected that making a success out of *Dante* would be no easy task. It was an enormous enterprise, with fifty players and more than a hundred nonspeaking spirits to people the circles of hell. It was also a mediocre play in thirteen interminable scenes. It was carried entirely by spectacle and what remained of Irving's drawing power; but here in the capital, even that power was no longer as great as it once had been.

When Irving had been knighted, some eight years before, the honor had seemed to confer some measure of permanence on that gilded age. In retrospect, it had actually marked the summit from which a descent would soon follow. A disastrous fire had consumed two decades' worth of scenery and properties in the railway arches at Southwark, wiping out the company's repertoire of productions and all the future income that would have flowed from them. Uninsured and in debt, Irving had signed control of the Lyceum over to a business syndicate. He was tiring. His health was beginning to fail. And yet, instead of being able to rest on his achievements, he now had to work to survive.

In Piccadilly, amid the white pillars and gilded mirrors of the Criterion's airy Byzantine dining rooms, Stoker went over the evening's arrangements with the restaurant manager. A few minor questions arose, and he was able to answer them all. When their business was done, Stoker took out his pocket watch and checked on the time. Then he thanked the manager and left the spacious grill room, descending a short flight of steps to emerge into Piccadilly Circus.

In the middle of the Circus stood the Shaftesbury Memorial, an ornate bronze fountain topped with a winged figure of Christian Charity. On the steps of its dais, with traffic all around him, Samuel Liddell Mathers waited.

He had not yet seen Stoker, and did not know from which direction he'd be approaching. This was as Stoker had intended. He wanted a moment in which to take a look at Mathers and assess the state of him.

He was, Stoker noted with some relief, dressed more or less normally. Too warmly for the weather, perhaps, in a thick coat that looked as heavy as a Persian carpet—and which might even have been cut from one, looking at it again—but nothing too embarrassing to be seen with.

He raised a hand to draw Mathers' attention, and having caught his eye he waited as the other man crossed through traffic to join him. They exchanged greetings, and then together they began to walk down Coventry Street in the direction of Leicester Square.

Stoker said, "How is Mina?" On closer inspection, Mathers' coat was almost threadbare. Mathers himself was quite gaunt inside it.

"She is well," Mathers said. "As am I."

"I have followed your progress."

"Then when you saw my note, you probably thought that I had come to visit London to ask you for money or patronage. Let me assure you that I have not."

"That's just as well," Stoker said. "The great days are gone, Mathers. The Lyceum company is no more. It pains me to say it, but the guv'nor is a lion at bay."

"If only you'd agreed to join us in those early years," Mathers said. "Then, who knows. The outcome might have been different for both of us."

But Stoker was having none of that. "You mean that together we could have magicked away misfortune?" he said. "Be serious, man. I had no inclination to involve myself with the members of any order. Let alone one whose life is a constant squabble over what to call themselves and how to organize. If it's not money and it's no other form of support, then what *do* you need?"

Mathers looked down at the pavement. "Crowley has betrayed me," he said darkly.

"That's exactly the kind of behavior I mean," Stoker said. Alick Crowley, or "Aleister" as he now styled himself, had gained some no-toriety in London circles before traveling out to Paris to join Mathers as a pupil.

Mathers said, "I sent an astral vampire to bring him down. He struck back at me with Beelzebub and an army of demons."

To Stoker, it was as if the traffic around them slowed into silence and all of the color drained out of the world. He stopped, and Mathers stopped with him. Stoker turned to look more closely at the other man.

Mathers was manifestly serious in what he was saying. But his eyes were dark-ringed, small, sunk back in his head as if by madness or mal-nutrition. They glittered, but not in the manner of a man filled with energy. More in the way of a man adrift. They were the too-bright eyes of a helpless stranger, far out of reach.

"An astral vampire," Stoker said.

"We battle with magic."

And he clearly believed it, too. Stoker looked at him. Mathers was not exactly a close friend, but Stoker had known him well and for many years. His manner now was dogged, earnest, entirely sincere. It was a heartbreaking sight to behold.

Stoker said, "How do you imagine I can help you, Mathers?"

"Don't do this," Mathers warned. "Don't pretend you don't believe. I have read your book." He reached inside the big coat and, from some capacious inner pocket, half produced a novel in yellow cloth binding so that just its corner showed. "They dismiss it as a shocker," he said. "But I know how close it is to the truth."

"*Dracula* is a fiction," Stoker said.

"Every fiction has its original," Mathers said, unwittingly echoing another novelist's assertion in the British Museum's reading room all those years before. "You tracked down the Wanderer. You found him. Don't try to deny it." He indicated the book. "This adventure you tell . . . it's a shadow play of what you really saw. Where is he now?"

"Who?"

"The Wanderer. The real one. I have a proposition for him."

"Don't," Stoker said. "Do not ask me this. Please."

"I helped you once, Bram. Perhaps I even helped you more than you can know. Did you think your good fortunes were all your own?"

Strange that Mathers should speak of his good fortunes, when in Stoker's own eyes so many of his hopes had fallen short of the mark. He'd thrown over his life for Irving, and imagined himself to be one of the great man's closest confidants; and yet when Irving had sold out the Lyceum to the syndicate, he'd told Stoker nothing of it until after the deal was done. And the work in which he'd invested all of his hopes of a serious literary reputation—Mathers was right, they called it a shocker, well done of its kind but with little of lasting merit, while his publishers had given it their shoddiest binding and done almost nothing to promote it to the public.

Even Irving, whose opinion mattered more to him than anyone's, thought it dreadful. If there was proof that Stoker's life was not enhanced by any magic, then there it lay.

He said, "Life has treated me well enough. I might have appreciated better. But I've never wished for anything more than I've deserved."

"Won't you help me, Bram?" Mathers pleaded.

Stoker drew in a deep breath, let it out, and looked down.

Then he said, "Call by the stage door at eight, when the curtain's gone up. I'll have something for you then."

He left Mathers in Leicester Square and walked back toward Drury Lane. He was fairly sure that he knew why Mathers wanted confirmation that there was a reality behind the Wanderer, and why he wanted to know where the current bearer of the title might be found. Mathers was a disappointed man, his life all but in ruins. He was unemployed, and probably unemployable. He and his wife had been living in near poverty in Paris. The organization that he'd helped to found had cast him out. His protégé was now his enemy. His reaction was the natural response of a desperate man: Only allow me the opportunity, and I will pay any price for the chance to turn my life around.

Any price. For in a position like his, it must seem that he had nothing at all to lose. What would it cost you to give up your soul, if your soul was a dead thing already?

Now Stoker was on Drury Lane, and across the road stood the Theatre Royal. It was no Lyceum, that was for sure. It had a big stage and good seating capacity, but on the outside its proportions were clumsy and lacking in symmetry or magnificence.

Back in that unfamiliar office, he returned his hat to the hook and settled again behind the desk. He'd have no time at home today. There was still much to do before the evening's performance. Irving planned to lead with *Dante* on his eighth American tour, and he had asked Stoker to prepare abstracts from the better notices for cabling ahead.

But first, Stoker drew out a blank sheet of notepaper and took up his pen.

My dear friend, he wrote. *If you would place so much faith in my word, be advised by me now. Forget these notions. Nothing you might find would be as you imagine. May your God go with you. Bram.*

He put five pounds in with the letter, and sealed both into a new envelope. He wrote Mathers' name on the front and took it down to the stage door, where he placed it in the care of the doorkeeper to await collection. He left instructions that Mathers was not to be admitted to the building, nor was Stoker to be sent for even if Mathers demanded it. If he should refuse to leave, the police were to be summoned.

It felt like a cowardly act. Whatever human flaws and frailties he might have possessed, cowardice had no part in Stoker's nature. But he could see no other way. At best he'd have to play the unhelpful brute, the treacherous friend. At worst, he might give in and tell Mathers what he wanted to know.

That would be, in its strongest sense, unforgivable.

He went back to his borrowed office, where he turned his attention to American tour dates.

THIRTY-TWO

n his suite of rooms on a second-floor corner of Murphy's Hotel, the young man known as Jules Patenotre was contemplating his shoes. He had them all out in a line, and was trying to decide which pair to wear today. All had been burnished until the leather shone. Not by his own hand, of course. Twice a week he had the houseboy come up and shine them while he watched. Watching the houseboy distracted his mind. Jules Patenotre's mind had a tendency to race and, if he did not take care to guide it, to seek out unexpected torments with which to entertain him.

Hotel living suited him, though. His needs were taken care of at the ring of a bell, and he was relieved of any need to keep a personal staff. He'd occupied these rooms for more than two years, ever since the Jefferson fire had destroyed his lodgings—and all his old shoes—there. No one had died, but the place had been gutted. They were rebuilding the Jefferson now. If this place should happen to burn down, he might move back in there.

When a knock came at the door, he made a quick decision and stepped into a pair of English Oxfords. He left the rest for the maid to deal with. By now, he'd have expected the visitor to have entered on a passkey. They had not, which suggested that it was someone other than hotel staff. He was expecting no one. This was awkward—one of the drawbacks of having no valet or manservant to deal with intrusion. He went to open the door himself.

A man stood there in the hotel corridor, his hat in his hands. He had a Slavic look to him. His head was shaven close, the gray stubble showing.

"Well?" Jules said after waiting for a few moments. "You knocked at my door. Do you intend to speak?"

"Sir," the man said, and seemed to stop there. Jules studied him for a moment, and then recognized him.

"You're Mary D'Alroy's man," Jules prompted. "I saw you at the Academy of Music."

"I am sent to inform you."

Again, Jules waited. "Of what?" he said.

"Miss D'Alroy—"

"Is a wonderful employer? That's very loyal of you."

He tried again. "Miss D'Alroy—"

"Has been discovered having carnal knowledge of an ape?" At that, Jules saw the man blush. "Forgive me," he said. "Go on."

"Miss D'Alroy told me to tell you. She offers that which you were seeking to collect."

"Ah," Jules said. He glanced to left and right, to see if they could be overheard. It would seem not. Without a hint of a smile and in a slightly lower voice he said, "And what must I do to collect it, then?"

"That I cannot say. But if you will follow me, I will take you to her."

"Oh. A jaunt. Do I need to bring money? Or is Miss D'Alroy a philanthropist today?"

"Any gift you care to make would be welcome. But mainly you would be obliging the lady."

"I'll bring money, then. Just in case she likes her obligations in hard cash."

The man dipped his head in a kind of subservient affirmation.

Jules found the pleasure of mockery growing very thin. The man was doing his best. Jules said, "You find this difficult, don't you? Do you disapprove of your mistress?"

The man said nothing.

"We all have to do things we do not care for," Jules said. "Sometimes due to circumstance. And sometimes when our nature demands it. But take heart from my example. If a shame remains a secret . . . then in what sense is it a shame? Wait there." He pointed to a chair that stood with a side table and a jug of fresh flowers on the other side of the corridor. "Sit if you want to."

The man was still standing when Jules emerged, fifteen minutes later, fully dressed and ready to go. As they descended the stairway to the foyer, Jules said, "Walk on ahead of me and wait for me outside. When you see me coming out of the hotel, set off and don't look back. I'll be there behind you."

They arrived in the foyer as strangers. The silent one was on his way out of the main doors as Jules approached the counter.

The clerk said, "Good morning, Mister Patenotre."

"Good morning, Charles," Jules said. "I need my box."

"Of course, sir."

The clerk reached under the counter and brought out the security ledger for him to sign. Once that was done, he handed over a key on a large ring.

Jules took the key around to the strong room near the counter where the guest boxes were. It was small, but gave privacy to residents so they could access their valuables without having them on public display. In the room was a bank of metal doors, each with two locks. The guest's key operated one of these but no thief could use it without also signing out the hotel's master, which opened the other. Jules turned both keys, swung open the door, and pulled out the long, shallow tray behind it. The room was reckoned to be proof against fire, and Jules preferred it to any bank. A bank expected you to keep to its hours; he was happier in a place that respected his own.

As he counted out some bills, he found that his vision was blurring and his hands trembling slightly. He stopped, until this settled. It was only anticipation, he knew, but he was annoyed at himself. His body was a rebellious servant, and often it disgusted him.

He dropped the house key off at the desk and went out into the street. The man sent by Mary d'Alroy was standing some way along the street, by a store window under a striped canvas awning. He saw Jules nod to him as he was approaching. When he turned and moved off, Jules followed.

The man walked for more than a mile. The sidewalks were busy until they turned north of Broad Street, into the area where most of the saloons were. These streets were almost deserted. It was too early in the day for most Richmond men to be out drinking, while no decent Richmond lady would want to be seen around here at all. In their gored skirts and leg-of-mutton sleeves, with parasols to shade them from the sun and preserve their unpainted, pale-and-interesting complexions, Richmond women tended toward lives of classic southern propriety.

On the face of it, at least.

They turned into a street where every building had been boarded and marked for demolition. One of the railroad companies buying up the land, at a guess. They'd already built a new terminus on Main Street, and the development wasn't going to stop there. These were mostly low-rise warehouse and office buildings but across the end of the street, its box office gutted and its marquee stripped to the bones, there stood the dead shell of a variety theater.

They entered it down a rubbish-strewn alleyway to the side, and the shaven-headed man secured the door after them. As far as Jules could see, the interior had been stripped of most of its fittings and anything else of value, but was dry and intact. At the back of the empty auditorium, they ascended to a suite of offices above the foyer. Here there was a wide lounge with an empty fireplace. As they entered it, a woman—Mary D'Alroy's other servant—rose to her feet. A moment later, Mary D'Alroy herself appeared in one of the doorways.

She was dressed in a plain off-white linen shift. Her hair was up and her arms were uncovered. She looked as if she ought to be barefoot on a riverbank somewhere, rather than walking the board floors of this ruin in the middle of a great southern city.

"You'd better come in," she said, and turned away. He followed her into the room.

"Close the door," she said.

He did as instructed, looking all around. There was a smell of old dust and horsehair. Light came from a skylight above, and through gaps in the thick boards that had been nailed across the windows. There was a mattress over in the corner, raised up a few inches from the floor on a wooden pallet. Alongside that were a chair, a table that didn't match the chair, and a water jug and basin on the table.

Knowing a squat when he saw one, Jules said, "I see now why you keep your address private."

The woman who called herself Mary D'Alroy ignored the comment. She said, "Before we begin, there's something you have to do for me."

Her tone began to stir something in him.

"Command me," he said.

"*Before* we begin," she corrected him. "Pen and paper. Over there on the table."

He moved to the table and saw that she'd laid out some sheets of good writing paper and a self-filling pen.

She said, "You keep a suite of rooms at Murphy's. I imagine your standing with them must be good."

"You want a letter of recommendation."

"I want to move to somewhere better than this. But hotel managers are a suspicious crew."

"Miss D'Alroy, you could charm a dog off of a butcher's wagon. I can't imagine the manager who'd turn you away."

"Write me the letter," she said. "Then we can discuss what you're here for."

He drew up the chair, sat himself down, picked up the pen, and then thought for a few moments before starting to write. After dating the note, he wrote quickly and without hesitation. When it was done, he picked up the paper and read it aloud.

"To whom it may concern. Please extend every courtesy to Miss

Mary D'Alroy during her time of residence. She is a personal friend of the Patenotre family, formerly of Iberville, Louisiana."

"Signed?"

"If you're happy with the wording." He added his signature in full. Then she took it from him and read it for herself.

"This is very impressive," she said. "And I have to say I'm honored. The entire Patenotre family?"

He made a wide gesture. "You're looking at them," he said.

"No other relatives survive?"

"Once upon a time we were one of the biggest plantation families on the Mississippi. Two hundred slaves and three thousand acres. After the war—slaves all freed, the crops on fire, and just widders and children left to watch 'em burn. I'm the last of the line. Well, I had two choices. I could spend my days in debt like my daddy, trying to hold together something that won't be held. Or I could do what I did. Which was to sell off whatever I could, borrow against the rest, and start spending the last of the fortune. When it's gone it's gone, and so are we all."

"That's a sad story."

"You should hear it with a violin."

He was still on the chair and she was standing close beside him. As she leaned over to slide the letter under a green book, she brushed against his shoulder. There was no mistaking that she was naked under the shift. In an instant, it was as if every fine hair on his skin was alive and bristling with static.

She said, "It must be very hard to carry the disappointments of all those generations on one set of shoulders. Stand up." He stood, the chair scraping back on the boards. "Does it help if you harm yourself?"

"It calms me down," he admitted.

"Let me see."

He hesitated for a moment. Then he took off his jacket and vest, and put both on the chair behind him. He pulled the links from his cuffs and the stud from his collar and unbuttoned his shirt. He dropped the suspenders that held up his pants and then pulled shirt and singlet together over his head.

He stood with his hands down by his sides, not meeting her eyes, knowing that she was studying him, sensing her gaze like the track of a burning glass across his skin. She was looking at his scars. Some of them were fresh, and not yet healed.

"I got more than this down below," he said.

"Show me."

"Please," he said. "Lock the door first."

There was no key, but the door had a bolt. By the time that she'd crossed the room, slid the bolt, and turned around to face him again, he was stripped to the skin from his head to his socks.

"Are you cold?" she said.

"No," he said. He was shivering, but he was not cold.

She came back and walked all the way around him, giving him a close inspection. It was almost as if she was taking an inventory of every mark and scar, noting every object, sharp and otherwise, that he'd managed to shove under his skin and which remained lodged there. He was no Adonis, but he was hard-muscled and thin. She couldn't miss the physical evidence of his anticipation.

He said, "How did you spy me out?"

From behind him, she said, "Like always seems to know like. Who can say what the signals are?"

"That won't explain it. My instincts aren't always good. I paid a woman in Iberville to horsewhip me. When we got to it, she said it was a disgusting thing to ask a Christian woman to do. She was one of the reasons I had to leave town."

"Only one of the reasons?"

"The main one."

She stopped and ran a fingertip lightly along a weal that crossed his belly, just above the pubic bone.

"And now you're here," she said. "Risking it all again. Is it the pain or the danger that you most enjoy?"

"You are nothing like her," he said. "I do not believe you would expose me."

"But I am a Christian woman, too. Do you think you deserve me?"

"I'll be damned if I do," he said.

"Very good," she said, and then turned serious again. "How would you like to feel clean?" she said. "Really clean for the first time in your life? How would you like to feel cleaner than you've ever felt before? That's something I can do for you. Kneel."

It took him a moment to realize that she'd instructed him. He knelt. She went over to the mattress and, with her back to him, drew off the shift in one single flowing motion. The body that she uncovered was long, lean, and rounded in its contours, pale and flawless, as white and smooth as newly worked marble. She folded up the shift and leaned over to put it in a safe place. She was not undressing for erotic effect. She was stripping for work.

She turned to him. She had the body of an alabaster Venus, toned and taut and entirely without blemish. His chest tightened so that he was hardly breathing.

"You need to know something," she said. "You should understand that this next hour will spoil you for all others. Perhaps even for all time. You can back out now before it's too late."

"No," he said, and the sound almost didn't come out.

"Very well, then," she said, and she turned away again for a moment and picked up something that had been lying out of sight alongside the low bed.

"You wanted to pay me for a kiss?" she said. "Then kiss this."

She walked across the room toward him.

hen Sayers returned from the barber and the bath-
house, Sebastian was immediately struck by the
change in his appearance. Even though the prize-
fighter's hair had been cropped so close for the ring that there was little to
be done to improve the look of it, a good shave and a sharpening up of the
sideburns had begun the effect. As it grew out, he would no doubt begin
to look even less of a crop-headed bruiser and more of a human being.

And not only that. The puffiness had left his features, and those cuts
were already starting to heal. Sebastian hadn't realized it at the time, but
when they'd met back at the boxing tent, the fighter had been in a steady
alcohol-sustained haze. Not drunk, but in the functioning state of the
habitual drinker.

Without its influence, he'd become more alert. His eye had cleared,
his hand was steady, and he didn't shamble anymore. He'd touched no
liquor since entering their house, and if he was suffering for it, he kept
that to himself. All in all, it was as if some new sense of purpose had
occasioned a return of the Tom Sayers of old.

Sebastian relayed everything that the bookkeeper had told him.

"She skipped without paying her bill," he said. "Oakes made a point
of mentioning the Pinkerton name, and the hotel people put him onto
the house detective. From what he'd been able to establish, she sent her
two servants to take her bags out of the back of the hotel while she was

walking out of the front door like it was just another day. The doorman remembered asking her if she wanted a cab, but she didn't."

Sayers, clearly no stranger to Louise's operating methods, said, "A hotel doorman knows all the cabmen. It would have made it too easy to track down the driver and find out what her destination was."

"But the hotel *did* locate the carrier who picked up her baggage from around the back. He had to deliver it to the waterfront for loading onto a steamer bound for Richmond. That's where the trail went cold. There was no Mrs. Caspar on any passenger list for that day or the next."

Sayers strode up and down. He ran his hand across the stubble on his head.

"Richmond," he said. "I've been this close and she's evaded me before. But never with such a strong lead to follow."

"I suppose you'll go after her," Sebastian said.

"I suppose I will," Sayers said. "But not blindly. I'll need to make a plan. Don't worry, Sebastian. You won't have to put up with me for very much longer."

When they heard Elisabeth and Frances returning with the boy, Sayers waited to offer a greeting. Then he picked up the parcel with his new clothes and went to his room, leaving the family to its family business.

If Elisabeth noted the improvement in Sayers' appearance, she gave no sign of it. She had other things on her mind. From the moment that she came in through the door, Sebastian could see that the afternoon had not gone well.

Her face was set. Frances was fussing around nervously, as if in the presence of some unstable device. In a quiet voice, Elisabeth sent Robert to the sitting room at the back of the house. He raced on up, and Frances took the opportunity to follow. Sebastian noted that the boy was carrying five new dime magazines.

"What did the doctor say?" Sebastian asked, rather dreading the answer.

"He offered Robert a place to live among the insane," she said, and then her fury boiled over. "He is not insane!" she said. "Nor is he handicapped or retarded! Why can none of them see it? I don't *want* him taken away. I just want him to have a normal life. All the pieces of a normal life are there. All he needs is someone to help him put them together."

She would have said more, but the creak of a board reminded her that there was a stranger in the house. Sayers was pacing again, making his plans.

Elisabeth made a gesture of exasperation, then turned away.

In a low voice, Sebastian said, "At least Sayers will be gone by tomorrow. With the news I just gave him, he'll need no urging."

It was poor compensation, but it was all that he could offer.

"Mister Sayers is our guest," Elisabeth said. "Tell him that he can stay as long as he likes. I wouldn't wish to embarrass him."

Supper was a subdued affair. Robert was excused early, but he stayed at the table, reading, his surroundings forgotten, away in the unknowable country of his unique imagination. For once, Elisabeth allowed it.

For his part, Sayers said very little. His mind seemed largely to be elsewhere, as well.

Later that night, when everyone had retired and the house was secured, Sebastian made his way up to bed and saw that a light was still showing under Sayers' door.

He lay alongside Elisabeth, knowing that she wasn't asleep.

Eventually, she said, "What are we to do for him, Sebastian?"

"Keep him happy. Keep looking."

"What about London?"

"Perhaps. Eventually."

It was all he could think of to say.

When Sebastian went downstairs the next morning, Frances was already in the kitchen. Robert was at the breakfast table but still in his nightshirt, bare feet swinging from his chair. He'd read all his new stories and was reading them again.

Frances said, "Has Mister Sayers left us already?"

"Has he?" said Sebastian. "I don't think he has."

"The door was off the latch and his outdoor coat is gone."

Sebastian went to Sayers' room and tapped on the door. After a few moments with no reply, he looked inside.

The prizefighter's cabin trunk was still there, but it was in the middle of the floor and all closed up. The dresser had been cleared of his personal items and the bed had been stripped, with the linen neatly folded at its end.

There was a sheet of writing paper on top of the upended cabin trunk. On it in large capitals were the words TO BE SENT FOR and under that *Sincere thanks for all your kindness, may God bless you all. Try not to think ill of me. That which I do is on my head alone.*

He must have been gone before the dawn. And he must have been pretty quiet about it, too, because the house was small and its walls were not thick. He'd probably carried his boots to the front door in order not to make a noise on the stairs.

Well, that was that. Sebastian returned to the kitchen.

"Looks like you'll be getting your room back, Frances," he said. "I'll put Mister Sayers' trunk down in the cellar until he sends for it."

"Oh," Frances said. But she hardly seemed happy at the prospect of a house with no Tom Sayers in it.

Elisabeth came in then, and Sebastian gave her the news.

"Richmond?" she said. "What does he expect to find in Richmond?"

"The Madonna or the Medusa," Sebastian said cryptically, "depending on the woman's mood. Let's not speak of it."

He declined breakfast. He'd pick up something from the Automat. He needed to get to the office before everyone else; Bearce had gone to Chicago and left Sebastian in charge of the keys.

"Is this a form of promotion?"

"More of a chore," he said. But she was right. It showed a new level of confidence from Sebastian's employers. The night janitor was responsible for opening up the main doors of the building, but the key holder was responsible for the office suite. Store cupboards, records, stationery . . . even the safe where the business accounts and the more confidential records were kept.

He buttoned his waistcoat, put on his topcoat, and went to his bureau. When he rolled back the top, the keys weren't there.

He moved a few things around. Opened one or two of the drawers. But he knew where he'd left them. No one else in the house ever used the bureau. Robert knew not to touch his father's papers, not to mention the Bulldog revolver that he sometimes left in the locked bottom drawer.

"What are you looking for?" Elisabeth called through.

"Nothing," he called back.

There seemed only one likely explanation, and he didn't like to countenance it. Sayers had needed writing paper for his note. Here was where he'd look.

That which I do is on my head alone, he'd then written.

Sebastian rolled down the top with greater force than he'd intended, and set out for the journey into town.

THIRTY-FOUR

When Sebastian got to the Chestnut Street building, it was open but still largely silent.

He climbed the stairs to the Pinkerton agency suite. If the key holder was delayed, the employees had to wait out in the corridor. If he didn't show at all, they'd have to fetch the building supervisor with his duplicates.

A key holder with no keys . . . well, that was something the system wasn't set up for.

No one was waiting outside yet. The door had an etched glass panel with the agency's name lettered on it. Sebastian stopped before it and listened, but heard nothing. Then he tried the door. It wasn't supposed to be unlocked. But it opened.

He stepped inside. "Sayers?" he called out, but something in the way his voice echoed through the rooms told him that he wasn't going to find anyone. No presence, no warm body anywhere. He'd hoped to catch Sayers here, but the man had already been and gone.

Sebastian went straight to the criminal department and the records room. Another door that should have been locked, but wasn't. The cabinets with all the records in them should have been locked as well, but they weren't.

Sure enough, there were gaps where some of the cards and some entire files were missing. The one on the man with the needles in his belly, for a start. Without a list, it was hard to say for sure what might have been taken.

At that point, Sebastian heard voices. As he emerged from the records office, two stenographers were passing through on the way to their room at the end of the hall. They were chatting animatedly, as awake and alert as a couple of sparrows. As far as they were concerned, the office had been opened up for them as normal. They broke off to bid Sebastian good morning and then carried on with scarcely a break.

"Good morning," he belatedly called after them. Even the stenography room was open. Sayers must have been right through the place.

When Sebastian reached his desk, he found his missing keys lying there, right next to the wooden bar with his name on it. With a guilty glance around, he opened the top drawer and swept them out of sight. Only when he'd closed the drawer did his heart stop pounding and the tightness in his chest begin to ease.

The loss of a few inactive files—that wasn't so bad. If Sayers had asked him for them, the answer would have been no—although, in truth, they were unlikely to be missed. Old files reached the end of their useful lives, just like old employees.

If that was all Sayers had taken, then the loss would be of no real significance. It was wrong, and it made Sebastian angry; he'd welcomed Sayers into his home, and now his hospitality had been abused. But the actual damage was small.

Never trust a drunk, or a man obsessed, he thought to himself. Plausible though he seemed, Sayers was both.

As more people arrived, Sebastian pulled out his chair, took a deep breath, and reached for the first of the papers that had begun to fill up his in-tray during his time out of the office. His initial panic aside, this was not quite the day of disaster it had threatened to be.

Awaiting his attention were some letters from potential clients that merited only standard replies. There was a cable for some information from an operative out in California. There was Oakes' claim for reimbursement for his tram fare yesterday. That would have to wait; only

Mr. Bearce could give authority for a payment from the office's petty cash reserve.

Sebastian went very still. Then he got to his feet.

He went into Bearce's empty office and around the manager's desk to the safe. It was a mighty cabinet of iron and brass, older than the building it stood in. It took the largest of the keys, and when the door swung open, it did so with the mass of a Babylonian gate.

"He took it," Sebastian said bleakly. "The cashbox was empty. The entire office cash reserve, including the money we keep to pay informers."

Elisabeth said, "Do you know how much?"

"Twelve hundred dollars and some change. Bearce keeps the record in a separate ledger so the informers' names won't get out."

Twelve hundred dollars. A dismayed silence prevailed as they considered the implications of Sayers' theft.

They were sitting on Frances' bed. After spending most of the day looking for some trace of Sayers at the railway terminus and asking around all the steamer offices in town, Sebastian had returned home and gone straight to his sister-in-law's room. There he'd broken into the prizefighter's cabin trunk and searched through it in the hope of finding some clue to the man's plans. After managing to stay calm for several hours, he now grew steadily more frantic.

He couldn't be sure at what point Elisabeth appeared in the doorway. He only knew that she'd been watching him for a while before she moved in beside him and interceded with a gentle hand, stopping his efforts and insisting on being told what was wrong.

"Your trust was betrayed," Elisabeth now said.

"I doubt that he even considered that," Sebastian said. "His obsession is his entire horizon."

"How long before the loss is discovered?"

"Two days. Three at the most."

"Maybe someone could have seen Sayers going in?"

"That isn't the point," Sebastian said. "I'll still be held responsible."

Twelve hundred dollars. In Tom Sayers' mind he'd have been taking the money from the agency, with no thought of any consequence to his host. But when Bearce returned and the money was found to be missing, Sebastian would be called to account for it. Blaming Sayers would not help him.

He looked down at the books and clothing that he'd strewn all over the floor. Nothing here was of any help. "I don't know what to do," he said.

Elisabeth said, "We have almost eight hundred dollars saved. And we've the certificates in my name from before we were married—they're worth about two hundred now. We can cash them in or I can borrow against them."

"To do what?"

"To replace what's missing before anyone else finds out about it."

"That's no solution, Elisabeth," Sebastian said. "That money's our future."

"If you lose your job and reputation," Elisabeth said, "we *have* no future. Take our savings, replace the money in the safe, and then go after Sayers and get back what he took. He's only been gone a few hours, and you know he's gone to Richmond. I know you can find him. He stole from the Pinkertons. How bright can he be?"

"It won't work," Sebastian said. "We can't raise enough."

"There's Frances. I know she has some money stashed away. I'll talk to her about it."

"No," Sebastian said helplessly, and put his head in his hands.

It *was* a disaster. How had it come to this, and in a matter of only hours? In his heart, he cursed Tom Sayers and he cursed the moment in which he'd turned around and gone back into the boxing booth, when he could so easily have walked away. Twelve hundred dollars was more than he'd earned in the past year. The sum was no great fortune to a business, but it was the kind of money that could make or break a family.

And now Frances was to be asked to pitch in. He knew why she put money away from the tiny allowance they were able to give her. Although she'd no beau and no immediate prospect of one, she was saving for her wedding.

Sebastian knew the worth of what he had. He'd endured a cold upbringing and a loveless youth, and he took none of his present happiness for granted. He'd once been ambitious, and sought success. Now his life was modest, ordinary, and filled with small pleasures—a less spectacular prize, but one he valued more.

Elisabeth said, "Everyone in this house depends on you. And God bless you, Sebastian, you've built a decent life for all of us. Let us support you now, or everything that you've worked so hard for will go for nothing."

She made him look at her.

"Get it back, Sebastian," she said. "Follow him. Tell them whatever you have to tell them and do whatever you have to do."

THIRTY-FIVE

om Sayers traveled by the Pennsylvania Railroad to Washington, and changed there for the Richmond train. The southbound service had three coaches, a diner, four Pullman carriages, and two baggage cars. For a while Sayers mostly wandered, restlessly, up and down the aisles. In his coach were a couple of families and a group of seven or eight men of business. The men all seemed to know each other, and were passing the journey by playing cards and talking politics. They wore middling-good suits and talked too loudly.

Outside, farmland gave way to wooded Virginia countryside. Sayers could see that his wandering was making the porters nervous. So he sat for half an hour, and fidgeted instead. When an attendant came through announcing lunch, he went along to the dining car, took a table, and ordered a steak. He could afford to live decently, at least for now. Dead broke and being punched daily for a living was no way to keep himself presentable for Louise. With each day that went by, he felt less like a dispirited slugger and more like the Tom Sayers of old.

He wondered if the Pinkertons had discovered their loss yet. Sebastian would be mad at him, for sure.

On the arrival of the plate, he found himself looking down at the food without much enthusiasm.

In a way, it was easier to keep on yearning for one's goal than to be taking such a definite step toward it. Day-to-day life could continue, and the goal remained a safe and distant dream. There'd be none of the uncertainty that he felt now; none of the fear that he might make a wrong move or a bad decision, and so wreck his hopes forever.

He glanced out of the window. They were on a trestle bridge passing over a wide, slow river. A flock of birds took off from the water as the train went by.

One thought sustained him. It was of that night back at Maskelyne's, when Louise had looked down from the stage and told him to forget her. She'd finally come to understand the truth of him. If only he could now make her see the truth about herself.

She was not lost. He couldn't believe that. Abused, manipulated, misled . . . all of these things. But never fit to be damned. All of the evidence so far suggested that her steps toward hell were no more than consensual games of harm, enactments of evil without the guts of evil in them. Charged with inflicting pain, she sought out those whom pain would make happy.

That might change, of course; the incident with the child in Yarmouth had pointed to a much darker prospect. Only sheer luck had kept the child alive that night. Louise might have taken on the role of the Wanderer and shaped it to suit herself, but she moved forward with the guidance and coaching of the Silent Man and his equally taciturn wife. They served Wanderers, not impostors. They would waste no opportunity to propel her ever closer to the edge and, if the chance came, to tip her over it.

Louise was not pure. But who was?

Sayers picked up his knife and cut into his steak. For a man with no appetite, he went at it pretty well from then on.

The train got into Richmond early in the evening, crossing the James River within sight of the old Tredegar Iron Works and entering Main

Street Station in a great cloud of venting steam. Sayers climbed down from the coach with his one small piece of luggage, then made his way toward the station building and the street. The building was recent, and towered above the elevated tracks like a brick château. Down below, horse cabs were lined up waiting for passengers.

Where to begin? He knew little of Richmond. Only that the city had been extensively reconstructed over the past few decades and, like the station, was mostly new; and that much of the new, like the great Monument Avenue, spoke of an obsession with what had been lost. The former capital of the Confederacy had been put to the torch when its troops had evacuated before the Union advance.

He first needed somewhere to stay. On Main Street, he began looking out for playbills. If he could find his way to the theater district, he could locate the watering holes that served it. Not those where audiences dined or drank, but the quieter ones where show people gathered. Sayers could usually spot a performers' haunt over a place that served the general public by instinct alone.

In any of those he'd be on his own territory, and could strike up a conversation with some stagehand or between-shows vaudevillian. He could learn where the cheapest digs were to be found and how the local scene was set. He might even get to hear something of Louise; a recent arrival herself, she'd be working just as hard to make her way—although not, he was sure, in exactly the same circles as he.

His inquiries took him to Broad Street and into the alleyways running off it. One promising-looking saloon became even more promising when he spied a couple of musicians walking out, wearing street coats over their pit clothes. It was an insignificant doorway in an unappealing spot, likely to be bypassed by anyone with no good reason to seek it out.

Once inside, Sayers faltered. Something wasn't right. This room was occupied by both white folks and Negroes, drinking peaceably side by side. His understanding was that the war had freed the slaves but that the races were still kept apart. Was Richmond's backstage world a common ground, where no segregation existed?

Then he realized that, of course, it was nothing of the kind.

Sayers stopped by one of the tables. "Excuse me," he said. "Would you be the Black Patti Troubadours?"

The seated man in blackface shook his head. "The Al Fields Minstrels," he said.

Sayers made his way to the bar. The bar was elaborately carved, with a spittoon by every footrail bracket. Before it stood a black waiter in a spotless white shirt, waistcoat, and floor-length apron, leaning on the brass handrail and talking to the bartender. As Sayers approached, the bartender finished the conversation and the waiter moved off to look for orders and pick up empties.

Sayers set his bag down alongside a bar stool and ordered beer. It came in a heavy crystal glass. He took one sip and then returned the glass to the bar.

He needed to take more care. It was as if that one sip had opened a door before him. Beer always led to a whiskey chaser and one whiskey chaser always led to another. They were the first notes in an extended melody that, once begun, would tease him onward and onward and would likely end with him facedown in the alley outside.

Once, moderation had been an option. No more. Now it seemed that his only options were total abstinence, or its equally extreme alternative.

He turned from the bar and looked at the room. His attention was drawn to a woman in one of the back-wall booths. She hadn't been alone when he'd walked in, but she was alone now. The sight of an unaccompanied woman was unusual in itself, but she was also the worse for liquor.

Sayers' guess was that she was an unsteady whore, here to work the crowd. The waiter seemed to think so, too, and stopped to engage with her. She started shaking her head. The waiter looked up and caught the white bartender's eye. The barman came out from behind his bar, and the waiter stood back while the bartender went about the noisy business of throwing the woman out. Those all around either ignored the scene, or did their best to pretend to.

Sayers studied the floor until the waiter and the barman came in from the alley, dusting off their hands. The waiter took a call from a nearby table and the barman returned to his station. Sayers saw the man eyeing his barely touched glass, and he beckoned him over.

"Something wrong with the beer?" the man said as he moved closer.

"Nothing at all," Sayers said. "Excuse me if I speak out of line, sir, but I'm glad to see you run a decent house here."

"And I'm happy to know it's appreciated," the barman said.

"Be assured that it is," Sayers said. "With all those playhouses just around the corner, I imagine you get quite a lot of the theater crowd."

"Some," the barman conceded.

"I'm in that line myself," Sayers said. "Looking for a place to stay with clean sheets and a management that doesn't fret or show too much interest in the hours a man keeps. Would you know of such a place?"

"I might," the bartender said. "Is one beer all you plan to buy?"

"Give me a whiskey chaser," Sayers said, "and pour one for yourself."

When the whiskeys were paid for, the barman reached under the counter and then slid a printed card across to Sayers.

Sayers tilted it to catch the light, then read it. The card advertised a small guesthouse with reasonable rates. Theatricals especially welcome. Sayers then said, "Thank you," and slid down from the bar stool. He picked up his bag.

"What about the drinks?"

"Both for you," Sayers said, and walked out.

In the alley beside the saloon, Sayers' first sight as he came out of the doors was of the ejected whore. She had fallen down, and could not get up. She could be seen from the end of the alley, but no one passing had felt moved to walk in and help her. Sayers went over. He lifted her to her feet, and guided her to where some crates were stacked against the opposite wall. Three of them came up at just the right height to make

her a seat. The empty bottles in them clinked together as he helped her
to settle.

"You need to get home," Sayers advised her.

"You take me."

"No."

"Damn you for thinking you can do better."

"I wasn't thinking any such thing." Sayers hitched himself beside her
and watched as she rearranged both her clothing and her dignity. It was
hard to say which was the more in disarray.

"Yah," she said dismissively. "You got a sweetheart. That don't
worry me. Everybody's got a sweetheart."

"You got one?"

"Used to."

"Me, too."

She looked at him. Contrary to the fashion, she was made up heavily. Instead of adding to her allure, it emphasized the coarseness of her
features and the bad condition of her skin. Sayers wouldn't have dared to
guess at her age. He reckoned she'd lived hard and probably looked much
older than she really was.

She said carefully, "I apologize. You were being a gentleman. You
stopped to help me and I'm calling you names."

"I didn't hear any names," Sayers said.

"I was doing it in my head. It's just that sometimes the drink stops
them making it to my tongue." She giggled. Smiling softened her, but
not by much.

Sayers said, "If you laid off the drink, you might attract more trade."

"If I didn't drink, I couldn't face the trade at all."

That was hard to argue with. "You've been around," Sayers said.

"That I have," she said, and stopped to look thoughtfully into the
distance. It was as if an idea of great import was starting to form, like a
ship coming forth out of the mist. A second later, she rose slightly and
cut a fart that rattled the empties in all three of the crates they were sitting on. It was as if the ship of thought had suddenly sounded its
foghorn.

The clanging bell of a passing electric streetcar echoed down the alleyway for a few moments, capping the fart like a cymbal shot and relieving him of the need to pass comment. She settled back, unperturbed.

Reckoning that he had a perfect opportunity and nothing to lose, Sayers said, "Can I ask you a question that would offend most women?"

"Ask away," she said. "I'll lay a hundred dollars that you can't offend me. If you'll furnish me the hundred."

"I can't do that," he said, "but let me ask you this. There's a certain kind of man who takes a certain kind of pleasure."

"Nances?"

"Not nances. I'm talking about the kind of man who looks to physical punishment as a source of gratification. Can you tell me where in this city might such men be found?"

"You want a beating? I can do that for you."

"It's not for me. It's complicated to explain."

"I'll bet it is," she said. And then she drew in a big breath and sighed and settled and gave the matter some serious thought.

"You want to find men with an appetite for that kind of thing," she said, "you need to look for the places where the rich ones gather. Get a bunch of 'em together and they turn into little boys. And those little rich boys . . . the only woman's touch they ever knew was being spanked by their nannies. That's their idea of paradise now they're grown men."

"What kind of places are we talking about?"

"The sporting clubs. Except there's more to their sport than horses and guns. That was easy. Give me a dollar and ask me something else."

"Okay," he said, and gave her two. "Say a woman has a child growing inside her. Someone presses her into ending that child's life before it begins. I imagine that would affect her. How long do you think it would take for her mind to achieve any kind of peace?"

She frowned. It was as if he'd suddenly broken into a foreign language, but she hadn't realized it and was struggling to construe the words in terms that she understood.

Sayers began, "What I mean is . . ." but she cut right across him.

"I heard what you said." With a sudden lurch forward, she rocked onto her feet. He stood up along with her. "I heard what you said and the hell with you!"

She took a swing at his face and he didn't really have to avoid it, because she missed him by a mile and lost her balance; he caught her arm to stop her from falling and she shook him off, violently. She grabbed the crates to steady herself instead, and then made a big effort and heaved the topmost one toward him. He skipped back as it crashed down onto the stones at his feet, the plank lid bursting off and broken glass flying everywhere.

She was screaming now, and sobbing at the same time, damning him over and over in language he'd never heard coming out of a woman before. People at the end of the alley were stopping to watch. The lower crates were open and she started pulling out empty bottles and lobbing them in his direction. Her face was a painted mask, fury and tragedy in a single design.

"Forgive me," Sayers said uselessly, and her answer was a flying bottle propelled by more abuse. He flinched and fended it off, taking another step back for safety. She was like a wild thing. He'd obviously started this, but he had no idea of how it might be stopped. If there was any way of stopping it at all.

Someone was pulling him away. It was the waiter from the saloon behind them. The door was open and people were looking out. He shoved Sayers' traveling bag into his hand and then hustled him back up the alley.

Sayers said, "I only asked her a question."

The waiter said, "I hope you got your answer."

Sayers glanced back over his shoulder.

"I think I probably did," he said.

THIRTY-SIX

he manager laid down her letter of recommendation and said, "Anyone held in such regard by Mister Patenotre is guaranteed a welcome at this hotel."

"I should think he'll be happy to hear it," Louise said. "I have two servants."

"Got a nice room for them in our annex. I assume they can share?"

"I would guess so. They've been married for longer than I can say."

"That's fine, then," the manager said. "For how long will you be staying with us?"

"It's hard to be sure. I have it in mind to find somewhere more permanent, but . . . you know how it is."

He got up from behind his desk and walked around it. His office was paneled and splendid and as badly lit as a chapel in a funeral home. She rose and took his offered hand and they shook on the deal like a couple of men.

He handed back her letter and said, "Please regard us as your home in Richmond for as long as you need one. We usually announce arrivals with a few lines in the *Dispatch*."

"In this case, I'd rather you didn't," Louise said. "It's not always the wisest thing for a woman who travels alone."

"I understand you perfectly. Can I help you in any other way?"

"Somewhere to lock up my trinkets would be nice."

"I'll arrange a deposit box. Stop by the desk the next time you're passing, and you can pick up the key."

She declined the assistance of a bell-hopper and made her own way up to the second-floor room, to where the Silent Man and his wife had already gone ahead with her bags. On show in the lobby was a plan for the hotel's expansion, intended for sometime in the near future. Instead of the modest low-rise building of the present day, the architect's drawing showed four great towers of seven and twelve floors, a footbridge linking two blocks across Eighth Street, and a Murphy's flag flying proudly on each roof.

So despite what the manager had said, it would not do to become too attached to the place. Like everything and everywhere else, all here was in flux, a fast-moving river that carried all before it toward a new tomorrow. She'd grown up in a world where values were constant, and could be relied upon not to change. Now it was as if nothing could be relied on at all.

The Mute Woman was alone in the suite. Louise's trunk was open and some of her dresses were already hanging in the closet. She went over to her trunk, intending to set out her few familiar objects on the dressing table in the way that she always preferred. But the Mute Woman closed the lid and stood there with her hand on it, holding it closed.

She pointed toward the floor above.

"Patenotre's rooms?"

A nod.

Louise left her, and ascended one floor. In the corridor she found the Silent Man, waiting. He'd already picked the lock on Patenotre's suite for her.

"The usual warning?" she said.

She let herself into the suite and closed the door behind her. As always she felt the steady pressure of their expectations, and the faint humiliation of their disapproval. From the beginning, they'd treated her the way that experienced sergeants might treat a raw young officer, their deference tinged with contempt. No, correct that; they'd held off until her failure to slaughter the child they'd procured for her. After that, the honeymoon was over. But by then, it was too late to change. The journey was well under way.

She knew that she was not their most cooperative student. She knew where this journey would lead. And if the outlook seemed bleak . . . well, what had she asked for?

She looked around. The sitting room had been tidied. It had that too-straight, untouched look. She went over to the writing table and tried the drawers, which she found unlocked. In them she found personal papers, unpaid bills, and some letters of no interest. There were a few items torn from newspapers and magazines, most of them making some reference to Patenotre's home county in Louisiana. She found a few loose coins, but no real cash or anything of value.

She didn't trouble to leave things as she'd found them. In fact, she went to the couch and punched a couple of the cushions, just to make them look sat-upon. At that point there came two taps on the wall, spaced a second apart.

Louise crossed the room in silence and spun into the bedroom, closing the door behind her. It had no lock, but it had a thumb latch that she slid across. Then she waited and listened. After less than a minute, she heard the door to the sitting room open and close. Then the sounds of drawers being pushed all the way shut, of cushions being picked up and slapped into shape.

When the bedroom doorknob was turned and the door rattled against the latch, Louise took a step back. She was not nervous.

She heard the maid on the other side of the door call out, "Mister Patenotre? Do you want me to make your bed up, sir?"

Louise pretended to yawn, making a sound that could have come from anyone—man, woman, even an animal—and which could have been intended to mean anything at all.

In the same raised voice, the maid said, "I'm sorry if I've disturbed you, sir," and went. Louise heard the outer door close a few moments later.

She looked at the bed. It was still made up from the day before. Jules Patenotre hadn't returned to his rooms last night, nor would he ever again. But it would suit her best if he didn't disappear just yet. She threw back the covers, mussed the sheets, and put a dent in the pillow, giving the bed a slept-in look. Then she searched the bedroom.

Shoes. How many pairs of shoes did a man need? Behind them in the bottom of the closet she thought at first that she'd struck lucky, because she found a locked box about the size of a gun case. Louise didn't have the Silent Man's skills, but she went and got the letter knife from the sitting room, and forced the lock.

The resemblance to a gun case was no coincidence. The box contained two guns. It also contained a collection of obscene postcards and a small number of books. She took out one of these and read the title: *A Treatise on the Use of Flogging in Medicine and Venery.* It was one of an edition of three hundred from a publisher with no address other than "Paris."

She left the box's contents as she'd found them. The damage to the lid wasn't obvious. The rooms had yielded nothing of use, but she wasn't done with Jules Patenotre yet. Before leaving, she took one last look around. She'd have the Silent Man or his wife come in and untidy them every day for a week or two. It would blur over any apparent link between her own arrival and her patron's disappearance. It wouldn't matter that his room key stayed behind the front desk, as long as the clerks didn't keep a record.

She went back down to the lobby.

"The manager promised me a strongbox?" she said to the clerk on duty.

"Right here for you, ma'am," he said, and reached under the desk to bring out a ledger. "If I can get a specimen signature in our security book."

"How does this work?"

"I'll walk you through it."

She signed as Mary D'Alroy, and then he led her to the small room just off the lobby where the wall of strongboxes was to be found. He showed her how two keys were used to open the door to her personal safe.

"This one you keep," he explained, showing her the key on the smaller tag. "It fits your box and no other. This second key is the hotel's master key. You need both keys to open any box."

With that, he left her alone. As soon as he'd gone, she dug into her clutch bag and took out the key that she'd found in the pocket of Jules Patenotre's coat. She tried it in each of the strongbox doors in turn, until she found the one that it matched. Then she took the hotel's master key out of her own safe's door and used it to open the second lock.

She drew out Patenotre's long tray and lifted the metal lid. This was more like it. There was a substantial amount of money, both in paper and gold coin. Her reaction was not of greed or of pleasure, but of relief. She transferred it all across to her own box. There was another key, a big one, with nothing to say what it was for. She took that. There were some pieces of jewelry, but she left these behind. Such things could be identified. The risk of that exceeded any value they might have—which, in all honesty, looked as if it wouldn't be much. She was no expert, but to her eye these were sentimental pieces, not heirlooms.

There were also some papers, legal documents—probably the last remaining records of a now-extinguished line. She was going to leave those as well, but she gave them a glance first in case there was anything involving stocks or shares. Without her close-work glasses, she had to strain a little. What she saw prompted her to stuff all the papers into her clutch bag for a closer reading later on.

She'd been in the room for about five minutes. Long enough. She slid both boxes back into the wall, closed the heavy doors on them, locked both sets of locks, and then took the hotel's master key back to the desk.

"Very ingenious system you have," she told the clerk as she handed in the master.

"We like to think it's pretty well foolproof," he said. "Good day to you, ma'am."

She read his name off his badge.

"And to you, Charles," she said, and went back up to her suite.

THIRTY-SEVEN

t was one hell of a gentlemen's club, that was for sure. Housed in a mansion built in the Victorian Italianate style, it stood behind fancy iron railings in the middle of the downtown area on East Franklin. The entire building was at the disposal of its members, who included a large number of Richmond's prominent and powerful. The rules governing membership were complex, subtle, and mostly unwritten.

Membership was for men only. Decent women of the town were known to turn their faces from the building as they passed it on their way home from church; to do otherwise was considered unladylike. The club was not spoken of, and it was generally understood that whatever happened within its walls, stayed within its walls. This was a place for the boys to be boys. The boys included bankers, factory owners, military men, and a significant number of the city's idler rich.

In a set of tails borrowed from the Bijou's costume store by arrangement with a fellow boarder, Tom Sayers pushed his way through the iron gates. He'd been advised to play up his English accent, so they'd think he was a gentleman, and to remember to take his hat off, lest they should spot that he wasn't.

Flaming torches lit the portico from brackets on either side of the entranceway. A black footman stood ready to open the door but hesitated, not recognizing Sayers as a regular member. But Sayers had taken advice for this moment, also.

"I'm a guest of the judge," he said.

It seemed that he'd been provided with a good choice of patron. "Justice Crutchfield?" the doorman said with an undercurrent of apprehension that bordered on alarm, and he all but jumped to admit him. Sayers could only hope that the footman would say nothing should the justice actually appear that evening.

He stepped into a marble-floored hallway with a staircase that swept around and up to a second-floor gallery and a dome of painted glass above. Another footman took his hat.

And where now? He couldn't appear to hesitate. Sayers chose the nearest set of doors, and found himself in a large, airy, and empty room the size of a gymnasium. It would have served equally well for dancing or banqueting.

A further set of doors took him into the dining rooms; these were spare and masculine, with hard wooden chairs and plain white linen tablecloths. The billiard room had five tables and electric lighting, and was entered through a curtained archway. Four of the tables were in use. He stood and watched one of the games for a while. Nobody addressed him or acknowledged him.

Finally, he reached the barroom, which proved to be the liveliest part of the club.

It was a dark room with a big fireplace, full of cigar smoke and well-dressed males. Some lounged on sofas but most stood in groups, each group back-to-back with two or three others, all having the loud conversations of men who are agreed that they're absolutely right about everything. Above the fireplace was the club's coat of arms, a wooden crest of shields, spears, and helmets with an incongruous clock face in the middle of it.

The air was thick and the room unpleasantly warm. Rather than stay in the doorway attracting attention, Sayers threaded a way through the crowd. Without meaning to, he jogged the arm of a big man addressing a small crowd of listeners. The man's fist had a drink in it, and some of the drink spilled. He looked around.

"Watch where you're going, sir," he snapped.

"Forgive me," Sayers said, but the stranger was not prepared to let it go so easily.

"I should think so!" he said. "Conduct yourself better, or get out of my sight. I don't care whose guest you are."

He was bullet-headed and barrel-chested, in off-white planter's clothes and with a waxed mustache. Before Sayers could speak again, a stranger had interposed himself between them.

"I witnessed the incident, such as it was, Mister Burwell," the stranger said. "I can tell you that no offense was intended or offered."

He drew Sayers away.

"Thank you, but you don't have to frog-march me," Sayers said as soon as they'd moved out of earshot. "I can see it when a man's spoiling for an argument."

"And I can spot when a man's ready to rise to one," the stranger said. "Calvin Quinn, at your service. I don't believe I've seen you here before?" Quinn was a spare-looking man of about his own age, and in a rather better suit.

Sayers gave his own name and added, "Just got into town a couple of days ago."

"Well," Quinn said, "if there's anyone you want an introduction to, just let me know. I've had dealings with most people here. I'm a lawyer. What line of business are you in?"

Sayers thought it best to mention no profession. He'd held down a range of jobs since the age of eleven. Bricklayer's boy, boxer, actor, theatrical business manager, warehouseman, fruit picker, road digger, carnival hand . . . none of them likely to win him much respect in a place like this.

So he just said, "I had a windfall. That's what I'm living on right now."

"Ah," Calvin Quinn said, and his interest seemed to increase. "So, what do you make of us?"

"I can't say I've been here long enough to form an opinion," Sayers said, glancing back as the noise level behind him continued to rise. The man who'd tried to provoke him was now trying to get a rise out of a young, good-looking man with a broad forehead and sideburns.

"Well," Quinn said, "don't form one based on the likes of him. That's Henry Burwell. He's angry, he's rich, and he was born unpleasant. It's not a healthy brew."

At the sight of that ruddy, aggressive countenance thrusting itself into the face of the younger man, Sayers was reminded of a belligerent Turkish wrestler he'd once had to share a trailer with. On a winter's morning, the strongman would strip to the waist and break the ice on one of the water butts, roaring loudly enough to wake up the whole camp as he splashed his bared skin with gallons of frozen slush. He would drink heavily, and when he got drunk he always wanted to arm-wrestle somebody. There seemed to be something about men of such build and temperament: the older they grew, the more hardened they became, and the more determined to seek out any opportunity to prove it in pointless competition.

Sayers said, "What's he angry at?"

Quinn could only shrug. "Who knows? We don't choose our natures. Any stranger is game to him. He spots an unfamiliar face and off he goes."

"Someone ought to stop him."

"Stop him? People contrive to get their worst enemies in here and then wait for the fireworks. You did well not to fall for it. So, what brings you to Richmond? Are you looking to invest some of that windfall money? I've got all the connections you could ask for, if you do."

So that was it. Quinn probably moved in on every stranger as a possible business prospect. Such contact was, after all, a main purpose of circles such as these.

"I'm looking for someone," Sayers said, and reached inside his borrowed coat. He brought out Louise's picture. "She came down from Philadelphia a few weeks ago. Might you have seen her?"

Quinn took the photograph and studied it politely. He seemed to grow quiet.

"It's an old picture," Sayers said. "She may have changed."

The lawyer handed it back. "I fear not," he said. "An actress?"

"On the British stage. In another life."

"I don't recognize the name."

"The name could be different now."

"How very mysterious."

It was then that the altercation behind Sayers grew so loud that the entire room began to fall silent and was turning to listen. "You seem to think you can insult your betters with impunity," the bellicose Henry Burwell was all but shouting.

"I insulted no one," the young man protested, raising his voice in response. "I never met a man so set on being offended."

"We shall settle this," Henry Burwell said, and gave the younger man a shove that sent him staggering back into his companions. It was a move that determined the only course that this confrontation could take.

"You seek a lesson?" the young man said, regaining his balance with the help of his friends. "You will have one."

It was as if someone had fired off a signal. The doors to the adjoining ballroom were flung open, and the entire club began to decamp from the bar. Sayers was carried by a human tide. He'd lost sight of his conversation partner by the time he'd reached the door.

There was something unsettling about the speed with which preparations fell into place. A rope was produced and run around a series of hooks, one on the inside corner of each of the ballroom's four wooden pillars. The crowd fell into shape around the ring that this formed. Burwell's seconds took his coat from him and had his sleeves rolled up before the young man and his friends had even taken in what was going on. Eager helpers propelled them toward one of the newly created corners, with everyone shouting advice.

One of the young man's friends called out, "Who's got the gloves?"

"Gloves?" Henry Burwell shouted back. "Only women fight with gloves!"

And a man somewhere close to Sayers' ear could be heard to say, "This has got to be the absolute best thing since the opera house did the naked nigger wrestling."

Sayers glanced around. Some of the clubmen were grinning while others were expressing disapproval, even though they were doing nothing that might interfere with the object of their annoyance. He'd seen this phenomenon before: those who decried a thing, while ensuring they missed none of it. Indeed, they'd seek it out in all its forms so that they might disapprove of it more thoroughly.

He eyed the young man in the makeshift ring, who was now down to his vest and shirtsleeves and was handing his watch and chain to a friend for safekeeping. He was narrow-hipped and wide-shouldered, with a nice taper to his form; he might well give the local brute a few surprises and make him think twice about issuing such challenges in the future.

And if he did not . . . well, who was Sayers to pass judgment? This hardly differed from the way he had made his living for at least five of the past dozen years. The goaded challenger, the unequal contest, the knockout blow. The only real dissimilarity was that Sayers had taken no pleasure from his victories.

He'd just taken the money, at the end of every day.

"I'd say you had a narrow escape," Sebastian Becker said from right beside him.

 s he spoke the words, Sebastian took a firm grip on Sayers' upper arm and held him fast. Sayers looked at him in astonishment.

"Sebastian?" he said. "What are you doing here?"

"Don't Sebastian me," the onetime policeman said. "You thief under my roof."

"I stole nothing from you!"

"You'd have ruined my good name if I'd let your crime stand," Sebastian said, his voice rising to compete with the racket all around them. "And I've damn near ruined my own family with what it's taken to cover for you. I'll have back what you took, and I'll have it right now."

With that, he turned Sayers around and started to shove him through the crowd toward the doors.

In among all the gentlemen, Sebastian was aware that he stood out in his travel-creased suit and his dusty shoes. He'd barely slept in two days and was sustained on a fuel of strong black coffee and indignation. He'd spent the past twelve hours canvassing every midtown lodging house in the public register, until he found the one where Tom Sayers' description was recognized. A fellow guest had directed him here. When the club's servants had tried to deny him entry, the sheer force of his response had been even more persuasive than any threat that he'd made.

He'd walked in just as everyone had been moving from the bar into the ballroom. He'd spotted Sayers almost immediately, and pushed his way through to his side.

Sayers said, "Wait, Sebastian. Please."

"So you can stay and watch the fight?" Sebastian said. "I don't think so. Console yourself with the thought that it'll be over before we reach the street. Can't you hear what they're all saying?"

"About what?"

"Those scars on the man's right hand."

Sayers looked back at Burwell. The big man's hand and forearm were slightly misshapen. His hand was like a bag of walnuts with fingers, his forearm marked with a jagged scar of old lightning. It didn't look like the kind of hand a man could fight with at all.

"Caught in a cartwheel and mangled," Sebastian said. "The surgeon fixed his knuckles with plates of Monell metal. Everyone in this room seems to know it. Apart from his opponent."

Sayers looked back again. The young man was limbering up by spreading his arms like a bird and stretching the muscles in his chest and shoulders. He had no idea of what he faced.

"That's a disgrace," Sayers said.

"It's not your affair," Sebastian said as the two opponents squared up. "I'm your only concern right now."

They reached the ballroom's double doors, but when Sebastian tried to open them, he couldn't. Someone saw him trying and called out, "The doors are always barred for a contest."

Sebastian spun around, dragging Sayers with him like an oversized errant child. He scanned over the heads of the roaring crowd, looking for another way out.

In the ring, the two men were circling each other. The young man tried a jab. Burwell blocked it and responded with an openhanded slap across the cheek. Then another.

"Fight like a man!" the younger man protested.

"Fight like a man," Burwell mimicked, mocking him in a girlish voice, and slapped him again. The young man responded instantly with

another jab, and this one took Burwell by surprise. It landed on his mouth, knocked his head back, and split his lip.

Sebastian spied a possible way out. It was through the dining rooms, and they'd have to go around the outside of the crowd to reach it. With a mutter of frustration, he jerked Sayers back into motion.

Burwell feinted twice and then smashed in a single right-handed blow to the young man's face. That hand, that twisted log with its hidden freight of stainless steel, was like a sack of bolts on a side of meat. Sebastian was no expert, but even he could tell that the cheekbone had probably gone in that moment. The fight was as good as over, but the young man struggled on, almost blind with pain and weaving like a drunk while the other man continued to play with him.

But Sebastian had other concerns. As they moved, he leaned close to Sayers' ear.

"Where have you stashed it?" he said. "And how much is missing?"

Burwell now had hold of the young man's shirtfront and was slinging him from side to side, spinning him about and then releasing him to lose his balance and fall. The noise from the clubmen was deafening. It was hard to see over the heads of the crowd for what happened next, but it seemed that Burwell dropped to one knee, pinned the boy down with his left hand, and pounded on his face with the right until the referee finally stirred himself and intervened.

"Calm yourself," Sayers said. "I still have most of it. You'll have it back. There's no need to handle me so."

The man in the ring was now challenging the crowd. Without any warning, Sayers jerked his arm and freed it from Sebastian's grip. In a second he was gone, diving in among the backs of the watching spectators.

Sebastian followed him into the sea of bodies, and immediately found himself thrown this way and that as the crowd raged. There was Sayers, a few feet ahead, bobbing his way toward the ring. What had looked like a move to escape was now beginning to look like something else.

Sayers was the bigger man, and more able to make his way. No one was letting Sebastian through.

Now Sayers was there in the middle of the room, ducking under the rope to enter the ring with a delighted-looking Henry Burwell.

"Oh no," Sebastian said, and felt his heart dropping like a filled bucket down a well.

He saw Sayers throwing his coat over the rope. Sayers didn't bother to roll up his sleeves. The young man's friends had removed him from the ring and were appealing to those around them for a medical man, but all seemed to be more interested in urging on the new contender.

Most of them probably considered Sayers a fool. For a man to enter the ring without knowing what he faced was merely stupid. To be driven in by anger after witnessing the danger . . . well, such a man deserved whatever was coming to him.

"Come on, then," Burwell called to Sayers, gleefully raising his voice above the noise of the crowd. His split lip had bled a little, but otherwise he was untouched. Even the wax on his mustache was still holding up. "Be a man. Avenge your friend."

Sebastian couldn't reach the ring. No one was prepared to yield his place. He stopped trying and stood, helplessly, watching the scenario unfold.

The same referee took charge, and the contest began. At first it looked to Sebastian as if Sayers was in for it, doomed to fall within the first minute. They squared up and he immediately took a couple of hard body blows.

Then it got worse. He punched, but he punched weakly. Burwell blocked him without trouble, slammed another into his side. Sayers backed off to regather himself, but it wasn't looking good. The passage of time and the years of abuse must have taken their toll. Perversely, it seemed as if cleaning up had done him no good at all. The deadening effect of the booze must previously have worked in his favor.

Another ineffectual exchange, another retreat. Sayers had made a terrible mistake. The fight was no more than two minutes old and the ex-boxer was getting visibly groggy. His only chance of survival seemed to lie in staying back out of Burwell's reach. The big man was getting annoyed; this was no good, all this chasing his opponent around the ring. The crowd was getting annoyed, too, and some of the clubmen were starting to boo and whistle.

Sebastian saw his chance and managed to get to the rope, from where he called Sayers' name. Sayers seemed not to hear him. He wove and stumbled as Burwell shepherded him, crowding him back toward one of the corners where he'd be trapped. The smile had gone from Burwell's face. This was one to be finished, as quickly and as cruelly as possible.

Sebastian tried to enter the ring, but more than one hand grabbed him and pulled him back. He heard cries of "Bad sport!" from those all around him.

Sayers was trapped in the corner, his balance going, his guard falling. He was an easy target. Burwell took aim. He let everyone see what he was doing. He drew his walnut-knuckled fist back beyond his shoulder and then let it fly with all his strength.

Sebastian could do nothing. Those who were holding him had let him go. He could make no difference now.

But something happened between the launching of the blow and its landing.

Sayers snapped upright. He leaned aside the exact distance required for the flying fist to pass harmlessly over his shoulder. Burwell's knuckles plowed straight into the wooden pillar, splitting the skin that covered them and causing blood to fly out in a spray. He screamed in pain.

Sayers, his face now only inches from Burwell's own, said loudly enough for all to hear, "And I'm not even his friend."

The metal plates had embedded in the timber. Burwell could not pull his hand free without a risk of tearing it apart.

Sayers now set about him with a precision that was almost scientific. It took three blows to break Burwell's nose, but with persistence it went. Sayers continued to snap Burwell's head this way and that until, finally, the man's hand worked itself free of the pillar and he staggered backward.

By some miracle, he did not fall. Sayers circled him as he stood there, arms hanging, body swaying, blood spattering down onto the wooden floor from a hand destroyed twice over. Then he put in one clean punch that dropped the big man where he stood. Once Burwell was down, he did not move.

Everyone cheered. The bully's seconds ducked into the ring to deal with their fallen champion. Then the rope fell and the crowd surged forward. Sayers held up a hand, trying to make himself heard. Those immediately around him stopped to listen to their new hero. Others paid no attention.

Someone gave him his coat. He searched around inside it and brought out a postcard that Sebastian recognized as the fighter's long-cherished picture of Louise Porter. He held it up for all to see.

They started to grow quiet.

It was after this that the real trouble started.

ebastian dragged Sayers into the dining room and turned to get the door shut behind them, only to find that two men had followed them through and were taking care of it. On the other side of the door, the uproar continued. Beyond the empty tables, waiters and club staff appeared from out of the kitchens and hesitated, looking worried.

The two clubmen turned and fell back against the door. They were laughing so hard that they could barely breathe. The Virginia lawyer was red in the face and his shorter companion was all but in tears.

"Well done, sir," Calvin Quinn said as he struggled to recover. "Well done. You win the heart and mind of every man in the room and then ask them for the whereabouts of a particular whore."

"That's nothing like what I said!" Sayers protested.

"But it's pretty much how everyone heard it. Come on, before they break the door down."

That seemed like a real possibility, so Sebastian went along with it. The four of them hurried out through the porticoed entranceway and down onto East Franklin, where streetlamps lit their way toward the extensive gardens around the capitol.

At a safe distance from the club, they slowed. "Oh my," Quinn said, recovering at last. And his companion said, "Thank the Lord I didn't find a fool to take my bet. What kind of idiot would I seem now?"

"Sylvester found a mark and lost a hundred," Quinn said, and that set them off again.

Through all of this, Sayers had been looking distracted and Sebastian hadn't cracked a smile.

Now Sebastian said, "This is far enough for me, gentlemen. We need to thank you for your help and take our leave. Mister Sayers and I have some business to address."

"Can't that wait?" Quinn said, and then he looked at Sayers. "You can't duck out now."

And his companion said, "We're taking you to the woman you've been looking for."

Through empty streets that were not the safest part of the city when the sun was down, the four men made their way to the abandoned theater of varieties. Night had turned it into a chalk and pencil sketch of a ruin, all shadows and silver. It faced the street like a skull in the moonlight.

In its foyer, they found a few burned-down stumps of candles. Quinn's companion hunted out a usable lantern. Both men seemed to know their way around.

Quinn stood in the middle of the foyer and called out, "Miss D'Alroy!" But this drew no response.

Long shadows danced across the auditorium as they crossed it. The stranger led the way up to the suite of rooms above the foyer. Sayers stayed close behind the stranger, whose name had not been mentioned. Sebastian stayed close behind Sayers.

"This isn't looking quite so promising," Quinn said.

They clattered up the uncarpeted stairs, emerging into the big room with the brick fireplace. There was a stink of food that had been left to rot; there seemed to be no doubt at all that this squat had been abandoned for some days.

Sebastian Becker crouched before the fireplace and picked over some of the ashes. He saw the half-burned remains of newspaper theatrical pages.

"She clings to what she knows," he said to himself.

Sayers turned to the stranger, who was standing by the doorway. He said, "She's actually been living here? Not just using the place for assignations?"

"That I can't say for sure. But it's the way that it looked to me."

A sudden sound from one of the adjoining rooms had Sebastian and Quinn reaching for the revolvers they carried. Sebastian moved to the door and called out, "I warn you! We have guns! Whoever you are, show yourself!" and then he raised his boot high and kicked it open, bursting the latch. Anyone on the other side would have been startled and at a disadvantage, but their lights revealed no one.

They advanced into the room with caution, stifling a cough at the dust raised by Sebastian's violent action. There was a table, a broken water jug on the floor, a pallet in the corner.

From behind them, the stranger said, "This was her room. The servants slept back there."

The sound came again.

"Rats in the walls," Sayers said. He went over to one of the dividing walls, its plaster long gone, and banged on the timber slats. There was an immediate flurry of panic and scuttling from the other side. More dust was shaken down, and a squeak or two helped to confirm the explanation.

Sebastian had Sayers raise the lantern high while he moved closer.

"Look at the boards," he said.

"What of them?"

"They're old. But the nails are not."

Sayers looked more closely. The nails weren't new, but their exposed heads showed clean metal. They'd been hammered sometime recently. He tested the slats, and they were firm.

He handed the lantern to Quinn and went over to the table.

"What are you doing?" Sebastian said.

"Stand back." Sayers lifted the table and carried it toward the wall. Sebastian understood his intention and took the other side, and together they swung it against the boards. Where the forward edge met, the wood splintered inward.

The timber wasn't rotted, or the job would have been easy. But with one of the slats broken, they could lever out the pieces and start on the board next to it. Something had been bundled into the space behind. Quinn and the stranger watched as the two men went at the work, uncovering an area of rumpled canvas.

"That's a backcloth," Sayers said. "Painted."

He and Sebastian both took a hold on the backcloth and tried to pull it out through the hole, but it was heavy and the glue size in the paint had stiffened the material. No matter how hard they tugged on it, the canvas stayed wedged inside the wall.

So they ripped out a few more slats to enlarge the hole and tried again, one on either side, each taking a grip. Sayers glanced back and saw Quinn and the smaller man standing there with an expression of dread.

Sebastian said, "On three. One, two . . ."

On the third count, they heaved on the canvas. It came out of the wall. With the backdrop came the body that had been wedged into the space behind it. It was naked, and male. It flopped out in a cloud of white dust, tumbling onto the floor as if from the back of a cart. There it lay, all hunched up, while plaster swirled in the air all around it. That smell they'd noticed as they'd entered the rooms—it was not the rotting of abandoned food. It was this.

Sebastian picked up the lantern and held it for a better look. Curled up as he was, it was impossible to say how tall the man had been in life. His hair was all mussed and dusty, and he had a long mustache in the same condition. His mouth was wide open, and his jaw was right down into his chest, as if he'd died trying to sing the lowest note of his life.

He'd been in the wall long enough for his skin to begin drying out and shrinking; the contracting flesh had begun to expel a variety of sharp objects used to pierce and penetrate it. It was hard to be sure what their purpose was, other than to cause lasting discomfort. The rats had been at him as well.

Sayers looked toward their two local men. Neither appeared to have been expecting this.

"Do you know this man?" he said.

Both of them went on staring. Neither of them said yes or no.

Sebastian said, "Someone will."

FORTY

ebastian hadn't been gone for more than a couple of minutes when Calvin Quinn and his nameless friend exchanged a glance and then quit the scene. Only Tom Sayers waited, along with the dead stranger. By the light of the lantern, he searched the rooms for some further sign of Louise. He found none.

Sebastian returned a short time later with a police party. He showed them the body and gave the best explanation of the circumstances that he could.

Over the Pinkerton man's protests, the officers arrested Sayers.

As they were taking him away, Sebastian called out, "Quickly, Sayers. Where's my money?"

Sayers, in handcuffs for the second time in his life, looked back over his shoulder and said, "Get me out of this and I'll tell you."

They took him to the Richmond City Jail, where he spent the night sharing a common cell with all the drunks, thieves, and vagrants that the night watch had scooped up in the course of their shift. They booked him as a suspect found in the presence of a murdered man, unable to give a satisfactory account of himself. He sat on the hard floor of a communal cell with his back against the wall, and he did not sleep. He hoped that Becker might appear and somehow get him released, but the hours passed without any sign.

The next morning, all were put in shackles and walked out in a shuffling procession to a wagon that would take them to city hall.

Richmond's city hall was a building that, on the outside, resembled
the Gothic whim of a mad Bavarian king. The shackled prisoners were
marched down into the basement where the police court was held.
Sayers was herded into a pen at the back of the room with all his
overnight fellows. They shared no sense of fellowship.

When the clerk of the court instructed all to rise, Sayers realized that
the presiding judge was none other than the man whose name had
caused such awe in the doorman that previous evening.

Justice John Crutchfield proved to be a spare, thin-lipped man in a
black string bow tie. He set about the business of the day with a terrifying if somewhat erratic efficiency.

After reading over the charges against the first prisoner to be called
before him, he looked up and said to the man, "Where you from, nigger?"

"North Carolina, sir," the prisoner replied.

"I thought as much," the justice said. "Thirty days."

It would be a while before they got to Sayers. So far, he'd had no
access to counsel. The only lawyer he knew hereabouts was Calvin
Quinn. He doubted that Quinn would be prepared to come forward.

Sayers had good reason to fear investigation. In England, he
remained a wanted man. The very information that might save him from
these charges would condemn him on the old ones.

Crutchfield's courtroom was like a marketplace with continuous
through traffic. The corridor outside of the swing doors was raucous; in
here it was more restrained, but still a fast-moving zoo. Justice John
seemed able to stay focused on the case before him without losing his
awareness of everything else that was going on around him, in sight or
just out of it.

Tom Sayers heard his name being called, and the bailiff prodded him
to move forward. The judge was reading some notes as Sayers took his
place before him. "And what's this about?" he said, looking not at Sayers
but at his clerk.

The court was told that the man found in the wall had been identified as Jules Patenotre, a native of Louisiana. He owned extensive property there, but he lived alone and kept a suite of rooms in Murphy's Hotel. There was some confusion over when he might have disappeared; the housemaids said that he'd definitely been seen around, but the desk staff said that he hadn't been picking up his key.

Now Justice John looked at Sayers. "Well?" he said. "What have you got to say about it?"

Before Sayers could speak, there was a movement at the other side of the courtroom, the scraping of a chair, a voice calling out, "I'm here to speak as counsel for the prisoner, Your Honor."

Sayers looked around in surprise. He was not alone; most heads in the courtroom were turning, too. Only the other prisoners were showing no interest at all.

Those who looked toward the public gallery saw a big man, bearded, in rugged tweeds and with his hat in his hand.

The judge said, "I saw you sneaking in there about half an hour back. And who the hell might you be?"

"Abraham Stoker, sir. A longtime friend of the prisoner. As to my qualifications, I was called to the bar in London, England."

"I know where London is. This is Richmond, Virginia, and you're in my courtroom. I hope you're not going to spoil my morning with a heap of legal argument."

"Not unless you particularly want me to, Your Honor," Stoker said. "As far as I'm aware, my client merely discovered a body and awaited the arrival of the police. I don't see the crime in that."

Bram Stoker?

Sayers was dazed, and finding all of this hard to take in. His sleepless night in the cells hadn't helped his powers of concentration. On the other side of Stoker, he could see Sebastian Becker, seated, and himself looking as if he'd skipped a night of bed rest.

The judge was sucking in his cheeks and considering Stoker. "I've met you before," he said. "Have I not?"

"You have, sir," Stoker said. "The Men's Club gave a dinner to honor Sir Henry Irving on his last American tour. I was with him then."

At that, the judge's face lit up. "You're Irving's man!" he said, and then a hint of disappointment. "And a lawyer as well?"

"I am, sir."

"Well, nobody's perfect. What can you tell me about this case?"

"Nothing at all, Your Honor. I arrived in town less than an hour ago and I've had no opportunity to consult with my client. But I know the defendant, and I can say with personal certainty that this man is no criminal."

Justice John's eyebrows went up. "That how they do things at the English bar?" he said. "Some lawyer stands up, says he doesn't know a damn thing about it, but swears that his client is aboveboard?"

"I'm a lawyer in that I passed the bar exam, sir, but I've never taken silk."

"Say what?"

"I've never practiced."

"That's more like it. We've got more than enough lawyers in this world, and I see far too many of them in this courtroom."

The judge studied his notes.

"Sayers," he said. "According to this, you had just shy of a thousand dollars on your person when they took you in."

"In a money belt," Sayers said. He didn't dare look at Sebastian Becker. "They took it from me at the jail."

"Care to tell me how you came by it?"

"No, sir."

Crutchfield looked up with his eyebrows raised and his pale blue eyes wide with an innocent wonder that Sayers knew he'd be a fool to take at face value.

"No?" he said.

But Sayers stuck to his word. "I prefer not to speak of it, sir. Don't I have a right to that? I believe it's in your constitution."

"In my courtroom," Crutchfield said, "you've got whatever rights I choose. You don't want to account for your situation here and now, fine. But account for it you will. I'm setting your bail at one thousand dollars. Bailiff, get him out of here."

Bram Stoker and Sebastian Becker walked out of the courtroom together. As they ascended from the basement into the ornate tan, cream, and gold four-story atrium of the city hall, Stoker said, "Our Justice John is a rum one. But at least Sayers has the means to cover his bail."

Sebastian said, "It's not his money, Mister Stoker. It's mine."

"Yours?"

"Why do you think I've pursued him all the way from Philadelphia?"

"I can't believe he'd ever steal from you," Stoker said. "Has he changed so much?"

"He didn't steal from me. He stole from the Pinkertons, and I had to make good the loss, or suffer in consequence. I don't doubt that he intended my family no harm, but harm was the outcome. It's this obsession of his. It blinds him to all else. The deeper Louise Porter sinks, the more she drags him after. Let's see what a spell in jail will do to his edge."

"You don't mean to leave him there?"

"I do."

A jangling of chains announced the approach of the prison party, shuffling up the stairs on their way to the transport. Each had been dealt with, and none looked any happier than before.

Sebastian looked the men over and then said to the guard alongside their column, "Where's Tom Sayers?"

"The Englishman?" the guard said. "He signed over his money and the judge signed the order. He's long gone."

FORTY-ONE

alvin Quinn was not hard to find. His law offices in the Chamber of Commerce building were listed in the city directory, and a three-figure telephone number along with them. Sebastian used a coin-operated telephone in the back of a drugstore. Quinn took his call, but when he realized what it was about, he cut off the conversation. So Sebastian waited outside his office until the end of the day, and followed his carriage back to his Church Hill home.

When Sebastian rang the bell by the door and stepped back, he saw movement at one of the windows, but no one came. So then he rang the bell again, and kept on ringing it until one of Quinn's black servants opened the door.

"Mister Quinn says that if you don't leave, he'll call in the police," the man said.

Sebastian said, "Tell Mister Quinn that if he won't speak to me, I'll fetch them myself."

A couple of minutes later, he was in Quinn's study. The lawyer left the study door slightly ajar. Sebastian was aware of at least one of the servants hovering outside in the hallway, presumably to eject him if called upon.

Quinn was already aware of Sayers' arrest. It was the reason for his nervousness. He'd no wish for it to be known that he'd led them to the old vaudeville house, or to make any public explanation of his own familiarity with its use as a venue for *le vice anglais*.

Sebastian told him of the scene in the courtroom, and the events that followed.

"I hurried to his lodgings," Sebastian said. "But I had missed him by minutes."

"And what of your thousand dollars?"

"I've lost it," Sebastian said simply. "The man's jumped bail and the money is forfeit. He's robbed me twice over. My family's savings, my son's hope of a cure, and a young girl's trousseau. All for his pursuit of that mad flogging whore."

"Steady on," Quinn said, and he got up and closed the study door.

Then he turned back to face Sebastian. "Why are you here?" he said. "Are you after replacing your money? I won't be blackmailed."

"Don't insult me," Sebastian said. "I won't take a penny. But you will help me."

He went on to explain his belief that the death of Jules Patenotre was related to at least two others of a similar character that had gone before: one in San Francisco, and another in Philadelphia. The woman now calling herself Mary D'Alroy was linked to each of them.

At the mention of Jules Patenotre's name, Sebastian had seen something change in Quinn's expression.

"You knew him," he said.

"I knew *of* him," Quinn said. "Patenotre was in the process of raising a loan against some property in Louisiana. He's been breaking up the old family estate and living off the proceeds. He's borrowed money before. Buyers don't always come along at the exact time when you need them, so he was using the plantation house for security whenever his funds dipped low. He'd pay off the loans whenever he sold more land. He always said that the house was the last thing he'd part with."

"His deposit box at Murphy's Hotel had been emptied," Sebastian said. "I believe by our so-called Mary D'Alroy after his death. The police don't know of her yet, and I want to keep it that way."

"You want to protect her? Why?"

"Not protect her," Sebastian said. "I need you to act for me. Contact each set of authorities and negotiate a reward. If I can't take my money back from Sayers, I'll get equal value from her. I can't do that if the police reach her first."

"How will you know where to look?"

"I reckon we can make a start by locating the Patenotre estate," Sebastian said.

NEW ORLEANS

December

1903

FORTY-TWO

er appointment was for seven o'clock that evening. At six-thirty, she left the St. Charles Hotel with the Silent Man following a few paces behind.

She was heading away from the French Quarter and into an even older part of town. Many of these houses had been the dwellings of original Creole families, and a few of their descendants continued to hang on. Their golden age was long past, the buildings run-down. The houses lined the streets in rows. Their owners stayed hidden away behind empty balconies and shuttered French windows.

She found the address, an anonymous-looking door in a brick-and-plaster wall. When she raised the iron knocker and brought it down, she heard it echo oddly on the other side.

While waiting for a response, she turned to the Silent Man.

"It's just a first meeting," she said. "I don't know how long I'll be."

He inclined his head and crossed to the other side of the street, where evening shadows were beginning to create niches of darkness in nailed-up doorways gray with cobwebs. The air was cool, but not unpleasant. Although this was December, it had the feel of a spring evening back in England.

When the Silent Man reached the far banquette, he turned. He barely appeared to move, but seemed to fade from sight as he eased back into a piece of the gloom.

Louise heard bolts being drawn, and faced the door. She composed herself. The door opened and before her stood a short, dark woman in immaculate linen and a folded headscarf.

"Miss Mary D'Alroy to see Mrs. Blanchard," Louise said. "I'm expected."

The servant woman stepped aside, and Louise went in. But instead of entering directly into the residence, she found herself in a wide passage-way of about fifty or sixty feet in length. It was paved, like a passage under a castle; halfway along it, from its vaulted ceiling, there hung an iron lantern on a chain. At its far end, an archway led to an inner court-yard with palm trees and a fountain.

After the anonymity of the street outside, the courtyard was a small paradise. A spot of total privacy, with flower beds and hanging baskets and benches for sitting out. There were ferns and oleander, as well as the palms, and a brightly colored parrot in a cage. The area wouldn't get much sunlight, but in the Louisiana summers that would be an advan-tage. Shade and a through breeze would be much preferred.

Balconies of filigreed ironwork overhung the courtyard at every level. Across it, another arch led to a stairway that ascended through each floor of the house.

Louise was led up and into a spacious drawing room that ran the full depth of the building. One end was open to the courtyard. The windows at the street end were shuttered, and candles had been lit there.

"I'll tell madame you're here," the woman said, and continued up to the next floor.

As she waited, Louise inspected the room. Alone in the middle of it stood a rosewood piano. The floor was polished timber, dark as pitch. The walls were of plain white plaster. A brass chandelier hung from an ornate plaster rose on the ceiling. Looking at the way that house had been put together, she was reminded of a shipwright's work: construc-tion that was solid to the point of crudity, yet shaped by its journeyman maker to follow lines of taste and elegance. Apart from the piano, there were two sofas and a few other pieces of mahogany furniture.

Louise went over to the piano. It was a London-made Broadwood, probably the Drawing Room Grand. She could imagine its journey, packed in boxwood and bound up with ropes to cross the ocean, then up the river by steamboat for unloading onto the levee, and then a final, rattling half mile on a wheeled cart to bring it here.

How did they get it up to the second floor? Probably over the balcony from the street, with block and tackle. Now here they were, Louise and the piano. Two exiled Europeans, a long way from home.

She did not sit and play. She could accompany herself, but not well. It was for this reason that she'd mostly made her living from recitation— it was a fairly simple matter to hire a meeting hall or a YMCA to give passages from *Les Misérables* and *The Mill on the Floss*. Hiring a piano and rehearsing someone local to play it involved complications, and complications meant added risk.

However, she'd been finding that they did not understand her so well in the South. In Philadelphia, her accent had been a professional asset. Here they asked her to repeat her words, and not just for the pleasure of hearing her speak.

For her part, she couldn't quite adapt to the local mixing up of language with French words rendered unrecognizable by American pronunciation. So out came the sheet music, and back came the vocal exercises.

She'd been exercising every morning. Whenever she could find a place to boil a kettle, she'd breathe in some steam. Louise had always assumed that her singing voice was something that she'd be able to call upon at will. But over the past few weeks, she'd discovered that it was just like any other neglected gift. She'd intended to keep it in use, but somehow over the years she'd never quite turned intention into action.

She sang well enough. Had she kept it up, she might now be sounding better than ever. But now she was coming to realize that she'd never again sing quite as well as she once had.

Well, as long as she could fill a room and please an audience. The smaller the room, the easier it was on both counts. Private events were the best of all—not only did she get to meet and charm her listeners beforehand, but the occasions made less of a mark in the public record. They might not be hugely rewarding, but for once money was not an immediate problem due to the contents of Jules Patenotre's strongbox. Right now, it was more important for her to seek out and meet people of use and influence.

Someone was coming down the stairs. It was Mrs. Blanchard. She moved slowly, one hand on the mahogany banister and the other being supported by the servant woman. Louise had only met her once before today, and then only briefly; one of her sons had conveyed this invitation and handled the initial arrangements. She was elderly and frail, and movement took so much of her concentration that it was impossible to guess at her character from her expression. She might be kind, forbidding, impatient—anything at all from sweet old lady to terrifying matriarch. Her hair was pinned up, and she wore a full cotton dress in a pleasing lavender shade.

Louise hovered awkwardly as the two of them moved to one of the sofas, where Mrs. Blanchard lowered herself with care. On the way down, she looked up at the servant woman and said, "Sophie, will you ask Euday to come?"

"He downstairs," Sophie said.

Mrs. Blanchard settled the last few inches and then, finally, was able to turn her full attention to Louise. "So, Miss D'Alroy," she said. "What will you take?"

Louise said, "A glass of water?"

"Take a cordial," Mrs. Blanchard said. "The water's not so sweet today."

Sophie left them, and there were a few moments of silence. Louise looked around and said, "Can I assume this is the room where I'll be performing?"

"Assume away," Mrs. Blanchard said. Her expression was stony, but her manner seemed warm. It was as if great age had robbed her face of animation and taken the strength from her limbs, leaving the person inside able to show herself in only small ways.

She said, "What do you think of my house?"

"I think it's fine," Louise said. "I think the whole town's very fine."

"Well, you can say that," Mrs. Blanchard said. "But you never saw the old New Orleans."

"I take it times have changed."

"Oh, have they. This was the richest city in America, and you knew it. We had the cotton and we had the river. Then came Mister Lincoln's war, and after that the railroads. Now it's one of the poorest. We can still put on a show, but it's not the place it was. There are some terrible people out there. I have Sophie lock the gates at night."

"Even so," Louise said. "There's something welcoming about this part of the world. I'm finding I feel at home here."

"And you've missed feeling that."

"Since I left my own home? I suppose I have. I've been away for a long time."

Mrs. Blanchard said, "You're a very pretty girl."

"I'm no girl," Louise said. "But thank you."

"And you sing like an angel. You're giving me the feeling that you think your heart is empty. But you're wrong."

"Am I?" Louise said, unaware that she'd given any such impression.

"Yes, you are," Mrs. Blanchard said. "People can lie. To others and to themselves. But I've heard you, and I'll guarantee that music always finds you out."

At this point, Sophie returned with a tray bearing a glass of cordial for Louise. She was followed into the room by a young black man in a brown suit with a high-collared shirt. He carried a brown derby hat in his hands and was in his twenties, no more than twenty-six or -seven.

Mrs. Blanchard said, "Euday, this is Miss D'Alroy. She'll be singing for the gathering this weekend. Do you have your music with you, Miss D'Alroy?"

"I do," Louise said, reaching down for the portfolio she'd brought along. "I'm afraid it's been rather well used."

The young man held out his hand for it and said, "I happen to believe that's no drawback in a good piece of music, ma'am."

He took the portfolio from her and carried it over to the piano. As he seated himself and took out the manuscript pages, Mrs. Blanchard raised her voice to say, "I had the tuner to it yesterday."

"I thank you for that, Miz Blanchard."

As the young man was looking through her pieces, Mrs. Blanchard said to Louise, "When Euday was ten years old, his mother came to my door and asked if I needed someone to clean my house. She was looking for a place with a piano. She needed somewhere they'd allow her boy to practice while she worked."

Louise, knowing that the young man was within earshot and unable quite to bring herself to speak as if he wasn't there, spoke loudly enough to make it clear that she was including him and said, "You taught yourself?"

"That's what he tells them in those terrible places where he plays of an evening. No, he didn't teach himself." She raised her own voice again. "You shouldn't be ashamed of a classical music education."

Euday grinned without looking up from the scores. "No, ma'am," he said. "Miss D'Alroy?"

"Yes?"

Now he looked up. "You've written something on 'The Last Rose of Summer.' Would it help if I were to transpose the key for you?"

"If you can do that."

"I can."

He carried on looking through. Mrs. Blanchard said to Louise, "Would you prefer me to leave while you practice?"

"It makes no difference to me."

"I'll just sit quietly, then. Forget I'm here."

The occasion was to be an afternoon's get-together of friends and family. There were similar events being held all over the city, both private and public, to mark the centenary of the Louisiana Purchase, the land deal of the century—this past one, or any other. The French had given up most of a continent for a pittance. Planned celebrations included a naval review on the Mississippi, a historical ball in the French Opera House, and what they were calling a "grand pontifical mass" at St. Louis Cathedral.

This would be a more modest affair. Cordials, conversation, and old-fashioned songs for old-fashioned people. Louise would sing in the drawing room and a quartet would play in the courtyard amid the jasmine and crepe myrtle.

Euday proved to be an expert sight reader and an accurate player. The only disappointment was the piano, a good instrument whose tone was beginning to go. Its sound was like everything else in the city: exuberant, warped, and slightly off-key. Tropical decay was in its timbers, as it was in everything else in this corner of the world where gilt always peeled, panels invariably split, and bright colors ran into one another.

They gave each of the pieces a going-over, adjusting tempo and clarifying the dynamics wherever necessary. Euday asked pertinent questions and anticipated many of the answers. His playing style was unique in her experience; where some pounded along, he seemed to float without effort.

It took them barely more than an hour. When they were done, Louise turned to Mrs. Blanchard, who, as good as her word, had said nothing throughout.

Louise said, "I hope you approve of the selection."

"The selection is fine," Mrs. Blanchard said. "What was that last one? I never heard it before."

"It's Italian. Something I used to sing when I first went on the stage. That was back in England."

Having gathered the printed music pages together, Euday now handed them back to her.

"Yours," he said.

"Don't you need to keep them?" she said.

"Just bring them along on the day," he said. "I think I've got them now."

He bade her a good evening. Mrs. Blanchard thanked him, and asked him to send Sophie up on his way out.

After he'd gone, Louise said to Mrs. Blanchard, "I've something to ask."

"And that would be?"

"I've been offered the use of a property. It's a house and some land outside town. I've never seen it, and I've no idea whether it's even livable. I could use the advice of someone who can look it over with me and say whether it's worth taking on."

Mrs. Blanchard considered for a moment. "I've a nephew who's a banker," she said. "Would he do?"

"I'm sure he would, if you're recommending him."

Mrs. Blanchard didn't seem entirely happy with her own choice.

"I'll think some more," she said. "Where are you staying? The St. Charles?"

"For now."

"Send the details over. I'll have someone look at them and then call on you."

When Louise emerged into the street, the Silent Man was at her shoulder within a few seconds of the door closing behind her.

Back at the St. Charles Hotel, she was handed an envelope along with her key.

"Who left this?" she said.

"I wasn't here when it came, ma'am," the desk clerk said.

She didn't open it there and then, but took it upstairs to open in her room. Louise disliked surprises.

The envelope contained a sheet of heavy cream paper that bore a fancy crest and read, *The Governor of Louisiana requests the honor of Miss Mary D'Alroy's presence at the Celebration of the One Hundredth Anniversary of the Transfer of Louisiana from France to the United States.*

It was a printed page in flowing script, with a space where her name had been added by a less-than-flowing hand. It would admit her to Sunday night's historical ball at the French Opera House. The evening included a gala performance with a series of allegorical tableaux at its conclusion.

She fanned herself with the paper, thinking. A kindness from one of her new acquaintances. She had no fine dress that was suitable. But influential people might be there. Rich people. Bored people. People of all stripes, and of all inclinations. She had dealt out no pain to any living soul since the last earthly moments of Jules Patenotre.

The thought sickened her, but not as much as it once might have. Nowhere near as much. Her first time had caused her weeks of nightmares. But repetition had blunted the impact of the deed, until it held almost no spiritual horror for her. She brought these people what they wanted, and so did her best to satisfy the terms of the Wanderer's unwritten contract. If she must do harm, she would do it only to those who sought it. When none offered themselves, she would wait.

And if the wait grew too long, what then?

She would accept the invitation, and she would go to the ball. There she would circulate, alone and anonymous. From among those who went out seeking pleasure in this strange, corrupt, and free-living city, she would find one whose needs matched her own. It would not be difficult. Like always seemed to know like. And in the event of an unlooked-for consequence, like the death of Jules Patenotre . . . well, on such nights there were always casualties, to be discovered and swept up in the morning with the fallen bunting and the beads.

Someone had laid out good money for this ticket. Her understanding was that they sold at a high price, to keep out the vulgar. Someone wished to see her there.

Like, perhaps, had spotted like.

On Saturday, she would sing. And on Sunday evening, join the dance.

FORTY-THREE

n Friday morning, there was a knock at her hotel room door and the bell-hopper called out, "There's a carriage awaitin' for you, ma'am."

She opened the door. She disliked it when the staff yelled her business for everyone to hear.

"I'll be right down," she said.

It was the Mute Woman's turn to shadow her. The street in front of the hotel was wide and paved, with rails for streetcars and a place for horses to stand. A victoria waited, just a few yards along. At the front, alongside the driver, sat her piano accompanist from earlier in the week. When he saw Louise, he climbed down and opened the carriage door for her. Louise stopped on the sidewalk, uncertain.

"Please, Miz D'Alroy," Euday said. "Climb on in."

Louise turned to the Mute Woman.

"It's a two-seater," she said. "And we've to pick up Mrs. Blanchard's nephew."

The Mute Woman did not move.

"It appears that you have the morning off," Louise said. "Let us both make the most of it."

She climbed into the victoria and settled on the buttoned leather, feeling self-conscious. The carriage had seen better days, but it was still transport that declared the importance of its passenger. Euday swung back up into his seat beside the driver. The whip cracked, and off they went.

Louise risked a glance back and saw the Mute Woman standing on the sidewalk, watching them go.

After a while, she began to relax. No one was paying any particular attention as they went by. They went through the Vieux Carré and within a few city squares they were passing along streets that she didn't recognize. At first she'd expected that they'd be stopping to pick up her adviser along the way. But after shops and office buildings gave way to warehouses, and the warehouses gave way to row after row of ugly wooden shacks with sagging windows and rotten verandas, she realized that they'd soon be outside the city altogether.

"Euday," she called forward. "Where's the nephew?"

The young man half turned in his seat. "Miz Blanchard reckoned I could advise you better. Only it won't do to announce that to the whole town. You understand what I'm saying." He suddenly remembered something, and reached inside his coat. "Here," he said, producing documents that she recognized. "You want to keep these safe. I've been looking them over for you."

He held them out for her to take. They were the deeds to Jules Patenotre's property. She'd had the Silent Man carry them over to the Blanchard house, effectively entrusting her stolen fortune to a stranger. But some risks had to be run. Of those in Louise's life so far, this was nowhere near the greatest.

Stowing them safely in her bag, she said, "No offense intended, Euday, but how come a piano player can advise me better than a banker would?"

"Music's not my living," he said. "I make that as a bookkeeper. When a banker mislays your money, it's the bookkeeper's job to find out exactly where he put it. So if you think it through, with me you got a better deal. Only drawback for you is, it's black folks and white folks. You understand what I'm saying?"

"I'm beginning to," she said. "If you have a regular job, why are you here instead of working?"

"The office is closed," he said. "For the celebrations."

"Then you could be celebrating."

"It's nothing to me," Euday said.

Throughout all of this, the carriage driver had sat hunched over his reins, playing no part in their conversation and paying it no attention. He was dressed in livery that would have looked handsome on some better-built and fitter man. As it was, he looked as if he was fleeing a famine by way of the dressing-up box. Euday leaned over and said a few words to him, and at the next fork in the road he tweaked at the reins and took a left, down a wide avenue of live oak trees hung with Spanish moss.

After another mile or two they saw the river, and a while later they saw it again—the road running more or less straight while the river snaked in and out of view. Patenotre had told her that his family's plantation was on land by the Mississippi. It was land that was flat, fertile, and likely to flood.

All along the River Road, they passed antebellum homes in various states of repair. Most of the bigger ones were in a Greek Revival style, century-old wooden mansions fashioned to resemble millennia-old stone temples. Sugar planters had built them in the years before the war. Theirs was an immensely wealthy economy, but one that had depended entirely upon slave labor for its vitality.

After a particular milepost, they came to a long driveway. It had been a dirt road, and now it was choked with grass that came almost up to the hubs of their wheels. The horses waded ahead, pulling the carriage along like a barge on a canal of greenery, trailing a neatly cut line down the center of the road. At the end of the driveway stood the gates to a mansion house.

The house seemed largely undamaged. The roof had lost a few of its red tiles and the white paint was peeling off, but its lines were fairly straight and the gallery didn't sag too much. It was two stories high and about eight rooms wide, with outbuildings beyond. As the victoria drew in before it, a stray dog on the porch scrambled to its feet and came down the steps, barking.

Euday said, "Don't get down till I chase him away."

"You can leave him be," Louise said. "He's doing no harm."

"They carry all kinds of diseases." He looked around for rocks, but found none. He found a stick and threw that. The animal dodged it, then turned around and picked it up and carried it a short distance to where it settled, gnawing at the stick to make it splinter. The dog was long-legged and rangy, some kind of a hound crossed with a spaniel.

Euday went to shoo it further, but it just moved a few feet, resettled, and carried on.

By this time, Louise had climbed down from the victoria and was approaching the house. The windows were all boarded up, giving the place a blinded look. The main entrance was secured with a chain, and the chain secured with a padlock.

She brought out the keys that she'd taken from Jules Patenotre. One had given her access to his strongbox. The other, larger one had been inside it.

The key from inside the strongbox fit the lock, but would not turn. She stepped back for Euday to try, and with a sound like old bones grinding together, he was able to get the lock to open. He unhooked it from the chain and drew the chain from the doors.

Then he opened the doors as wide as they would go.

Louise stopped on the threshold. The house was gloomy, but not dark. Although the windows were boarded, there was a skylight dome at the top of the main stairway. This created a perpetual twilight in the center of the house, falling away into shadow as one moved off into other parts.

She took a few steps forward. She'd been expecting a ruin. But this house was merely neglected, and compared to some of the places where she'd been forced to hide out—Richmond's theater of varieties or that empty grocery store in Oregon, to name a couple—it was more than habitable. Some of the plaster had come down and there was an odor of sweetness and rot in the air, but there was nothing here that couldn't be fixed, disguised, or ignored.

From behind her, Euday said, "A lot of these places got burned."

She looked around. He was standing there squinting up at the dome. "In the war?" she said.

"People didn't wait for the soldiers to come. They dragged all the cotton bales out of the warehouses and onto the levee so they could set light to them. Then they fired the ships at the wharves and cut them loose to float downstream. My granddaddy remembers steamboats burning on the river. Imagine that. You'd think it was the fleet of the devil himself sailing through."

"Was your grandfather a slave?"

"No ma'am. My granddaddy was a free man."

From the central hallway, she moved through a wide arch and into one of the reception rooms. It was big enough to dance in. There were thin stripes of sunlight across the floor and up the walls, streaming in through gaps in the planking. They picked out odd details: a plaster cornice, some hanging wallpaper black with mold, the pink marble of an elaborate fireplace whose full splendor would only be revealed when the boards came off the windows.

Euday didn't follow her into the room, but from the archway said, "Looks like the furniture went."

"It was sold," she said, her voice echoing. "I've got all the receipts. I may see if I can buy it back. If it hasn't already been sold on."

She could do it, too. She had the money as well as the paperwork. The furniture had gone for a song. Let her servants object, with their subtle pressures and their poisonous looks. She'd have her way.

Louise continued through the rooms, and Euday went upstairs. She could hear him above her, knocking on walls and stamping on boards.

Toward the back of the building, she found signs that someone had managed to find a way in. There were cold embers from a long-dead fire, and scattered animal bones that had been barbecued over it and picked clean. But that was all. Someone had camped here and moved on. In a scullery, she found the broken window they'd got in by. She found birds' mess and pigeon feathers in the room.

She couldn't dislodge the picture that Euday had planted in her mind. As she moved back through the house, she kept imagining what it must have been like to stand on the riverbank and watch burning ships go by. Rudderless, unpiloted, fully alight as they came into view around the bend. One Flying Dutchman after another. Roaring bright and yellow from masthead to waterline, the wash of their heat blasting the watcher as they passed . . . and as the current bore them on downstream, still more of them coming into sight.

In their blazing majesty, they must have been like a glimpse of something greater. A devil's fleet, indeed. A peek into the abyss.

Louise found no other signs of intrusion. Whoever had broken in here that one time, he'd found little reason to stay. It made for an intimidating squat, and there was nothing here to steal.

She went back to the hallway and out through the front door. Euday had found an exit onto the second-story gallery, and was descending some outdoor stairs with a hand on the rail.

"Doesn't look as if the rain's been getting in," he said.

Louise backed off from the house a few steps and looked up at it. "I can imagine living here," she said.

"Still needs some work."

"I've got people."

She sensed that he was probably in broad agreement, but in no rush to commit himself without seeing more.

He said, "Let me take a look at the cistern."

While he went off to check on the water supply, she walked around the house and out into the land behind it. A broken fence showed the outline of a kitchen garden. A riot of bushes and weeds now grew within its boundary, so dense that it was impossible to enter. The outbuildings hadn't weathered so well as the planter's house. There was a privy and a pigeon tower, and beyond the garden a frame structure that might once have been guest quarters or an overseer's cabin. The roof was off it now.

A hundred yards or more from the main house, screened from it by trees and with a wide dirt road running through, there stood two rows of slave cabins. These were wooden shacks with pitched roofs and overhanging porches, raised from the ground on brick pilings. Their un-painted woodwork had turned silver with age.

Something moved behind her, and she looked back. The dog had followed her out. He was keeping his distance but he seemed to be look-ing for a signal, some indication of welcome that would allow him to approach. But Euday was right. Stray animals carried all kinds of diseases. The dog would have to look elsewhere for the human company it craved.

"Shoo," she said. "Go."

But it didn't obey.

Following the dirt road back to the mansion, she passed the slaves' cemetery. At least, she guessed it was. It was a clearing in a ring of trees with recognizable grave mounds, set out in rows just like the slave houses and with stones to mark them. That was all they had: stones to mark them. Some had been roughly shaped, but none bore any inscription.

It was here that Euday caught up with her. He said, "You notice the graves all face to the east?"

She hadn't, but they did. She said, "What's the reason for that?"

"So their spirits could fly home to Africa."

They started to walk back. The dog was keeping pace at its usual dis-tance. It flinched a little when Euday tried to scare it away, but didn't take him any more seriously than it had Louise.

Louise said, "You weren't born in Africa. So where will *your* spirit fly home to?"

"Wherever my kinfolk happen to be," Euday said. "Same as yours."

"Mine are gone," she said.

"Most of mine, too," he said. "But that doesn't matter. It's all about those you love and the ones who love you. Dead or alive. That's your country to me."

Their driver was still waiting out front. He'd fed and watered his horse and was stowing the feed bag in a locker between the wheels of the carriage. If she came to settle this far out of the city, she'd need to invest in some transport of her own. And whatever the skills it might take to maintain a trap and look after a horse, the Silent Man and his wife would have to acquire them.

She said to Euday, "Well, what do you think? Would it be practical to open the house up again?"

"Take a lot of time and money to put it back the way it was."

"I'm not talking about putting it back the way it was. Just opening it up to live in as it is."

Euday looked toward the house, and reluctantly committed himself to an opinion. "Well," he said, "I don't see why not. First thing you want to do is have your people clear the dead birds out of your drinking water. Unless you want to catch the yellow fever and join those folks back there." This was said with a nod in the direction of the cemetery.

He went in and secured the broken window, and then he closed up the house. As they descended the steps to the driveway, he promised to list his observations and send a note of them along to her hotel. These would include such repairs as were needed, and costs and taxes that would have to be taken into consideration.

He also suggested that she might have the deeds amended to show title in her name. Did she have some way of proving transfer?

"I have this," she said, and took out a letter.

They'd reached the carriage now. Standing alongside it, he opened up the letter and read it aloud.

"To whom it may concern. Please extend every courtesy to Miss Mary D'Alroy during her time of residence. She is a personal friend of the Patenotre family, formerly of Iberville, Louisiana."

He refolded it and handed it back.

"Would that be enough to satisfy a lawyer?" she said.

"I expect so," he said. "If you pick the right one."

FORTY-FOUR

here was no looking glass in the room, but there was a mirror out on the landing. At this hour of the day there was barely enough light in the stairwell to see by, so Sayers took the mirror from the wall and brought it in. He had a *chambre garnie* on the top floor of a house kept by a colored woman on Dauphine Street. It was a *chambre* with very little *garnie* about it. It was, however, his for fifteen dollars a month, with gaslight and heat extra.

The mirror wasn't a true mirror, but a framed piece of window glass painted black on one side. Sayers turned himself back and forth, looking critically at the fit of his tails.

In the glass, he looked like Pepper's ghost. But he supposed he'd pass. This was the suit in which he'd fled Richmond after his night in jail, having no opportunity to change until he was safely out of town. Another of his many betrayals of trust; the suit should have gone back to the Bijou after use. Stoker had spoken up for him in court, but in his pursuit of Louise he'd let down many who could have spoken against.

He hadn't imagined that he'd need it again. But tonight was the night of the governor's ball.

For once, Louise had been easy to locate. Almost absurdly so. The New Orleans Transfer Company met all trains and steamships coming into the city, and would check and deliver baggage to private residences and hotels at twenty-five cents apiece. Sayers had gone to their offices, taking the part of an Englishman who'd traveled out to join his sister. She was supposed to have found them a place to stay, but he'd received no message. A little footwork to draw out the name she was using without revealing his own ignorance of it, and there she was—Mary D'Alroy at the St. Charles Hotel.

Mary D'Alroy? After Richmond, she'd have been safer with a change of identity. But she could not have known that Jules Patenotre had been found.

His first impulse was to run over to the St. Charles and make himself known. But the impulse was mixed with a tremendous and unexpected fear of the moment.

And it would not do. Haste could prove fatal—literally so, if the Silent Man should be there. So instead he found himself a spot across from the hotel to wait for a sight of her.

Time passed. They had not met in so long. What exquisite irony, if she were to walk straight by him with neither knowing the other! It could happen. In his heart and in his memory, she was forever the Desdemona of the photograph that he carried.

Then he saw her. Returning from somewhere. It lasted no more than a few moments; she came into view on the sidewalk and then, with a swish of her long skirts, she was entering the hotel and gone. As Sayers had predicted, the Silent Man was right behind her, the pistol in his waistband pushing his coat out of shape.

The brevity of the sighting was of no consequence. If it had been a second or an hour, his sense of shock could have been no more or less profound.

She was little changed. Not so thin, but only as might be expected in a grown woman rather than a girl. It took him a moment to match the two, one overlaying and replacing the other; and by the time the hotel doors had swung closed behind her, Sayers' mental picture was revised and complete.

He felt shaken. He'd been wise not to attempt to confront her. He'd have been hopeless.

But now, with that moment out of the way, he could begin to prepare.

That evening, still new in town, he went looking for a game. He was broke, apart from an emergency five-dollar bill that he'd kept in his shoe for so long that he'd almost forgotten it. Gambling was no longer allowed or licensed in New Orleans, but it still went on. Secretly in the part of the city around Canal Street, and openly at Bucktown and along the Carroll-ton levee.

Sayers had learned his play from circus folk. By midnight he had nearly sixty dollars, a promissory note that he knew he'd never collect on, and a ticket for the governor's ball that one card player had thrown in when his cash had run out.

The next morning, he mailed thirty dollars to the Becker family. Then he scratched out the owner's name on the ball ticket and wrote in Mary D'Alroy's before delivering it anonymously to the St. Charles.

Which brought him to this. Tonight.

The night of the governor's ball.

Toulouse Street, down by the side of the French Opera House, was a jam of carriages and nervous horses. Men and women in spectacular finery were crossing into the grand old building. On the sidewalk opposite, a large crowd of people had gathered just to watch the arrivals.

Sayers walked on to the wing of the theater where the offices and dressing rooms were. There he joined a line of artistes and theater staff at the stage door. Some of the front-of-house people were in stiff shirts and tailcoats like his own. The line moved slowly as the doorkeeper checked off names under the eye of a private policeman. There was a lot of walking wealth in the French Opera House tonight, and nobody wanted any of it to walk off in some rogue's possession.

Sayers was on the employee list; having no ticket of his own, he'd signed up as a waiter. His lack of experience wouldn't matter. The moment he was inside, he planned to desert and join the revelers.

And so it went. Once backstage, instead of going to pick up his tray and an apron, he found his way to the pass door and entered the auditorium.

He had to stop and take it in. The opera house auditorium was a wide oval in shape, of extraordinary breadth. The house rose up in five gilded tiers to a high-domed ceiling of decorated panels. Sayers had never seen anything quite like it. It had to seat two thousand or more. Along with all the gilt the decor was crimson and white, and there were flowers set up everywhere. A temporary floor had been laid over the stalls, transforming the lower level into a ballroom. An orchestra was playing, and the dancing was under way.

There was enough jewelry on show to finance a small war. The men were all in dark evening wear rather better than his own, apart from a few in military uniform so gorgeous that it might qualify as fancy dress. The women wore the real plumage, and they glittered. Gems around their necks, diamonds on their wrists, jewels in their piled-up hair. As the couples danced, they swept by him in a wash of taffeta and expensive silk.

Sayers made his way around the dance floor, observing all the women as he went. After that glimpse of Louise in the entranceway of the St. Charles, he knew that he would recognize her. And this time he'd be better prepared. For a moment, she'd stopped his breath, and all but stopped his heart.

But he did not see her anywhere. At the back of the auditorium was a large foyer that was mostly used for promenading between acts. Now it was steadily filling up with new arrivals. As people came in, they spotted friends or groups of friends, or others that they merely wished to impress.

Sayers was conscious that he moved alone. Even the young men hunted in twos and threes. He felt a pang of envy for all of them: For years, he'd known no society other than the company of carnival folk, and even they'd merely accepted rather than embraced him.

When he finally spotted her, it was because she was a still point in all the free-flowing gaiety.

She was standing by a pillar, gloved hand raised to cover a small cough. Her effect on him was still powerful. Without taking his eyes from her, Sayers moved to a spot from where he could watch.

Louise.

Louise, Louise, Louise.

And no one to step between them.

Her gown was adequate for the occasion, but fairly plain. She seemed to be waiting for someone, and he found himself using this as an excuse to hold back for just a little longer.

Her manner was that of a person among strangers, aware of all around her, smiling briefly at anyone who met her eye. Sayers wondered who she might be waiting for. After a minute or so, she moved.

After watching her watch the dancing for a while, and then seeing her move again to another spot, Sayers concluded that she was alone and waiting for nobody. That was an act. She was changing her position lest it become apparent to all that she had no one to speak to, and nowhere in particular to be.

He was finally raising the nerve to approach when some man asked her to dance. She accepted with grace, but not before Sayers had seen her give a telltale glace around and beyond her would-be partner, as if checking for witnesses. They vanished onto the dance floor, and Sayers lost sight of her for a while.

He found her again about fifteen minutes later. Again, she was alone. The dance had been no more than a dance. The liaison had clearly not flourished.

Watching her was almost painful to him. Has this been your life, Louise? Your reward for the Wanderer's burden? It was a strange kind of predator that waited to be asked.

He could hold back no longer, and moved forward from where he'd been standing.

He positioned himself on her eyeline, and waited to be seen.

FORTY-FIVE

ouise was idly studying the crowd all around her. For a moment, she was looking straight at him. Then her gaze moved on, and left him unrecognized.

Sayers started forward. He saw her become aware that someone was approaching. He saw her composing herself, the beginnings of a polite smile. Then he saw the smile fade as he drew nearer and recognition dawned.

"Tom," she said as he finally stood before her.

No words seemed quite adequate to the moment, so he simply said, "I see that your eyesight hasn't improved."

She'd grown pale. "Tell me that this is just some incredible chance."

He shook his head to assure her that it was not.

She went blank for a moment and then said, "You sent me the invitation."

"How else would I catch you without a bodyguard?" he said, and then to reassure her he added, "I'm here alone."

She studied him narrowly. He could see that she was trying to work out what his presence implied.

"How did you find me?" she said.

"Mary D'Alroy? The name of your part in *The Purple Diamond*? You might as well have sent me a signal. I was in Richmond. They found the man who died there. Don't worry, I'm not going to turn you in. But there's a Pinkerton man who will if he gets the chance."

"You seem to have me where you want me," she said, and glanced all around as if trapped.

"You don't understand," he said. No one was paying them any attention, but anyone close by might overhear their business. He said, "I've much to say to you. Can we go somewhere else?"

From the lobby behind the foyer, staircases led to all parts of the house. The various tiers were named in the French manner, from *les loges* for the Dress Circle all the way up to *le paradis* at the top of the house. They ascended one level and found relative privacy in the Circle.

The dance went on below. A few couples had come up here to rest and flirt. The great opera house stage loomed before them, its cloth painted and lit to represent a starry night sky.

She was tense and wary, but seemed to have recovered from the initial shock of seeing him. They took a couple of seats in an empty section but even as they sat, the Dress Circle was starting to fill. People were coming up from below in anticipation of the tableaux.

She said, "You're looking well, Tom."

"Am I," he said, not really believing it.

"Yes, you are. I'm glad they didn't hang you."

"Not half as glad as I."

She smiled for a moment, but it didn't stay. "So, tell me," she said. "Why, Tom? Why are you here?"

He hesitated, and glanced down at the dancers. Each couple moved with their own purpose but, seen from above, all combined into a swirling pattern like a stream passing over stones.

He said, "There's something you have to know."

"If you've chased me halfway around the world to declare your love for me," she said, "don't. It's wasted on me. I can never deserve it."

Sayers said, "I thought we were great friends, once."

Her cheek twitched as she recalled. "My devoted servant," she said.

"I know I had some small place in your affections then," he said, "but I was no James Caspar. Do you still believe I took him from you?"

She looked away, out toward the stage. "No," she said. "I know exactly what I was to him. And what he would have done to me, had I given him the chance. It can make no difference now."

"I'm here to tell you that you can return to the world. If you'll choose it."

"Believe me, Tom," she said. "There is so much you cannot know."

"You thought you would marry. He seduced you ahead of the wedding. You saw no wrong in it and felt no shame. But in the weeks after he died, you found yourself with child. Whitlock procured an abortion for you."

She seemed about to deny it, but he said, "I saw you, Louise. I followed you that night. I saw you go into that doctor's house, and if you pressed me I could tell you exactly what went on inside."

She stared. "You've always known this?"

"What do you think I would do? Consider you spoiled, and turn away? Caspar set out to destroy you for his own amusement. Whitlock continued the work so you could serve a purpose of his own. But Louise, you are not destroyed. You think you're cursed beyond forgiveness. I know all about the life you've led since. But if I can pick myself up from in front of a train and forgive you . . . If I can face the loss of my name and my reputation and forgive you . . . If I can live in dirt and love no other and still forgive you . . . You don't have to love me, but will you not do me the sheer common courtesy of at least trying to forgive yourself?"

She opened her mouth to speak. But he could see that she was at a loss.

She looked away. Her hand flew to her lips. She tried to draw a breath but could not take one deep enough. Her color had become alarming.

When she started to sway, he quickly gathered her up, catching her as he had on that moving train so many years before. She was now a little more substantial, and he was a little less spry.

No matter. Looking to remove her from public view, he carried her into the narrow passageway that led all the way around the backs of the loges.

He pushed open a door and took her inside, settling her onto one of the four ornate chairs that he found there.

These boxes offered more privacy than most. Each was screened from the rest of the Dress Circle by a lattice. Total seclusion could be obtained by the release of a velvet curtain that was tied back with a tasseled silk rope.

When Louise began to revive after a minute or so, Sayers said, "No wonder you fainted. Forgive me, but I loosened your stays."

"The dress is a size too small," she admitted. "I rented it."

"This suit is from Wardrobe," Sayers said. "I got in as a waiter."

"What a sorry pair of frauds we are."

Then, after the thought had sunk in, she said, "You loosened my stays? There was a time when you were embarrassed to look me in the eye."

"Life with the carnival can knock the innocence out of a man," he said. "I pulled three drunk women naked out of a river one Christmas Eve."

"What were they doing?"

"They called it frolicking. I call it drowning. Or freezing to death. Take your choice."

"Did they thank you?"

"With abuse the like of which you have never heard. Two of them had husbands. We were chased out of town."

She sighed and looked down. "You'd still have your old life if it wasn't for me," she said. "I wish I deserved you."

"Old life, new life, it's all one," Sayers said. "Nothing stands still. Don't you hear yourself? How does that square with the soulless thing you suppose yourself to be?"

Down below, the waltz ended and the orchestra struck up a patriotic song. Attention began turning toward the stage.

Louise said, "I kept the name of Mary D'Alroy because of a document I needed to use. I had some foolish notion that I might be able to stop moving around and find myself a new place in the world. That's the kick in the Wanderer's curse. It's not the commitment you make in a moment of self-hatred. It's when the moment has passed, and you realize that you've traveled too far down your chosen road to go back."

"Suppose there were no such road. I have a friend who would argue that the Wanderer's contract is only a construct of the human imagination. One by which we once lived, but whose day has now gone."

"What use is that to us, Tom? We're creatures of our time."

"What time would that be? I've been living for tomorrow. You for yesterday. You're right, Louise. We *are* a sorry pair of frauds."

The stage lighting came up on the first of the tableaux down below. The house applauded. Sayers barely gave it a glance. Something with ships and waves and Napoléon.

As the cheers rang out below, she said, "I think I knew that James Caspar was rotten when I fell for him. Then, when he died, I just continued to fall. I saw no way out. I came to consider myself a lost soul."

"Lost to whom, Louise?" he said. "Never to me. In all these years, there has not been an hour in which I have not thought of you."

"I've taken life."

"With intent? I don't think you have. Be honest, Louise. Name me one man that you've actively struck down."

For a long time, she watched the stage. Her expression gave no indication of what was going through her mind, but he did not want to interrupt her. Down before the audience, the French army was on the march. Spain was involved in it, too, somewhere, and the Spirit of America under an enormous waving banner.

"I know how the games work," he said. "I know how they die. No one seeks it. But sometimes it happens. The risk is the pleasure. And the risk is their own."

"Tom," she said. "I've told you I cannot love you. I believe that all possibility of love has died in me. But I do wish it were not so."

She looked at him then. He understood that look.

While it was true that he had loved no other, his had not been a life entirely without female company and the occasional rehearsal.

"What are you saying?"

She closed her eyes for a moment, as if reaching deep into her memory, and said, "That there can be passions and appetites which are neither loathsome nor unnatural, but which celebrate God and the way that he meant us to be."

Then she opened her eyes again.

"Here?" he said.

She looked around the box and said, "Why not?"

"No, Louise," he said. "Not like this."

"It's not wrong."

"It is if you feel nothing for me."

"That's my point. No other has loved me. I cannot say what I may feel."

On the stage, the actor playing James Monroe was holding up a rolled parchment to represent the treaty. Louise stood up and unhooked the silk rope so that the box's velvet curtain fell free. Then she drew the curtain all the way around and across, screening them not only from the Dress Circle but from the rest of the theater as well. That vast auditorium was suddenly reduced to one small and private space. Now they had no light other than that which spilled in from around the edges of the velvet, and the fan of yellow from under the door to the access passageway behind them.

She stood there, a shadow in shadows.

"Wait," he said, and he got up and moved to the back of the box where he threw the latch on the door.

Then he turned to her and said, "Louise, you ought to know there is no way I can refuse you. But do not enter into this just to reward me and then walk away."

"Tom," she said. "That's not my intention. I tried to extinguish my own spirit. You make me think it still lives. Bring me back. If anyone can do it, you can."

Off came her gloves, and then she reached for the fastening on the rented gown.

"Help me with this," she said.

He could barely keep his hands from shaking. A few moments later, the gown slithered to the floor of the box.

He said, "I have dreamed of this moment in one form or another."

"I know," she said. Stitches tore in his frock coat as he struggled out of it. On the other side of the door, there was a heavy-footed rumbling in the corridor; someone rattled it against the latch and then moved on to try elsewhere, with muffled voices and giggling.

"Please," he said, "don't be offended by the tattoo. A moment of folly from my drinking days."

"I think that's enough talking for now," she said.

Sayers began to explain how the Chinese tattooist had come to misspell her name. But he seemed to lose the power of speech as she drew the last of her layers over her head and off. She held out the chemise and let it fall at arm's length. It was not so dark that she did not glow, pale as white moonlight. With her arm outstretched and her weight resting on one foot, it was as if she knew exactly the effect that her pose would have on him. So profound was Sayers' appreciation of it, he thought that he would faint.

The floor of the opera house box was of hard, painted boards.

As if that mattered.

FORTY-SIX

ut on Bourbon Street, at the corner where it met Toulouse, Sebastian Becker stepped into a saloon for a schooner of beer and to listen to some piano, and very soon realized that the place he'd chosen was not a respectable one. The restaurant section for unescorted ladies was little more than a showroom for the bordello that seemed to be operating upstairs. He fended off a couple of approaches, declined a street hawker who tried to sell him a booklet, finished his beer quickly, and departed, leaving a nickel on the bar.

The day had been a washout, frankly. A public holiday was not the best time to be rolling into town. He'd found offices closed, and no explanation given. Given the scale of tonight's celebrations, he rather feared that the next morning would be no better.

Elisabeth had once voiced an interest in visiting New Orleans, but he reckoned he'd be reluctant to bring her here. It had all the color and romance that she imagined, but it was a disconcerting town. The areas she'd probably enjoy most were the very ones a woman needed to be kept away from. The Creole heritage of the Vieux Carré was fading fast, and a strange, new kind of immorality had taken its place. It was like a better world, but turned entirely upside down. Sinful deeds were conducted with the strictest courtesy. The finest mansions and parlor houses advertised themselves, not as brothels, but as "sporting palaces"; their madames were "entertainers" and the girls were their "boarders," and their trade was carried on openly and with the most elaborate decorum.

Outside of the old quarter, the greater Crescent City ran its business like anywhere else. Department stores had opened and skyscraper-style buildings were beginning to rise. But Sebastian found that it was this part of town, this continuous unmasked ball of discarded inhibitions, that commanded the attention. He'd been told that they held a Carnival on these streets, every Mardi Gras. But how would one ever know it? Making his way through the nighttime crowds, hearing different music from every bar and dance hall that he passed, it was as if Carnival ran all through the year.

It might have been tailor-made for Louise Porter: a place where a flogging, strangling, and choking whore could engage in her perverted endeavors alongside the regular trade, and draw no attention to herself at all.

The biggest gathering was outside the French Opera House. A floating collection of people, constantly losing numbers into the taverns and being replenished with new faces from the same source. They were here to watch society go by, to spot the prominent citizens and marvel at the expensive gowns. Those who passed before them were people they'd never know, leading lives they could only imagine. Imagining those lives was their evening's entertainment. A large number had packed the sidewalk to watch the arrivals, and a lesser number now stayed around to catch the departures.

He'd gone to the telegraph office that afternoon. He'd sent a wire home so that Elisabeth would at least know that he was well. But he'd said nothing of setbacks, or the increasing bleakness of their situation.

The crowd around him showed a sudden interest when a uniformed footman opened one of the entrance doors to the opera house. Some people were coming out. That was all.

But in having his attention drawn, Sebastian saw something that he otherwise would have missed. Or rather, he saw some*one*.

Striding along on the raised wooden banquette at the fringe of the watching crowd, fists balled by his side, pacing like an ape and with his anxious gaze fixed on the doors for his mistress, was a man whose appearance he remembered only too well. Last seen in Maskelyne's, many years before, letting rip with a revolver with which, fortunately, he'd shown no great proficiency. Shaven of head, bony of skull, and not much changed at all. Whitlock's so-called Silent Man.

He seemed to sense that he was being watched, because he looked and saw Sebastian in that same moment. Sebastian turned away. Was he too late? He doubted that the Silent Man would know him after all this time. But to be stared at always arouses a man's suspicions.

He risked a glance back. The Silent Man was watching him now. Damn! Sebastian broke the eye contact again quickly, but it was probably too late. That second look would have given him away.

So he abandoned any attempt to conceal his intentions, and started toward the Silent Man.

The Silent Man broke from the crowd and started to cross the street. Sebastian tried to change direction to intercept him, but that wasn't going to work. The man was too far away and too far ahead of him. Now he was at the doors and going in.

Sebastian didn't see what happened then, but when he entered the foyer he saw a uniformed man down on the floor and a well-dressed group of people gabbling in shock, as if a banshee had just ripped through them. Of the Silent Man, he saw no sign; up at the top of the carpeted stairs, the doors to the auditorium were still swinging.

Or maybe that was just his imagination, and the way he'd remember it later.

Sebastian grabbed the nearest usher and had him call for the house manager. When the manager appeared, Sebastian showed his Pinkerton credentials and told him that he was in pursuit of the man who'd just entered the building. When one of their private policemen had tried to get in his way, he'd come to violent grief.

"I believe he's trying to reach and warn his mistress," Sebastian said, "who herself is a dangerous woman. For the security of your guests and their property, give me two of your best men and let me go inside. I will promise you the minimum of disruption."

With one man down and bleeding, he was met with no argument. Before they went in, he switched coats with one of the ushers in order to be less conspicuous when he was out on the floor.

Two of the biggest employees were assigned to Sebastian. The rest of the staff dispersed throughout the house to look for signs of trouble.

The tableaux and the speeches were all done with, and the dancing had resumed. As he emerged onto the outskirts of the horseshoe-shaped arena and looked up at the vast interior of the building, Sebastian realized that a search here would be no small task.

It was hot. The dancing men and women were all as flushed as they were eager, and it was as if a red haze hung in the air around all the lights. Sebastian eased his way through the people around the outside of the dance floor, ignoring the dancers but looking closely at the watching faces. The two theater employees followed him, waiting for instructions.

After he'd scanned the watching crowd, he looked up at the Dress Circle. The temporary dance floor had raised the ground level of the theater so that the proscenium boxes were at a walk-in level, and the lower edge of the Dress Circle ran just above them.

One of the ushers was signaling for attention. Others in different parts of the house had seen him and were moving his way. The man pointed across the Dress Circle to where one of the loges was curtained off. No other was.

Sebastian turned to the man behind him.

"Are boxes supposed to be closed up like that?"

The man said not usually, no.

It was as well that Sebastian had his two guides. Otherwise, he'd have been lost within a minute. They led him to the staircases and to the narrow corridor that ran behind the boxes. The passageway ran in a curve, following the line of the Dress Circle. Three ushers were there already, but the house manager had yet to arrive.

The back wall of the boxes was flimsy, and the numbered doors in it were flimsier still. They got to the one they wanted and then Sebastian kicked it open.

It wasn't secured. It flew back and bounced off the wall with a bang like a gunshot. There was feeble light from the passageway, and it fell across disarranged chairs and a heap of old clothing. Out from under the clothing, there stuck a bare arm.

Sebastian dropped to one knee and drew the tailcoat aside. It had been laid over the unclothed body on the floor, draped with some care like a blanket.

"Sayers!"

Sayers was lying on his back. His body was pale, his face was dark. On one side of his bared chest there was a tattooed heart with the word *Louse* woven through it.

There were some other surprising details as well, but for the moment Sebastian didn't take them in.

For the moment, all that he could register was a length of silk rope with tassels on its ends, wound twice around Tom Sayers' neck and twisted tight.

FORTY-SEVEN

n Tulane Avenue, at the corner of Johnson Street, stood the Hotel Dieu. As often had to be explained to tourists, this was not a hotel at all, but a private hospital run by the Daughters of Charity. Begun with only five patients and growing until it occupied most of a city square, it had been the only institution of its kind to stay in operation throughout the Civil War. After a few more years of running it as a hospital for seamen, the Sisters had decided to expand the building further and had accomplished this by means of having the entire structure raised up on jackscrews with the patients still inside. It was a hospital used both by visitors to the city, and by citizens without homes. Charges for those who could pay ranged up to five dollars a day, but that included meals, medicines, and the price of medical care.

One of the city's most eminent doctors had been present at the Centennial Ball and had been summoned to the fallen man's aid. Sebastian had the cord off the fighter's neck by the time the doctor had been located, but he was unable to find a pulse.

The doctor had served as a contract surgeon with the U.S. Army during the Spanish-American War. He'd once saved a man after a summary hanging. He checked Sayers' windpipe for any crushing injury and got him upright. Sayers' color immediately began to improve. The physician determined that a pulse was there, but it was weak. Pressure on the jugular veins had caused blood to back up in Sayers' brain, causing rapid unconsciousness and then a slow decrease in respiration. Fatal asphyxia had been only minutes away. Already the damage might be too great.

A horse ambulance was sent for. Sayers was transferred to the Hotel Dieu and the doctor returned to the ball. Sebastian followed the ambulance to the hospital and waited around for a while, but it was late and the sisters made it clear they didn't want him there.

He'd been through Sayers' pockets and knew where he was staying. He went over to the furnished room and spent an hour going through Sayers' clothes and luggage.

He found little there to guide him. And there was nothing left of his money, of course. But at least he now had somewhere to spend what remained of the night.

The next morning, Sebastian began his inquiries. In the afternoon, he returned to the hospital, jumping onto a Tulane car when he saw it coming to a stop on Canal Street. The car was full, and he had to stand next to a man in a grimy ice-cream—colored suit who lurched into him every time the car started out. Each time he begged Sebastian's pardon, and every time the car moved he stumbled into him again.

As Sebastian climbed the public stairs to the male ward, two men were coming down. One had a gun in his belt and they seemed to have somewhere else to go. They were talking about horse racing.

Sayers was in a bed at the far end of the ward. He was propped up on pillows and looked as if he'd been exhausted by some enormous struggle that had left him unmarked, but almost drained of life. He showed no surprise when he saw Sebastian approaching.

One of the nurses explained his condition to Sebastian. He could drink, but not eat. He'd been given medicines to thin his blood and had been forbidden to speak above a whisper.

As soon as the nurse was out of earshot, Sebastian said, "I saw two men leaving. They looked like detectives. Were they here? Did they speak to you?"

Sayers nodded.

Sebastian pulled over an empty chair from beside the next bed and seated himself upon it. "What could you tell them?" he said.

Sayers shook his head, and raised his hand to make a flat-out gesture. *Nothing.*

Sebastian said, "She tried to throttle you and then left you for dead. Don't protect her. It's gone beyond that now. I realize there's more to this than I can ever know. But you can't draw it out any longer."

Sayers looked down.

Sebastian said, "Last night. At the opera house. When we sat you up, I saw those old scars you've been keeping covered. I saw new ones that have barely healed. Were those things that were done to you? Or am I right in thinking that you inflicted them on yourself?"

Sayers didn't look up.

"And then back at the room," Sebastian said. "I looked in your bag. I'm sorry, but it seemed as if you might not survive. I found the razors."

Sayers did not move.

"Tom," Sebastian said. "Your business is your own. I can see that this is dark country. I will not pretend that I understand the half of what I've seen. But nor will I try to stand in judgment over you. Yours has been a hard road. I cannot begin to imagine what it must have taken to sustain you in your journey. What I am saying is that every road needs to reach its end."

Now Sayers raised his head, and looked at him steadily. His were the eyes of a man who'd looked into darkness, and seen a place for himself out there.

"She checked out of the St. Charles Hotel this morning," Sebastian said. "But I know where she'll be going. She's buying back furniture for the plantation house on the Patenotre estate."

Sebastian got to his feet and looked down at Sayers.

"You had your shot with her," he said. "Now she's mine."

FORTY-EIGHT

n this old part of town, every one of the houses had been built over a street-level shop. Many of the shops had been boarded up, and even the occupied apartments looked empty. The furniture store was easy to spot by the rocking chairs standing out on the banquette and the dusty shapes behind its windows. Its doors had been thrown open to the street, like a saloon's.

Louise climbed down from her rented carriage.

"You can leave me here," she told the Silent Man. "Go back to the hotel for the rest of the bags. Come and get me when you're all loaded up. I should be done with business by then."

He'd not yet acquired the skill to turn a horse and rig in the street using only the reins, so he climbed down and began to lead the animal by its bridle. It was a dapple gray, and it seemed to dislike him. As far as the Silent Man was concerned, the feeling was mutual.

Some of her New Orleans acquaintances had suggested that if she planned to settle in the town, she could get rid of the Silent Man and his wife and hire colored help with more skills for less money.

How little they understood.

She had no idea of how Edmund Whitlock had come to acquire the two of them, or when. Nor did she know what now bound them to her, or why. She'd once tried to draw the Silent Man on the subject. She knew that he could speak English almost as well as he understood it. Both of them could. But when she attempted to quiz him, his grasp on the language mysteriously became less firm.

She walked in through the doors and found herself in a long room that carried on deep into the building. There was a narrow way down the middle of it, between barricades of desks and tables piled high on either side. Every few feet along the ceiling hung a different style of chandelier, some of them tied up in sacks. There was a glassed-in office halfway down and, just alongside that, an open staircase winding up to other floors.

It was a very spare-looking office—a desk, ledgers, bills on a spike, and a wall clock so big that it had probably come from a railroad station. There was no one in charge, but there was a brass counter bell on the desk, which she rang. Then she waited.

She'd paid her hotel bill that morning. She always paid when she had the money, and only skipped when she had to. Where they'd give her credit, she stayed in the best places. Otherwise, she camped in the meanest, and took care that no one got to know about it. Appearance was all to the circles in which she'd moved.

She was about to go back into the office and ring the bell again when she heard footsteps from above. A few moments later, a thickset, red-haired man came down the stairs, pulling on a jacket over a long brown apron that he wore over a vest and tie. It was as if he'd forgotten the apron in his hurry to make himself presentable.

Louise said, "I'm Miss D'Alroy. I'm here about the Patenotre furniture."

"Forgive me, but I wasn't ready for you," the store manager said. He was a man of about forty, American-Irish, and with blue eyes paler than a wall-eyed collie's. His stare was disconcerting, but his manner was friendly enough. He said, "Had you specified a time . . ."

"It suited me to bring my plans forward. Can I inspect whatever's still unsold?"

"Of course you can. Excuse me," the man said, and he turned from her and stuck his fingers in his mouth and gave an ear-splitting whistle down the length of the store. He followed it with an equally wince-making call of "Henry! Get down here."

Turning back to her as if nothing was amiss, he went on. "Henry will show you. Some of the nicer pieces went early, but I think you'll find that most of it's still there. Not many people are looking to open up the big houses these days. Most of the old families are selling up and closing them down. Anything else you need, just look around. You'll probably find it. Come see me in the office when you're done."

Henry was a gray-haired Negro of indeterminate age, and he wore a similar brown apron to that worn by the boss. He led her toward the back of the building, where a few twists and turns revealed further unexpected rooms and yet more antiques, treasures, and plain old dross from a hundred broken-up households of varying scale and prosperity. A courtyard linked to another building, older and even worse-lit and with the furniture stacked even deeper.

But the room they ended up in was much lighter than any of the others and would have been big enough for public meetings in its day. There was even an upper gallery running around it with space for three rows of seating. The seats were gone, and all the broken items from the other rooms seemed to have been dumped up there. Down on the main floor, all the biggest pieces of furniture were stacked high in warehouse rows.

"Which ones?" Louise said.

"Ever'thing wit' a green ticket," Henry told her, and waited at a distance while she took a closer look at the unsold Patenotre haul.

The green-ticketed goods took up more than an aisle. Some of the more expensive and vulnerable-looking pieces had been wrapped in burlap before storage. There were long carpets, rolled and bound with twine. Tea chests filled with porcelain all nested in wood shavings and screwed-up old pages from the *Daily Picayune*. Four-poster beds, broken down into their component timbers. There were mirrors and paintings and even family portraits, a ready-made sense of place and history with no survivor to lay claim to it.

She suddenly realized where it was that this place called to her mind. It was the scene dock at the Theatre Royal in Bilston, the properties graveyard of busted companies where Edmund Whitlock had picked up his settings for *The Purple Diamond* at bargain prices.

She looked toward Henry.

"If I were to take it all, could you deliver everything back to the house?"

Henry shifted his position, saying nothing but leaving her with the impression that he was saying yes, they could.

There really wasn't much more to be done, other than to go back to the owner and work out a price. She knew from the receipts how much he'd paid for everything, and she knew he'd need to profit. He'd probably start out by naming some outrageous figure. But if business was slow, she need not expect to get skinned over it.

She had not dared hope it. But it was all coming together.

With a decent home set up, she could hide out along the River Road and look to her future in a way that she never had before. A nomadic existence of short dates and rented rooms had been bearable for a while, but she was growing weary. A young woman, with no ties and all of time to play around in, could put off thinking about tomorrow. But she no longer thought of herself as a young woman.

She wanted to believe that Tom Sayers was right. That there really were no Wanderers—only those who believed in their damnation, living in their own heads and looking for something to call themselves as the world changed around them.

If it was true, then she might yet leave their company. If it was not too late.

She saw Henry straighten up, as if he'd just seen someone approaching. Before she could look around a voice behind her said, "Miss Porter."

She didn't turn quickly. She hesitated first and then turned slowly, as if the name meant nothing to her.

A man stood at the far end of the aisle. He wore a brown suit and his shoulders were set with his hands held out slightly from his sides, giving him a tense and challenging look. He was no one that she could recognize. He was somewhere in his forties, dark and starting to show gray.

"I'm sorry," she said. "I believe you've mistaken me."

"We've met before. Through Tom Sayers."

"Tom who?" she said. "I don't know him."

"Then who did you meet at the opera house last night?"

"I really don't know what you're talking about," she said, and turned her back on him. She walked around to the next aisle. He moved along a row and reappeared at the far end of it.

"He survived your attentions," the man said. "In case you're interested."

"Why?" she said. "What happened to him?"

He was worrying her now. Sayers had mentioned a Pinkerton man. The Silent Man had spoken of a stranger, showing interest. Could this be the one?

This man said, "You left him in too much of a hurry. I got to him just in time. He'd started choking on the cord."

She stopped and looked at him. Hard. She couldn't place him at all.

She gave one last try at brazening it out.

"I tell you, you've mistaken me. My name is Mary D'Alroy."

"Sayers may live. But there are others who didn't. Why don't you make this easier for both of us?"

Was that a British accent? Or was it New England? She'd spent so long here, and moved around so much, that she could no longer say with certainty.

She said, "I don't know any Tom Sayers. I don't know you. My name is Mary D'Alroy. I'm here to furnish my house. Now *go. Away.*"

She set off back toward the office. The stranger was following. She was beginning to feel angry and hunted. Louise was strong, and might surprise him if he tried to restrain her. But she wished that the Silent Man or his wife were here. Normally, she found their close supervision oppressive, and seized any opportunity to be alone. Who would have expected trouble in a furniture store?

As before, the little office was empty. She hit the bell so hard that her hand stopped it from ringing. She hit it again and stayed at the counter, her hands braced against it, looking down.

He was there behind her again, and he wasn't giving up.

He said, "Were you planning to settle? You know you can't do it. Aren't you the Wanderer? You can't ever stop."

That was it. That was the limit. She whirled around and angrily faced him. He'd stepped up behind her and she stopped him in his tracks.

His face registered astonishment, and he looked down.

After a moment, she followed his gaze. The base of the bill spike from the counter had somehow fixed itself to his chest, right in the center of it above his stomach.

He looked up at her. Then down again.

She realized that she'd put it there.

The speed and the drastic nature of her response had surprised even her.

"There, now . . . ," she said, haltingly and without conviction. "See what you did?"

Still disbelieving, he reached for the wooden base and, taking hold of it, pulled. The spike seemed to come out as easily and as painlessly as it had gone in. Bloodstained sales dockets rained down onto the floor, where they scattered around his feet.

He looked her in the eyes. She didn't know what to say. This was not something she'd consciously intended. But there was no denying that she'd done it.

"I'm sorry," she said.

He staggered and fell.

Upstairs and over her head, someone was crossing the floor. The owner would be here at any moment, expecting to close their deal.

Down before her, the stranger was slowly curling in around his wound, as if to protect it from the air. His knees were drawing up, his shoulders hunching in. Blood was spreading out underneath him. He coughed once, and the pool rapidly doubled in size.

There was no point in her staying. The spike had pierced something vital and he was done for. She might regret it, but there was nothing she could do for him now. Pinkerton man. Or whoever he might be.

The furniture in the warehouse, the Patenotre house on the River Road, the home and the future on which she'd been setting her sights . . . all that was lost to her now. She felt almost no disappointment. It was as if she'd known all along that it could never be, and that it had only been a matter of time. If it hadn't been this, it would have been something else. Perhaps sooner, maybe later. But it surely would have come.

She looked around for the man called Henry. Had he seen what had taken place? Had he run to tell someone? It hardly mattered if he had. All that was left for her now was to dump her dreams and go.

Someone was descending the stairs. She had to step over the man on the floor to get out of the office before he arrived.

It was true what they said, Sebastian was thinking. Your mind stays clear, and everything else grows cold. He could only wonder how they knew.

It didn't hurt.

Ice becomes ashes.

He was vaguely aware of the woman leaving, of someone else arriving, and then of others arriving as well. But only vaguely. Someone leaned right over him and shouted something at him, but he paid them no attention. His attention was an increasingly precious thing, and he had none of it to spare.

He felt himself being pushed back and forth. Someone was going through his pockets. They seemed to find what they were looking for, because then everyone started shouting a name. It might have been his own. It was hard to be certain.

Sebastian wasn't listening. He needed his attention for the important things. The things he had to take with him. The wife that he'd never felt he deserved. The life they'd made together. The way dust motes danced in the sunlight in their bedroom on a summer Sunday morning. The smell of books. The taste of cold water.

He'd often wondered what this would be like. He needn't have worried. The final priorities took care of themselves.

Down on the office floor, with people shouting over him and the light slowly fading, Sebastian Becker was remembering the rare look of awe in his boy's eyes, shaking the hand that once shook the hand of Buffalo Bill.

FORTY-NINE

he first that Tom Sayers knew of it was when the nurses came around asking for volunteers to provide blood for transfusion, and even then he didn't realize that Sebastian Becker was the emergency case in question. Only when a cross match had confirmed his suitability and they trolleyed him down for the procedure did he discover the identity of the recipient.

Sayers wasn't the only donor. Five other volunteers were lined up, all able-bodied and noninfected, and all of them were needed to get Becker through the surgery.

Afterward, Sayers told the medical staff all he knew of their patient. Which was actually little beyond Sebastian's home address and the name of his wife, but enough for them to be able to send off a wire.

He had to stay around the hospital. Becker remained in danger, and there was a chance that Sayers might be called upon again. Blood couldn't be taken and stored, but needed direct transfusion. After his second session, he all but fainted when he tried to stand. They put him in a chair and took him back to his bed, where he slept for fifteen hours straight.

One of the Sisters told him of Elisabeth Becker's arrival. She'd come all the way down from Philadelphia alone, an epic journey involving more than two days of hard travel. After what he'd done to their family, Sayers didn't dare face her. No apology could suffice.

Oh, God . . . if Becker died now. She'd be turning around and taking her dead husband home. They'd had a boy killed on the road once, half his head taken off by a flying cable, and his widowed mother had come all the way out to the tent show to take his body back with her. They'd all followed the hearse down to the station, and he remembered the sight of the baggage car with the casket on board. It was ebony black with silver handles, raised from the boarded floor on two firm trestles and lashed so that it wouldn't slide around. An empty chair stood alongside it.

If that was to be Sayers' gift to the Beckers, after all the other blind damage that his obsession had brought . . . then let the Lord take him now, for in his time on this earth he'd surely done nothing but harm.

Anyway, he didn't need to worry about seeking Elisabeth Becker out. She came and found him. He was dressing to leave, but the effort was exhausting him. He looked up, and there she was.

"How is he?" he said. His injury was healing, but his voice still didn't sound like his own.

"Spare me your concern."

"I'm so sorry."

"Sorry does nothing for me, mister," she said. "I had a home, a good man, and a family with a future. Now I've got this."

"The fault is all mine," Sayers said.

"And may you never be forgiven for it," she said, and then turned her back on him.

FIFTY

fter Sayers had quit the hospital, he set out on foot for the River Road. He rode a streetcar to the end of the line and then struck out toward the river country beyond. Even hitching a ride on a wagon, it took him most of a day to get to the Patenotre plantation.

The grass in the long driveway was all beaten down, and in places it had been churned into raw dirt. As he walked toward the house, he saw that the gates were wide open. When he went through them and stood before it, he glanced down and found that he'd acquired a dog.

The animal followed him as he circled the house. He was looking for a way in. When he climbed the outside stairs to the upper deck, he found that someone had neglected to secure one of the doors. The dog followed him, and promptly set off on its own to explore. He could hear its claws on the boards as it trotted elsewhere in the house, occasionally crossing his path in some hallway or on some landing.

The tour told him little. It was an old place with no life invested in it. He descended the main staircase under the domed skylight, and sensed no presence other than his own and that of the animal that had followed him.

When it came time to leave, the dog was at the door waiting.

He left the place more secure than when he'd found it, and walked out into the grounds behind. It was there, near a row of cabins, that he met a young black man of around eighteen or nineteen. He was in baggy field hand's clothes, leading a horse by its bridle.

The young man stopped and watched him until he'd drawn close enough to hail.

"Ain't nobody here," the young man said.

"You're somebody."

"But it ain't me you're looking for."

"Who *am* I looking for?"

"Same woman the sheriff's men came looking for? They didn't find her, neither."

They started to walk together down the track. Sayers said, "Why do you think that is?"

" 'Cause there ain't nobody to find."

Sayers looked at the horse he was leading. It was a dapple gray. He said, "Yours?"

"What of it?" the young man said.

"Woman I'm looking for hired a wagon, and a horse just like that one along with it. Nobody's seen either since."

"I wouldn't know about that," the young man said. "This one's mine."

"You got papers for it?"

"Horse don't read," the young man said. "Keep looking. But don't waste your time looking here. Try on down the river."

Sayers looked at him sideways. "Yeah?"

"Yeah. Out past the next bend. About three, four miles. Look for a yeller church. That's what I'd do."

"Thanks," Sayers said.

He had an hour or two of daylight left. He started to work his way outward through the estates on the River Road, staying off the road itself and sticking to paths and dirt tracks.

Shortly after leaving Patenotre land, he came upon the burned-out remains of a wagon in a lane. Nothing remained but the ironwork among the ashes. But it was recent; the smell of the burning still hung in the air, and it would take a rain or two to wash it away.

He'd expected to lose the stray's company when he reached the limit of its territory, but the dog stayed with him. It kept a slight distance in case he should suddenly turn and run it off, but otherwise it seemed happy to tag along.

Most of the big houses along here had burned just like the wagon, or else they'd been pulled down or had their roofs taken off. Occasionally, there'd be one that still had a family living in it, but they'd be like survivors camping in the ruins of an older civilization. The houses showed all the signs of having been abandoned by those who'd built them, their planks springing and with goats and chickens wandering in and out.

The land that he crossed was still being worked, but the big estates had been divided up into smaller holdings. Subsistence was now the aim, where once had come forth riches.

As darkness fell, he settled for the evening in the abandoned shell of an overseer's house. He lit a fire in the empty grate, then broke out the provisions he'd brought.

He didn't see the dog for a while, but then it came back carrying something dead, which it settled down with and tore up while he was eating. By now it was too dark for him to see what it had caught. The dog would retch on the bones and gristle, cough them up for further chewing, and eventually strangle them down again. This process seemed not to bother it at all.

Afterward, Sayers wrapped himself up in the blanket that he'd been sitting on, and bedded down with his pack for a pillow.

Sleep was a strange journey. It was as if he rolled off ledges into deep crevasses of insensibility, to be borne back up again by some rising force. He'd come so close to waking that his senses returned for a few moments, although the power of movement did not.

During one of these brief episodes, he was aware of the dog sitting in the doorway of the ruined cabin, looking up at the full moon. It turned its head to look back at him. Then he rolled off into the depths again.

FIFTY-ONE

hen Sebastian Becker awoke in his hospital bed for the second time that day, it was to find himself looking up at the very face that he'd left behind in his dreams. Waking and sleeping, life and death; in that moment, the two states seemed to merge and become one.

"Hey," Elisabeth said.

"Hey yourself," he tried to say, with only partial success.

She reached over and smoothed away a couple of strands of hair that had become sweat-plastered to his forehead. He closed his eyes again for a moment, the better to experience her touch.

"How do you feel?" she said.

"Pretty good," he said, opening his eyes. This time the sound came out more or less as he meant it to, and the words held together.

"That's the morphine," she said, managing a damp-eyed smile. "Don't get too fond of it."

She made a sudden sound of protest when Sebastian tried to flex his shoulders and raise his back from the bed. His bandages felt too tight. His entire chest felt too tight, and his stomach felt as if it had been punched with unbelievable force.

But, thanks to the morphine, this caused him no distress. When they came to withdraw the opiate, he'd feel differently. But until then . . .

He subsided onto the mattress. Small though the movement had been, the effort had all but exhausted him.

He took a breath and then said, "I had my chance at the reward, Elisabeth. She was right there before me and I missed it. She walked away from me. I've let everyone down."

"Sebastian," she said with a note of warning, "don't say that. I won't hear it."

"But we've lost everything."

"You've kept your name. You still have your reputation. And, by God, though you came within an inch of losing it, you've hung onto your life. Your son has a father and I have a husband. What compares with that? Anything else, we can rebuild."

"I don't know how."

"Don't worry about how. We're the same people we were before. What we managed once, we can achieve again. Let Sayers pursue that blighted creature if he must, and let Sayers take the consequences of the chase. They're no part of our lives now."

One of the Sisters came to check Sebastian's dressings, and Elisabeth stepped away for a few minutes.

When she returned, she studied him with some concern and said, "Is this tiring you, Sebastian? Should I leave? You won't need to worry. I won't be far away."

He shook his head, and reached for her hand.

She settled again onto the chair beside him and said, "I've spoken to Mister Bearce. He's a very nice man."

After a moment, she said, "You must try not to laugh, Sebastian. You might cause yourself some damage."

"I'm sorry," he said.

She said, "As soon as I can get you home, I'll find us somewhere cheaper to live. Shhh," she added before he could object. "Mister Bearce will hold a position for you. He promised me. And perhaps I can find some kind of employment as well."

"Work? You?"

"I'm sure there are all kinds of things I could do for a living."

"Maybe Sousa needs a euphoniumist."

"I was thinking of something behind a counter at Gimbel's," she said. "I've dealt with those women often enough. I've seen what they do. Yes, ma'am, no, ma'am. How hard can that be?"

"Before anything else," he said, "we have to pay back Frances."

"Frances understands. She has no regrets."

He tried to tighten his grip on her hand, using what little force he could muster.

"Aren't I lucky," he said.

She gripped it back with enough strength for the two of them.

"Aren't we just," she said.

here was an old frame church out in the middle of a cane field. It had been painted yellow, and from a distance it looked whole. Only when Sayers drew nearer did the reality begin to show. The roof had been stripped down to its laths and the window openings were like holes in a skull. No one had prayed here in some time. But someone had moved in.

He saw the Silent Man at about the same time the Silent Man saw him. Sayers was crossing the field toward the church, way out in the open. The Silent Man was pumping water and he stopped, resting his hand on the pump handle and watching as Sayers drew nearer. After about a minute, his wife, the so-called Mute Woman, came out and stood on the stoop. Both continued to watch him, and neither moved as he drew closer.

Sayers had grown so used to the stray dog's presence that he now sensed when it wasn't there. It had peeled away and moved to a spot about a hundred yards from the building, where it seemed happy to stay for now.

As Sayers got closer, the Silent Man took his hand from the pump and straightened up.

Sayers said, "Is she inside?" but the Silent Man continued to stare at him. Sayers noted that the man hadn't shaved in a few days, and his clothes had grown shabby. Over by the church, his wife was looking no better. Once lithe, she'd gone to fat. Of all of them, she was the one who had changed most over the years.

Sayers said, "How is she?" and the man glanced toward the building. He seemed to be looking to his wife for guidance. Sayers saw her make the faintest move by way of response. If it wasn't a shrug, it was intended to mean more or less the same thing.

Sayers met with no interference as he covered the last few yards to the church, but he was aware of the Silent Man abandoning the water pump and following him.

The Mute Woman stepped aside as he entered the building. Sayers remembered her eyes. They hadn't changed. Dark, and intense. They were on him as he passed.

It wasn't one of those simple one-room churches. In its day, it must have been something. The nave was a jewel box of a hall, with a curving balcony and fancy detail in the rails and paneling. There had been a real pipe organ, but that had been ripped out. The pews were all gone and it looked as if animals had been kept here for a while, leaving a mess that made the ground floor unusable. Sayers climbed a stairway to the organ loft and found Louise in a room behind it.

One of the old pews had made its way up here and she was sitting on it, feet apart. She was looking rough and hollow-eyed. There was a bowl of water on the floor before her. Her hair was up and her blouse was more or less white. Her skirt was nondescript and her boots were dusty. She'd been splashing her face, and had nothing to dry her hands on.

She wiped her face on her sleeve. She didn't seem surprised to see him.

"Tom," she said.

"Have you been keeping up with the news?"

"They're looking for me," she said. "I know."

The Silent Man and the Mute Woman came around from behind him and stood by her, one to either side.

Louise looked down in utter dejection.

"You tried, Tom," she said. "And for a minute you almost made me believe it. Then I had to go and ruin it all. No excuses this time."

"I don't know what these two have told you," Sayers said, "but Sebastian Becker didn't die."

Louise raised her head.

The Silent Man was to the left of her. Sayers drew the Bulldog pistol from his coat and shot him once in the chest. He swung around to cover the Mute Woman and fired again. This time he shot high, but it didn't matter. Blood and brains flew up the wall. She was starting to crumple before her husband hit the floor.

Louise was frozen in the middle, hands half raised, eyes glancing from side to side as if she was frightened to move her head.

The Silent Man was writhing and making an unpleasant noise. Sayers went over and shot him again in the head. His entire body bucked once and then he stopped moving.

Sayers returned to his place in front of Louise, and carried on as if nothing had happened.

"There," he said. "Less for you to worry about. Think of it as the end of an era. You're going to walk out of this place and not look back. You know what the book says. Go forth and sin no more."

"No!"

Her sleeves had been rolled back for washing. He reached forward and gripped her arm above the wrist. It was slender and wiry, her hands long-fingered and powerfully tendoned. They were the hands of a grown woman, not a soft girl. The nails were bitten.

"Look at you," he said. "You're not lost. Your guilt's devouring you. The longer you stay away from the world, the worse it's going to get."

She pulled her arm away. "I'm a destroyer," she said.

"You're no destroyer," he said. "And now you're no Wanderer, either. Look at us. You were right about one thing. You and I are creatures of our time. There's only one way forward for us now."

He reached out and touched her cheek, where a tear ran.

He said, "If love can redeem, then you should know that you are redeemed many times over."

He transferred the tear to his own cheek, as she'd once taken the blood from Edmund Whitlock's.

"What are you doing?" she said.

"You are loved," Sayers said. "By your own confession, I am not."

She jumped to her feet and almost fell back over the bench trying to get out of his reach. "Tom," she said. "Don't do this."

"Too late," he said. "Come on."

Louise didn't move. So he took her by the shoulders and turned her toward the doorway. He walked her past the bodies of her onetime servants. She gave no resistance as he steered her to the organ-loft stairs and down.

She just said, "You mustn't. You mustn't do this," while allowing herself to be guided.

Sayers' dog was waiting down in the nave, looking up toward the organ loft. It watched as the two descended the stairs, which were narrow and turned awkwardly.

Sayers walked Louise to the door of the church. There he stopped and turned her to face him. He held her at arm's length so that he could look into her eyes, and he studied her for the very last time.

"I release you," Sayers said. "It's all on me now." And then he shoved her out the door.

"Go."

FIFTY-THREE

n Friday, the first of January, 1904, the British theatrical knight Sir Henry Irving received a note at his Washington hotel. Acting manager Bram Stoker opened and read the mail as usual, and conveyed the message to his master. It came from the White House, inviting him to attend the president's reception later that same morning.

For over a century, it had been a New Year's custom for the president of the United States to receive all government officials based in the capital, along with all the ambassadors and any common citizen who cared to turn up and get in line to pay their respects to the nation's chief magistrate. Irving's invitation specified that he should go to the private entrance around the back of the White House. From there, he and Stoker were led straight up to the Blue Room, where Irving was given a place in line after the officers of the Marine Corps.

The reception marked the launch of the official social season, and with close to seven thousand hands to be shaken there was an unusual level of personal security for the president. Secret Service men and extra police were all over the building. No one was allowed to approach the receiving party with hands in pockets, or concealed in any way.

As soon as President Roosevelt saw Irving and Stoker, he stopped the line and they conversed for several minutes. To Stoker's delight, the president remembered him by name from the time when he'd invited him to share the bench at a New York Police Department disciplinary hearing.

Some felt their patience tested as the line was forced to wait. Others wondered if the canny Roosevelt had seen the ideal opportunity to call a halt for a few moments and conserve the presidential stamina. Extra attention for this official or that ambassador might be construed as unequal treatment, but an eminent actor stood outside such considerations.

When the conversation had to end, Irving and Stoker were invited to join Roosevelt's friends and family behind the velvet rope.

They stayed for about an hour. Much was made of Irving. Occasions like this one had been helping both men to rise above the feeling that this eighth American tour was but a ghost of the great ones; Irving was fussed over and feted as always, and the venture would turn a profit, but the expensive failure of *Dante* had taken any sense of triumph with it.

Stoker's reverence for his employer had never diminished. But as they pressed ahead, working their way through thirty-three cities on a five-month schedule, with the sixty-six-year-old actor playing only roles that he'd created some thirty years before, Stoker would feel the occasional rueful twinge. He couldn't help but wonder if this was all some kind of reckoning for the time when he'd once stood on a station platform and considered his lot superior to that of Edmund Whitlock's man.

When he checked the next morning's newspapers, Stoker found that the president's reception had been displaced to the inside pages by reports of a devastating theater fire in Chicago. Close to six hundred people had died in the disaster at the Iroquois Theater, where staff had been untrained, the asbestos fire curtain had stuck fast in wooden tracks, and inward-opening exit doors had jammed or been frozen shut. Many had been trampled. Some of those who did not panic or run had perished in their seats. A trapeze artist had died, stranded high above the stage. Stoker, never one to be able to resist the spectacle of a blazing building, was torn between feelings of horror and fascination. He also wondered if there would be any impact on their tour schedule. Many theaters were being closed for a safety review.

Among that day's letters was a bulky envelope that was addressed to him by name, and that had been delayed by at least three redirects.

He opened it, and found a dozen sheets of onionskin paper each filled on both sides with some of the closest handwriting he'd ever seen. No longer blessed with the eyesight he'd once had, he fetched a magnifying glass. The letter was unsigned, but he knew its author from the opening lines.

For an hour the guv'nor's affairs were forgotten as Stoker read and reread the story in those pages.

When it was done, he took out his tour diary and began to work out how best to steal a few more days from the itinerary, which would be keeping him busy from here until March.

This was not easy to pull off. Stoker's responsibilities covered just about every practical matter involved in getting the company from one place to another, as well as serving as the guv'nor's round-the-clock factotum. But the same skills that kept the company moving now came into play to squeeze out time where there appeared to be none.

So it came to pass that one day later that month, Bram Stoker arrived alone in the small town of Iberville, Louisiana, and hired a horse-drawn taxi carriage to take him out as far as a crossroads within sight of a distant yellow church. The track that once led to the church had now been plowed over. He had the driver wait—he'd taken the carriage for the day—and set out across the cane field toward the building.

Even before he reached it, he could hear the flies. They hovered in a cloud over the body of a woman. She lay about thirty feet from the door of the church. Her face was in the dust, and could not be seen.

Stoker pulled out a handkerchief and covered his nose and mouth as he passed her. Where the flesh of her bare forearms showed, some animal had been tearing at it.

The church door was unsecured. It was cooler inside, but there was a rankness in the air. Near the foot of the loft stairs was the raggedy-puppet body of a long-dead man. He hadn't been dragged as far as the woman. He'd been left propped against a pillar, sitting upright with his legs thrown out before him. His chin was down on his chest, but Stoker could see that the flesh was drawn back from his teeth and his eyes were sunken right back into his shaven head. A morbid humanity remained. He looked as if he might yet rise and speak.

"Up here, Bram," Stoker heard from the direction of the organ loft.

Stoker ascended, trying not to breathe too deeply. In the room at the back of the organ loft, he found Tom Sayers. He was sitting on a hard chair behind a plain table. On the table before him lay a double-action Bulldog police revolver. On the floor beside the table lay an actual dog.

"Well, Tom," Stoker said, eyeing the revolver. "What's this?"

"Can't say for sure, Bram. Having it around seems to calm me down."

"Any plans to use it on anyone?"

"The thought sometimes crosses my mind."

Stoker studied him. Sayers wasn't meeting his eyes, which made it easier. The former prizefighter's skin was gray and sheened with sweat. He didn't look as if he'd seen sunlight in ages. Stoker would have been prepared to believe that he sat in this room, on that chair, for days on end, just waiting for someone to arrive and speak to him. Like an interview room in hell, manned for all eternity.

Stoker said, "What happened to the people downstairs?"

"They were bothering a lady. I had to defend her."

Stoker drew out the second chair and sat down.

He said, "I made the inquiries you asked of me. The authorities here are still looking for Mary D'Alroy. Last week, Louise Porter sailed for England under her own name." Stoker took a breath. "Tom . . ."

"I don't sleep," Sayers said abruptly. "I can't eat. This Wanderer business, Bram. There is a substance to it that you cannot imagine."

"Can you not simply . . ."

"Deny the reality of it? No. I thought perhaps I could. But you cannot enter into something because you believe in it, and then choose to stop believing. With the belief comes the obligation to do ill. The urge will turn outward or inward. But turn it must. It is a creature of my own making. But of which I am not the master."

Stoker still had his eye on the revolver. Sayers wasn't touching it, but he had it within reach. The barrel was pointing toward Stoker. He could see the tips of the rounds in the chambers, so he was in no doubt that it was loaded.

He said, "Do you need money?"

"No."

"Doctors."

Sayers shook his head.

"Then what would you have me do?" Stoker said. "You must have some purpose in bringing me out here. Please do not ask me to find you a successor. You cannot hand this on. There must be some other way."

Now Sayers looked him in the eye. "A way to avoid seeing the evil continue?" he said. "There is only one. Which is to take it out of this world for good."

Stoker was beginning to understand. "You mean go," he said, "and take it with you." Without disengaging from Sayers' gaze, Stoker reached over and quickly slid the revolver out of his reach. "No, Tom," he said.

"If the Wanderer is a thing of the mind, then it dies with the last one to believe in it."

"And if that sends your soul to hell?"

"I am there already. Help me, Bram. This one last favor."

So that was why Sayers had not reacted when he had taken the weapon. He had meant all along for Stoker to have it.

Stoker said, "Tom, I am in awe of your courage. And the enormity of what you propose. But abet a man in putting his soul beyond the reach of God for all of time? No. Do not ask."

Sayers rose from his chair. "It's a gamble for me, Bram, but it's a calculated one." He began to move around the table. The dog raised its head and took an interest, but without further movement.

Sayers said, "She does not love me, that I know. But she has to know what I've done for her, and in time, when her heart thaws, she may come to look differently on my memory. Wherever I am, if that day ever comes, I will know of it."

Now the two men were standing face-to-face. The police revolver was in Stoker's hand. Sayers placed both of his hands over it. There was a click as he thumbed off the safety catch.

"I swear to you, Bram," he said. "This is the only way. If it does not end here today, tomorrow I'll continue it in town."

He held the barrel up against his chest.

This was not the errand that Stoker had expected. But what could he do?

"God bless you, Tom," he said.

"One more thing," Sayers said. "When it's done, I want to go home."

FIFTY-FOUR

n a spring morning in the year of nineteen hundred and eleven, the same morning—entirely by chance—that the transatlantic steamer bringing Sebastian Becker and his small extended family to England made its arrival at Southampton dock, a woman and a child passed through the bastard mix of castle wall and cathedral windows that was the gatehouse of Highgate's Western Cemetery. They made their way through avenues of memorial stones and mausoleums toward the upper terrace.

Highgate Cemetery, on London's Highgate Hill, was not always the place of romantic decay that it has now become. It was then a city of the decent dead, a privately run enterprise kept in order by the constant attention of a team of landscape gardeners. Graves that are now engulfed by creeping ivy stood out on open hillside. Today's soot-stained, derelict vaults were originally scrubbed and solid, like provincial banks with their assets in bones. Statuary gleamed with the purity of new marble. Urns spilled over with flowers, where they would one day brim with dirt and moss. Its neatly kept and winding ways ran from the sunken catacombs of its Lebanon Circle, all the way up to the high terrace with its view across London as far as the East End.

The woman knew where she was going. The child did not, and stared about her. This place was both captivating and disturbing. It was as if she had dreamed of a garden of toys and playhouses, all drained of life and color.

The path climbed a grassy slope. Then the gravel way leveled out and they passed along a row of monuments, each an act of morbid imagination. Stone women wept, petrified torches burned with sculpted flames. Stone angels spread their wings and raised their arms, their majesty frozen as if stilled by a curse in mid-exaltation.

The child did not know why she was here. She carried a small posy of flowers that her mother had given to her before they left home, and which she suspected she would soon have to give up. No matter. She was tiring of them.

Her mother seemed to have found what she was looking for. The monument at which they stopped was far from the biggest or the grandest, but it was one of the most intriguing. A plinth had been raised to a height of about two feet. On the plinth stood a granite sepulchre with sloping sides and a pitched-roof lid. The mason had made a couple of gestures toward classical detailing but the overall effect was homely, like an upturned bathtub.

At the foot of the sepulchre lay a stone dog of indeterminate breed. Its head was on its paws and the sculptor had managed to infuse it with a sense of enormous dejection. The child looked at it and thought how sad its eyes were . . . although, of course, it had no actual eyes at all. Its body was smooth and muscled. She feared to touch it, lest it proved to be more than stone.

On the end of the tomb above the dog was an inset circle. It framed a relief carving of a man's head in profile, like a king on a coin.

"Who's buried here, Mother?" she said.

"A good man," her mother said. "The best I'll ever know."

The child stared at the relief. Whoever he was, he lived in history now. All kinds of people lived in history. None of them was ever quite real.

Her mother told her to lay down the flowers. She put them on the plinth. Her mother moved them to the middle and turned the posy around the other way. Then she stepped back and stood there for a long time without saying anything.

The girl moved her weight from one foot to another, until her mother's silent touch on her shoulder made her stop. She didn't move again. What if every time she moved, she had to start the wait all over again from the beginning? They'd be here forever.

So she watched a bird. It came and went a few times. One of the times, it had a twig in its beak.

She wondered if it would be wrong to take some of the flowers from the graves that had many, and place them on the graves that had none.

Finally, her mother said, "Come on," and took her hand.

They descended toward the gatehouse. She looked back once, before the monument was lost to sight. Her mother didn't say anything, and she didn't break the silence herself, in case she spoke out of turn. She sensed that this was not the time for it.

It had been an odd day out. She'd had to dress in her best. She never found out why. Over the next few years, her mother would sometimes ask her if she remembered that morning. But she was growing fast, and new things were happening all the time. She would always pretend that she did, although most of it had soon faded.

She would remember the mixture of anxiety and fascination she'd experienced walking through that gated necropolis. That feeling would never leave her. But for the rest of it . . . she grew to accept there were mysteries about her mother that she could never hope to understand. If she ever recalled a purpose to the visit, it would only be in the vaguest of terms.

She'd think of it as just another of those odd remembered things in a child's world.

Usually as the day that she left some flowers for a dog.

Sources and Acknowledgments

The historically aware may already know that Tom Sayers was a living person, a bricklayer and bare-knuckle boxer who rose to fame in the 1850s. After basing a stage act on his sporting achievements and taking it on the road, he died in retirement at the age of thirty-nine.

Sayers lived again in the imagination of Amalgamated Press writer Arthur S. Hardy, who resurrected and mythologized him in the pages of a weekly story paper titled *The Marvel*. Hardy (real name Arthur Joseph Steffens, born September 28, 1873) had been an actor-manager and a sportsman before working for the penny dreadfuls. He began writing in his dressing room while waiting for stage calls. Sayers the bricklayer became Sayers the contemporary gentleman, the bare-knuckle fighter became a Queensberry Rules boxer, the circus turn became a legitimate stage actor and performer in Music Hall boxing sketches.

Hardy's writing was fresh and lively, his storytelling driven by the moral certainties of his era. Any expression of thanks must begin with him, and with Eric Fayne, editor of *The Story Paper Collector's Digest,* and all the other "Old Boys" of both genders who once welcomed an eager thirteen-year-old Sexton Blake fan into their company.

By the latest count, there are at least four major Bram Stoker biographies. The first to be written, by sometime ghost-hunter Harry Ludlam, created a template for those that have followed. Ordered and useful, it lays out most of the basic facts with no attempt to decorate or interpret.

The next, by Daniel Farson (a great-nephew of Stoker's) is rambling and padded but contains some additional secondhand material and some useful flashes of family lore. Barbara Belford brings academic method, some new discoveries, and a modern psychological approach; I should add that Professor Belford was also a friendly and encouraging correspondent. Paul Murray's equally valuable work approaches its subject from a more personal angle. Laurence Irving's landmark biography of his actor-grandfather Henry Irving mentions Stoker only occasionally, but effectively gives us a month-by-month schedule for his working life. Taken together with Stoker's own *Personal Reminiscences of Henry Irving,* these documents help to bring into focus a hardworking writer and man of the theater who might otherwise have been remembered chiefly as one of nature's devoted lieutenants.

Once the project was off the ground, I was aided in my initial search for material by Richard Dalby, Stoker collector and definitive bibliographer. As well as giving generously of his time and allowing me access to his collection, Richard supplied me with photocopies of Stoker's pamphlet *A Glimpse of America* and of *Snowbound,* Stoker's (then) hard-to-find anthology of linked stories about a touring theatrical troupe. *Snowbound* has since been republished by Desert Island Books.

Scott Meek and Archie Tait, then of Zenith Productions, took an option on film rights that sponsored most of the research that followed.

Another generous correspondent was the late Leslie Shepard of the Dublin-based Bram Stoker Society, with further help from secretary/treasurer Dr. Albert Power and David Lass of The Bram Stoker Club. In New York, I was grateful for the chance to visit Dr. Jeanne Keyes Youngson and her private museum of memorabilia. President of both The Count Dracula Club and of The Bram Stoker Memorial Association, Dr. Youngson also made my day by letting me hold the Oscar awarded to her late husband, *Days of Thrills and Laughter* silent movie anthologist Robert Youngson (and yes, they're as heavy as they look).

Dr. Michael David Chafetz, one of my oldest friends, took on the job of setting up contacts for the U.S. leg of the research.

My first point of contact in Philadelphia was the ball of fire/bundle of energy that is Sharon Pinkenson of the Philadelphia Film Office. Thanks also in Philadelphia to Richard Tyler at the historical commission, and the staff of the Historical Society of Pennsylvania. Leslie Mars looked after me at the Rosenbach Museum, where I enjoyed the rare privilege of being able to go through Bram Stoker's working papers for *Dracula*.

In Richmond, I was guided by the sharp insight and hyperefficiency of Catherine Councill of the Virginia State Film Office and her co-worker, Marcie Kelso, both of whom engaged with my needs so thoroughly that their enthusiasm seemed to exceed even my own. Further thanks to Laura Oaksmith, and to LuAnne Brannen at the Metro Richmond Motion Picture and Television Office; to Roy Proctor for his company at dinner and his chronology of Richmond's theatrical scene from 1890 to 1910, and to Miles Rudisill at the Byrd Theater and Doug Selzer at the Empire.

Also in Virginia: thanks to Kathy Walker Green at the Governor's Mansion, Teresa Roane at the Valentine Museum, Kip Campbell and Carolyn Parsons at the Virginia State Library and Archives, and Frances Pollard, senior librarian with the Virginia Historical Society.

In Louisiana, my gratitude goes to Konita Berthelot at the Louisiana Film Commission in Baton Rouge, and to her coworker Phil Seifert, who came on the road with me for a couple of enjoyable days spent exploring estates and old plantation houses along the Mississippi. Further thanks to Jessica Travis at the Historic New Orleans Collection, and to the staff of the Howard Tilton Library on the Tulane University campus.

Returning home, it's thanks to Marian J. Pringle, senior librarian at the Shakespeare Birthplace Trust, and to Christopher Sheppard at the Brotherton Collection, Leeds University Library.

And after I'd pulled it all together, it's thanks for guidance and management to Julia Kreitman, Howard Morhaim and Kate Menick, Shaye Areheart and Anne Berry, Abner Stein, and Mike Moorcock for the final steer that has led me, over the past three or four years, to this unexpected place.

And, finally, a special nod to a correspondent whom I only ever knew as "Scary Gary" and who, in the early days of this project, supplied me with Xeroxed material from his own archives of weird and bizarre material from throughout the ages.

Gary, wherever you are . . . thank you. But stay right there. That's close enough. Okay?

About the Author

Stephen Gallagher is a British novelist and screenwriter. He was born in Salford in the northwest of England and studied drama and English literature at the University of Hull. Married with one daughter, he lives in Lancashire's Ribble Valley.

For in-depth information on the research and background to *The Kingdom of Bones,* visit www.thekingdomofbones.com.

About the Type

Bembo is an old style serif font based on typeface cut by Francesco Griffo for Aldus Manutius' printing of *De Aetna* in 1495. Today's version of Bembo was designed by Stanley Morison for the Monotype Corporation in 1929. Bembo is noted for its classic, well-proportioned letterforms and is widely used because of its readability.